UNSEEN . . . AND UNINVITED

There was a loud creak, and for a moment Mark ignored it. But it was followed by another, softer sound this time. The priest froze in the pew, his ears straining to listen. He remained absolutely still, scarcely breathing, waiting, trying to pinpoint from what direction the sound was coming.

The silence seemed interminable, but then it came again—a soft footstep. This one was followed by a bump, as if a leg slightly grazed a chair. Mark's heart was racing. He was having a hard time hearing anything over the blood pounding in his ears, and he could feel the hair on his arms beginning to stand. There was definitely someone else inside the dark church now. Someone creeping slowly, cautiously, obviously aware that he was no longer alone.

D0034170

Other Father Mark Townsend Mysteries by
Father Brad Reynolds, S.J.
from Avon Twilight

THE STORY KNIFE
A RITUAL DEATH

CRUEL SANCTUARY

A FATHER MARK TOWNSEND MYSTERY

FATHER BRAD REYNOLDS, S. J.

AVON

TWILIGHT

AVON BOOKS, INC.
1350 Avenue of the Americas
New York, New York 10019

Copyright © 1999 by Father Brad Reynolds, S.J.
Published by arrangement with the author
Visit our website at **http://www.AvonBooks.com/Twilight**
Library of Congress Catalog Card Number: 98-93310
ISBN: 0-380-79843-3

First Avon Twilight Printing: January 1999

AVON TWILIGHT TRADEMARK REG. U.S. PAT. OFF. AND IN OTHER COUNTRIES, MARCA REGISTRADA, HECHO EN U.S.A.

Printed in the U.S.A.

WCD 10 9 8 7 6 5 4 3 2

A.M.D.G.

And for Terri, Bill & Karen,
who make it look easy

ACKNOWLEDGMENTS

As always, my appreciation extends to everyone who provided helpful information and encouraging support. Chris Lydgate's insightful article in the *Willamette Week* focused my attention on gutter punks at a propitious moment. And Mickey LeClair at WARM and Dana Blue at the Children's Home Society assisted my research into adoption and the awkward, complicated process of finding birthparents. Mike and Maureen Chamness, two of Seattle's finest, once again guided me through police procedurals. I'm also grateful to Donna West and Jim Ziegler for sharing their fingerprinting expertise; to John Miller and his brother, Frank; to Kevin Healy; and to Melanie Loveland and her son, Dan. Thanks to my agent, Ellen Geiger, and my editor, Ann McKay Thoroman for their guidance and support.

And then there are the Jesuits. Thanks to my Provincial, Bob Grimm, for the time to write this book; and to Scott Coble and the Jesuit community at Gonzaga University for the use of their hideout in Idaho. And for assists with the detail work in this book, I'm grateful to Eric Zuckerman, Jack Bentz, Craig Boly, and the entire staff at St. Joe's.

PROLOGUE

She was walking backward up the hill. The road was steep and slick with mud and ice, and the girl carefully planted one foot behind the other, cautious less she slip in the oozing slime. In thick shade beneath birch trees, old snow, remnant of a long winter, lay in sooty mounds. Below the girl, trekking slowly, an old woman followed. The knees of her blue jeans were already mud-caked. She was dragging a child's battered red wagon, and the extra weight made her slip. When she did, the girl would stop, crouch down and make a photograph of the old woman kneeling in the mud. *Click.* Then she would help her to her feet. Those were about the only moments the girl lowered the camera from her face. The rest of the time she kept it trained on the old woman while walking backward up the hill.

Her grandmother did not seem to mind. For the most part, she paid no attention to the girl. She smoked her cigarette and pulled her wagon. That seemed like enough. Let the child do what she needed to do.

Grandmother stopped long enough to straighten her back and look past the girl at the road ahead. There was still a long ways. She glanced back at the wagon, its wheels thick with mud. Scraping it off was senseless, a dozen more steps and the wheels would be coated again. Nothing was so sticky as Yukon mud. She threw down her cigarette and continued pulling.

"Is it much farther?" Her granddaughter had the camera glued to her face like some shaman's darkest mask. She was wearing fancy cowboy boots that were now coated with mud. The old woman had tried discouraging her, had offered her an old pair of moose-hide *mukluks*. The girl took one smell and declined.

"Yes," Grandmother answered. She was concentrating on the wagon's weight and remembering an earlier time, when dogs pulled sleds. Sometimes her own Grandmother would let her ride up the hill behind the dogs.

She heard the camera click again, then the girl's sudden intake of breath, and she knew her granddaughter had finally stopped focusing long enough to see. She would be looking to the west, seeing the river from up here for the first time. The old woman stopped to turn and look, too. Just below the hill, the Yukon River curled and writhed like a brown and white snake. This was only May, so the brown water was still choked with slowly twisting ice churning downriver. Over four hundred more miles until it reached the Bering Sea. God help anything, anyone in its way.

Grandmother lit another cigarette. She passed the girl still standing in the mud, watching the river.

"Close your mouth, child," the old woman warned, "before mosquitoes fill it up."

Her granddaughter dallied long enough to make several pictures of the river, then slogged up the road until she was at her side.

"Do you want me to pull the wagon awhile?"

She was acting polite and the old woman shook her head no.

"I don't understand why you have to bring so much food," the girl said. "I mean, it's only, like, a symbol, right? You don't need to do a whole meal, do you?"

Grandmother continued her steady pace, her fingers wrapped tight on the wagon's handle.

"My children are not symbols." She did nothing to disguise the hardness in her voice. "They are real. So I feed them real food." She stopped, but only long enough to gaze into her granddaughter's brown eyes. Her lashes were too thick. "You don't understand our ways," she told her.

"I'm trying to," the girl whined. "I mean, that's why I'm here. We're studying about the old ways in anthro class. I told you that before."

"Yes."

"I mean, it's not like mom is going to teach me. And Anchorage isn't exactly brimming over with Athabscan elders or anything."

"No."

She went to Anchorage once. Too much of everything, she remembered that. Buildings taller than hills, and too many cars. The air smelled, and the people's eyes were dead. She came home as soon as her daughter was well.

They were almost to the top and she could see the grove of birch and just make out the blunt points of the picket fence. When the snow finally melted, the men would have to paint it again.

". . . and you do this every year?" The child never ran out of words, and she had that camera in her face again. "Every Memorial Day?"

Grandmother nodded. Just a few more feet. Her arms ached and her mud-encased feet felt heavy and tired. She was having trouble breathing.

"We don't speak so much up here," she told the girl. "And we talk quieter." Maybe her granddaughter would listen. Maybe she could learn.

Frozen snow was piled at the base of the picket fence, and the wooden gate was packed tight. The sun's rays were still too weak. Grandmother let go of her wagon and, with both hands clutching the top of the fence, care-

fully climbed the snow until she could step over the
pickets. She was in the cemetery now.

"Hand me those boxes," she ordered.

Her granddaughter set her camera in the wagon and
lifted the first of the cardboard boxes out, carefully passing it over the fence. Grandmother carried it a few feet
to a patch of bare earth, then returned for the second.
She came back again for the paper sack, but her granddaughter was already carrying it across the fence herself.
She wore the camera around her neck.

"Thank you." Grandmother set the bag next to the
boxes of food.

The girl was turning in a circle, looking down at the
wooden markers. "So these are my relatives?" She was
standing on her uncle.

"Move," Grandmother ordered, pointing to another
place. "Stand there."

The girl stood where she was told, her arms hanging
uselessly at her side. A look of hurt washed across her
face and Grandmother saw it. The child did not know.

"It's okay," the old woman soothed. "Yes, these are
my children; your uncles and two aunties." She began
pointing to the markers. "My oldest, Gabriel. Sonny is
there. Then Mary. Behind you is your Auntie Emily. She
was only two when she died. Over there is Matthew.
That's your Uncle Samuel, where the cross is knocked
over. He always kicks it over, every winter. Sammy
hated going to church, so maybe he still does."

For once she did not raise her camera. Maybe she
could learn.

"How did they die?"

There was a sharp and bitter pain in the old woman's
heart and she could feel her throat begin to tighten. She
swallowed hard and turned to Gabriel.

"Gabe was shot," she whispered. "Mary fell out of
a boat. Maybe she was drinking. They say that she was.
I already told you Emily. Matthew was on his way to
Galena and his sno-go broke. He froze. And Samuel . . .

Samuel was drinking and walking on the river and the ice broke.''

''What about Sonny? How'd he die?''

Grandmother turned back to her second oldest. He was her favorite, although she would never say so. Not here, not in front of the others. ''He got shot, too,'' she said quietly.

''Two shot?'' Her granddaughter was speaking too loudly. ''What were they, like, hunting or something?''

''They shot themselves,'' the woman replied.

The girl said nothing. Grandmother waited, then knelt in front of Emily's grave. Leaning forward on one hand, she began clearing away the twigs, leaves, and debris that cluttered the earth above her daughter. She cleaned in silence, her thoughts far away, to another time.

Her granddaughter watched, knowing any offer to help would be refused. When she figured the old woman was completely lost in what she was doing, she stepped back a couple of feet, knelt, and raised the camera to her eye.

The lens was wide enough to take in not only her grandmother hunched over the old grave but the wooden cross behind it and farther back, the tall, lean white trunks of birch trees. She angled the camera slightly downward to catch the old woman's hand plucking at twigs and pressed the shutter. *Click.* She was too caught up in making the image to see her grandmother flinch.

They cleaned all six graves. The old woman working slowly and methodically; the girl making her photographs just as methodically. She paused in her chore only as long as it took her to change rolls of film. The bulge of canisters in her coat pocket grew as the afternoon wore on.

The six graves inside the picket fence were arranged three to a side with a wide aisle for walking down the center. Three crosses on the right, three on the left; Samuel's tilted onto its side. Grandmother spent several minutes straightening his cross, propping it up with rocks.

"You leave this alone now," she scolded her son. "This is for your protection. And so I can find you. Why you always push it away?" She leaned heavily on the crossbeam, trying to force it farther into the frozen ground. "Now, leave it be. You hear, Sammy?"

Her hands started to shake when she realized her grandmother was speaking to the dead boy, but she forced herself to keep shooting. Grandmother's mouth was set in a firm, narrow line and her eyes blazed as she leaned harder on the cross. She bent her head, pushing with all her strength. *Click.*

"Good." The old woman moved back to the center, where she had discarded the dried grass, twigs, and leaves from the graves. Kneeling in the mud, she used her fingers to rake them in a pile.

Click. The old woman's hands were red with the cold and her blue parka spattered with mud. The red kerchief was pulling back from her thinning gray hair. The girl's hands were cold, too, but she continued shooting.

"What are you doing now?" she asked Grandmother.

"Making fire," she answered. "Hand me that sack."

Grandmother tore long strips of brown paper, threading them under the twigs, into the middle of the dried grass and leaves. She wove several tendrils of the torn sack into the pile, each leading to the heart of the mound. Then, leaning back, resting on her heels, she took out her matches. First she lit a cigarette and took two long, deep pulls. The smoke filled her lungs and she slowly blew it back out while looking up, seeing birch limbs and sky. *Click.*

Annoyed, she lit another match and held it to the paper. The flame caught and she moved her arms to the left, lighting around the pile. *Click.*

Ignoring her granddaughter, she slowly raised herself and dragged the two cardboard boxes closer to the smoldering fire. There were crackles as some of the smaller twigs started to catch. A narrow tendril of smoke began to rise. *Click.* Flames grew up from the paper, leaves and grass, and there was a louder pop as a dry branch burst bright. *Click.* Grandmother began removing the tinfoil covering the bowls in the boxes.

She made all their favorite foods. She had brought paper plates and, with her own hands, began piling food onto them. Thin slices of moose roast, and baked salmon, and ptarmigan, whitefish, potatoes, and canned beets that she bought in Galena two months before. Grandmother had cooked greasy meat from the one who sleeps in winter and whose name they never say. She had made fry bread that morning and brought enough for all her children.

"I'm giving you little bites, Emily." Grandmother shredded the salmon in her fingers, searching for the fine, white bones that she plucked and threw into the fire. She broke a piece of potato and mashed it. "You never ate too much solid stuff," she told her daughter, "so go slow with this." *Click.*

Reaching into another bowl, the woman scooped out a white, pasty stuff and mounded it onto Emily's plate. "You always liked *agutuq*," she told her daughter, "even when you ate nothing else."

Finished with the plate, Grandmother lifted it slowly until she held it just above the fire. Then carefully, she lowered it into the flames. *Click.*

She spoke to each of her children as she fixed their plates, remembering which foods they liked best, giving them extra portions. Mary loved canned beets and ptarmigan. Samuel got extra fry bread. Sonny liked moose.

The girl recorded it all, stepping around the old woman, moving far enough back to picture the wooden crosses above the graves, the birch trees behind the low picket fence, the frozen mounds of snow, and Grandmother heaping food onto paper plates and placing them on the fire. She was lost behind the small rectangular piece of cut glass, not attending to where she was. Stepping back, her leather boots slipped on the snow and the girl started to fall. Letting go of her camera, she reached out, trying to grab on to the picket fence. She missed and fell heavily, her cheek just grazing one of the rocks at the foot of Samuel's cross.

"Be careful, child!" Grandmother was beside her, scolding even as she dabbed at the blood with her wet thumb. "There's too many graves already this year."

When she was done serving the food, Grandmother reached into her parka and pulled out a small pint bottle of whiskey. Walking to the far grave, Gabriel's, she knelt and, with her left hand, began digging a shallow hole.

"You can put your camera down now." She did not look up as she dug. "You don't have to photo this." Then she poured some of the whiskey into the hole.

Mary's grave was next, and the old woman did the same. Her baby's, Emily's, was next and the old woman passed by. "You're too young," she told her, then she knelt in front of Samuel's. When she had poured each of her children a drink, Grandmother went back in front of Mary's. The whiskey she had poured was already gone, soaked into the mud.

"You always were the thirsty one, Mary." And she emptied the rest of the bottle into the hole.

She knew her granddaughter was watching, wanting to protest. Alcohol killed all but Emily, and here she was, pouring it into their graves. But this was not about judging. This was about remembering. Her granddaughter would not learn that for many more years. But she needed to see it before she could begin to know.

Grandmother had one more task. Past Matthew's grave there was an open spot, and she knelt there. No marker, no cross, but still she set to work, clearing the ground of debris. She worked quickly.

"What are you doing, Grandmother?" The girl watched her intently. "Is someone buried there?"

Grandmother shook her head.

"Then why are you clearing it?"

The old woman slowly stood. She was tired and her muscles ached.

"Next year we will have a Stick Dance," she explained to her granddaughter, "and we will say goodbye to everyone who died since our last one. We will feed them and make them new clothes and sing them our traditional songs. You come back here then, and you bring that camera. There will be plenty of snow and no mud yet, and the river will be frozen so hard that the people can drive their snowmachines all the way to Kaltag. You and me, we'll have snowshoes, and we'll come up here." Grandmother pointed down to the ground she just cleared. "There will be a new grave here then. We will need to sing."

ONE

Wolf worked five grommets, mostly in Pioneer Square and along Seattle's waterfront. Today he put Weasel and Chuey outside Bayview Books. The Wease couldn't spaynge worth jack, but Chuey was a pro.

With big wide eyes that were a soft brown, Chuey had a look of intelligent innocence. Wolf made him chop his hair short, wear glasses, and keep his pants up. Readers liked to think he was a school kid spaynging for bus fare or something. They gave him cash like he was their own son. The Wease, on the other hand, was thin and sly-faced and copped an attitude. He looked like he would just as soon poke you as kiss you. So folks pretty much steered clear of him. Wolf put him leaning against a trash can right in front of Bayview, staring straight into customers' faces as they left the bookstore. Most shifted their eyes, trying to avoid his threatening looks. And when they turned their head, there was sweet Chuey, an innocent smile like a girl's, his hair short and his pants up around his waist, where they belonged. Wolf had him hold a couple of books in one hand, and people almost stood in line to hand him their coins. Meanwhile Wease just slouched there, glaring hard and mean. Chuey and Wease made a good team.

The other grommets Wolf didn't trust as much, so he wanted them close by, where he could keep his eye on them. Today he had them spaynging coins in front of the ferry terminal. He called it Kids and the Kitties.

The setup went like this. Tool was another mean kid like Weasel, and Wolf put him right in front of the terminal's entrance. Made him stand there and look dangerous. He was big kid, heavy and slow on his feet. Dumb, actually. But he could look dangerous in his Doc Martens, black jeans, and long black overcoat, so Wolf used him for that. He hung a smiley around Tool's neck—a heavy chrome chain and padlock that caught the sun and looked bad against his black clothes. The kid only bathed, like, once every month, so his smell added to the effect.

Wolf positioned the youngster, Red Pup, off to the left side, about twenty feet from the ferry terminal's entrance. He had him squat down on his skateboard to look even smaller than he was. The kid was part Indian and looked it. He had a goofy haircut. The back was cut short, but on the sides it hung down over his ears. He parted it down the middle, so in the front both sides curled into points of hair that stopped right where his cheekbones started. Pup was a quiet kid who watched a lot. He showed up at the start of the summer, and Wolf had a hunch he would leave at the end. Another "burb wanna-be," kicking with gutter punks for the summer. But what the hell.

The one who called herself Slash got the kitties. She sat right on the sidewalk just outside the ferry terminal's entrance. Folks almost had to step on her to reach the ramp leading up to the terminal lobby. Either that or circle around the girl. But that put them close to big Tool, and most people would do anything to avoid walking near him. The girl was just a little bitty thing, probably about fifteen. Jail bait, for sure. She came out of Denver and had hooked up with Wolf and Chuey last January in San Diego. A sharp kid, and quick, too. Today she wore coveralls and a pink T-shirt that made her look cute. She was into piercing big time, and she had rings in her belly button and both nipples. Wolf made her take most of the studs out of her ears and the two in her nose when they were spaynging. Too much metal turned people off. They avoided looking at a pretty little face loaded with hardware, and that made getting their money all the harder.

Between her legs the little girl held five scraggly, skinny kittens in a cardboard box. Wolf made her a sign: PLEASE HELP ME FEED MY KITTIES. Underneath he wrote in smaller letters, almost like it was an afterthought: A CAR KILT THEIR MOM.

Folks ate it up.

They made most of their cash panning the people leaving the ferries. The ones heading into the terminal were usually rushing, too harried to stop and search their pockets for coins. But coming off the ferry ride, it was like they were mellowed out, just looking for places to drop their change. Slash was right there to help them. PLEASE HELP ME FEED MY KITTIES. Between Chuey and the girl, they made enough to get by. Wolf bought them ten-sacks and teeners and kept them safe at night. He made sure they had good food and lots of it. If you kept your grommets well-fed and happy they stayed with you. Most gutter punks never wanted to bother with a bunch of grommets hanging out and acting like they were real. But most gutter punks were content with squats under freeways and Dumpster diving. Wolf wanted more, and these grommets were his way to get it.

A ferry horn split the air with its loud blast. The *Spokane*, coming from Bainbridge Island, was approaching Pier 52, and on the opposite end of the terminal a crew was readying the dock. Wolf was readying his crew, too. Late afternoon of a warm August in downtown Seattle meant lots of tourists. Mucho tourists with mucho cash. Slash grinned at Wolf and plucked a kitten from the box, hugging it to her cheek and making soft mewing sounds.

Cute. An old lady hurrying into the terminal spotted Tool. She stopped in alarm and stepped aside. Seeing the girl holding the cat, she smiled down at the child. Pausing long enough to fish in her purse, the lady handed her a dollar. Slash thanked her sweetly and tucked the bill in her coverall pocket. She had close to thirty-five bucks now. Wolf looked past the old lady, watching the top of the ramp. Foot passengers coming off the *Spokane* would be heading down in a minute.

Ferries docking at the Washington State Ferry Terminal are off-loaded on two levels. The lower deck is for auto traffic, and a wide steel ramp has to be lowered and secured before cars and trucks can drive off the ferry. Meanwhile, up above, a much smaller ramp is slid onto the ferry's deck for foot passengers. A mob of them wait, bunched up like cattle, while the ferry crew gets the ramp in line. Then they are turned loose to lope toward downtown Seattle. Some cross the footbridge that connects the terminal with First Avenue. But those heading toward the waterfront will usually come straight through the terminal—and today, right into the arms of Wolf and his grommets.

Shoving his way to the front of the pack impatiently standing on Spokane's upper deck was a short, fat man. He was dressed like a tourist and kept looking nervously over his shoulder. He had on khaki pants and a too-small orange knit shirt stretched over a too-big belly. He wore a tan vest with about twenty zippered pockets on it, and tennis shoes. The man was in his late forties and nearly bald. The top of his head was a bright pink turning to red. Either he had forgotten his hat or lost it. Off his left side hung a forest green shoulder bag. It was made of padded canvas and looked heavy. Around his thick neck, on a thin strap, hung expensive camera equipment, real top of the line stuff; a Nikon F4 with an autofocus telephoto lens. The nervous little, fat bald man kept looking around as the ferry crowd surged forward, acting like someone was sneaking up behind to steal his camera.

Wolf left his spot next to the curb and circled behind Tool. The kid was slouched against a light pole, his face slack and his eyes nearly closed. Sidling up behind him, Wolf slugged him hard and sharp in the back.

"Wake up, butthead!"

He kept on walking and positioned himself farther down the sidewalk, about ten feet behind Slash. On the other side, Red Pup sat up straight on his skateboard. He had spotted the punch Wolf gave Tool.

The fat bald man with the expensive camera was hustling along the terminal's outside walkway, heading for the footbridge that crossed above Alaskan Way. He was almost halfway along the side of the terminal when a tall man in blue jeans stepped around the corner of the building in front of him. Baldy spotted him and stopped in his tracks. He looked back over his shoulder and spotted another tall man trailing about thirty feet behind him. Matching threats. A door leading into the terminal's lobby was to his left. Raising his camera, he pointed it at the man in front of him and fired off two frames before ducking into the lobby. Both tall men began moving forward, following him inside.

Wolf idly scratched his crotch. The ferry folks were starting down. Red Pup lifted his plastic cup and shook the coins inside. A business man flipped him a quarter. Slash was poking at her kittens, making them mewl, smiling up at the people hustling past.

In the center of the terminal's lobby, encased in glass, is the Colman clock. A huge, mechanized antique of mostly gears and pendulum, it passes time as passengers skirt around it to buy their ferry tickets. Baldy ducked behind it, his head cranking back around like one of the clock's gears. He was headed toward the terminal's other side exit when another tall threat appeared in that doorway. This guy was black and wearing shades and had his hand tucked inside his jacket, which is never a good sign. Baldy lifted his camera again and fired, then turned the corner back around the clock. The other two were just coming inside, blocking his way. He fired off another frame of film. There was only one way out of the terminal now and Baldy took off toward it. A long, wide hallway led to three sloping ramps that emptied onto the sidewalk in front of the ferry terminal. The ramp to his left had people coming up toward the lobby and the ramp to his right was clogged with people leaving. When it was working, the ramp in the middle was supposed to move people up the incline to the lobby, like an escalator. Today it was standing still and Baldy chose the center ramp. He was hustling as fast as his short, little legs would take him, his tennis shoes slapping against the rubber surface of the ramp, his forest green canvas bag slamming against his side, his Nikon bouncing off his belly.

He was halfway down when the three tall men started after him. Two of them had hands inside their coat and the one in shades already had his hand back out. He kept his eyes fixed on the back of Baldy's sweating pink head, a gun hidden in the hand he held close to his leg.

The little girl in the blue coveralls and pink T-shirt readjusted her sign asking for help and smiled up at the ferry passengers spilling out of the terminal a few feet in front of her. She held out her small cupped hand for coins and tried her best to look waiflike. One of the kittens was crying and that helped. Near the bottom of the ramp she spotted a man headed her way, his face like a big pink balloon about to burst.

Baldy was near the bottom of the ramp and planning to dash down the sidewalk, hoping to lose the three tall threats in the crowd. He spotted a kid with a box smack in front of the terminal entrance and prepared to dodge her.

The three tall men were only halfway down the ramp and could see their prey was on the verge of getting away. There were too many people on both sides and in front of them, but the one with his gun out sighed an oath and raised his arm anyway. A woman screamed when she saw his gun, but he kept his focus on the pink head and squeezed off one, two shots. The sound was loud and echoed in the rampway. People started dropping to their knees. There was a lot more screaming.

Cats. The girl had cats in the box. Baldy was allergic to cats and he didn't like little girls much, either. The first slug hit his left shoulder and the second hit his neck, severing his spinal cord and hurling him the rest of the way down the ramp. The dying man's arms flew out in front of him as he tumbled ahead and the forest green canvas bag left his shoulder and sailed out onto the sidewalk. The top was open and a long black camera lens rolled out and across the sidewalk until it came to rest in front of Tool. The boy stared down at it, trying to figure out why it made those two loud popping sounds. The rest of the bag's contents went flying in all directions.

Red Pup was on his feet, one foot holding his skateboard in place, checking out Wolf to find out what the punk wanted him to do. Slash was still sitting, the box of kittens between her legs, her mouth wide open as she watched the short, fat bald man rolling down the ramp in front of her. Baldy's camera strap broke and the Nikon F4 skittered away from him, coming to a stop next to a litter barrel. The three tall men were shoving people aside, trying to reach the bottom of the ramp.

When Slash spotted blood on Baldy's face she screamed and jumped up, kicking the box of kittens onto its side. All five let out piteous, frightened cries. The girl took one last look at the fat man bleeding on the sidewalk and took off running, dropping Wolf's sign on top of a bewildered calico.

Wolf yelled at Tool to grab the lens. The grommet obediently bent down and picked it up. He turned and took three steps in Wolf's direction when the tall man with the gun spotted him with the lens and shot him dead. Tool and the lens fell in the gutter. Wolf saw the tall man fire and the grommet fall, and he turned and ran. Slash was already ahead of him, screaming bloody murder.

Red Pup saw everything too. One tall man running toward Tool, one bending over the green canvas bag, and the third rolling the fat dead guy onto his back. Wolf and Slash both running away. And the Nikon camera lying by the litter barrel.

Shoving off on his board, the kid scooted past the barrel, bending low enough to snag the camera's strap with one hand. Planting his right foot firmly, he changed his direction ninety degrees and pushed off, shooting between two cars and into the street. Pup was kicking hard, gaining speed, and he shot his board across all four lanes, dodging through traffic. The South Jackson Street trolley, filled with rubbernecking tourists, was rolling past, and the kid jumped the curb and across the tracks directly in front of the oncoming trolley. He was so close he could see spit flying out of the conductor's mouth as he cursed him. Pup cut onto Columbia, narrowly missing a fire hydrant. A yellow cab screeched to a halt, brakes squealing as he raced under the viaduct, pushing hard past the Polson Building. He ollied up the curb again at Western, shot up the block, and hung a sharp right onto Post. The ferry terminal was out of sight now, and hopefully the shooters, too. Running up fifty feet, he suddenly crossed the street and steered his board into a bank's parking garage. Inside, it was dark and cool. But Pup was sweating hard, and he grabbed the hood of a 1997 Mercedes, yanking the car's distinctive round ornament off the car's hood as he swung his board left. The bank's elevator door was open and Pup shot in, his heart racing. He hit the button and the doors rolled shut. While the car rose one level, the boy spun his board around and waited. The doors silently slid open and he headed back out, now onto First Avenue. At an alley past Cherry, he shot across the road, jumping high to clear a brick island in the street's middle. Careening onto the crowded sidewalk, he deftly threaded his way around meandering tourists, shoppers, and business people. A few yelped in surprise as he flew past. The kid whipped by the totem pole in Pioneer Place Park and looped left, under the cast-iron pergola. The kid crossed the intersection at James and Yesler Way, then swung right onto a street called Occidental. Down a block to Washington, he jumped the curb again, slowing down as he entered Occidental Park.

The bench in front of Tsonoqua and Bear was already occupied. An old Indian, his long gray hair matted and hanging down over his face, was hunched over, his arms propped on his knees. His heavy parka was shiny with dirt and sweat. The old man did not look up when Pup dropped beside him. Behind them, the black carved totem figures, Tsonoqua and Bear, faced off, either ready to attack or embrace. From the way they stood, Pup was never sure which.

The grommet was breathing hard and his heart was racing. The camera was sweaty in his hands and he turned it over, examining its surface for nicks and scratches. There were hardly any. He held it up to his face, closing one eye and cocking the other to peer through the eyepiece. Things looked closer inside. He pointed it at the art gallery across the street, and there was a mild whir as the lens automatically refocused. He could see details in the camera he could not see with his naked eye. Turning in his seat, he aimed it at the top of the old Indian's head. The camera whirred and dirty strands of gray hair swam into focus.

"Cool."

He checked the dials and knobs. The counter showed eighteen pictures were taken. Holding the camera back to his eye and aiming at the Indian beside him, Pup fired. Nineteen. Turning around, he fired over the back of the bench at Tsonoqua. Twenty. He held his finger down and twenty-one, twenty-two and twenty-three ripped off faster than he could count.

"Pretty cool."

Spinning around once again, he planted both feet on his skateboard and looked at the old man.

"Hey, mister!" Pup said loudly. "Hey, mister! Wanna buy a camera?"

He held the camera low, where the old Indian's bleary eyes could see it. The man stared at the Nikon for a long minute. Finally he lifted his head. The young kid looked like an Indian but with an ugly haircut and eyes that were too big and soft. He looked a lot like a girl.

"You wanna buy this camera, mister? Fifty bucks."

He looked at the shiny black Nikon in the boy's hands, then back at the kid's soft face.

"You gotta be shitting me," he wheezed.

TWO

Father Mark Townsend was enjoying a little death. That was what he called his walks through Lake View Cemetery. On warm sunny days, when he could, the priest escaped the ringing telephones and constant stream of visitors to St. Joseph rectory for an afternoon's quiet stroll among the dead. Helen Hart, St. Joe's vigilant receptionist, had spotted him heading for the door. Grabbing a handful of pink message slips, she started flapping them at the departing priest.

"Where do you think you're going?" she wanted to know, waving her pieces of paper at his back. "These people are waiting for you to call. And don't forget you've got a two o'clock."

"I'll be right back," Mark promised, waving over his shoulder at the woman. "I just need to clear the head. Maybe enjoy a little death."

Helen sighed and dropped the messages back on her desk. That meant Father was headed for the cemetery. There would be at least five more phone messages waiting for him before the Jesuit returned. But priests need time off, too, and she was not going to begrudge Father Townsend his few minutes out of the office. She knew he had been up since 5:30, in time to celebrate the 6:25

Mass. After which he came directly to the office to begin his working day. Since then, he had spent two hours writing his homily for Sunday, attended a community-life planning meeting, fielded seven phone calls, reviewed the parish financial report for July, written two letters, and spent an hour counseling a Holy Names nun who saw him for spiritual direction. Now he was skipping lunch to stroll through a quiet haven with green lawns, tall trees, and lots of dead people. Helen Hart smiled to herself. Father Townsend deserved his break today.

Mark had two routes to the cemetery. The direct one took him past St. Joe's and down Eighteenth to Galer, where he turned left up to Fifteenth and the entrance into Lake View. But when he had the time and wanted to meander and people-watch, he headed up Aloha to Fifteenth, and crossed the street into Volunteer Park, the eighty-acre green refuge perched on top of Capital Hill and bordering the south end of Lake View Cemetery. The park was home to Seattle's Asian museum, one of the better conservatories in Seattle, a nifty bandshell, a water reservoir, flower gardens, and plenty of wide open spaces. And on a hot sunny day in early August, the museum, conservatory, bandshell, gardens and open spaces were crawling with the park's patrons. About the only place left unoccupied in Volunteer Park was the water reservoir—and that for obvious reasons. But from Frisbee-throwers to sunbathers, the rest of Volunteer Park was crowded with people of every age, race, creed, and persuasion. The park was also popular for drug deals, sexual cruising, and, after dark, muggings. Today Mark took the short route, up Seventeenth. He had seen enough people already and his day was only half over.

Seattle's temperature was in the low eighties and by the time he arrived at the wide gates opening into Lake View, the priest was sweating. His black clerical shirt was soaking up the sun's rays like a sponge. He could see no long lines of cars or clusters of people in the cemetery, so Father Townsend was reasonably sure he would not be crashing someone's funeral. He always felt a little uncomfortable hiking past a funeral when wearing his Roman collar. Those awkward occasions earned him some strange looks from mourners at times. He worried that they might think he was scouting extra business for himself. But this afternoon, Lake View looked pretty dead. Mark spotted some couples strolling arm-in-arm through the graves, a few cars slowly circling around the lanes, and ten or so people making earnest searches for particular plots. But no funerals that he could see. Mark passed through the cemetery gates and followed a narrow road leading to the right, toward the shade of a row of tall elm trees.

Lake View was one of the oldest cemeteries in Seattle, established by the Masonic Lodge in 1872. Subsequently it became the final resting place for some of Seattle's first and famous families. There were Borens, Dennys, and Rentons resting there. Princess Angeline, the daughter of Chief Sealth, after whom Seattle was named, was buried in Lake View. As he wandered, Mark passed the marker for a distinguished Chinese woman who served on the city council. The cemetery had quite a few Chinese graves. The most famous of all was Bruce Lee's, buried next to his son, Brandon. Hardly an hour went by without someone paying a visit to Bruce Lee's grave. Busloads of pilgrims sometimes pulled into Lake View, unloading people from around the world who came to stand a few minutes in front of the actors' upright slabs. They often left tributes to the men: flowers, balloons, stuffed animals, hand-written notes, coins, even articles of clothing.

Mark spotted a car near the Lee's grave site and veered off in another direction. He was there for solitude and quiet and presumed others were wanting the same. Against the slope of a slight hill near the fence separating Lake View Cemetery from Volunteer Park, Father Townsend spotted a new grave, the mound of dirt cov-

ered by large sprays of flowers that were now wilted and
drooping in the summer's heat. He headed toward the
grave site he had blessed five days earlier. Lorna Madsen
had not been a member of St. Joseph, but her daughter
was. And since funerals are more for the living than the
dead, when Penny Metcalfe asked him to bury her
mother, Mark quickly said yes. His two o'clock appointment was with Pen Metcalfe. Mark was prepared for
doing grief counseling with the woman. Her mother was
seventy-four when she died and Pen was her only child.
The father, Edgar, had died several years earlier, so now
Penny was without either parent. That always brought
its own kind of grief, Mark found.

He stopped in front of Lorna Madsen's grave and
stood silently while offering a prayer for the repose of
the old woman's soul. Her husband was buried next to
her, and Mark prayed for Edgar, too. And while he was
at it, he added a prayer for Pen and her husband, Lyle.
That duty done, the priest turned and headed back down
the lane.

Parish life was supposed to slow down in August, but
this year seemed to be the exception. Although many of
the families in the parish were away on vacation, both
Mark and his associate, Father Dan Morrow, were keeping busy. Luckily, Dan had taken his own vacation earlier in the year, so was still around to help out. The other
three Jesuits in their community were away on vacations.
Mark had hoped to get time to visit the Jesuits' lodge at
Hayden Lake, but his vacation would have to wait until
his calendar cleared a little more. Perhaps in January,
after the madness of Advent and Christmas. That was
still nearly half a year away, but fall and early winter
were some of the parish's busiest times. However, come
January, someplace warm with temperatures about like
this would feel mighty fine. Mark stretched out his arms
and threw back his head, relishing the thought. If he
could hold out that long, some sun and warm weather

in January might just be the ticket. The Jesuit priest began to whistle.

Two young lovers, hand-in-hand, stopped their whispered secrets to glance back at the priest wandering down the roadway behind them. He was a tall man in his late thirties, still slim and fairly fit. The priest had gentle gray eyes and a long drooping mustache that hung down to the edges of his mouth. His light brown hair was cut moderately long, too long for summer. He was swinging his arms and staring up at the sky while loudly whistling a children's Christmas carol: "Frosty the Snowman." Giggling at the unusual sight, they veered off the road and began tripping between the gravestones, glancing over their shoulders at the funny priest behind them. Neither one looked down to notice the grave they were walking over belonged to Forrest B. Richardson, whose children's book, *Frosty,* made him one of Lake View's minor celebrities.

As he left the cemetery, Mark glanced at his watch. A quarter after one. Dan had wanted to speak to him, and Helen had that fist full of phone calls. If he hustled back, he might be able to take care of one or two before Pen showed up. Mark trotted across Fifteenth and turned down Galer on his way to St. Joe's.

THREE

"I'm back," Mark announced, bursting through the rectory's door. "Did you miss me?"

"Your name again?" Helen Hart grinned at the priest as she gathered up her collection of phone messages.

"Two," Mark told her firmly. "I've got time for two. And Dan wants to see me. Any idea where he is?"

"Over in the church," the receptionist replied, hurriedly sorting through the pink slips. "Here, there's three, but they all sounded important."

Mark scanned the slips Helen handed him. The chancellor for the Archdiocese had called at 10:30; the president of the parish council called at 9:17; and Rev. John Davies at Trinity Lutheran had called fifteen minutes ago.

"Only two," Mark said, handing her back the chancellor and heading toward his office. "And if Dan comes in, tell him I'm back."

Father Townsend threw himself into his chair and swept aside several sheets of yellow notepaper on his desk. Remembering they were his text for Sunday's homily, he slowed down long enough to sort, stack, and file them in his top drawer. Then he grabbed the phone.

"Reverend Davies, please," he told the woman who

25

answered. "Father Mark Townsend, returning his call."

High feminine voices doing Gregorian chant told him he was on hold. Impatiently Mark drummed the top of his desk. They were good, but Mark liked his chant sung a couple of octaves lower.

"Mark, thanks for calling back!"

"Good to hear your voice, John. How's life at Trinity?"

"We're holding our own. Yourself?"

"Busy," Mark told him. "For August, it's real busy."

"One of the penalties for being popular," the Lutheran pastor joked.

Mark took another glance at his watch. "What do you need?"

"There's a group of us getting a vigil together for those street kids. The ones in the paper?"

Street kids. Paper. Mark was drawing a blank.

"Yeah?"

"We don't think the city is doing enough for these kids anyway, and these latest tragedies confirm it. So we're organizing a prayer vigil for Friday. Can we count on St. Joe's?"

Street kids. Still a blank. Mark realized he had not read a newspaper in two days. What was happening with street kids? He flipped open his desk calendar, paging to Friday.

"Tell me about the vigil," he said, stalling.

"We'll do it at the courthouse," Pastor Davies told him. "We're starting at four-thirty, which is when people are heading home from work. It's also a good time for TV. We may be able to get a station to do some live coverage for their five o'clock news."

Davies had good media-sense and a lot of contacts.

"The main message we want to convey is that kids are dying, figuratively and literally, and no one is doing much about it."

Street kids dying. Bingo! Mark remembered Dan

Morrow talking about some kids recently turning up dead. There were three or four in just the last few days. He grabbed a writing pad.

"John, my own calendar is filled, I'm afraid." Mark was scheduled for a dental appointment, so he was not lying. "But I'll see if someone on the staff can be there. Would that do?"

"What about Father Morrow?"

"I'll ask."

"Maybe some parishioners?"

On a Friday afternoon? Fat chance.

"I'll spread the word." Mark made a few notes. "Friday, four-thirty, the courthouse. And if Dan can come, I'll have him give you a call."

"That'd be great, Mark."

The two men said their goodbyes and hung up. Father Townsend checked his watch. Pen Metcalfe was due to arrive in twenty minutes. Another phone call or Dan Morrow—which would it be? At that moment, his associate arrived at the door.

Dan Morrow was almost twenty years older than Mark Townsend. In a former life the Jesuit priest had served as a marine sergeant. That was thirty-five years ago, but he had kept himself in good shape. Better than Mark, if the truth were known. He wore his graying hair clipped in a short brush cut. His face was chiseled a little too sharply and his demeanor looked a little too stern. But his tough-guy looks and rigid discipline had served him well when he worked as vice-principal of Gonzaga Prep in Spokane. However, it was a burn-out job, and after fifteen years of playing the heavy in charge of discipline, Father Morrow had put in for something new. After a year of retooling in theology and pastoral ministry, he was assigned to St. Joseph as Father Townsend's associate. Mark felt the two made a good team. He grinned up at his fellow Jesuit and motioned to a chair.

"Come on in, Dan. What's up?"

Father Morrow shook his head, still standing outside Mark's office.

"If you've got a minute," he said grimly, "I'd like you to come over to the church."

Mark looked down at his watch. "If it won't take long."

The two priests went out the side door of the rectory, heading toward the church. A tall hedge of honeysuckle along the walkway was in full bloom and the sweet scent of the orange flowers was intoxicating.

Mark followed Dan through the vestibule and into the church proper. Father Morrow started up the aisle toward the sanctuary, peering into the pews to his right as he walked.

"Right up here," he called back to Mark, while he continued ahead.

He stopped about twenty pews up and looked back expectantly.

"Here," he said. "This is it."

Mark joined the priest and looked into the pew. Morrow was pointing to a pile of trash on the wooden seat.

"So?" Mark was not quite sure what this was about.

"It's garbage, Mark. Someone's coming in here to eat and they're leaving their garbage."

Father Townsend took a second look. There was a flattened brown bag, an empty Pepsi can lying on its side, and another crumpled bag. He entered the pew and fingered the crumpled bag. Corn nuts.

"I told you about this last night. This is the third time this week."

Townsend had a vague recollection of last night's conversation. He had come in from a late marriage preparation with a young couple and found Morrow planted in front of the television. First searching out a cold beer from the refrigerator, he had dropped down on the couch, happy to stare at whatever was flickering on the tube. That was when Morrow started in about food in the church. The TV was loud, the beer was cold, and

Mark was too tired to pay much attention to what Dan was saying. He let it go in one ear and out the other, figuring that if it was important he would hear about it again. Apparently this was important—at least to Dan.

"I think there's someone camping in here," Dan told him. "Yesterday morning it was a pizza box." Father Morrow stepped into the pew and began gathering up the trash. Mark gave him the empty bag of corn nuts along with a grin. "Laugh all you want, but there's someone having picnics in here."

As the two priests headed back to the rectory, Mark told his associate about the prayer vigil planned for Friday. Morrow was shaking his head before Townsend even finished.

"No can do. I've got a late-afternoon appointment on Friday. Sorry. Why don't you check with Jack?"

Jack Abel was St. Joseph's Social Ministries coordinator. A former seminarian, he worked full-time on the parish staff, organizing and running the church's social outreach ministries. One of those was providing meals once a month at the Haven, a service center for homeless youth in downtown Seattle. He was an obvious choice to represent St. Joseph at a vigil for street kids, and Father Townsend made a mental note to ask the young man to attend the ecumenical vigil on the courthouse steps.

The antique clock in the rectory hallway showed three minutes to two. Mark was about to head into his office to make his second call when Helen Hart caught him.

"Penny Metcalfe is waiting," she murmured quietly. "Shall I send her in?"

"No need." Mark loped down the hallway toward the front lobby.

"Pen." The woman stood up from her chair and Mark gathered her in his arms for a pastoral hug. "How're you getting along?"

She was a tall woman with blond hair, which grazed against Mark's cheek in the embrace. He could not see her eyes through the sunglasses, but her red nose and quivering lips told him she was feeling lots of emotion. Penny Metcalfe was the only child of the Madsens. And Lorna and Pen were as close as any mother and daughter Mark ever knew. Lorna's death had hit her hard. The suddenness certainly did not help. Although in her seventies, Lorna Madsen was far from feeble or debilitated, and she was leading a full and active life right up to her death. But one night while sleeping, her heart just stopped. When she did not answer Pen's phone calls, the daughter went over in the afternoon and found her mother's body lying in bed.

His arm still wrapped around her, Mark led his parishioner down the hall to his office. He ignored the smaller room just off the lobby that they used as a visiting parlor. When he was seeing strangers or younger people, he used the parlor. For older and familiar friends, Father Townsend took them back to his own office. Lyle and Penny Metcalfe were some of the first people Mark met when he was assigned to St. Joseph parish. They had gone out of their way to introduce themselves to him. Not by standing in a long line after his Mass, but coming right over to the residence one evening, carrying a cake and bottle of wine. And before they left they invited the new priest to their home for dinner. Mark was flattered by their attention, and in the months that followed, he grew quite close to the handsome couple. Only later, after learning Lyle was on Seattle's City Council, did he suspect that their first visit was probably as much good politics as it was Christian charity. But by then they were friends, so it really did not matter why or how they first met.

Mark closed the door to his office. A lectionary and commentary on the gospels were stacked on the easy chair and he lifted them off and offered the chair to Penny. The woman lowered herself in the seat while dabbing at her nose with a crumpled handkerchief. Mark dropped down in his own chair and leaned forward, his eyes full of concern.

"How are you, Pen? You look like you're still hurting."

The woman shook her head and bit her lip. Her emotions were obviously still close to the surface. The priest could see tears coursing down her cheeks from beneath her dark glasses.

"Take your time." He leaned back in his chair and offered her a patient and sympathetic smile.

Pen Metcalfe was struggling to control her emotions, but it was not easy. She shook her head in frustration, her fists clenched tightly, one holding the soggy handkerchief and the other clutching a soft leather notebook. Exasperated with herself, she leaned her head back in the chair. Her hair cascaded back over her shoulders, and from under the glasses, Mark caught a glimpse of moist, dark eyes blinking up at the ceiling. She was wearing light cotton tan slacks and a simple, short-sleeved silk white blouse. A gold chain with one solitary diamond hung from her slender neck. Lyle had given her the necklace at a surprise thirty-fifth birthday party he had orchestrated for his wife two months ago in their elegant home a few blocks from the parish. Even though she was caught totally by the surprise, without an opportunity to dress or prepare for the party, she was easily the most beautiful woman there.

"I'm sorry," she finally managed to say, although only in a whisper. "This is so difficult."

Mark nodded and offered her another reassuring smile.

"I thought I was done crying," she continued, her voice clearing slightly. She took a deep breath. "This is so painful for me."

Father Townsend's eyes filled with concern. The woman was hurting a lot more than he had imagined. He leaned forward in his chair and spoke in a low, gentle voice.

"I know how close you were to your mother, Pen. So I realize her death must be hard for you."

The woman turned her head toward the window and looked out. She managed a small, sad smile and took another deep breath.

"Yes, it's very hard. But mother lived a full and happy life. And her death was peaceful." She turned back to her priest. "But that's not what this visit is about, Mark."

Pen sat forward in her chair and began unfastening the clasp of her notebook with hands that were trembling.

"I've started going through mother's things." Her fingers were having trouble with the small clasp. "Maybe I should have waited longer, but I wanted to get it over with. And I thought it might help." The latch popped with an audible click. She sniffled and looked up at the priest. "My mother was a very tidy woman, quite organized. And she never kept a lot of things she didn't need. If she didn't use it at least once a year, out it went. Everything in her apartment is so clean and orderly."

She was looking at the closed notebook in her lap but continued talking. "I started in her kitchen because I figured I wouldn't be quite so emotional about pots and pans." Pen gave a small laugh. "Boy, was I ever mistaken about that. Everything I picked up seemed to have a story attached to it. I was trying to put together a pile of things for St. Vinnie's. I would put a bowl or pan in the box but then remember something about it, some little story about mother, and end up taking it back out. Crying the whole time, of course."

Father Townsend's parishioner leaned back in her chair and crossed her legs. He could see some of the tension leaving her body. Pen Metcalfe finally removed her sunglasses. Her eyes looked red and swollen, and she offered the priest an apologetic smile.

"I must look a fright," she murmured. Mark shook his head.

"Finally I left the kitchen and started in on the bathroom. The same thing happened. Into the box, out of the box. With more tears. Always more tears. Mark, there was no place I could go in that apartment that didn't get me crying." She clasped her hands and raised them to her chin, resting her elbows on the notebook. "It was awful. I finally ended up crying myself to sleep on top of mother's bed."

Father Townsend cleared his throat. "Everything in the apartment reminds you of good times with your mother, Pen. And the loss of her from your life is so recent. It sounds like right now it's just too painful for you."

The woman nodded. "I know," she said. "You're right." She put her hands down to her lap and held the notebook. "But I can't seem to stop. I open drawers, cupboards, closets, take a look inside and start to cry. And then yesterday morning I opened Mom's cedar chest."

One tear drop fell onto the notebook's cover and the small, perfect circle it made turned a dark chocolate color as it soaked into the leather. Pen turned and looked back out the window.

"I found her wedding dress, folded up at the bottom. I lifted it out and draped it across the bed." Her hands opened the notebook and lifted out an envelope. "This was tucked inside of it, Father." She held the envelope out to the Jesuit. He cocked his head and looked quizzically at the packet in her hand.

"Mark, these are papers for an adoption." Penny Metcalfe was fighting hard to hold back her tears. "I think they're mine."

FOUR

Father Townsend studied the bulky envelope Pen Metcalfe was holding out, then looked back up at her face. Her eyes were locked onto his, her chin was quivering.

"Pen, are you sure they're yours?"

"I'm not sure of anything," she answered. "But the name and date of birth are the same." She handed Mark the envelope. "You can read it."

Three sheets of paper were stapled together. The pages were yellowed with age and the creases at the folds were beginning to tear at their edges. The first two lines of the document proclaimed:

IN THE SUPERIOR COURT OF THE STATE OF WASHINGTON
IN AND FOR MASON COUNTY

And beneath that

No. 0183734
DECREE OF ADOPTION

Mark lowered the pages and looked up at Pen. She was watching him closely, waiting for some response. For once, he could think of nothing to say. He turned back to the pages and continued reading. The text was legal jargon, but the meaning was quite clear. An infant girl, born in Shelton, Washington, was being adopted.

"You see the date?" Penny asked him. "The baby was born in Shelton on June 11, 1963. That's my birthday. Who else could it be, Mark?"

Father Townsend stopped reading. "And your parents never told you about this?"

Pen raised one eyebrow. "My parents? My parents? According to this, they're not my parents."

He watched her as her face began to tighten. She closed her eyes, but tears squeezed out and coursed down her cheeks. Her lips trembled, and Penny Metcalfe raised her hands to her face and started sobbing uncontrollably.

Priests think of themselves as healers. To the best of their abilities, they try to ease people's pain. Not so much the physical as the spiritual and the mental. But the three are seldom very far apart. Penny Metcalfe was crying loudly, doubled over in the chair, her shoulders quaking. She was gasping for breath. Mark let her cry. Pain this bad had to come out on its own. He rolled his desk chair closer to the sobbing woman and gently laid his hand on her back. He could feel her skin tighten momentarily as she felt his touch, but her cries went on unabated. Pen's grief was welling up from deep inside the woman, and Mark knew the time for healing was going to have to wait.

When she was able, she sat back up and Mark rolled back to his place next to his desk. He slid a box of tissues across to her. She took several and began dabbing at her face.

"I'm sorry, Father. But I feel so lost right now."

"I think that's a natural feeling, Pen, given the circumstances."

"I just can't believe they never told me. All these years . . ." She took more tissue. "I can't believe it."

Mark turned the pages of the Decree of Adoption. At

the bottom of the second page there was more information about the adoption.

Baby Girl Metzler was legally granted the name of Penelope Jane Madsen. Her determined date of birth was June 11, 1963 and her place of birth was Shelton General Hospital. Full names of the petitioners for adoption were Edgar James Madsen and Lorna Jean Cantrell Madsen.

The final page provided the name of the presiding judge and the attorney representing the petitioners. There was an additional line that read: "DONE IN OPEN COURT this 28th day of June, 1963."

Mark slowly folded the pages and placed them in the envelope, handing the packet back to her. Penny Metcalfe tucked the envelope into her notebook and refastened the clasp.

"So what do I do now?" she asked.

Mark knew better than to answer. "What does Lyle think?"

His friend shook her head. "I haven't told him," she replied. "I don't know what to tell him." She turned her hands over and studied her palms. "Your wife's parents aren't her real ones. Your wife doesn't even know who she is. You don't know who she is. The woman you've married is a stranger." She stopped speaking but kept her eyes cast down. Mark waited to see if there was more she wanted to say.

"Lyle loves you very much, Pen. He loves you and he knows you. He might not be aware of this one fact about your life, but that isn't going to effect what he feels for you. You are still just as real and just yourself as you ever were. Being adopted doesn't change that. And your parents loved you, too. Whether or not they were your birth parents doesn't effect what they felt for you. I didn't know your father, and only met your mother those few times, but I know she loved you very much. You know that too, Pen. Being adopted doesn't change that."

Her head dipped slightly and Mark took that as acknowledgment.

"I can imagine what a shock this must be to you. And you're probably feeling very confused about this. I know there's all sorts of emotions boiling around inside, and they're mixed in there with the feelings you have about Lorna's death and missing her. There's so much going on inside, I don't imagine you can sort it out by yourself right now."

Pen gave a decided nod of her head.

"One thing that might help is to share this with your husband. It's too much to be carrying by yourself. Let him help. Will you?"

She raised her tear-stained face and nodded twice.

"I'll try," she said. "He knows I'm upset. But he thinks it's just about mother's death. And it's true, some of it is. But I haven't said anything about this other matter. I don't know how."

"You did it okay with me," Father Townsend told her with a smile. "And if you can tell me, I know you can tell Lyle. He'll understand."

"I know that, Mark." Her voice sounded stronger. "I know that Lyle will understand that I'm adopted. He can probably accept that even better than I can right now. What I don't think he'll understand is how that makes me feel. And at this moment, I don't even know how I feel." She uncrossed her legs and self-consciously began smoothing her slacks. "Your word is probably the right one—confused. I'm just very, very confused."

They had been in his office for fifty minutes already. Penny Metcalfe seemed calmer, but obviously nothing was getting resolved. Except perhaps that she would share this discovery with her husband. And maybe some of her pain.

"Shall we get together again?" Mark asked her.

She smiled slightly and nodded. "I'd like that, yes."

He checked his calendar, searching for an open spot. Tomorrow was too soon.

"How about Friday at ten?" he suggested. "Is that a good time?" .

"That'd be fine, Father. It'll give me a chance to talk with Lyle and maybe sort through some of this for myself. Friday at ten."

"Pen, you might put off going through your mother's things for a while. Maybe it's a little too soon."

She was nodding as he spoke. "I've already decided that." She put her dark glasses back on as she got to her feet. "The thought of opening any more drawers or cabinets gives me the chills. Lord knows I don't need any more little surprises in my life right now."

"You're going to be all right?" he asked.

She gave him a hug and pecked him on his cheek. "Thanks, Mark," Pen murmured. "Thanks."

"God bless."

Father Townsend escorted Penny Metcalfe to the front door and saw her out. Her walk was determined as she left the rectory steps and turned toward her home.

In former times, the doors to Jesuit residences were watched over by Jesuit brothers; men who did not want to be priests but still wanted to be part of the religious community. Their job was listed as porter. Their's was a privileged position as they watched the comings and goings of community members, as well as the arrival and departure of all guests to the house. The brothers who made the best porters had eyes like the blind and ears like the deaf. They needed the wisdom of diplomats, the discretion of confessors, and, at times, the strength of lions. Next to the community's rector, the porter probably knew more about what was going on than anyone else in the house. And if the truth were known, he probably knew more than the rector. If you needed to know where Father X was, or who he was counseling, or who was counseling him, the porter was the one who knew. The man with the keys was the man with the news.

Rectors knew that a good porter with discretion was worth his weight in gold.

Helen Hart perched behind her desk, her hands on her computer's keyboard, her eyes fixed on the monitor in front of her. St. Joe's modern-day porter gave no indication she was even aware of Father Townsend and Penny Metcalfe passing through the lobby. Now in her late fifties, Helen had grown up in St. Joseph parish and knew the names of most of the registered members by heart. She had worked as the receptionist for twenty-three years. When a young man and woman walked into her lobby hand-in-hand, giggling and cooing while they waited for Father, Helen did not have to be told to check the church calendar for available Saturdays in May. When older, married couples walked in and waited in silence for the priest, she knew better than to ask about their family. So when Penny Metcalfe walked into her lobby to see Father Townsend and failed to remove her sunglasses, Helen was pretty sure she knew what was going on behind them. And she knew better than to look at the woman's red and swollen face when she told the priest goodbye.

Penny was married to Lyle Metcalfe, the city councilman, and lived in one of the brick mansions on an elm-lined street just outside Volunteer Park. The Metcalfes were generous contributors to St. Joseph. The husband served on the parish finance committee and the wife was on the building committee. Mrs. Metcalfe was always dressed impeccably, with her hair and makeup done perfectly, no matter what the occasion. The same could be said of Mr. Metcalfe, whose face regularly appeared in the newspaper and on TV. Helen knew that Penny Metcalfe's mother had just died. And when she saw the sunglasses, the red nose, and the wad of tissue balled into her hand, Helen was sure that the poor woman was still suffering from her recent loss.

In this case, Helen Hart still had a thing or two to learn.

"Is Jack Abel upstairs?" Father Townsend was standing at her desk, and she turned as if just noticing his presence.

"I think he went out about half an hour ago," she informed the priest.

Mark told her about the vigil on Friday. Neither of them knew what Abel's calendar looked like, but Helen offered to check with the young man when he returned. Before the priest was able to get away, she snatched the remaining pile of messages off her desk.

"Your sister, Pam, called," she said, thrusting the slips of paper at the priest. "And the chancellor tried again. He said he was out the rest of today, but that you could reach him in the morning."

With a look of resignation and with genuine reluctance, Mark accepted the pink pile as if it was his fate. On average, each innocuous piece of paper represented fifteen minutes of his life. He dreaded the chore of returning phone calls. Years earlier, when he once manifested this distaste of his to the provincial, the grim old man, who must have been beleaguered with a pink pile four times the size of Mark's, informed him with something close to theological certitude that he was sure the fires of hell were fueled by millions of blazing pink message slips.

On the same arm holding the papers, Mark resignedly checked his watch. If he worked the phone until dinner, perhaps the flames would burn a degree or two cooler.

FIVE

Mark had the 6:25. Leonard V. Michael's mellifluous baritone voice penetrated his veil of sleep, praising the coming day in glowing terms. Bright sun, blue skies, and temperatures in the mid-to-high seventies. A perfect Seattle day for early August. The radio announcer shifted his attention to other parts of the Pacific Northwest and Mark rolled over onto his back. Morning light was already seeping into his room; outside his window he could hear a robin begin an incessant four-note song. His clock radio glowed at 5:31. Slowly the priest kicked back his bedding and began his morning routine.

Father Townsend had left his lectionary open on his desk last night and one of the first things he did was flip on the desk lamp to refresh his memory with the text. The first reading scheduled for the day's Mass was from Numbers: *Moses is at home in my house. How have you dared to speak against him?* It was not a pretty story; Aaron and Miriam bad-mouthing Moses and God getting mad at them. After a sound scolding, He left Miriam a snow-white leper. An Old Testament *Take that!* Moses himself intervened on her behalf, but even then, God made the poor woman seclude herself for seven days before she was cured. No doubt the seven days Aaron

and Miriam had to spend apart put a lid on some of their
backbiting ways. The gospel account out of Matthew
had Jesus walking on the lake during a storm and Peter
climbing out of the boat to go to him. *Order me to come
to you across the water.* Peter was great with ideas; it
was his executing them that got him in trouble. Father
Townsend padded down the hall to the bathroom, trying
to come up with some connection between Miriam the
snow-white leper and Peter the sinking apostle.

The number of people who showed up at St. Joseph
for Mass at 6:25 on a weekday morning was not large,
twenty-five to thirty on most days. The worshipping
community was small and their faces were familiar to
one another. Very seldom was there an unfamiliar face.
Over the years, Mark had learned their names and most
of the reasons that brought them out of their homes and
into the church when other people were just beginning
to think of getting out of bed. Rain or shine, whether
dark or light, the same faithful few showed up to begin
their day with prayer.

Father Townsend and Father Morrow took turns praying with them. One took the 6:25 Mass and the other
got an extra thirty or forty minutes in bed. They kept
the schedule flexible and traded back and forth whenever
the need arose. The early morning worshippers were
never quite sure which priest would show up to lead the
liturgy.

Their small number would be lost inside the cavern-
ous church, so weekday Masses were celebrated just inside the front doors, in the vestibule. On weekdays the
lobby was transformed into a small chapel with chairs
and a portable altar that could be stowed in a matter of
minutes if the space needed to be cleared. On the weekends the vestibule was always left clear for the larger
crowds who dutifully filed into the church.

After shaving, showering, and donning his black clerics, Mark had time to grab a quick cup of coffee. He
still had no great insights into the readings and only the

vaguest idea of how to talk about them. Fortunately, homilies at the early morning Mass were not expected to run longer than five or six sentences. Most of the attendees were heading to work right after the Mass, and a significant number of them were in a hurry to catch Bus 14 when it arrived at the bottom of the hill behind St. Joseph at 6:55. So if the priest was taking too long, the people started giving nervous and pointed glances at their wristwatches. And if Mass ran any longer than twenty-five minutes, the faithful flock began fraying at the edges as one by one they slipped out of the church and down the hill.

During his theology training, one of Mark's professors warned his students that the length of a homily was a surefire indicator of how much preparation went into it. The longer the preacher rambled, the shorter the time he spent preparing. Saying anything sensible under six sentences at 6:30 in the morning took more preparation than most people suspected.

As always, Mrs. O'Keefe was waiting at the side door when Mark left the house at 6:15 and crossed the street to unlock the church. The little old widow had a rosary tightly wrapped around one hand, and even from the sidewalk Mark could see her lips moving. When he reached the door she gave him a small, patient smile but continued murmuring her silent prayers. No matter how early Mark arrived at the door, Mrs. O'Keefe was there to greet him. Even on the darkest, coldest, and wettest winter mornings, she stood there, rosary in hand, waiting for Father to unlock the door. Several times over the years both Mark and Dan had offered the woman a key to the church, but she always declined. Evidently, there was more grace in suffering.

The two entered together, Mark pausing just inside to flip on the lights to the vestibule. Mrs. O'Keefe headed straight toward her usual chair, second row back on the aisle. She settled in, regularly clicking off the pale blue beads in her small fist.

The Jesuits used a small side room inside the church as the vestry where they kept their vestments and articles for the altar. This morning the door was unlocked. Both priests tried to remember to click the lock when they left, but they both occasionally forgot. Mark carried the lectionary and sacramentary books out to the altar. Dr. Wallace was already lighting the candles on the low altar in front of the half-circle of chairs, and Gary and Sue Budd were just coming into church. Mark greeted them with a smile as he returned to the vestry.

He selected a gold paten and chalice and placed an unconsecrated host on top of the paten. Turning over two small beakers next to the sink, he filled one with water. The Mass wine was kept in a small closet and Mark searched the shelf for the bottle. Yesterday morning he had left a bottle that was half-full, and this morning it was gone. He tried to recall if Dan Morrow had said anything about a larger-than-usual liturgy later in the day that would have emptied the bottle. But even if that were the case, it was not like Morrow to empty a bottle and not replace it. Mark had to thread his way the length of the church to the larger sacristy behind the main altar, where the cases of wine were stored. And as a consequence, the 6:25 Mass at St. Joseph did not begin until 6:29. And because of that, and a homily that ended up running over ten sentences, at precisely 6:50 Mark earned six nervous and very pointed glances at wristwatches and one baleful sigh from Mrs. O'Keefe. Mark felt a lot like Miriam.

Morrow was already pouring his third cup of coffee from the pot in the rectory kitchen when his fellow Jesuit wandered in.

"Morning, Mark," he said, lifting a cup from the shelf and holding it out.

Mark nodded as Dan poured. "There wasn't any wine left in the sacristy this morning," he complained.

"There should have been," Dan told him, "I left a full bottle in there after yesterday's eleven-thirty Mass."

"But yesterday morning there was one over half-full," Mark replied.

"Well, it wasn't there," Dan replied. "I had to go get one."

"Did you remember to lock the sacristy?"

Morrow shrugged. "It was unlocked when I went over, but I thought I locked it when I left."

"We gotta remember to do that," Mark told him as they left the kitchen.

Jack Abel was waiting for Father Townsend outside the priest's office. The social minister was an intense, dedicated young man. His priestly vocation and his days at the diocesan seminary both drew to a close shortly after spending a summer building houses for the poor in Tijuana with a group of college students. While there he met a young woman named Kathy, and now the two were engaged and planning their marriage for next summer.

"Helen said you wanted to see me about some vigil?" Jack said it as a question.

"Yeah," Mark answered. "Come on in."

Both men made themselves comfortable in the priest's office as he searched the top of his desk for the notes he had taken during his phone call to the Lutheran minister.

"They're trying to get something going about these street kids getting killed," Mark told him, still searching his cluttered desk. "The pastor over at Trinity Lutheran called yesterday. They have a vigil planned and want us to join. Both Dan and I are booked, so I was wondering if you could go." Mark found his notes and leaned back in his chair. "Friday, four-thirty, at the courthouse downtown."

Jack started to blush.

"Uh . . . yeah, well . . . uh . . ." His voice trailed off and he gave the priest a sheepish smile.

"You've got a conflict?" the priest asked.

"Yeah, well . . . uh." The young man shifted in his

chair. "Kathy and me were going up to the San Juans for the weekend," he confessed.

An awkward silence fell across both men.

"Well . . . ," Mark began.

"But . . ." Jack started to say, "I could change . . ."

". . . don't change your . . ."

They offered each other foolish, embarrassed smiles. The priest knew perfectly well that many couples engaged in prenuptial sex. And in his premarital counseling he usually brought it up as a point of discussion. But stumbling across the fact with one of his own staff members, a former seminarian, was awkward. For both of them. And there was a long silent pause as each man tried to find some graceful way around the topic.

Father Townsend offered his social minister an inspired smile. "I wouldn't want you to hold up the group to attend the vigil," he told him. "I know it would disappoint your friends."

Relieved, Jack nodded. "Thanks, Mark. Maybe I can find someone else on the committee who could go. I can make some calls."

"Let me know if you find somebody. I haven't been following the story about these kids, so I'm not really up on the situation."

Jack was, and he eagerly leaned forward to tell the priest what he knew. Seattle's population of homeless youth, especially during the warm summer months, is quite large. Some estimates put it at over two thousand kids. Most are runaways and some of them are as young as nine or ten. A few service agencies do what they can for them, but the population is much larger than anyone can adequately handle. As a consequence, the kids end up scrounging whatever and however they can to survive. Drugs, prostitution, and child pornography are not your usual childhood occupations, and neither are muggings, breaking and entering, and even murder. But all of them are familiar to many of the youngest denizens living on Seattle's streets.

St. Joseph's parish outreach brought Jack Abel and his helpers in regular contact with the city's street kids, and the involved parishioners shared a common concern over how little was being done for them. Over the last week and a half, Jack told Father Townsend, four kids had been found murdered. One boy was gunned down right in front of the ferry terminal during a shoot-out. Another boy's body was dumped off a pier into Elliott Bay, and a young girl was found lying under a freeway overpass with her throat slit. The last kid was killed just two days ago. The newspapers said he was tortured and beaten to death. His body was found in an alley near Pioneer Square, stuffed behind a Dumpster. Jack said the police were trying to decide if the killings were connected in any way, but so far it did not appear they were working the investigation with any real energy. At the moment they were still trying to find out the kids' names and where they were from. Most street kids are as separated from their real identities as they are from their families.

Mark Townsend pursed his lips and tugged at the ends of his thick brown moustache as he listened to Jack's description of the killings. He glanced over at his calendar listing his afternoon dental appointment on Friday. Unconsciously, he probed his back molars until he found the rough edge of the cavity near the bottom of his tooth. His dentist had been after him to come in for the past four months. But maybe he ought to cancel his appointment.

"What's that?"

Jack was looking at him, waiting for an answer.

"I'm sorry, Jack. What'd you say?"

"I asked if you wanted to come down with us next time we serve dinner at the Haven. We feed about a hundred and fifty kids. A lot of the churches take turns cooking and serving them meals."

"Yeah, it'd probably be good for me to see that."

Mark was looking at a calendar already hopelessly over-booked. "When'd you say it was?"

"I didn't, Mark." His young staffer smiled patiently at his Jesuit friend. He knew the condition of the priest's calendar and the demands placed on his time. Townsend never even had time to clear the top of his desk. There were at least twenty-five phone messages stacked up beside his phone. And letters, some opened and some not, were scattered in untidy piles across the desk. "We won't plan another meal down there until after school starts up in September. I'll let you know the date."

Father Townsend looked relieved.

During the next forty-five minutes, Mark managed to whittle his phone messages down to twenty-two. And that included fielding three new ones that rang in while he was working. His stomach was grumbling, and he was about to push away from his desk and head for lunch when Father Morrow showed up at his door, looking grim.

"What's up, Dan?" Mark asked.

"I found your missing wine bottles." He held up one hand with the necks of two green bottles twined in his fingers. "Along with the rest of someone's lunch." His other hand lifted a greasy red-and-white cardboard box. A well-gnawed chicken bone slipped out the end and fell onto the carpet.

"In the church again?" Mark bent over and tossed the bone into the trash.

"Right up by the main altar," Morrow informed him. "There were bones and crap all over the pew."

"Well, we're going to have to watch things a little closer, I guess."

His response did not satisfy Father Morrow.

"We've got to do more than that, Mark. This is getting out of hand. The next thing you know, we're going to have people camping out in there."

He was not going to admit it, but over the years Mark

had occasionally come across people doing exactly that. Often they were homeless men who hid until the church was closed and locked for the night. Usually it happened in the winter, when the cold and wet weather forced them into finding any shelter they could just to survive another night. Mark tried to remain gentle, even as he firmly escorted them to the door. Only once had he found a parishioner sleeping inside. He was a widower, quite elderly, and had lain down in a pew near the front and fallen asleep. A month later he was diagnosed with Alzheimer's, and his children quickly moved him into a rest home.

"Let's make sure we double-check the doors, Dan," he suggested to the priest. "And maybe search through the church before we lock up. We sure wouldn't want folks sleeping in there at night, would we?"

SIX

Part of the legacy St. Ignatius left his followers was the Examen, a sort of daily spiritual compass-reading that was intended to refocus the Jesuit's attention and direction back to God. The procedure is simple self-reflection: what directions has my life taken during the last few hours, which were the right turns and which were wrong, and where was God in all of that? The hard part comes with answering honestly. As a prayer, it does not take long, about the length of time it takes to walk around the block or play three games of computer solitaire. Each Jesuit, as he grows familiar with the procedure, finds ways to adapt it to his own circumstances and life. Ignatius cautioned his men that if they found themselves too busy to do anything else spiritual, at least they ought to hang on to the Examen.

For practically his entire time as a Jesuit, Mark Townsend had managed to hang on. Even when his morning prayers, the Divine Office, and spiritual reading were stretched almost to the point of becoming nonexistent, he managed to cling to those few minutes that had become so vital for his balance and self-preservation as a Jesuit and a priest. He usually squeezed in three Examens a day; one right before noon, a very brief one late in the afternoon, and a grand, final one before shutting down for the night. If he had the time, Mark liked to make his final Examen in the quiet darkness of St. Joe's before heading across the street to bed.

When night falls, a terrible stillness descends inside a church. No matter whether a cathedral or a small country chapel, the insides of the building turn quiet and calm, as if the entire structure is holding its breath, waiting. If there is any noise at all, it seems amplified to the point of sounding sacrilegious. Footsteps, a cough, the creak of a pew, even the growl of a car's engine from outside sounds like an unholy violation. Unless you can sit inside a dark church at night without making the slightest sound—not even a breath's sigh—you will feel out of place, as if you are trespassing. That is the feeling.

Moving in and out of shadows cast by vigil candles, blood red sanctuary lamplight, and whatever pale glow penetrates stained glass, are spirits. At night, they occupy the empty, hallowed space of the church as their own—and during daylight, they surrender it to the broken, lonely, and weary who seek refuge there. They wait for the dark, when the church becomes theirs again.

If you come into such a place to make your Examen, you had best be serious about it, and do nothing to disturb the church's spirits or their sanctuary.

Father Townsend sat quietly inside a pew halfway up the long aisle leading to the altar. The light from a few red vigil lights flickered against the high cement walls to his left. Soft light glowed from the high stained-glass windows on either side. Suspended from above, just to the left of the altar, the red sanctuary lamp burned steadily. From far beyond the thick walls he heard one quick bleat of a car's horn. He heard the church take a breath, and from above, the sound of a rafter issuing a sharp complaint. Then silence settled back into the church.

His day had been long and the priest was tired. Starting up at 5:30 and trying to run straight through until 11:00 was too much. He meant to get out for a walk after lunch, perhaps to enjoy a little death for a few minutes. But his homily for the coming weekend anchored him to his desk. Probably it would have gone better if he had taken the break. But anytime he moved toward the lobby, Helen Hart was there, flapping phone messages, demanding his attention. Mark felt a twinge of resentment for the woman. He was making her responsible for those pink intrusions into his life, as if she were telephoning people, recruiting them to call back just to impinge upon his time. That was foolishness, and now the priest acknowledged it. There was a responding creak from something in the church. Helen had her own work at the front desk, and the calls coming in for Mark, Dan, and the rest of the parish staff must feel intrusive to her, too. Yet anytime she answered the phone, she managed to sound pleased to hear the voice on the other end. As a receptionist she was courteous and welcoming. Mark's resentment was misdirected.

He lifted his arms and stretched them out, draping them along the edge of the pew's back. Tipping his head, he stared into the darkness overhead. Voices drifted in from outside; a man's and a woman's, talking excitedly, happily, as they moved down the sidewalk past the side of the church. God bless Helen Hart and the work she does.

Townsend smiled, recalling Jack Abel's visit to his office. His wedding was still a year off. The young man was deeply in love. They were both embarrassed while talking about his romantic plans for the weekend. Maybe there was some way he could have handled that better. Mark sat patiently, waiting for the spirits to tell him what it might have been, but nothing was coming. Young engaged couples have sex before they're married. In the grand scheme of things, how awful was that? Mark knew what the Church thought. He and Jack had been discussing the deaths of four young people. Next to those murders, how bad was making love? Mark let a long sigh escape from deep inside him. His sound swept through the church, from the very back of the choir loft to the tiled mosaic in the sanctuary. There was a stirring and he heard the church sigh back.

So much about what he did as priest still felt like a mystery. And sometimes the mysteries felt like burdens.

Tomorrow he would meet again with Penny Metcalfe. Still mourning her mother's death, she now had to deal with the uncertainty of who she really was—and why she was never told about her adoption. In silence, Mark prayed for the woman. He tried imagining what it would feel like to suddenly discover the people you thought were your parents were not. That your life, as you knew it, was not based in truth. There would be so many questions, so much doubt. The priest brought to mind his own parents. They were retired now, living happily under the warmth of the Arizona sun. What would he feel if one of them called tomorrow and announced, "Mark, it's time you know the truth. You're not our son." How would he react if he was told he had no biological ties to his sister, Pam?

Mark prayed for his family, and mentally added another pink message to the pile on his desk, reminding himself to call his parents over the weekend.

He could feel the day's tiredness seeping into his bones and he relaxed against the pew, stretching his mouth in a wide, silent yawn. He had watched an old man do the same thing during his homily last Sunday. Then it had looked so rude. Tonight it felt so good. The priest stood up suddenly and his foot kicked the kneeler as he did so. In the silence, the sound was like a shot. And from around the edges, he could hear the noise ricochet into the shadows. Mark made a quick, half-hearted genuflection in the aisle and turned to leave. But he caught himself in midstride and turned around again to face the altar. Cocking his head, he listened to the silence in the church, trying to peer into the darkness in front of him.

St. Joseph has eleven different entrances to the main

body of the church. Four of them open from the sanctuary. The other seven are spotted at various points around the room. Each of those eventually connects to doorways leading outside. Some lead downstairs to the parish hall and the gymnasium used by the grade school. Two stairways on either side at the back of the church wind up to the choir loft. In the vestibule itself there are three other entrances from the outside. To trot around and check each door on each level of the church would take Mark nearly half an hour, and a lot more energy than he could summon at 11:15 on a weekday night. Nevertheless the Jesuit priest cautiously negotiated his way around the platform built beneath the dome and climbed the stairs into the sanctuary. He tried the doors on either side of the sanctuary and, satisfied they were locked, headed back toward the main aisle. Genuflecting to the tabernacle once again, Mark moved across to the church's north side to double-check the vestry door. He gave it a good tug and found it locked. Satisfied, the priest turned once again and peered into the church's darkness.

"Good night!" he sang out loudly.

He waited a moment, in case any of the spirits wanted to reply. When they did not, he continued into the vestibule. After checking the locks on all three entrances, Mark left via the one closest to his house.

In the darkness inside, the church spirits once again relaxed. The priest's footsteps faded into silence and everything was still. One of the vigil candles sputtered, flickered twice, and extinguished itself with a small hiss. Then from a narrow dark alcove along the south side, a small piece of the blackness broke free and began slowly and quietly edging down the aisle.

SEVEN

"Corn nuts!"

Mark was hunched over his desk, staring intently at the yellow notepad in front of him, trying to figure out how to preach about the concept of living bread without sounding trite, weird, or like a thousand other sermons on the Eucharist. Father Morrow's loud and angry voice actually lifted the priest off his chair.

"What the hell are you talking about, Dan?"

Taking his question as an invitation to come in, the older priest moved from the door into Father Townsend's cluttered office, thrusting out his right arm and displaying his palm under Mark's nose. His hand was filled with brown nuggets.

"These were scattered all over the back of the church." Morrow's voice was indignant and his face was flushed clear up to the roots of his short hair, now bristling in outrage.

"So someone spilt corn nuts. It's not the end of the world."

"Not spilt," Dan Morrow complained. "These things are scattered clear across the back. You can't take a step without crunching some of them. These weren't spilt, Mark. Some fool is throwing corn nuts in church!"

Father Townsend shrugged. Right now his worries with living bread kept him from getting too concerned with crunching corn. "It was probably a couple of the boys, throwing them at each other."

"I don't care if it was the angel Gabriel! Corn nuts don't belong in church. This whole food thing is way out of line. We've got to put a stop to it."

This was Dan Morrow the high-school vice-principal talking, with more than a little of Marine Sergeant Morrow thrown in for good measure. Mark knew he was going to have to wait some until Father Morrow the pastoral presence made an appearance.

"What would you suggest we do about it, Dan?"

"We need a notice in Sunday's bulletin," the marine ordered curtly. "And I think we should put up some signs on the church doors," urged the vice-principal, "No Food or Drink Allowed in Church."

Mark looked down at his notes on living bread, then grinned up at his associate.

"Dan, the whole point of coming to St. Joe's is for the food and drink inside."

Father Morrow threw the handful of corn nuts into Mark's trash can, angrily brushing the crumbs from his hands. "You know what I mean, Mark. It's not just the mess. Food like this is going to attract rats. We're going to have problems if it continues."

"You're right." He sighed. The image of rats scampering across the feet of worshipping parishioners convinced Mark that the priest was right. "Let me think about it some. I don't think we're to the point of putting up signs, but we've got to do something. I'll think about it a bit."

Mollified only slightly, Father Morrow left his office.

Distracted from living bread by scampering rats, Mark lifted his empty coffee mug and headed for the rectory's kitchen. He had an hour before Penny Metcalfe was due, time enough to come up with one or two ideas for a homily. But not without coffee. Helen Hart was standing with her own coffee mug, leaning over the kitchen table while engrossed in the morning's paper. She was shaking her head as Mark eased past her to the coffee machine.

"What you reading?" he asked.

The receptionist lifted her head. "They found another one of those poor kids dead," she told him. "That makes five."

Mark leaned over her shoulder. "A boy or a girl?"

"A girl this time," Helen told him. "They found her near the beach out by Golden Gardens."

A boxed, two-column story was set into the lower right corner of the front page of the *Seattle Post-Intelligencer*. FIFTH STREET YOUTH FOUND SLAIN. There was no photo with the story, but at least it was on the front page.

"There's some mighty sick people in this world, Father." Helen rinsed her cup in the sink. "Why would anyone be killing those children?"

Mark was still scanning the story, looking for details, as she returned to her post at the front door. The newspaper's report was sketchy. Early Thursday morning, a jogger in the park had discovered the body of a young teenage girl. The police were releasing few details and were not going to give out the girl's name until her family could be notified. But the jogger told the news reporter that it looked to him like the girl had been beaten up. He said the body looked fully clothed, and he could not tell how she died. The police refused to say if the girl was sexually assaulted. A paragraph near the end of the story mentioned the rally being planned for that afternoon at the courthouse. Mark's tongue crept back toward his mutinous molar as he again considered canceling his appointment with the dentist. But if the appointment was not too long, perhaps he could get to the rally before it ended.

Try as he might, Mark was having a hard time getting back to living bread. He forced himself to remain at his

desk, trying to keep his eyes trained on his notepad. But
the Jesuit was finding he kept getting hung up on the
image of bread. Why bread? Why not some other type
of food? There are about as many references to fish in
the gospels as there are bread. Why not living fish? Even
as he thought it, Mark knew the idea was ludicrous. *I
myself am the living fish come down from heaven* . . .
Ridiculous! But as an approach, it might catch the people's attention. Why not fish? Why not a vegetable? Or
dessert? Or for that matter, why not corn nuts?

There was something about what Dan Morrow said
that was still bothering Mark. Without actually intending
it, his thoughts shifted away from living bread and back
to Morrow's complaint. Tugging at the ends of his mustache, the priest tried to recall what it was that had
caught his attention. But whatever it was Dan had said
was not coming back. Helen's phone call, announcing
the arrival of Penny Metcalfe, wiped away all thoughts
of bread and corn nuts.

She looked more composed than she had two days
ago. There were no sunglasses hiding her eyes, and her
face looked smooth and untroubled. Mark noticed Pen's
deft touch with makeup—the pink gloss on her lips and
the blush she had added to her cheeks. Whatever she
was feeling today was better disguised. That did not tell
him anything about his parishioner's mood, but it did
mean she was in more control of her emotions. Her sleek
hair was pulled back into a ponytail, held tightly in place
by a bright red ribbon. Pen was wearing white bermuda
shorts, which deepened the tan on her long legs. A kelly
green knit shirt and espadrilles completed her ensemble.

''I hope you don't mind me looking like this,'' Pen
said, smiling at Father Townsend, ''but I'm meeting
Lyle at the club after we're done. The Powells have
invited us out to lunch on their boat.''

Ron and Judy Powell were a couple of St. Joseph's
wealthier parishioners. Stingiest, too. Which probably
explained how they could afford their many expensive

playthings, including their fifty-five foot *Emerald Lady* moored in Lake Union.

"You look a lot more relaxed today," Mark observed.

Pen dipped her head in acknowledgment. "Staying out of mom's stuff has helped. You were right about it being too soon."

Mark nodded and waited.

The woman in the chair crossed her legs and looked around his office. Her eyes fixed on a dusty Ninja Turtle puppet propped up on one of Mark's bookshelves and she pursed her lips.

"Have you ever wondered why Lyle and I don't have children?"

Mark had. The Metcalfes were a healthy couple, socially and financially established, and in a marriage that appeared relatively secure and happy.

"Lyle doesn't want them," Penny told him bluntly. She leaned forward. "He never has. He told me that before we married and I went along." Her eyes shifted back to the puppet. "I thought he would change his mind once we were settled. But now he thinks children would slow us down." She looked at the priest. "He wants to be mayor, you know."

Mark did not know, but her statement came as no great shock. Lyle Metcalfe had served on Seattle's City Council for three successful terms. He was a recognized political force in the city, so it was not surprising to hear he aspired to a higher post. "He may run against Wes next election," the councilman's wife confided. Wes Dixon was Seattle's current mayor.

"And he thinks children would get in the way?"

Pen nodded. "And at this stage in our lives, he's probably right. Between civic obligations and socializing, we probably don't spend more than one or two nights home a week. There would be no way we could raise a child unless we were to change our lifestyle." The smallest tip of her tongue flicked tentatively at the edge of her upper lip, and she lowered her eyes to study some point on the floor just beyond her legs. "But I don't know," she said softly, "maybe there is some way we could do both."

"It sounds like this is still an open question for you."

Again she nodded.

"Have you raised it with Lyle?"

"Yes. And again last night. We were discussing my adoption and that evolved into another argument about children."

This was the first time she had used the word *argument,* and Mark's ears pricked up. He was expecting Pen to come in and talk about her feelings around discovering she was adopted. Hearing her talking about children surprised him. Now a new element was being introduced; tension between Mr. and Mrs. Metcalfe. Mark felt the ground of the conversation beginning to shift. He remained silent, letting Penny decide the direction they would move.

"If he decides to run for mayor, he doesn't want anything to get in the way."

"And that would include children?"

The woman began shaking her head no, then stopped and nodded. "Yes, no children," she agreed. "But he doesn't want me doing anything about my adoption, either." She stopped and searched Father Townsend's face. Discovering confusion, she pressed on. "I told him I wanted to look into it, to try and find out more about my background. He said absolutely not. He told me to let it go."

Mark's chair let out a loud creak and he realized he was pushing back as far as his desk chair would let him. He caught himself putting greater space between himself and his parishioner, and he quite consciously righted his chair and rolled it a couple of inches closer to the woman. This was no time to be distancing himself from her or her troubles. But for some reason he had caught himself recoiling from what she told him.

"I'm surprised," he confessed. "I didn't think Lyle would react that way."

"Me either, Mark. I was stunned when he asked me not to pursue it." She crossed her arms and drew them in tightly beneath her breasts. "We were driving back from a dinner at Hunt's Point and were on the bridge. I was telling Lyle that all evening I felt like a stranger at our friends' house, like I wasn't really sure who I was. It was the strangest sensation, and it would catch me at the oddest moments. For instance, one of the women was talking about growing up in Omaha, and she described her earliest memory of having a picnic beside a river when she wasn't any more than two or three. And I sat there realizing that I have no early memories of my real parents. My first one is of walking between mother and father in Volunteer Park. Except now I know that there were two other people who had me before that memory."

Penny Metcalfe stopped talking but held her mouth open, staring at the priest. "I don't know who those people were, what they were like, or anything. And I don't know why they did not keep me. That's what I mean about feeling like a stranger. It's like I have discovered this huge locked box in my life. Inside it are all sorts of secrets about myself, and I have no way of getting it open. And now my husband is telling me to ignore it."

She uncrossed her arms and laid her hands in her lap. Her eyes were flashing, and Mark could see she was tightening her jaw. He waited. Penny was looking straight into the priest's eyes, and Father Townsend did not let his own eyes waver as he looked back. Neither one spoke, and the silence in the room lasted for a full two minutes.

"I'm not going to do it." Pen Metcalfe decided.

"You're not going to do what?"

"I won't ignore the fact I was adopted," she said firmly. "If I do, that leaves me with too many unan-

swered questions about myself. There are things that I
want to know—'' she stopped herself. ''There are things
I have a right to know. And I'm going to find them out.''
Having made her decision, Pen uncrossed her legs,
planted both espadrilles firmly on the floor, and gave
Father Townsend a bright smile and a look of determination. Mark smiled back.

Pastors often find themselves in the position of counseling parishioners. There is not a seminary in the world
that does not offer at least one course in pastoral counseling, teaching the fundamentals of how to become an
effective counselor. And every minister and priest with
any experience at all knows that the line between what
is spiritual and what is psychological counseling can be
razor thin. That line gets crossed all the time, in confes-
sionals and rectory parlors everywhere. Good pastoral
counselors know how hazardous razor-thin lines can be.

''It sounds to me,'' Mark began, ''like you've made
a decision.''

Pen bobbed her head in agreement.

''Then what I'd like to suggest,'' the priest continued,
''is that you take a little more time to rest with your
decision. Give it some more thought and even a little
prayer.''

''My mind's made up, Mark.'' She was still smiling.
''I'm going to go ahead with this. I'm going to find out
who I am.''

''That's quite clear, Pen. And I'm not trying to change
your mind. All I'm suggesting is that you hold off acting
on your decision for a little bit.'' Father Townsend
leaned forward, resting his arms on his knees and clasping his hands together. ''In Jesuit language, we would
say that what you've done is made an election. You've
decided on a course of action. The next step is to seek
confirmation. That means taking a little more time to
consider your decision. It doesn't mean you're going to
change your mind.''

Pen interrupted, ''Then why wait?''

"It's like pudding." Mark grinned at her. "You commit to making it, but then you have to wait until it firms up, don't you?"

The woman laughed out loud. "Mark, sometimes you astound me! Who in heaven's name would ever believe a Jesuit is comparing something spiritual with pudding?"

Father Townsend was on a roll. "But that's sort of what it's like, Pen. In spiritual discernment you first make an election, then you wait for confirmation. And that's my field. If you come to see me for advice, you're going to get spiritual direction. I'm suggesting you wait for confirmation before acting on your decision."

Penny Metcalfe stopped laughing and was listening to what the priest was telling her. "So I wait," she said, "and do what?"

"Just rest with it," Mark suggested. "See if it feels as right tonight as it does this morning. And tomorrow, when you get up, check the feeling again. You might even try bringing it to prayer."

She shrugged. "I could do that, I suppose. For a couple of days anyway."

"Through the weekend," Mark urged. "If you feel the same way on Monday, then go ahead with your plans."

"And what about Lyle? What do I say to him?"

Mark checked the line. It was very long, very thin, and razor sharp.

"Let me pray about that," he answered weakly. "I'll get back to you."

"Canceling appointments only postpones the inevitable, Father." Mark was being scolded. "These things don't go away on their own." His dentist's eyes twinkled. "Unless you've got access to the miracle hotline over at St. Joe's."

Dr. Garry continued poking and prodding against Mark's upper gum. The Novocain was a thick blanket protecting him from pain, but all the activity in his mouth was uncomfortable, and Mark found himself tightly clutching the arms of the chair to avoid squirming in his seat.

"We're almost ready here. I just want to get a little more."

Mark watched the dentist reach for his drill. He hated the drill. He tried distracting himself by thinking of other matters. His conversation with Penny Metcalfe earlier in the day continued to disturb him. The Metcalfes were two of his closest friends in the parish, and the priest was uncomfortable in knowing there were tensions between them. From the way she had described it, there was more than one issue at stake. A central one was the disagreement over children, but her wanting to look into her adoption sounded like it might displace the one about kids, at least for the time being. It was not until after lunch that Mark realized he had neglected to ask Lyle's reasons for not wanting his wife to investigate her adoption. He was mildly irritated at himself for missing that obvious question.

"I need you to open your mouth a little wider, Father." Mark was frowning with a mouthful of fingers. At least the drilling was stopped. His mouth was going to be sore for a few hours. He had purposely planned on having dinner at home tonight, knowing he was going to be picky about what went into his mouth. Nothing hot, nothing cold, not too hard. If Morrow found any more corn nuts he would have to eat them himself. Mark winced just thinking about the pain of biting down on one of those.

"Wider, please!" Dr. Garry's voice was tinged with a note of impatience. But on a Friday afternoon, at nearly five o'clock, it was understandable. Mark knew he was probably not the dentist's most cooperative patient.

There was something about Father Morrow's brief morning visit to his office that had been bothering Mark all day. Whatever it was hovered right beyond the edge of his consciousness, just out of reach. Like this damn cavity, it was not enough to distract him totally from his work but just enough of a bother to keep him on edge.

He could hear Garry giving his assistant instructions. Asking for this or that while rubber-gloved fingers kept flitting above Mark's face, darting into his mouth momentarily and then back out again. How much longer were they going to take?

The young woman sitting on his right, just beyond his line of sight, leaned a little closer and cooed into his ear, "I need you to bite down on this, Father." He felt a flutter go past his lips; it felt like a butterfly had flown into his mouth. "No," she instructed, "not quite yet." Whatever it was had settled over the tooth Dr. Garry was working on. "Now," she ordered, "move your jaw around, back and forth." Mark made a few tentative thrusts with his jaw. "You'll have to do it harder than that," she encouraged. He ground his teeth together and was rewarded with a pleased look from the assistant. "There we go. Open wide." The butterfly flitted out and Dr. Garry's puckered brow hovered into view. He peered in and went to work with something that felt like a tiny belt sander.

"I'm just smoothing the filling to match your bite," he offered. He sanded a few more moments, then waited while his assistant went through a similar exercise with Mark biting down and grinding back and forth again. This was a mysterious procedure and one the priest could not recall doing before. As his dentist went back to sanding, he tried to figure out how the two activities were related. Flutter, bite, and grind. Then sand. Flutter. Bite. Grind. Sand. Whatever he was biting down on must be leaving some sort of mark, showing the dentist where the tooth still needed further smoothing. Something like carbon paper, Mark guessed. It probably marked the tooth, showing his dentist where he needed to go.

That was it! Flutter, bite, grind, then sand! Mark had it! Despite the tools and fingers, his mouth formed into a wide grin. Above and behind his head, Dr. Garry and his assistant exchanged puzzled glances. This had a been a long week, and the priest was their last patient. After fighting them through most of the procedure, his mouth was now stretched into a wide smile.

The dentist shrugged at his assistant and turned his attention back to the priest. "Father," he scolded, "you're going to have to open just a little bit wider."

EIGHT

The front door was open and through the screen Mark heard the crack of a bat. Morrow was watching the Mariners. He bounded into the living room, startling Dan, who was just lifting a can of beer to his mouth.

"Dammit, Mark!" he barked, brushing spilt foam off the front of his clerical shirt. "This was my last clean shirt."

A bat cracked and both sets of eyes automatically shifted to the television. Another Griffey homer.

"What's the score?"

"That makes it three to two," Father Morrow replied, forgetting the stains on his shirt for the moment. "Top of the third. Maybe the boys are going to pull one off."

Griffey tagged home and while the camera pulled back and panned the Kingdome crowd, a beer company's logo spread across the television just before the screen switched to a commercial for pizza. Mark's tongue touched lightly on his new filling. Pizza, if it was cool enough, might be okay.

"Tell me about those corn nuts again, Dan."

"What?" Father Morrow was thinking about pizza, too. "What about 'em?"

"Tell me where you found them."

"They were scattered all over the back of the church."

"The vestibule or the inside of the church?"

Dan Morrow shifted his position on the couch so he could look directly at Mark Townsend. He knew he had been at the dentist's, maybe it was the Novocaine.

"Inside the church, through the lobby and into the back. They were all over the floor."

Flutter, bite, grind, and sand. Mark had a wild grin on his face.

"What's this all about?" Father Morrow asked.

"I think I figured out why they were there," Mark told him.

"This morning you said kids were throwing them."

"Yeah, but I was wrong. I think someone spread them back there on purpose."

What for?"

The game came back on just as a pitch was thrown. There was another loud crack and Dan Morrow's head swiveled back to the set.

"As an alarm," Mark told the back of his associate's head. "I think they were there on purpose."

Father Morrow was more interested in the Mariners than he was corn nuts, at least for the moment, and he declined Mark's invitation to go with him to inspect the church. So Father Townsend crossed the street and went into the side entrance of the vestibule by himself. The doors were still unlocked; it was only a little past six o'clock. He entered the main body of the church through the wide double doors in the center of the vestibule. There was still plenty of light outside, and the inside of St. Joseph was bathed in soft colored lights filtering through the rows of stained-glass windows set into the church's cement walls. The pews were empty as far as Mark could see. There were a few rows in both transepts that he could not see from the very back of the church. He listened for any human sound, but the church was quiet. Father Townsend looked down at his feet. The cement floor was swept clean. He walked along the back wall toward the north, searching the floor until he arrived at the other set of doors leading to the vestibule. No sign of any corn nuts. Mark doubled back and walked to the other set of doors on the south side. Nothing. He stopped walking and stared toward the main altar. As far as he could see, there was nothing amiss inside the church. And yet, he knew there was.

Someone was living inside St. Joseph church, the Jesuit was convinced of it. The empty food containers over the last week or so meant that whomever it was had been in here for some time. And the corn nuts on the floor were meant as an alarm. If anyone tried walking into the church, he or she would step on them. The way Morrow described finding them scattered across the floor, there was no way you could avoid them. Inside the quiet church, the sound of the loud, brittle crunching would have carried into every corner of the building, warning whoever was hiding inside that someone had just come in. If you were in the church and were afraid of being turned out, the sound might give you time to duck out of sight. The nuts were a cheap but effective alarm system. Mark continued searching around his church. Someone was there, all right. He was sure of it.

Greeks make the best pizza. And Olympic Pizza was so close to St. Joe's that you could almost hear the mozzarella bubbling. At the top of the seventh, the Mariners and Twins were tied. Mark placed their order for a large number twenty-five with extra pepperoni and, while Dan yelled at Griffey for another long one, quickly drove the five short blocks to pick up their order. He was back in time to see the Twins run onto the field for the bottom of the inning. And as the sunlight slowly dimmed across Seattle, the two Jesuits munched their large number twenty-five, drank two more beers apiece, and cheered as the Mariners won by two. Mark's tooth felt fine. By the time the game ended, the night sky was completely dark and a cool breeze was beginning to blow through the screen door.

"You want to take a walk?" Mark suggested.

"Let me grab a jacket first," said Dan.

The priests set off down Eighteenth in the opposite direction of the church. Despite the dark sky, there were enough street lights to see that there was still plenty of activity in the neighborhood. Warm summer nights in Seattle are wonderful gifts, rare enough not to be undervalued. And while the sidewalks were hardly crowded, there were plenty of people still outside. Halfway up the block, an army of small children were engaged in some sort of game that required lots of running and screaming. And on a lawn across the street, four teenaged girls were crowded around a CD player, talking excitedly over the heavy bass booms coming from the box. Someone's sprinkler made soft swooshing sounds as it swept back and forth across the lawn.

The two men were easily recognizable. Father Morrow, by his tall, erect stride and the stiff brush cut that made his silhouette so distinctive; Father Townsend was just as tall, but his body drooped more, as if there was a huge weight pushing down on his shoulders. And he ambled. Parishioners seldom saw Father Townsend striding anywhere. But he was a great one for ambling through the neighborhood. Voices called out greetings to the priests as they wandered through the neighborhood. They politely turned down two requests to join families on their porches, preferring their own company as they toured the streets around their church.

Mark had already explained his theory behind the corn nuts while they watched the baseball game and ate pizza. Morrow was inclined to agree that someone was camping inside St. Joseph, given the amount of trash they were finding in the church during the past few days. As they meandered through the neighborhood, the Jesuits speculated who could be hiding in their church. Both were convinced it was a single person. Morrow was positive that their guest was female. A woman was more inclined to hide in a church, he reasoned, considering it as a place of safe refuge. Men, on the other hand, were not afraid to brave the elements. They would be more likely to find a place to sleep in Volunteer Park, he claimed. Whoever she was, she was smart enough to think up the trick with the corn nuts. That implied at least some education and intelligence. So this was not one of the homeless and disturbed women you saw pushing shopping carts and muttering to a doll, Father Morrow theorized. This woman had her wits about her. He was guessing it was a someone hiding from an abusive boyfriend or husband. Or maybe her life had been threatened. And she was not Catholic. No Catholic with a conscience, Father Morrow believed, would dare leave messes like they were finding inside their church.

Mark had his doubts. Not about it being a single person; but Morrow's scenario of an educated and abused non-Catholic woman sounded like too much guesswork. Father Townsend had no idea if the person inside St. Joe's was a man or woman, nor how educated he or she might be. There was one thing he felt pretty sure of, though—this person had a good reason to want to hide in a church. Anything beyond that was merely guessing.

"How about a little counterinsurgency?" Father Morrow suggested.

This was the marine coming out in him, Mark was sure.

"What do you mean?"

"Let's try sneaking into the enemy's camp," urged Dan. "Maybe we can catch her by surprise."

Father Townsend started pulling hard at his mustache. "You mean like an ambush?"

"Yeah!" Dan said excitedly. "Let's go back and see if we can't surprise her. You go in the front and I'll sneak in through the back."

Mark checked his watch. It was after ten o'clock. Earlier in the evening he felt sure someone was still inside the church, although he had neither heard nor seen anything that gave any clue as to where the person might be hiding. There were too many nooks and crannies inside the old church to search them all. But if their mystery person came out from hiding at night, she or he might be in the open now—which might explain why the nuts were scattered across the floor. If you were going to stay hidden, why bother rigging the messy alarm system?

"What do you say? You wanna try it?" Even in the dark Father Townsend could see his fellow Jesuit's eyes gleaming. "Let's go do it."

They were on Sixteenth now, heading in the direction of the church. Mark had to hustle to keep up with Dan's long strides. He was more amused by the older priest's sense of adventure than anything else, and he had very little expectation that their gambit would prove successful. Still, what could it hurt? And they had to lock the church for the night anyway.

When they reached the sidewalk in front of the rectory, next to the church, Dan held up a hand and stopped. In a conspiratorial whisper, he planned their joint attack. Fortunately they were standing in a dark spot on the walk, so Father Morrow could not see his companion's amused grin.

"I'm going to cut around to that basement door on the side," he was saying. "Then I'll go up the stairs to the church. Give me five minutes to get into position."

Mark was trying hard not to giggle. He felt like he was twelve again, staying out late on a summer's night, getting in one last game of Army with his friends before being called into his house. Dan Morrow was trying to see his face in the dark, so Mark quickly summoned a look of serious concentration.

"Meanwhile," the priest continued, "you go in through the vestibule. If you can do it quietly, get just inside the back door and wait for me there." He stopped and laid a hand on Mark's shoulder. "You'd better go in the side door, not the center. There's that light right over the middle door and she might see you. Wait in the back corner where it's dark, and I'll come out the front. If we're lucky, we'll trap her between us.''

Mark bit down hard to avoid another laugh. A sharp and sudden pain from his new filling drove away all thoughts of humor. But Father Morrow saw only the wince.

''Don't worry, Mark. We'll be perfectly safe.'' With that he gave the priest a reassuring slap on the back and broke into a jog as he headed around the corner of the church. Father Townsend strolled to the side door closest to the parish office.

Once he slipped into the vestibule he began having second thoughts about their plan. It was much darker inside than out on the sidewalk. He tried listening for any sounds coming from the church. He thought he heard a shuffle, but perhaps not. Mark laid his hand against the cool concrete wall and slowly inched his way forward in the blackness. He looked at his watch, but in the church's dark interior it was impossible to see the time. Dan said to wait five minutes. He had two or three more to go. Mark's fingers felt the wood of the door that opened into the body of the church; he let his hand glide down the grainy surface until it grasped the brass handle. His palms were surprisingly sweaty. And again he had the impulse to call this off. But Dan would already be inside and was probably already creeping up the stairs from the basement. He could step inside and yell for the priest and that would end it. Mark was cautiously opening the door when he heard another noise. Several loud clicks sounded from somewhere near the center of the church. Pulling back the door, he quickly slipped inside. He stayed in the corner as his eyes tried to penetrate the darkness around him. The priest heard another shuffling movement from somewhere near the front altar. The door gave a groan as it finished closing behind him. Too late, Mark had forgotten to slow the heavy door's movement with his hand. Now there was absolute quiet. He listened carefully. Nothing. The inside of the church felt tense, as if poised and waiting. Where was Morrow?

Mark strained to see into the darkness. But other than the small red glow coming from the vigil lights in front and the pale exit sign over the far doorway, there was nothing more he could see. His ears were picking up no sounds, either. The church was absolutely still. Time slowed, seeming to stop, and Mark could hear his own shallow breaths. In the silence they sounded loud and heavy.

Dan Morrow burst through the doorway near the church front with a loud bellow. The sudden noise startled Mark even though he was expecting it.

"Mark! Mark, are you back there?"

"Right here, Dan." The two priests were yelling loudly and their voices reverberated throughout the building.

"Do you see anything?" Morrow shouted back.

"I don't see anything," Mark loudly answered, "but I thought I heard some sounds coming from the other side of the altar."

"Which other side?" Father Morrow was starting to move. Mark heard the Jesuit shuffling forward. At least he thought it was the Jesuit.

"On the St. Joseph side," he replied. There were two mosaics flanking the sanctuary in the front of the church: Mary to the north, Joseph to the south.

"All right," Dan shouted back. "I'll cross over in the front and you start up from the back." He was making no attempt to speak softly; his plan was to flush out anyone who might be hiding. Or get them to give up. "Start walking forward. Now!" Morrow ordered.

Mark headed up the side aisle. He spotted a tall dark shadow striding in front of him, coming from the left, opposite him. Morrow was moving, too. He would reach the pews in front of St. Joseph before Mark. "Do you see anything?" Mark called to him.

"It's too dark," Dan yelled back. "I'm going to hit the lights."

In the darkness in front of them there was a sudden scurrying. Both priests heard footsteps as someone started to run.

"Where is she?" Dan cried.

Mark stopped moving, trying to see in the dark. His eyes searched the blackness in front of him. A shadowy streak passed between him and the vigil lights.

"She's coming toward you," he shouted out.

From the other side he heard Morrow rush toward the center aisle. Mark started running forward himself. There was a sudden loud clatter from directly in front of the altar, followed by a rolling, clicking sound. Something was moving across the concrete floor, down the center aisle. Mark quickly darted into the pew beside him and started hurrying toward the center, hoping to catch up with whomever or whatever it was. The clacking sound was growing louder and Father Townsend realized he was about to intercept whatever was coming his way. About six feet before he reached the end of the pew, his foot caught on a kneeler that was left down and the priest felt himself sprawling forward. His hands shot out to break his fall, but his body crashed onto the kneeler in front of him. The priest's right ankle twisted sharply and he felt a sharp stab on the palm of his left hand as it slammed against the edge of the pew. He felt his flesh tear as he pulled his hand away. With his head just inside the end of the pew, Mark managed to lift his eyes in time to see a dark figure rolling past.

Dan Morrow heard his friend fall and called out.

"I'm right here, Dan," Mark answered the priest, trying to lift himself up. The clacking noise was at the very back of the church now and there was a sudden, loud scrape as the sound shifted direction. Mark caught sight of a moving figure just before it disappeared into the dark shadows at the far north end corner. Whomever it was had found the door in back and pushed it open. The rolling suddenly stopped, quickly followed by footsteps hitting the stairs leading down into the church basement. At the bottom of those stairs was a doorway opening to the outside, and Mark slowly eased himself onto the pew, knowing further pursuit was futile.

"What the hell was that?" Dan Morrow was at his side. "Are you all right?"

Both men were breathing hard, and their hearts were racing. Mark's hand was beginning to throb and his foot felt like it might be sprained.

"I'm okay," he managed to say. He gingerly touched his left palm. "I think my hand's bleeding, though. I fell over the kneeler, otherwise I think I could have got him."

"What was that?" Morrow asked again. "Could you see it?"

In the darkness there had not been much to see. Only the shadowy figure moving much too quickly into the back of the church. Nothing to see, but plenty to hear.

Mark could feel the wetness of blood on his hand.

"It was a skateboard, Dan. The kid was on a skateboard."

NINE

If you hang out in the dark long enough, your eyes get used to it and you can see quite a bit. The same thing happens if you are in a place where darkness creeps in gradually until you feel like you are swallowed up by it. But then you don't have the feeling of not being able to see at the beginning, because your eyes begin adjusting to the lower light right from the start. That's how that works.

So like if you are in a church when it grows dark outside, and you don't have any bright lights to distract you, probably you are able to see and move around inside pretty good. And your hearing is good, too, because your ears aren't so used to a lot of noise. Churches are mostly quiet when no one is inside them. No one besides yourself, that is. So if a car drives by or someone around the church is playing a radio, you can hear it real loud, like it's right there next to you. Or even if someone unlocks a door in the basement. They don't think you can hear the loud click of the lock and the door opening, but if you're listening, you can. And then, because you know they're coming, you can hear soft footsteps creeping up the stairs.

The best thing to do is have a hiding place already

picked out. So if you hear a sound like that, you can go there. And because your eyes are used to the dark, you can move quickly, without bumping into stuff. But if you start to go there and then your eyes catch just a thin sliver of light in the back corner of the church, and it only lasts a second, you can figure someone else is sneaking inside through the back door in the corner. You're sure of it when you hear the door bump close. And then you know they're trying to trap you. Only they probably already have because the one door on your side is locked and you know that because you've tried it before.

Now you need to think of something else. But your throat is dried out and it's hard to swallow, and your heart is beating real fast and loud and it's harder to think. You can't hear anything coming from the dark in the back, but whoever is coming up the stairs is getting closer because you can hear that. And you're too late to try and climb up and hide on top of the boxes where they hear confessions, but maybe you can get inside one and they won't think to look in there. You figure you'll start to go there, but then someone crashes in from the door on the other side and yells real loud. And then the one in the back yells. Now your mouth is really, like, all dried out, and you're so scared you can't even move anymore, even though you can hear both of them coming right at you. It's like you're paralyzed.

When the one on the side says he's going to turn on lights, you come back to life. You know that if those lights come on that you're dead, so you decide to make a break for it. And you slam down your board and push off for the back, only away from where the guy is. And you pick up some speed when you can see the light over the door in the back that you're aiming for. You know the door on the side is unlocked and you know where those stairs go, so you rip as fast as you can down the concrete, which is pretty smooth. There's a guy cutting through the benches to head you off and it looks like he's going to make it, only then he falls and you shoot by him, aiming for the back. You hang a hard right and head for the door. There's voices behind you, but they're way back now, in the middle of the church, and you know you're making it and you hit the door, flying. Your foot slams the deck of your board, and when it flips up you catch it on the fly and take the stairs two at a time, running down until you hit the outside door. This time you don't wait to block the latch so it doesn't lock behind you. You hit the sidewalk and jump back on your board. You have a choice to go up or down the hill, but it's no contest because you're rushing now and you aim down and shoot the steep sidewalk to the bottom of the hill, stopping long enough to look behind you.

The street is deserted and you can't see anyone running out of the church. But you're still scared and you're not going to hang around, so you push off and roll down the street to put some distance between you and them. Your mind and your heart are both racing, and you're, like, so glad to be out of there. No way are they going to catch you now.

After a couple of more blocks you can slow down and begin to think a little. Whoever the two guys were, they knew you were in there. They knew right where to find you, so that means you are probably going to have to find some place else to hide. But you know you need to go back to that church one more time. Getting in and out is no problem. But if they're waiting for you, it could be harder.

If you knew they were priests, you might not have run. If you weren't fourteen and you weren't so scared of someone trying to find you and maybe kill you. If you weren't quite so alone. If you weren't all those things, and you knew the two guys were priests, maybe you wouldn't have run but stayed and, like, let them catch you.

TEN

Saturdays were the one day of the week when the priests at St. Joseph could sleep late. And they usually did. There was no Mass until late in the afternoon. There were still meetings and appointments, and oftentimes a wedding, but both Mark Townsend and Dan Morrow took the opportunity to stay in bed longer than usual. For Father Morrow, that meant sleeping until six. But Father Townsend was never a marine, so he felt none of the same compulsion and, on most Saturdays, usually managed to lie in bed until seven. There may have been a few residual twinges of guilt left over from his novitiate training, when the novice master informed them that only the idle rich could afford to sleep past sunrise. But novitiate guilt is more pleasurable than ordinary kinds, and so Jesuits usually take delight committing the peccadilloes their novice master warned them against. Sleeping-in and eating between meals were two of Mark's favorites.

This Saturday he was also feeling stiff and sore. His mad dash through the dark church had left him with a twisted ankle and an achy hand. He stayed in bed a little longer and, when he finally did get up, moved a little slower. When he eventually made it down to the kitchen,

Dan was already on his third cup of coffee, finished with the Seattle paper, and halfway through the front section of the *New York Times*.

"How you feeling?" he grunted.

"Sore." Mark headed for the coffee.

"You really ought to exercise more, Mark. You're beginning to get a belly."

"Yeah, maybe." Townsend finished pouring his coffee and was poised to turn back toward his room if Morrow was planning to pursue this conversation. He did not need a lecture this morning. But the Jesuit's nose was back in his *Times*, so Mark wandered to the table and dropped into a chair.

"Any news?"

Father Morrow shook his head. Mark rested his chin in his hand and idly stared out the window while slowly sipping his coffee. From where he sat he had a good view of one side of St. Joseph. He could see the basement door where the kid ran. Both priests had known pursuit was useless, so they had not tried. Dan went through the church, checking all the doors, while Mark limped home and wrapped a bag of ice around his ankle. When Morrow returned, he reported finding two of the basement doors propped open with pieces of cardboard wedged into the locks. Father Morrow was convinced that he had secured the church and had announced it was locked up "tight as a drum." Father Townsend sipped more coffee and looked across at the open window in one of the rest rooms. He considered pointing it out to Dan but decided the silence was more pleasant.

By 8:30 he was in his office, shuffling the papers on his desk. He rifled through the phone messages, sorting out any that looked as though they could be returned on a Saturday. There were not many. The dog-eared yellow pages with his homily notes poked obtrusively from his desk drawer, and finally with a sigh of surrender, Mark pulled them out and set to work. He had eight more hours to come up with something about living bread.

The first Mass of the weekend began at five o'clock, and that was his deadline.

Although the parish offices were ostensibly closed on Saturday, there was a constant flow of visitors into the rectory. There were no weddings scheduled that day, but the place was still busy. The youth minister came in, leading half a dozen teenagers up to her office on the second floor. As they filed past Mark's office, there was a chorus of *Good morning, Father,* and *Hi, Father Townsend.* There was even a *Yo! Padre!* from one of the boys. At a quarter to twelve, Helen Hart materialized at his door.

"Good morning," she said brightly.

Mark looked up from his notes and smiled back at the receptionist.

"What are you doing here on a Saturday?" he asked.

"I'm dropping the bulletins off. They weren't ready yesterday. Anything exciting going on?"

The priest shrugged. "Nancy's got a group of kids upstairs and I heard some voices back in the kitchen awhile ago." A twinge in his ankle reminded him. "Oh yeah, Dan and I almost caught our church mouse last night."

"The one who's leaving food?"

"It was a kid on a skateboard."

Helen pursed her lips. "What would a child be doing in a church? Was it a boy?"

"Dan thinks it was girl, but I couldn't tell," Mark admitted. "Whomever it was, was fast. You should have seen him shoot out of there. I think we scared the bejesus out of the kid."

Maternal concern softened the woman's face. "I can't imagine a child hiding in our church," she told the priest. "Where are the parents? We've had trouble with derelicts before, but never a child." She wagged her head at the wonder of it.

Mark stayed planted at his desk until after one, finishing up his homily. Not one of his best but hopefully not a clunker, either. He would know in a few more hours. He fixed himself a sandwich in the rectory kitchen and quickly ate it standing at the sink. The sun was hot and he could feel the heavy dry air pushing against him from the open window above the sink. He had time before Mass to get some of that exercise Dan mentioned. Leaving through the front door, Father Townsend headed for Volunteer Park.

The neighborhood around St. Joseph consists of mostly old two- and three-story houses built in the late 1800s and early 1900s by Seattle's more established medical, business, and civic leaders. After about fifteen years of dowdy and dangerous decline during the sixties and seventies, when suburbs like Edmonds and Bellevue became the more fashionable addresses, families started returning to Capital Hill, reclaiming the old homes, once again creating neighborhoods where children could safely play and oldsters could walk to the store without fear. After nightfall the area is still no time to be out walking alone, but during the day the neighborhood around St. Joe's is peaceful and relatively quiet.

Volunteer Park is only four blocks from the church and, on a hot Saturday in August, crowded with visitors. In its earliest days it was simply referred to as the City Park. But before becoming a park it was a pig farm. Funeral caissons had to roll through the muddy yard to reach the property owned by Doc Maynard, which was becoming Seattle's main cemetery. When the town's citizens decided to build the park, they bought the farm and moved some of the closest graves out of the way. And after the Spanish-American War, the park was rededicated to honor Seattle's volunteers who fought in the war. A water reservoir was dug near the center, and a tall red-brick water tower was erected nearby to add pressure for all the tubs, sinks, and flush toilets going into the homes surrounding the park. Cedar, spruce, and cherry trees were planted throughout the park, and a bandshell was built in a large open lawn. What was once a pig farm was now becoming an idyllic, bucolic spot for Seattle's gentry. A few years later a conservatory, modeled after London's Crystal Palace, was built near what was then the entrance into the cemetery. The reservoir, water tower, and conservatory are still there, now joined by the Seattle Asian Art Museum. The museum stands at the park's highest point, overlooking Elliott Bay and offering a great view of the Seattle Space Needle. Two large stone camels flank the entrance into the building and, as Father Townsend wandered past, he spotted the usual pack of small children clamoring over the tops of the stalwart stone beasts.

Across the street, an arc of water shot high into the air above the water reservoir. Mark slowed to catch the view of the Space Needle through the hole in the huge black granite sculpture perched on a ledge above the water. Formally titled *Black Sun*, most locals simply referred to it as the Doughnut. A cluster of Asian tourists were crowded around its base for a photo, posed with the Needle lined up in the hole behind them. They were not exactly the first ones to think of that photo op. Father Townsend smiled and walked on. The lawns all around him were dotted with couples, kids, and dogs. Frisbees were flying through the air, and the rhythmic beat of drums boomed up from the direction of the bandshell. The day was way too hot to wander through the humid interior of the conservatory, so Mark circled the bronze statue of William Seward and turned east. The children's play area was crawling with tots, and their squeals drowned out all other sounds, including the loud drums. The water in the shallow wading pond looked like it was boiling as dozens of little feet churned through it. From the look of things, as much water was splashed onto the walkway around the pond as was still in it. A couple of the parents spotted their parish priest and called out a greeting. Mark smiled and waved but pretended not to notice their arms motioning him to join them. He was enjoying the pleasure of his own company this afternoon and had no need or desire to stop and visit.

Once he hit the street that ran past the park's entrance, he turned left, in the opposite direction of St. Joe's. There was still time to enjoy a little death, so Mark headed for the wide iron gates of Lake View Cemetery. The original entrance into the cemetery had been located just a little up the hill from the children's wading pond, but now it was sealed off with a chain link fence and shrubs that separated the park from the cemetery. The oldest graves were toward the back, and Father Townsend headed in that direction. As he strolled further into the cemetery, he could see several cars parked along the drive near Bruce Lee's grave. He heard flute music as he drew closer, and saw three tight clusters of people standing around the site. Whatever was going on was nothing he wanted to become involved in, so the priest kept walking straight, avoiding the crowd.

One of his favorite plots was in front of him, and Mark paused a few moments to pay his respects to the Pontius family. In 1889, the Pontius family owned the building that first caught fire and resulted in Seattle burning to the ground. Chicago has Mrs. O'Leary's maligned cow, and Seattle has the glue pot in the basement of the Pontius Building.

By the time he returned to St. Joseph it was after three o'clock. The priest was tired and sweating in the heat. Dan Morrow was in front of the television again, engrossed in the first game of a Mariner's doubleheader. He barely glanced at Mark as he headed upstairs. Father Townsend had the Saturday Mass, which meant he did not have the leisure for watching baseball. By the time he showered and shaved, dressed in his clerics, and once more reviewed his homily, it would be time to begin setting up for Mass. The routine was familiar enough that Mark did not feel any urgent need to rush, but he knew better than to park himself in front of the television. Getting distracted by a baseball game was not a good idea.

By 4:20 he was changed out of blue jeans and into his blacks, his homily notes neatly organized and sorted, and heading to church. Morrow wished him luck and informed him it was the bottom of the ninth and the Mariners were going down in flames. That kind of news made crossing the street a little easier.

Father Townsend was about to enter the center doors of the church when he heard a familiar sound behind him. At first there was nothing that he could see, but then on the sidewalk in front of the school, coasting his way, he spotted two boys on skateboards. They looked about ten or eleven years old. Both had on baggy jeans, cut off and frayed just below the knees. One was wearing a black T-shirt at least two sizes too big for him, with *Metallica* scrawled in large letters across the front. The other had on a white Sonics tanktop and a black baseball cap worn sideways. His narrow white shoulders and thin arms protruded awkwardly from the shirt as he propelled himself down the sidewalk behind his buddy. The kid in black was obviously more comfortable on his board; the Sonics one had to work hard to maintain his balance and keep up with his friend. Mark recognized neither of the two, but he stopped to watch as they drew closer. He closed his eyes, listening to the wheels, trying to tell if either sounded like the skateboard he had heard in the church the night before. But the sidewalk was rough, not smooth like the church aisle, and there were too many other noises outside. He opened his eyes in time to watch the youths glide by. Judging from the size of them, either boy could have been the dark shadow he spotted in the church. But these were not moving with anywhere near the speed that he had seen—or at least heard—the night before.

Inside the vestibule, Father Townsend changed direction and crossed to the side door he had entered the previous night. He stood just inside the church, as he had in the darkness, and stared ahead. The interior was light of course. He could see everything perfectly well, from the long rows of pews in front of him to the altar and beyond it to the mosaic of Christ Triumphant on the back wall of the sanctuary. The priest shut his eyes again, trying to recall the sequence of the night before. Everything was quiet right before Father Morrow burst through the side front door. Mark peeked and located the door. He let his eyes drift across to a point where he guessed the kid was standing, then closed his eyes again. Dan Morrow let out a lőud yell and Mark had answered. Both priests started moving forward, Dan from the side and Mark from the back. The church was still silent and there was no sound coming from the kid. Not until Dan had said he was turning on the lights. That was when the kid started running. Mark opened his eyes again and moved up the aisle, watching as an imaginary kid in baggy shorts and a black T-shirt darted out from the right side of the church. The kid ran in front of the altar and turned down the main aisle, heading toward the back. Mark knew if he cut through one of the pews that he could head him off. If the kneelers were up and if it was light in the church. Dashing between pews in the darkness was a stupid move, but the kid was trying to run past them. By now, Mark recalled, he was on his skateboard. Where did that happen? And how?

The Jesuit cut across the church and into the center aisle, watching the floor as he walked toward the altar. He remembered hearing the running feet and then the sudden clatter of the skateboard as it hit the concrete, and then the loud clack of the wheels as the kid shot down the aisle. Father Townsend stopped and looked to the back. Whoever had raced by him was good, very good. Much better than the two awkward skateboarders he had just watched in front of the church entrance. This kid, in the dark, had managed to throw his board to the floor while still running, jumping on it and tearing through the blackness while being pursued by two grown men. It did not take a professor in logic to reach a couple of sound conclusions. One, this kid was extremely comfortable on a skateboard. And two, this kid had courage.

Weekend liturgies in a church the size of St. Joseph, which holds upward of seven hundred worshippers, are not simple affairs. Simple neither to organize nor carry off with any semblance of order. Jesuits are not famous for being great liturgists. In fact, there are some who claim a Jesuit's Mass is both valid and licit if he can manage to get through it without injuring anyone— which might explain the numbers of people involved with planning, organizing, and conducting a weekend liturgy. At St. Joseph, as in most parishes, the preparations began much earlier in the week. The liturgy committee reviewed the scripture readings and decided the theme for the coming Sunday. Mark was given some ideas to mull over for his homily and suggestions were made to the music director. Then the various tasks were assigned: greeters, lectors, eucharistic ministers, musicians, ushers, altar servers, acolytes, and celebrant. St. Joseph had four weekend Masses, which meant a list had to be prepared for each. The church's liturgies would involve anywhere from sixty-five to seventy-five parishioners every weekend.

Although each person supposedly knew the rubrics for his or her assigned task, there were always a lot of last minute consultations—hurried, loud whispers in the back of the church—and the rounding up of one or two pinch hitters from the pews. Weekends in August were notorious for no-shows. But somehow it was pulled together at the last minute; and with the priest and his entourage lining up in the vestibule as the final peels of St. Joseph's bells echoed through the neighborhood, the organist hit the first loud notes and Mass was underway.

The church was a little less than half-full; and as Mark processed up the aisle, he nodded to the few familiar faces that glanced up from their hymnals as he passed. A lot of the regulars at the Saturday night were absent, probably taking advantage of the long days and good weather. Mark did not blame them a bit. Besides, most would show up at one of the morning Masses tomorrow.

His homily went about as well as he expected. No one walked out or, as far as he could see, fell asleep. But there were no loud *Amens* or bursts of applause, either. The Jesuit explained some of the theological concepts of living bread, touched a bit on the good Lord's intentions, and wrapped it up by reminding his congregation of the need for living bread in their own lives. Solid, yes; inspired, no.

There were not too many young people in the church, but as Mark continued with the liturgy, facing the congregation, he found himself searching out the younger-looking faces, examining them, trying to decide if any might be the mysterious night visitor. If one of them rolled up to communion on a skateboard, he could be reasonably sure they had the culprit, but Father Townsend was pretty certain it would not be that easy. His eyes roamed over the heads and searched the darker corners of the church, checking for a youngster's pale face looking lost and alone. But as near as he could tell, no one in the church fit that description. The kids in front of him were either familiar members of the parish or obviously attached, however reluctantly, to the adults in the pew next to them. And there was no sign of any skateboards in the church.

He stood on the walk outside the thick bronze doors after Mass, greeting parishioners as they trooped past. Most were anxious to get home for dinner, so few tarried longer than the moment it took to shake the priest's hand and murmur something fairly noncommittal about the Mass, the music, or his homily. The Jesuit noted there were not too many murmurs about his homily. Perhaps he could find an extra hour tonight to polish it a bit more.

As always, old Mrs. O'Keefe was one of the last to leave the church. The widow stayed after to finish her prayers, usually kneeling in front of the image of Saint Joseph as she did. She had probably lit a couple of the vigil candles: one for her dead husband, Joe, and one for the daughter who, as Mrs. O'Keefe insisted on reminding him, was still living in sin. Once a month she asked the priest to offer a Mass for her second oldest child, Katy, who had been living with a man since 1973. The couple had never married and now had three children. Mrs. O'Keefe continued to harbor hopes for a church wedding and every Saturday lit a candle and offered prayers for that intention. Her candles were as much a part of her spirituality as a Buddhist's prayer wheel or a Jew's mezuzah.

Mrs. O'Keefe was wearing a long black raincoat, much too heavy for the summer's heat; and as she approached the priest she reached into the side pocket. Father Townsend smiled down at her but earned only a withering frown for his efforts.

"Our church wasn't very clean this evening, Father," the old woman scolded. "Maybe you need to have a few words with the janitor."

She extended her arm and dropped a couple of objects in Mark's outstretched hand. The first looked like a chrome peace symbol, large and heavy. The priest studied it a moment before recognizing it as the shiny and distinctive hood ornament off of a Mercedes Benz. The other item in his hand was easily recognizable and much more familiar: a half-empty bag of corn nuts.

"Where'd you find these?"

"In my pew," she informed him, "right in plain sight. I would think the trash could be removed before Mass, don't you?"

She did not wait for a reply but set off down the walk. Mark watched her tottering figure for a moment, then went back inside. Once in the vestry, he quickly removed his vestments. The church was empty and he headed up the side aisle. Twenty pews from the front,

Mark turned and entered it, moving to a spot about seven feet in from the center aisle.

For as long as he had been at St. Joseph's, Mark Townsend had only seen Elizabeth O'Keefe sit in one spot. Twenty rows back and seven feet in. The old woman was always one of the first in church, so there was never a question of anyone being in her place. And if the pew got crowded, late-comers had to excuse themselves and step around the old woman. She would never budge from her spot in that pew. Father Townsend had no doubts that Joe and Elizabeth O'Keefe had sat together in that same place for most, if not all, of their forty-three years of married life together. The priest dropped down in the O'Keefe pew and stared ahead at the altar. But his thoughts were not focused on the old woman who usually sat there, nor her long-deceased husband, nor their forty-three years together, nor the daughter "still living in sin." Instead Father Townsend was thinking about a an invisible, anonymous youngster with guts, balance, and apparently, no place to call home.

He laid the ornament and bag of nuts on the seat of the pew, then stood, genuflected, and headed back to his house.

ELEVEN

Father Morrow had the nine o'clock Mass Sunday morning. Mark was preaching at all the weekend Masses so he left the house at the same time as Dan. But before he vested, he checked Mrs. O'Keefe's pew. Both the Mercedes hood ornament and the corn nuts were gone.

The Jesuit had no way of knowing where the kid was hiding. The few parishioners arriving early were surprised to spot the tall priest standing inside one of the pews, turning slowly as his eyes roamed over the walls of the church. They knew this was not part of the liturgical rite, but were at a loss as to exactly what he was doing.

As they vested, Mark told Dan about the hood ornament and corn nuts he had left in the pew the evening before. Their young visitor was obviously still around, so the ambush the two of them had staged two nights before had not scared the kid away. But with three Masses in front of them, both priests knew this was not the time to begin a search. Nevertheless, as the organ sounded and the procession started up the aisle, both men were scanning the younger faces in the pews.

* * *

Mark celebrated the eleven o'clock Mass by himself. By now his commentary on the living bread sounded stale and dry even to himself. As he preached, Father Townsend could hear an apologetic tone creeping into his voice. He redoubled his energy, trying to inject some leaven into a homily that refused to rise.

In the bad, old days the priest, flanked closely by his faithful altar boys, offered a quick genuflection at the conclusion of the Mass and, with a final rustle of his silk chasuble whispering in the air behind him, quickly exited stage right, directly into the sacristy. There was no processing back down the aisle and standing around to exchange pleasantries with departing worshippers. In the old days, Father could get away with saying anything he wanted from the pulpit, knowing he did not have to face any of his people afterward. So there were a lot more scoldings from the pulpit back then, and a lot more bad sermons. But when you have to stick around and wish folks a good morning, you are less inclined to scold them. And if your sermon stinks, there are some in the congregation who are more inclined to let you know it.

His parishioners were kinder than Mark deserved. They shook his hand, wished him a good day, and some even urged him to get out and enjoy the nice weather. A couple of people thanked him for his words, but that was about as bad as it got. No one said, *Nice try* or *Better luck next week*. Father Townsend was grateful for Christian charity.

Lyle and Penny Metcalfe were at the eleven o'clock, and they waited until the crowd had thinned before approaching the priest. Lyle Metcalfe's handshake was firm, but his smile was fairly weak. His wife looked nervous.

"Pen says she's told you about this situation of hers," Lyle Metcalfe said in a voice low enough not to be overheard.

Mark nodded. "You mean her adoption? Yes, we've talked."

Metcalfe looked over his shoulder, apparently checking to see if anyone was close enough to hear what they were saying.

"We've talked about it, too," Lyle said. "I think she should drop it."

Lyle Metcalfe was as tall as the priest, and he was one of those men whose physical presence exuded power and confidence. Mark never felt unduly impressed by Lyle, but this morning there was something about the councilman that felt intimidating. His tan face looked tight, and the smile he offered the priest was thin. He had sandy hair, tinted blond on top by the summer's sun. He was dressed in tan slacks and a blue blazer over a crisp white cotton shirt and blood red tie. He pulled himself erect and moved closer to the priest. Mark's impulse was to take a step back, but he forced himself to stand his ground.

Pen stood about three feet away from her husband's right side but closer to Mark than to Lyle. She was wearing a yellow cotton dress, and her blond hair was pulled back and tied with a bow that matched her dress. She had said nothing so far.

"Pen?" Mark smiled at her.

The woman tipped her head at the sound of her name and then looked up at her husband. "I told Lyle this is something I want to do. I don't want to let go of it."

Her husband jerked around to his wife and his smile grew even thinner.

"We obviously have some disagreement about this," he turned back to the priest, "as you can see."

"Would you want to get together and talk?" asked Mark.

Pen began to answer but her husband interrupted. "That'd be good, Mark, but I'm heading out of town early tomorrow and won't be back until later in the week. But maybe then."

Pen's eyes flashed as she listened to her husband.

"I have time now, if you want," the Jesuit offered.

Metcalfe glanced down at his watch, shaking his head as he did so. "Won't work," he informed the priest. "We're due at a brunch and are already running late." He gave Father Townsend a depreciating grin. "Your homily ran a little long this morning." Lyle looked over at his wife and then back at Father Townsend. "I've asked Penny not to do anything until I get back. Then we can talk this all out." He moved even closer to the priest. "I hope you'll back me up on this."

Mark did step back this time. Lyle Metcalfe was crowding him, physically and verbally. Up to this point his wife remained fairly quiet, although her initial nervousness was now replaced by a look of determination. When she spoke, Pen's voice was calm and even.

"And I've told Lyle that if I decide to look into my adoption, then that's my decision to make."

"Honey," her husband replied quickly, "that's the type of decision that effects us both, and I think we need to talk about it first."

"We have talked about it, Lyle." Her voice was louder and Lyle looked around to see who was listening. "We've talked a lot about it. And every time you've told me to drop it. You don't want me even to say the word adoption."

Lyle covered his anger with a silly exasperated look of despair, shrugged his shoulders, and held out his hands. "What can I say?" he asked the priest. "I want to talk some more, she doesn't." He stepped to his wife's side and draped his arm over her shoulders. Pen Metcalfe stiffened at his touch. "Mark, promise me you'll keep an eye on her while I'm gone. Will you do that for me?"

The priest was tugging at the end of his mustache as he watched the couple. Another family had moved up behind the Metcalfes and were waiting to speak to him. Father Townsend nodded to them and, stepping beside Pen, began moving the Metcalfes farther along the walk.

"Pen, why don't I come over for coffee tomorrow?

That'll give us a chance to talk some more." He wriggled his eyebrows suggestively. "Call me when your husband's left the house, okay?"

Lyle Metcalfe let out a short bark of laughter. "Great!" the councilman said, trying hard to sound enthused. "Now I can't even trust my own priest around my wife." He slapped Mark on the back of his chasuble as he took his wife's arm and began leading her away. "You two talk, work things out, then the three of us can get together when I come back. We'll get this all figured out."

As they hurried down the block, Pen Metcalfe turned and shot Mark Townsend a worried look. He gave her a small wave and mouthed the words *Call me* before turning back to the family still waiting by the doors.

He had really intended to do something about the homily before that evening's Mass. All it needed it was a little tweaking, perhaps a couple of fresh images. The spirit was willing, but the flesh was weak. Father Townsend had lunch first; a ham sandwich with a cold beer. Then he took the *New York Times* crossword puzzle out to the chaise lounge in the backyard, intending to do no more than half of it. But in the warm sun the priest relaxed, began to nod, and finally succumbed. His nap was long and satisfying and would have gone on even longer if the sound of a skateboard had not startled him awake. Mark jumped up and ran to the hedge to look over, but whoever was riding by was already down the hill and out of sight. The priest rubbed the sleep from his eyes as he wandered back into the house.

Those who showed up for the five-thirty Mass were a motley bunch. Sun-baked and tired, at least half of them had just returned from a day out on the water or in the mountains. There were people still dressed in dusty blue jeans and some with baggy shorts pulled over swim suits. Latecomers continued straggling in even after Mark's final words on the living bread. They were probably the fortunate ones, he ruefully decided, watching as a sunburnt family noisily crowded into a back pew. He lifted up the bread and began reciting the prayer of offering.

That night Mark got hooked on a television movie with a cross-country car chase and rode it to the end. There was nothing urgent on the eleven o'clock news so he clicked off the set. Dan Morrow was already in bed and Mark checked the lock on the back door. He quietly left the house through the front door and headed up to Fifteenth. He turned right, intending to walk toward the park, but after a couple of blocks he doubled back. There was a grocery store a few blocks away that stayed open around the clock. He was surprised how many people shopped that late on a Sunday night, but Mark quickly found the aisle he was looking for and picked out the biggest bag of corn nuts on the shelf. On his way to the checkout stand, he grabbed a can of Pepsi.

"A little late-night snacking, Father?" Lucas Rochford was the night manager and a member of the parish. He rang up the priest's purchase and handed Mark his change.

The spotlights were on, brightly illuminating St. Joseph's bell tower. Father Townsend knew the front center doors would be locked, but he was guessing the side nearest the rectory might still be opened. He guessed wrong, but the key was in his pocket.

The priest made no effort to muffle the noise he made going inside. In fact, he put a little extra effort in pulling the door closed behind him, and made sure to bump against the inside wooden door before opening it. Once inside, he coughed loudly. His footsteps echoed throughout the church as he marched down the center aisle. When he reached the parquet stage supporting the main altar, Father Townsend mounted the steps, setting each foot down with extra weight. As he reached the top he turned and peered back at the darkened church. Mark stood quietly and listened. The church's silence was imposing. Nevertheless he stayed in place and continued to listen.

Finally he sat down on the top step of the platform and cleared his throat.

"My name is Father Mark Townsend." He spoke in a loud voice but tried to sound conversational. "You've probably seen me around. I was one of the priests who came in here the other night." He paused, his eyes searching the blackness in front of him. "I'm sorry we scared you like that."

He stopped speaking. A car passed by and inside the quiet church it sounded as loud as a jet plane. Mark waited until the sound disappeared.

"I don't know why you're in here, but I'd like to help you if I can."

The paper sack in his hand rustled loudly as he opened it. Mark lifted out the can of Pepsi and bag of nuts and set them on the floor.

"I brought you some more corn nuts," he called out, "and something to drink. I'm leaving them here in front of the altar." He stopped. Father Townsend had no idea if anyone was there to hear him or not, and he was beginning to feel a little foolish, talking out loud to a dark, empty church, putting out food for a kid who might or might not be there. "There's a garbage can in the bathroom," Mark continued, "and it would help if you'd throw your trash in there instead of leaving it in the pews. A couple of people have talked to me about it."

The silence around him felt oppressive. He started to say more but did not. He clasped his hands in front of him instead and sat quietly, waiting. Except for a few indistinct creaks, there were no other sounds. The priest continued to wait.

The founder of the Jesuit order, St. Ignatius Loyola, was not a particularly patient man when it came to waiting for other people. He had big dreams and plenty of plans, and having to wait until others understood and agreed with him often proved an aggravation for the saint. But gradually, over the course of his lifetime, Ignatius learned there could be some benefit to giving others enough time to think things over. Especially if it meant they ended up agreeing with him.

Father Townsend sat on the steps and waited ten minutes. Ignatius probably would have waited longer, but Ignatius was a saint. Mark rose to his feet and called out, "I'm coming right back." Then he went to the back of the church and found the light switch in the vestibule. The chairs were already back in place for the regular weekday Mass, and he was not going to try walking about in the dark. Near one of the doors, he found a St. Joseph collection envelope, put out for visitors to the parish. He grabbed a hymn book and a pencil and sat on one of the chairs. Resting the book on his knee, he scrawled a note on the front of the envelope.

Please don't be afraid. I would like to talk to you. I live across the street from the church.

Underneath, Mark signed his name and then printed his address and phone number. He hesitated, then added another line.

P.S. Here's $20. If you need more, come and see me.

He took a twenty out of his wallet and stuffed it in the envelope, then went back into the church and up the main aisle to the altar. He picked up the paper sack but left the envelope underneath the Pepsi can. Then he turned and faced the pews.

"I've left some money here for you," he called out. "It isn't much, but it'll buy you a couple of meals. If you need more and you want my help, then come and see me. I live just across the street. My address and phone number are on the envelope. I don't know why you're hiding, but I want to help. Please let me."

When he was finished speaking, the priest left the altar and went back down the aisle. He switched off the lights in the vestibule and made certain all three sets of doors were locked as he left. Mark was about to cross the street when he stopped and turned back. He hesitated a moment, looking back at the side entrance to the church. Then he cut across the lawn to the side door leading into the church basement. He had difficulty seeing in the dark, but his fingers felt along the door until they found the handle. Tugging gently, he felt the door begin to open. He moved his fingers along the edge of the door until they felt the lock. Cautiously he lifted out the folded cardboard wedged into the crack, then carefully replaced it, letting the heavy door slowly settle back into place.

TWELVE

He had intended on getting up before Dan Morrow. But it was after one by the time Mark fell into bed, and he tossed and turned for nearly another hour before finally falling asleep. He spent a restless night dreaming of bad sermons and skateboards, and when he awoke it was after seven. Dan would be through with Mass already. Mark hurriedly shaved and showered. He heard the front door open and close as he finished dressing, and once downstairs, found Morrow just settling in at the kitchen table.

"Good morning." Dan greeted him, lifting his filled coffee mug in salute. He already had the newspaper open to the sports page and was about to plunge into his favorite part of the morning.

"Hi," Mark replied, "I thought you were going camping." Monday was Morrow's day off, and he usually left the house as soon as Mass was over.

"Yeah, in a bit. I'm going up by Stevens Pass."

"How was Mass?" Mark asked.

"Typical." Morrow was trying to read the baseball scores.

"Did you check out the church by any chance?"

Father Morrow raised a quizzical eyebrow but kept his focus on the newsprint. "For what?"

"I wondered if there was any sign of the kid," Mark replied.

"Not that I saw, but I just went into the vestry and back out."

Morrow was no help, he would have to check for himself. Mark entered through the side door. Even from the back he could see that the can of pop and the bag of nuts were missing. He assumed the envelope was taken, too, but he went up just to check. Everything he had left in front of the altar was gone, but lying in their place was the hood ornament off a Mercedes Benz. The priest grinned as he reached down and pocketed the gift.

Shortly after 9:30, Helen Hart buzzed Mark's intercom to inform him Penny Metcalfe was on line two.

"Hi, Penny."

"Are you ready for that coffee?" the woman asked brightly.

"Give me ten minutes," Mark replied.

Her front door was open and through the screen Mark could hear her voice coming from the kitchen. She called out when he rang the bell, so he walked in.

". . . I'm going to be around all day," Pen Metcalfe was saying into the phone, "so call if you find out anything." She waved to Mark and motioned him toward the coffee. Mark helped himself as she continued speaking.

"That's fine. And I'm sorry for the inconvenience." She paused, listening. "That's right," she said. "I'll wait for your call."

She smiled at the priest as she hung up, gathering together some loose pages of paper arranged on top of the kitchen counter.

"Sorry about that, Mark." Penny looked a lot happier than she had yesterday at church. He hoped it was not just because Lyle was out of the house.

"You seem happy this morning."

"I'm better," she said, dropping into the chair next to his and laying the papers on the table in front of her. "I'm going ahead with my search, I've decided."

She was watching for Mark's reaction.

"And Lyle? . . ."

"And Lyle can go to hell!"

She was smiling as she said it, but he could see both doubt and pain in her eyes.

"So nothing got resolved."

"Only that we disagree." Pen took a tentative sip from her coffee. "We spent all of yesterday arguing about it. He can't understand why I want to do this. It's like we're talking on two different levels."

One graceful hand curled around the coffee cup while the other began idly sorting through the adoption papers on the table. She kept her eyes on the pages as she continued speaking, refusing to look at Mark.

"This feels so important to me, Father. I can't understand why he won't support me. If there was ever a time when I needed him, it's right now. And he's not there. He keeps talking about his career and our future and what a sensitive time this is. It's like I timed my mother's death and finding these papers just to annoy him."

Mark waited until he was sure she was finished speaking.

"Maybe he's afraid."

"Lyle? Afraid?" Pen gave the priest an incredulous look. "Afraid of what? My God, all I want to do is find out who I am. It's not like this is going to change anything."

There was no doubting her sincerity, but Father Townsend knew that making choices inevitably leads to change. Certainly Penny Metcalfe was smart enough to realize that. She was asking some of the most fundamental questions about herself, questions that most people grow up never having to ask. No matter what answers she might find, they were bound to change her. And probably her husband, too.

"He might be afraid of what this may do to you, Pen."

"It's not going to do anything except give me some answers." She held the pages up. "There was a woman named Metzler who gave birth to me in Shelton in nineteen sixty-three. Was that Mrs. Metzler or Miss Metzler? Do you know?" Her eyes were bright and stared straight into Mark's. "Was my mother married? Then why did she give me away? Maybe, maybe her husband was another Lyle who didn't want kids. Or maybe a baby wasn't safe around him. I want to know why I couldn't stay with my mother. And I'm going to find the answer. Tell me, how is that going to change me, Father?"

How do you begin answering a question like hers? Do you start with her feelings? Pen was still engulfed in the emotions of her mother's death. Was it possible she was bargaining away her grief in hopes of finding a replacement for her mother? When people feel out of control, the natural tendency is to find some way to take charge. Perhaps searching for her birth mother was a means to that end. Mark had counseled enough people who, facing unpleasantness in their lives, found projects to distract them from facing the real issue. The more unpleasant the real issue, the more important the distraction becomes.

His reply was measured and he watched her closely as he spoke. "Talk about what is most important in your life for a moment. As you consider yourself and your life, what are the key elements that define Penelope Metcalfe?"

"You mean, like my husband, my house, and things?"

"Tell me what's important to you, Pen."

She looked at him doubtfully for a moment, then shrugged her shoulders and plunged in.

"Well, Lyle, obviously. And my mother and father."

Her hand left the papers and moved upward to begin twirling a strand of her hair. "And I'd say my house and the stuff in it." She paused a moment as she thought, her brow wrinkled. "My faith. St. Joseph parish and the people there . . . my friends"

Her list ran out. Father Townsend waited patiently, letting her work at her own speed. She was showing no emotion as she continued pondering what was important about her life. Pen Metcalfe sat at her table and tried to imagine what else was important in her life. Gradually tears began to pool in her eyes.

"It's important in a negative way," she sniffled. "Not having any children of my own." She fished into the pocket of her pants for her hanky and dabbed at her eyes. "That's an important part because of the way it hurts."

The priest nodded.

"I think I've let Lyle decide what is and isn't important in our lives. He's always said that politics and children are not a good mix, and I guess I've gone along with that without really believing it. We know a lot of politicians, Mark, and most of them have children. They're something that's important to me, but I've put them aside for his sake."

Her hand left her hair and returned to the papers in front of her. "But this is something I don't want to put aside. I'm tired of doing what's important for my husband. I want to do what's important for me."

"I was waiting to hear you say this was important, Pen."

"It is." She looked down at the pages. "It really is."

Their coffee was cold and she poured them new cups. While she was up, she informed the priest that the phone call he had overheard was with the Metcalfe's attorney. She had called him to ask how she could begin the process of locating her birth mother.

"I gave him the information off the Decree of Adoption," she told Mark, "and asked him to find out whatever he could. Evidently Washington State keeps adoption records confidential. He said they're sealed records and to open them means having to go to court." Her mouth pulled down in a frown. "I'd rather avoid that," she told the priest. "Lyle's not going to be too happy seeing me go to court."

"What's the alternative?"

"He said there's ways to do a private search. And there's also some organizations that specialize in finding parents or children lost through adoption. Those sound like better ways to go, especially given Lyle's attitude."

"He feels that strongly about this?"

Pen Metcalfe rolled her eyes. "You wouldn't believe how strongly! I told you we argued about it for most of yesterday. Last night got really ugly. I was upset and crying, and we were both saying some pretty hard things. Lyle as much as admitted that he thinks my adoption would affect his campaign for the mayor's job."

"In what way?" asked Mark.

"If I'm illegitimate." Pen was blushing. "He's worried about what people will think if he's married to someone illegitimate."

"But that doesn't have anything to do with you or your husband's politics," Father Townsend objected.

"I know that and you know that," Pen replied. "Lyle knows it, too. But in a political race, stuff like that can get used against you. It happens all the time."

"But Lyle is your husband."

"Who is also on the city council," Pen reminded him. "And he doesn't want anything to upset his plans for running for mayor. Last night he made that damn clear. In fact, he didn't wait around until this morning. We were arguing so hard that he finally packed his bag and left last night."

"Not this morning?"

She shook her head. "I told you things got ugly."

"Do you know where he went?"

Again Pen shook her head. "He had a flight to Denver this morning, but I don't know where he spent the night.

Probably at one of the hotels. Or maybe on the couch in his office. I don't know. And right now, I don't care.''

"You don't really mean that, do you, Pen?'' Even as he said it, Mark recognized he was reacting more as her friend than a priest. And he was growing uncomfortable with mixing his roles.

Penny was, indeed, regarding him more as a friend than a priest right now, and she picked up on the concern in his voice. As the wife of a political figure, Pen Metcalfe was accustomed to displaying a public persona, even to someone as close as her parish priest. But Mark Townsend was a friend, too, and it was to the friend that she answered.

"I'm afraid I do, Mark. Things haven't been very good between us for quite a while now. In fact . . . I haven't told anyone this . . . but Lyle and I are sleeping in separate bedrooms now.'' She bit hard on her lower lip, then kept going. "We still talk and do things together, but there isn't much romance in our relationship anymore.'' She stopped again and looked him squarely in the eyes. "To be honest, there never really was.''

Mark Townsend was hearing more than he wanted to know, certainly more than he was prepared for. And he was having a hard time sorting through his own responses, both as friend and as priest.

"I'm sorry to hear that. I . . . I didn't know,'' he managed to stammer.

"No one does,'' she told him.

An awkward silence fell over the two of them. Both sat at the table, wondering where to take the conversation next. Boundaries were already crossed, and they were both intelligent enough to recognize that they needed to be restaked.

"Is there anything I can do for you two?'' Mark asked.

The woman paused and thought. "Pray for us, I guess. And try not to let this get in the way of being friends. Lyle would be very hurt if he knew I told you.''

Mark nodded. "No, this stays between us. I won't say anything."

"Thank you."

The phone's loud ringing startled them both. Pen answered and listened for a moment before handing the receiver to the priest.

"It's Helen Hart," she told him.

The receptionist's loud voice sounded worried. "Father? There are two people here to see you."

Mark had left his appointment calendar sitting on his desk. He tried visualizing the day's schedule.

"Am I late for an appointment?" he asked her.

"No, no," she assured him. "They just showed up at the door. But, Father? They're the police. There's one who says he knows you and asked me to find you." Father Townsend heard someone speaking to her in the rectory office. Helen was answering whomever it was. "What? What? Oh." Then her voice was back on the line, loud and shrill. "His name is Peter Newman," she told the priest. "He wants to talk to you."

A flood of memories rushed over Father Townsend. He had not heard from the homicide detective in more than two years, but he remembered Peter Newman very well indeed. When he was just starting out in homicide, the detective and the priest became embroiled in a murder case, traveling to Alaska, to a Yup'ik village on the Bering Sea coast. Mark Townsend knew Peter Newman very well.

"Father Townsend?" The detective's voice sounded older, but it was still familiar.

"Peter! What a terrific surprise! How are you?"

"I'm fine. How about yourself."

"Just great. How's your family?

"They're fine, too." The detective's voice sounded serious, as if he was not as pleased as Mark to be having this conversation. The priest picked up on his tone.

"Peter, is there something wrong?"

"Father, this is awkward over the phone. But I'm here

with my partner in an official capacity. We're here to talk with you."

Penny was rinsing their cups in the kitchen sink, her back turned to the priest.

"I can be back there in about ten minutes, Peter."

"That would be fine. We'll wait for you here."

Father Townsend hung up the phone and explained that he had someone waiting for him at the rectory.

"I'm sorry to have to cut this short, Pen."

She gave him a quick smile. "That's okay, Mark. I think I said about all I should have, anyway. Maybe a little more."

"Can we talk again?"

"That'd be good. I should hear back from the attorney, perhaps by this afternoon. Why don't I give you call and let you know what I find out."

"Do that, please."

The walk back to St. Joseph was a short one. Ordinarily after a conversation like the one he had just had with Penny Metcalfe, Mark would take a longer route home, perhaps wandering through Volunteer Park, pondering what they had discussed. But an old friend was waiting back at church. And while Father Townsend was unaware of it at the moment, he would soon discover that the park was the last place where he wanted to be seen.

THIRTEEN

Parks in cities of any size have their problems. You never leave your car unlocked in city parks, you do not let small children wander off by themselves, and you do not ordinarily stick around after dark. At least in the United States, in the closing years of the twentieth century, those are unpleasant but accepted facts of life.

Lots of parks, Volunteer included, have signs posted at their entrance, forbidding anyone to enter after certain hours. The signs at Volunteer Park prohibit people from going in between the hours of 1 and 6 A.M. But they do anyway.

Teenagers, cocky immortals that they are, sneak in after hours, their contraband beers tucked inside coat pockets. Couples, lost in love, wander in to find some secluded site to snuggle. And there are the occasional insomniacs, often with dogs on leash, who stroll along the park's inside perimeters. Seattle's police will occasionally patrol the park, and if they spot the teenagers, lovers, or dog walkers, they remind them that the park is closed, that this is no place they want to be so late at night. They warn them there are others in the park as well, others whose reasons for being there are not quite as innocent.

Behind the bandshell, just north of the reservoir, are public rest rooms that are good to avoid. And after dark, the roadway running past the tennis courts is not the best one to walk along. There are growths of dense shrubbery around the Asian art museum, where people have been known to hide, and sometimes strange-looking men loiter near the children's wading pool. Another public rest room is located between the play area and the conservatory, and it is only a little better than the one behind the bandshell. The police do what they can, but everyone knows that parks in cities of any size have their problems.

Craig James did not like breaking laws. You would not work too long as an airline pilot if laws did not have much meaning for you. So if a sign demanded he keep right, Craig James kept right. If you are instructed to climb to 32,000 feet, you climb to 32,000 feet.

The sign posted on Fifteenth clearly stated that Volunteer Park was closed from 1 A.M. until 6 A.M. His digital watch showed 5:45 A.M., but the sky was already bright and cloudless and it was only fifteen minutes before the legal opening. The airline pilot felt positive there would be no risk if he raced through the park fifteen minutes early. He was due at Sea-Tac Airport in three hours for a flight to Salt Lake. After his jog, he planned to shower, dress, and have a leisurely breakfast with his wife before helping her wake and dress their two little girls. By cutting through the park, he would shave nearly ten minutes, enough time for a second cup of coffee with his wife. Clearly, disregarding the sign was not that big of a deal.

Besides, he needed to use a bathroom. Stopping along the road and trying to pee behind a tree was too risky, besides being illegal. Even this early, there were other people about. But he knew there was no risk in the park. After all, the park was closed and no one would be inside. James jogged past the sign and up the road leading into Volunteer Park. There was a rest room just past the wading pool on his right, but the pilot had gone in there once before. The place gave him the creeps. Rude graffiti and bad smells drove him back out. But he knew there was space behind the rest room, between the building and the cemetery fence, with plenty of privacy. With a growing sense of urgency, he left the road and trotted across the lawn toward the fence. He held his head up and breathed deeply as he ran, making sure to watch all around him.

A lot of the chain-link fence separating the park from the cemetery was covered over with thick, green ivy, and the tendrils trailed down off the fence and across the ground. The grass ended about fifteen feet from the fence, where the ivy took over. As Craig James drew closer to the edge of the grass, he saw something in the ivy that he knew did not belong there.

The body was facedown, lying on a path that coursed from the edge of the grass through the ivy to the foot of the fence. The runner stopped at the edge of the grass and peered ahead. He saw no movement, no sign of life. He could not tell for sure if it was male or female, although he surmised the person lying there was fairly young. Thin arms were extended out in front of the head, and the torso looked small and underdeveloped. The legs were underdeveloped, too, and the butt was small and lean. Black jeans were pulled down to the ankles as were the white cotton briefs. He guessed it was a boy. The youth's hair was black and hung down, obscuring both sides of the face. He took three steps forward and stopped next to the body. Before crouching down, he checked around in case anyone else was in the vicinity. Then he knelt beside the body and slowly, hesitantly, lightly placed the finger tips of his right hand against the neck. The smooth skin felt cool, almost like he was touching porcelain.

Craig James forced himself to look at the naked lower half. He was embarrassed to be staring at the naked flesh of a stranger, and he looked around again. The park was still closed, and no one else was in sight. The young bottom was smooth and unblemished. There was a faint bit of fine hair on the legs. James guessed the youth was not much older than eleven or twelve. Thirteen, at the very most. The jeans looked dirty. The black T-shirt was flecked with dirt and small blades of grass and bits of leaves. On the feet were red, high-top tennis shoes.

James was more disturbed by the youth's nakedness than anything else, at least initially. His first impulse was to reach out and pull the pants back up. In fact, he did reach out one hand to do so before quickly yanking it back. Shocked, he jumped to his feet, realizing for the first time exactly what he had discovered. A low cry of fear escaped Craig James lips as he stood beside the corpse. Although it was wrong, he knew he had to pee real bad, and right then.

FOURTEEN

Father Mark Townsend tried bounding up the front steps of St. Joseph's rectory, but his ankle was still sore and he only made it onto the second step before he faltered. The priest ended up limping through the front door. His friend, the detective, was sitting in one of the upholstered chairs just inside the doorway, and he jumped to his feet as Mark entered.

"Peter!" Mark exclaimed, "it's so good to see you again. It's been ages. How are you?" He was pumping Newman's hand eagerly as he spoke. "You haven't changed a bit."

Mark was being truthful, the detective had not changed since they had last met. His pale blue eyes still blinked up at him through the same round tortoise-shell frames. His red hair might have been a little shorter than Mark remembered it, but the scattering of freckles across his face still gave him the appearance of a man at least ten years younger than his thirty-one years. The day was already too warm for a jacket, and Newman's tan sport coat was draped over the arm of his chair. He had on blue cotton twill slacks, a white shirt, and a dark blue silk tie.

"Father, it's good to see you, too." The detective's

face wore a look of concern, and his voice conveyed little of the enthusiasm or delight of Mark's. He turned aside and gestured to a woman occupying a second chair in the rectory's lobby. "This is my partner, Detective Gail Draper. Detective, this is Father Townsend."

She was a young woman in her late twenties, solid-looking, with cropped, dark brown hair and brown eyes. She had on gray slacks that were stretched tight, and a cream-colored jacket over a white blouse. Detective Draper stood when Newman introduced her. She thrust out her right hand to shake the priest's while in her left she extended the silver badge clipped inside the black leather wallet.

"Nice to meet you, Father." Mark looked first at her face, then down at her badge. "Detective Newman's told me quite a bit about you."

Draper had a square jaw and a nose just a bit too large for her face that took a decided curve to the right. For a homicide detective, she looked the part. Mark greeted her and got a grim, tight-lipped smile in return.

Helen Hart was trying to look busy and disinterested, but for once she was failing. The parish receptionist sat at her desk, her hands poised above the keyboard of her computer, warily watching the two police officers as they shook hands with Father Townsend. She recalled Peter Newman from several years past only because of the dramatic way he forced their parish priest to accompany him to Alaska. She had not approved of how she involved Father Townsend in his investigation of that lawyer's murder, and she was wary of Newman's motives for visiting the priest today. This was obviously not a social call, not with that chunky-looking woman with him. Like the faithful Jesuit porters of old, Helen Hart was on full alert.

Mark was also aware that this was not a social visit. Newman's tone of voice, when he first spoke to him over the phone, had made that clear enough. And the somber way he was greeting him now confirmed it. The priest caught a glimpse of the receptionist's worried face out of the corner of his eye.

"Why don't we go in here to talk," he suggested, pointing to the visitors' parlor, "it's a little more comfortable."

Father Townsend closed the parlor door behind them, but Helen Hart was still not able to return to her work. Something about the detectives' attitude left her feeling uneasy, nervous. She did not consider herself as the overly protective sort, but after twenty-three years as the receptionist at St. Joseph, she had a sixth sense about which visitors meant trouble for her priests. Helen was starting to regret interrupting Father Townsend's visit to the Metcalfe's house.

Gail Draper was not the sort of detective to waste much time easing into an interview. And she was more than a little uncomfortable knowing that her partner had some previous history with this particular individual. Granted, the priest had, some time ago, provided helpful assistance to Newman during an investigation. Nevertheless that was in the past. Draper was determined to keep this interview focused on the present.

"Father Townsend." She spoke first, before Newman had a chance. "We're investigating a homicide in Volunteer Park that took place last night or early this morning."

"Oh, my Lord!" the priest exclaimed. That explained Peter's seriousness, and why he was here with his partner. Mark was suddenly aware of how intently both of them were watching him. He realized the woman detective had more she wanted to tell him. "This isn't about a parishioner, is it?" Father Townsend's mind was racing as the names and faces of troubled parishioners flashed through. He leaned forward in his chair.

Peter Newman cleared his throat and looked at his partner. "No. No, Mark, we don't think the victim was a parishioner." He stopped, not sure of how to proceed, wearing a helpless expression on his face. Draper saw

Newman's uncertainty as her opportunity to continue.

"Probably not a parishioner," the woman confirmed with a curt nod, "but we do have some questions for you."

The priest leaned even farther forward, more out of concern and curiosity than nervousness. "Sure," he shrugged, "any way I can help."

Detective Draper glanced at her partner before continuing.

"Our victim is a young male, approximately thirteen or fourteen years old," she began. "Possibly Amerasian or Native American. He's four foot seven, about seventy pounds; black hair, brown eyes. He has a small black-and-white stud in his right earlobe, that Oriental symbol for the yin and the yang . . ."

The priest nodded that he was familiar with the symbol.

"That's about all we have at the moment," the woman quickly concluded.

In the silence that followed, Peter Newman spoke up. "He was discovered in Volunteer Park early this morning, Mark, beaten up pretty bad. The coroner's initial report says he had some broken ribs and a ruptured spleen. Death was probably from internal injuries."

Mark was slowly shaking his head as he listened to Peter's description.

"Was this one of those street kids?" he guessed.

The two detectives exchanged looks and Gail Draper jotted a note onto her pad.

"Perhaps," she said as she wrote. "We're not sure if this is related or not. There are some circumstances that indicate maybe it's not."

Father Townsend was growing increasingly uneasy. There was a lot these two were not telling him, although they were obviously feeding him certain pieces of information. The fact that they described the boy in some detail seemed to indicate they might think Mark could identify him. But describing his injuries did not make sense. His question about the boy being connected with the other youngsters who were murdered had caught their attention. Jack Abel came to mind; did anyone from St. Joseph attend that rally on Friday? Mark felt guilty about letting that slip by him.

Detective Draper was studying the priest's expression. A look of consternation swept across his face, but she had no way of interpreting what it meant. She checked her partner to see if he had caught it, but Peter was looking forlorn, staring down at his hands. She was more convinced than ever that Newman's presence was a mistake.

"Father Townsend," she continued, "does anything about this boy sound familiar to you?"

Peter looked up at the priest.

Mark shook his head. "Not so far," he replied. "He doesn't sound familiar."

"This doesn't sound like someone you've met. Maybe here at the church or maybe elsewhere. Perhaps over at the park?"

Detective Newman was watching the Jesuit intently. He scarcely breathed, waiting for Mark to reply. The priest took his time, trying to recall if he had seen someone like the boy they had described. Finally he shrugged.

"I'm sorry," he said. "I just don't recall seeing anyone like that. Perhaps if there was a picture."

Detective Draper reached into her bag and extracted a small cardboard folder. She removed two Polaroid photographs and held them out to the priest.

The first was the boy's face, with just a few inches of his upper chest showing. The head appeared to be lying on a stainless steel table and Mark presumed the photo was taken at the morgue. The child's left eye was swollen shut from what appeared to be a long, deep gash across the brow. The right eye was open but staring ahead lifelessly. Both the upper and lower lips were badly swollen. The mouth was pulled back on the right, and Mark could see small bloody teeth between the lips.

The small ear stud, with its black-and-white curved tear-drops, was still in place in his right earlobe.

The second photo was of the boy's naked torso. Mark cringed. His skin was a dusky gray hue, and there were dark bruises on the chest, across the belly, and a large one on the front of the right thigh. His genitals were small and he was not circumcised. Mark shifted uncomfortably in his chair and flipped back to the first picture. The close-up of the face contained all the information Mark needed. He suspected Draper had handed him the second photo to shock him. The priest bought time by intently studying the boy's face. He looked more Indian than Asian, at least to Mark.

"There was a black T-shirt and black jeans." Draper's voice was intrusive. "And he was wearing red tennis shoes."

Still disturbed by the photos, there was something about the way she described his clothing that sounded odd. Mark looked at her, puzzled.

"What is it, Father?"

"Was he dressed?" Mark asked.

Newman let out a long, low sigh.

"Why would you ask that?" Detective Draper wanted to know.

The priest shrugged his shoulders again. "Just the way you said it."

"Mark, his pants were down around his ankles." Peter Newman's voice sounded harsh, impatient. "And his underwear."

Mark took one last look at the small, bruised, violated body and handed the photographs back to the police-woman.

Mark masked his revulsion with another question. "Is there more?"

Draper nodded. She pulled folded sheets of paper from her bag and began opening them.

"When the medical examiner went through his pockets," she said, her voice flat and noncommittal, "she found these.'' The detective handed Father Townsend four sheets of paper.

The top two were copies of a twenty-dollar bill, front and back. The third sheet revealed the front of a collection envelope from St. Joseph Church. A pencil sketch of the church's front and the bell tower was printed on the left side. The name of the church was clearly visible. Mark had no need to examine the fourth page, he already knew what was on it. His hands began to shake as he turned it over.

Please don't be afraid. I would like to talk to you. I live across the street from the church.

FIFTEEN

Mark was trying to explain as precisely and clearly as he could. Detective Draper looked up occasionally, but for most of his narration she remained hunched over her notebook, writing copious notes. As for Peter Newman, he tried to look reassuring as the priest struggled to describe his relationship with the dead boy. Or rather, his lack of relationship. But the more Mark talked, the longer Peter's face began to look.

Maybe he was overdescribing the situation. Maybe he was not being clear enough. Townsend redoubled his efforts as he started describing his one close encounter with the boy. He now knew that his earliest suspicions were right. The boy hiding inside St. Joseph was scared for his life. Scared and alone. Mark Townsend had as many questions as the police. But he also had valuable information that he knew could help the two detectives, information he was trying to share with them now.

"Dan wanted to try and catch whoever . . ."

"Dan?" Draper interrupted, pencil poised.

"Morrow," Mark said. He thought he had mentioned Morrow's first name earlier. "Father Dan Morrow." She nodded and returned to her writing.

"Dan suggested we sneak into the church and try to

catch whoever was hiding in there. So I went in from the back while he went around the side. We figured we might be able to surprise the person leaving the messes."

Detective Draper interrupted again. "At this point, Father, did you know there was a child hiding in your church?"

"We didn't know who it was," Mark replied. "Father Morrow thought it might be a woman . . ."—he paused, remembering—"At some point I thought the corn nuts were being thrown by some of the students from the school."

"Anyone in particular?"

Mark waved his hands. "Just some of the kids." She nodded and he continued.

"We could hear someone moving inside the church, and we started going toward him. Dan said he was turning on the lights and that's when the kid took off running. Then he jumped on his skateboard and rode to the back of the church. I fell over a pew or I probably would have caught him."

Peter cleared his throat. "There was a skateboard?"

"Yes," Mark confirmed. "He had it with him inside the church. That's how he got away."

"Can you describe what it looked like?" Newman asked.

The priest shook his head. "I heard it. But it was too dark to see anything."

Draper again. "What was he wearing."

"I don't know. It was dark."

"Do you know if Father Morrow saw him?"

"He didn't. He didn't know it was a skateboard until I told him. And he thought it was a girl. Or a woman, rather."

"So neither one of you can say for sure that the person in your church was actually this boy?" She motioned to the photos lying on the table in front of her.

The principles of logic, strictly applied, will bog down

anyone's story, no matter how good it is. Logic makes the narration lurch in fitful starts and sudden stops. Backtracking is inevitable, and to the one telling the story, it begins to feel like plodding through cement. You wonder if you will ever reach the end. By now Father Townsend had lost all sense of his narration. What had started out as a rather clear and dramatic tale of hiding, discovery, and escape was turning into a long, painfully drawn out recitation of times, descriptions, and uncertainties. About all that was left for Mark was to answer their questions and try to help them make sense of this terrible tragedy.

"I think the fact that he had my note in his pocket proves he was the boy in the church," Townsend told them.

"Why is that, Father?" Gail Draper was a plodder and she trusted logic. What she did not trust was the way this Jesuit was trying to apply it.

"That was Saturday night when we chased him out of the church," Mark recounted. "On Sunday night I went back and left the note and the money in front of the altar. Oh, and I put a can of pop and a bag of corn nuts there, too. So whoever picked those things up had to have been in St. Joseph."

Peter Newman was listening closely to the priest's explanation. He watched as his partner made careful notes of what the priest was saying. Gail Draper was good and she was thorough. And Father Townsend's story had holes big enough for Boeing jets, he reluctantly decided.

"Mark," he began hopefully, "Father Morrow will be able to confirm all of this, won't he?"

"Sure," the priest replied quickly. Too quickly. "Uh, no. Yes. I mean, some of it."

Gail Draper had stopped her scribbling and Detective Newman was looking at him doubtfully.

"What I mean is, Dan can tell you about the ambush part on Saturday night. He was there for that. But he doesn't know about the note or anything on Sunday. He was already in bed when I went over there, and I did that by myself.''

"So all Father Morrow knows, or can tell us, is that there was somebody in the church when the two of you went in Saturday night. And he heard something that you think was a skateboard,'' Detective Draper summarized.

"It was a skateboard,'' Mark said sharply. "I heard it and I saw the kid streak by me.''

"You said you didn't see him,'' she reminded the Jesuit. "It was too dark.''

Mark knew that he sounded confused. But he was telling the truth. "I saw something, Detective Draper. It scooted by me when I tripped on the pew. I looked up and saw a dark figure, and there was the sound of wheels. He was not running. He was riding on a skateboard.''

"You believe it was a he.'' Her tone was argumentative. "You don't know that for sure. The other priest suspected it was a she.''

Mark bit down hard on the inside of his lower lip. He was trying to be helpful.

Newman watched his partner. Gail Draper was doing nothing to disguise her animosity. Peter knew the murders of these kids was getting to her. Bodies of beaten, tortured youths were showing up all over Seattle. About all that any of them had in common was that each kid was identified as homeless. Three of them had arrest records, but with the others it was harder to learn much about them. The street people they contacted usually knew gutter punks by their nicknames. Who they really were and where they were from was proving difficult to discover. Only this latest kid provided anything like a solid clue. A name, address, and telephone number found in a pocket were about as solid as clues could possibly get. Unfortunately Father Mark Townsend's name, address, and number were already familiar, not only to Newman but to his superiors. If he was not already working the other cases with Detective Draper, this one would surely have been reassigned. But on the chance that the boy in Volunteer Park was connected to the girl at Golden Gardens, as well as with the others, Peter Newman and Gail Draper were given the case. Draper more eagerly than Newman.

Peter leaned forward in his chair. "Maybe we ought to bring in Father Morrow," he suggested. His partner shot him a pointed look.

"I don't think we're quite finished with Father Mark yet, do you?"

"I was thinking perhaps Father Morrow could add to what Mark is telling us," Peter explained.

The priest was shaking his head. "Dan's not here right now," he told them. "It's his day off. He won't be back until tomorrow."

"Is there someplace we can reach him?" Draper's pencil was poised above her notepad.

"I'm afraid not," Mark told her. "He's off hiking in the Cascades."

"He probably doesn't carry a cell phone."

Mark had to grin. Both priests hated them. "Afraid not," he told her.

Detective Gail Draper heaved a loud, dissatisfied sigh. "Let's go back to last night, shall we?"

Whatever was going on in there was taking much too long. Helen Hart fixed her eye on the clock above her desk. They had been in there for over an hour. Three calls had come in for Father Townsend; one from the daughter of an elderly parishioner at Swedish Hospital. Helen had hoped it was an emergency, but the young woman assured her she only wanted Father to keep her mother in his prayers. Twice she had gotten up for coffee. But they were talking so quietly that she only heard murmurs as she passed the parlor door. Once she thought she recognized the priest's voice, loud and insistent, but the visitors' parlor was well-insulated and the door was solid wood. Few sounds escaped, and never any secrets. The old woman sat at her desk and fretted. Police at a church was never good news.

Their interview continued another twenty minutes. Draper's hand was sore from clutching her pencil and Peter Newman's anguish was evident across his freckled face. Father Townsend was frustrated. No matter how hard he tried, he could not seem to convince the policewoman that the young victim discovered in Volunteer Park was hiding in St. Joseph Church out of fear of something or someone. To Mark, it seemed so apparent. To the detective, it seemed so suspicious. For every assertion he tried to make, she had another question. If he tried to answer, she asked another. She had even questioned him about his twisted ankle and the bandage on his hand. Townsend reminded her that Dan Morrow was in the church when he fell.

"And he'll be back tomorrow?" was all she said, making it sound like Mark had him hidden away somewhere.

The priest's goodbyes to the detectives as they left the rectory were not nearly as effusive as the welcome he had uttered an hour and a half earlier. Helen pursed her lips and studied her computer screen intently. Father Townsend looked drawn and tired and his voice sounded flat. He assured the young-looking policeman how glad he was to see him again, but to the policewoman he only said goodbye. Not even a *Nice to meet you.* She waited until she heard the door close before she turned in her chair. Father Townsend was watching out the window as the two detectives made their way down the walk.

"Can I get you something, Father?" she asked in a gentle voice.

"Thanks, Helen. No." He continued looking outside.

"Did something happen?"

Mark turned back to his receptionist. He saw her look of concern.

"There was another kid found dead," he told her. "They found his body in Volunteer Park. It's possible he was the one hiding in the church."

The old woman blanched and let out a long, sad sound. "I'm so sorry," she told him. "Do they know who did it?"

He shook his head, feeling confused, tired. "I don't think so," he mumbled. He stumbled forward as he started down the hall to his office. The receptionist did not hear him add, "I hope not."

SIXTEEN

The remainder of that Monday passed too slowly. By midafternoon the temperature had climbed into the low nineties, and the insides of the tan brick rectory turned hot and stuffy. Seattle seldom gets that hot, so air-conditioners have never been big sellers. Usually a breeze blows in from Puget Sound, and opening a couple more windows is sufficient for cooling down hot rooms. But on that Monday in August there was no breeze, and the hot summer air hung heavy and solid inside St. Joseph's rectory. Helen Hart dozed fitfully in front of her computer, her damp palms slumbering on top of the keyboard. The phone was asleep. Most of the other parish staff members were either on vacation, taking the day off, or attending to business away from the rectory. Only Father Townsend shared the heated building with her. And since the detectives' departure, he had remained in his own office with the door closed.

With his door closed, Mark was sweating badly. After the detectives left, his first impulse was to hurry to Volunteer Park. From Peter Newman's description, the priest recognized the area where the body was discovered. The boy was found lying in shrubbery near the public rest rooms, off one of the main drives into the park. The Jesuit wanted to go see the site for himself, but he knew it was not a good idea. Like everyone else who watches television crime shows, Mark was aware that the bad guy always returns to the scene of his crime. How many shows had he watched where the cops spot the arsonist as he hungrily studies the flames of his own handiwork? Or the murderer, returning to the blond's apartment to recover the dropped tie clip that can implicate him? No, even though he was innocent, it would be best if Mark stayed away.

So he sat in his office and sweated. Working was futile. Dan had next weekend's homily, so there was nothing for Mark to prepare. Other than his earlier meeting with Penny Metcalfe, he had no other appointments. And apparently no one was trying to reach him because Helen had not buzzed his office once. He wondered if the old woman was still out there. If so, she was probably napping. He had letters he could write and phone calls he could answer, but the priest was too distracted. He tried to blame his lack of energy on the heat, but what Father Townsend was really sweating was the boy on the skateboard.

He must have been hiding when Mark sat down on the altar steps. Unless he was in the basement, he had to have heard the priest's voice. He had to have heard Mark's offer of help. What prevented him from standing up, stepping out from the shadows and saying, *Here I am, Father. Yes, I need your help.*? Why did he stay hidden? Why not come out? Was he suspicious of another trap? The night before, they had tried to ambush him; catching him by surprise, yelling loudly, then chasing him out of the church. Now one of these same priests was back, offering help—while the other one was hiding in a back pew, waiting to pounce? Maybe it made sense that the kid stayed hidden.

Father Townsend leaned back in his desk chair, pulling at the ends of his mustache. Heat made it itch; maybe it was time to shave it off. Mark was purposely distracting himself, imagining what he would look like without his mustache. He had grown it seven years ago, long before coming to St. Joseph. Would his parishioners even recognize their priest without his mustache? Maybe he should show up at Mass next Sunday clean-shaven and see what happens. With a start, Mark sat upright in his chair. This was probably not the best time to be thinking about altering his appearance. What would the police think if he shaved it off?

"You're paranoid, Townsend." His own voice hissed like water over hot coals inside the closed office.

Father Morrow was still not back and it was too hot to cook, so after watching the evening news, Mark quartered an apple, sliced some cheese, and drained a glass of cold Chablis from the box in their refrigerator. Feeling vaguely European, he carried his meal out to the back steps off the kitchen, away from the sun. Mark was wearing a white T-shirt with Seattle University emblazoned across the front, and he had dug around in his dresser until he found an old pair of gym shorts. They felt a little tight; maybe Morrow was right, maybe he was putting on a few pounds. He went barefoot and it felt good. The priest was not expecting company, so he was not concerned about the way he looked. Sitting on the lowest step, where he could not be seen over the back fence, he began munching on his apple.

The local news did not make a big deal out of the story. In fact, there was nothing until after the second commercial, and then it was only the Japanese anchor-woman who reported police were investigating the death of another homeless youth. They did not even bother showing any footage of the park or yellow police tape wrapped around the trees while little children played in the wading pool a few feet away. Just the announcer's talking head, and then her partner asking how many deaths this made and her answering, without even having to look it up, that this made six. The segment was over in less than a minute and then there were more commercials that lasted three times longer. You have to sell a lot of soap in order to tell folks about a dead boy in Volunteer Park.

Mark was just finishing his apple and was only half done with his wine when the doorbell rang.

"Damn." He looked down at his T-shirt and shorts as he got to his feet. Whoever it was would have to accept the fact that priests sweat just like everybody else. Mark set his plate and wineglass on the kitchen counter as he passed through. The sun was hitting directly onto the front porch and all he could make out through the glass in the door was a silhouette. Either a woman or a short man, Mark could not tell until he opened the door.

"Peter!"

Detective Newman had removed his tie, but otherwise he was dressed exactly as he was earlier that day. His eyes ran up and down Mark's tall frame, taking in the priest's skimpy attire.

"Did I catch you at a bad time?" Newman asked with a nervous smile.

"Yes, as you can see, I'm dressed for a dinner with the Archbishop," Townsend replied with a look of clerical solemnity pasted to his face. "We were just about to go running through the sprinkler. Care to join us?"

The detective self-consciously tugged at his shirt. "I'm afraid I'm a little underdressed," he worried.

"I'm sure His Excellency has some extra purple shorts you could wear."

Newman chuckled. "It's good to see you again, Mark."

"You too, Peter."

"You've spruced the place up a little, haven't you? I seem to remember the yard looking pretty cruddy last time I was here."

Mark stepped aside and motioned his friend into the house. "One of our parishioners, Mr. Lee, is a retired gardener. He lives in an apartment now and comes over here to keep his hands in dirt. It's good for him and makes our place look a lot better.'' He led Peter into the kitchen. ''How about some wine? It's a new box, just opened.''

''Beer?''

''Got it,'' Mark said. He pulled one out and tapped some more Chablis into his glass. ''Let's go sit out back where we can pretend it's cooler.''

The two men pulled lawn chairs into the shade of the house and made themselves comfortable. Each was aware of the distance that too much time apart had put into their friendship. But policemen and priests are used to people coming and going from their lives, and neither felt overly guilty about it. At another time, and in another place, they came to rely heavily upon each other. Mark had saved Peter's life, and the detective, although unintentionally, had helped the priest heal some old, personal wounds.

Peter Newman raised his beer. ''To good times in Soognyak!'' he remembered.

Mark toasted in return. ''Were they? Good times, I mean?''

Peter took a pull from his bottle. ''Yeah, I think they were. That's a case I'll never forget. Do you ever hear from any of those people?''

''Not really,'' Mark admitted. ''Once in awhile I'll see one of the Alaska Jesuits when they come down. But the Eskimos aren't great letter writers.'' Newman was nodding. ''So how's your family? Anne? Justin? He's okay now?''

Peter smiled, grateful to the priest for remembering. The Newman baby had nearly died while the two of them were in Alaska.

''They're both great,'' Newman told him. ''Justin is almost three now. And smart as a whip.''

''He must get that from his mother,'' Mark teased.

''I hope so. Both his brains and his looks, because his old man is shy on both counts.''

Peter Newman had a self-assurance about him that Father Townsend did not recall. In the past couple of years he seemed to have gained confidence. Homicide detectives must either learn to have confidence in their skills as well as their instincts or get out of the field. They face too many life-and-death decisions. Peter had just started out in homicide when Mark first met him, and Townsend recognized the maturity a couple of years can make.

"You didn't bring your partner?" The priest did little to disguise the relief in his voice.

"We're off-duty," Newman replied, "so this is social, not business." He lifted his beer as if to prove it. "If it was business, I would have to bring her along."

"But it's okay to talk about the case?"

"I was hoping we could," Peter answered. Two years ago his lapses in following proper police procedures were out of ignorance. Tonight they would be out of friendship and what Peter was coming to call gut instinct. "Gail and I are still trying to piece together the sequence of events. Tracking this kid is a pain."

"Do you know who he is yet?"

"We're getting closer. His nickname is Red Pup, and he hung out with a group of street kids downtown. They call themselves gutter punks now, an awful name. This boy seemed fairly new, not too many knew him. At least two of the other kids we've found dead were part of this same gang."

"So the deaths are related."

Newman hesitated before answering. "Possibly."

"But you're not sure?"

"This one has some differences, Mark." He took two long sips from his beer, putting off the inevitable. "We're not sure they're connected."

Peter set his bottle on the lawn beside his chair and leaned forward. He began ticking off the differences with his fingers. "This is the only one whose clothing was pulled aside. When we found him, he had his jeans and his underwear down around his ankles. None of the other kids were undressed like that. And his location, in Volunteer Park, makes it look more like a sex crime. We know that some of these kids turn tricks; this could be one that got out of hand. And finally, most of the others were tortured before they were killed. The first one was shot, but the rest were tortured.''

"But he was beaten, wasn't he?'' Mark interrupted. "I saw bruises in the pictures.''

Peter nodded. "But not tortured the way the others were. Some of them had broken fingers, like they were bent back until they snapped. And there were slices from a blade across their arms and, a couple, also on their faces. Those kids were tortured, this one was beaten.''

"Was he . . .'' the priest hesitated, ". . . was there anything sexual?''

"There was no semen on, in, or around him.'' The detective spat the words quickly and roughly. The subject was as distasteful to him as it was to the priest. "There wasn't anyone else's pubic hair on the body and no bruising or wounds on the sexual organs. So if it was sex gone bad, it happened before things got too far along.''

The two pictures Detective Gail Draper showed him flashed before Mark's eyes again. They were so vivid, Peter could have been holding them in his hands. Red Pup's bruised and battered face looked young, too young for such violence. And his naked little body was far too immature for the types of things Peter Newman was describing. Kids that age should be home with their families, and their worst fights should be arguments with brothers and sisters. They ought to be playing baseball and mowing lawns and riding their skateboards—not hanging out in parks and pulling down their pants for money. Father Townsend's face looked grim.

"What can I do to help?'' he asked.

This was what Newman was waiting to hear.

"What I have to do,'' he began, speaking slowly and

methodically, "is establish the sequence of events that takes him out of St. Joseph, where you say he was, and into Volunteer Park, where he was found. Somewhere in that time frame is when this kid met his murderer."

"You can't be talking about too many hours," the priest observed. "I left the church right before midnight. And you said the boy was found before six in the morning."

"Right. The coroner says he wasn't dead more than three or four hours when he was found. So that's not a huge amount of time we need to work through. Unfortunately, though, those few hours are big question marks. So far you're the only one with any ties to the kid." Peter looked hopefully at the priest. "I need to know exactly what happened, Mark."

Father Townsend hesitated. Peter Newman was a friend, but he was also investigating a murder, and the priest was fearful. "Let me ask you something, Peter. As a friend." Mark's voice faltered, "Am I a suspect?"

Newman heaved a sigh and his shoulders sagged as he stared down at the ground. His answer was obvious, but he voiced it anyway.

"At the moment, you're the only person we know who had any contact with this kid." He looked up at the priest's glum face. "I don't think you're involved, Mark. But until we can figure out what happened, your name's on the list."

"It sounds like a short list," observed Townsend.

"It is," Newman admitted.

The Jesuit stood up from his chair. "Then let's do something about it," he said resolutely.

Newman stood, too. "Meaning?"

"Come on," Father Townsend commanded, "I'm going to take you over to the church and walk through this with you."

Mark took time to change into jeans and put on shoes, then he led Peter out the front door, across the street and into St. Joe's vestibule. They stopped just inside the door.

"We have Mass back here during weekdays," he informed the detective. The chairs and altar were arranged in a semicircle. "That's at six twenty-five. The priest who says the Mass unlocks the church."

Peter looked around the church lobby. "How many doors are there into the church?"

"Almost a thousand," Mark replied. Newman jerked his head around. "Actually, probably around fifteen. There's these three main ones back here, but then there's some others along the sides that enter through the basement. I've never bothered to count them all." He turned into a short hallway. "I want to show you something."

There were two rest rooms just off the vestibule in St. Joseph, and Mark took Peter into the closest one.

"Look," he said, pointing to the window. The latch was lifted and the window was cracked open. "That window's been open for at least a week, every time I check it." He started to reach over and close it.

"Don't!" Newman ordered. Mark turned toward him. "Let me get someone out here to dust it for prints. If the kid climbed in and out through here, his fingerprints should be all over it."

"I can show you another place he came in," Mark informed him, leading Newman back through the vestibule.

He took him into the church, stopping at the back to show him where Father Morrow found the corn nuts scattered across the floor. Heading up the main aisle, he pointed to the pews where they had picked up trash the days before: pizza boxes, pop cans, chicken bones and empty bags of corn nuts. Mark stood next to the pew where Mrs. O'Keefe sat.

"The last stuff we found was in here," he told Peter. "There was another bag of nuts and a hood ornament."

"A what?"

"Off a Mercedes," Mark explained, "the circle that

looks like a peace sign. One of our parishioners found it in this pew."

"Do you still have it?"

The priest told him about replacing both, only to find them gone the next morning. Then later, after leaving the can of Pepsi and bag of corn nuts on the steps for the kid, discovering the Mercedes circle lying in their place, as if in payment.

"I've got it over in my office," Mark said. "I'll give it to you before you go."

Newman nodded and turned toward the main altar. "And up there is where you left the pop and nuts?"

"On the first step," Mark told him. "And I put the money and note underneath the can."

Detective Newman turned back to the priest. "I've got to tell you, Mark, that wasn't such a good idea." He was watching the Jesuit's face as he spoke. "That note can be read in a couple of different ways. You and I know you were trying to help the kid, but not everyone is going to think so."

"Not everyone—meaning your partner," Father Townsend guessed.

"Gail reads it differently," Peter admitted, tipping his head in acknowledgment. "To her it sounds like someone trying to make a connection . . ." Peter was uncomfortable continuing, but he did, "for illegal purposes."

Mark dropped into the pew and sat, looking off at the vigil candles flickering beneath a picture of Mary. He was silent for a long time, then looked back at Peter.

"Let's say it straight out, Peter. She thinks I wrote the note to try and meet this kid for sex. And that I met him in the park. That's what she suspects, isn't it? Because, like everyone else, she's read about priests doing that stuff."

"She doesn't know you like I do, Mark."

Mark turned back to the candles. "You're right, she doesn't."

He described for Peter how he locked the front doors

as he left the church the night before, then how he went around the side to check the basement door and found it propped open with the piece of cardboard.

"Show me," said Newman.

Mark led him down the inside back stairway to the door, reminding him that these were the same steps the boy raced down when he escaped the priests' ambush. Mark stopped in front of the door and Peter Newman knelt down to study the lock. He nudged the heavy bronze door open with his elbow, reluctant to touch it with his hands, and a folded piece of cardboard fluttered to the ground.

"There!" Mark exclaimed. "That's what I was telling you about. He kept the door from closing by stuffing that cardboard in the lock."

The sun was already dropping behind the range of mountains to the west, but the air was still hot, and there was plenty of light. "Let's walk up to the park," Peter suggested. "Show me the best way to get up there."

"It depends on which side of the park you want to get to," Father Townsend pointed out. "You can go right up to Fifteenth and over, or you can go along Eighteenth, then cut up to the park. That'd bring you about to the place where the boy was found."

"Show me the best way if you were riding a skateboard," Peter told the priest.

He took him up Eighteenth, past the fine old homes lining both sides of the street. Some of the people outside recognized the priest, but the red-headed man was a stranger; and because the two of them were obviously engaged in serious conversation, they did not call out or greet Father Townsend as he passed. When they reached Galer Street, Mark steered them to the left.

"You start going uphill here," he told Peter, "but it's not that steep. A skateboard could roll up here easily." The two men continued their walk.

"Mark, we haven't found a skateboard yet."

Townsend stopped in his tracks. "It wasn't by the body?"

"We haven't found one," the detective repeated. "We've searched the area, and there's no skateboard." The priest was tugging his mustache. "You told us this afternoon that when you chased him out of the church, he jumped on a skateboard while he was still running down the aisle. Could you be mistaken about that? You did trip and take a fall. Maybe that was something you imagined."

Father Townsend shook his head. "No, there was a skateboard. I heard the wheels, and the kid was gliding when he went by me, not running. Don't forget, Morrow heard something, too. I'm sure it was a skateboard."

Peter Newman looked skeptical. "It'd help if we could find it, then. But at this point, we're not sure where we should be looking. I didn't say anything earlier, but we did find an empty can of Pepsi and a wadded corn-nut bag. We're checking them for prints, but my guess is that they are the kid's.

"Where were they?"

Peter coughed and looked across the street, away from the priest. "They were on a bench, right where you go into the park."

"So that proves the kid was in the church before he came up here," Mark deduced.

The detective looked back at the priest, sadly shaking his head. "If we can tie them to the boy, it proves he had a can of Pepsi and a bag of corn nuts. And the autopsy may report traces of the nuts in his stomach. That means he had them, and it substantiates your claim that you gave them to him. But it still doesn't prove he picked them up inside the church."

The implications of what Peter was telling him were not lost on the priest. The police could prove that Father Townsend wrote the boy a note, asking to meet; and that he offered him money as well as a can of pop and a bag of nuts. What no one could prove, including the Jesuit, was the how or the why.

"Let's keep walking," Mark urged. "I want to see where you found the body."

SEVENTEEN

There were still plenty of people inside Volunteer Park, walking, playing, enjoying the last vestiges of light before returning to their homes. Father Townsend and Detective Newman crossed Fifteenth and started up the drive into the park. As they did so, Newman stopped and pointed to a small outbuilding set back off the roadway a few feet. A small bench was built into the building's side. He told Mark that was where a policewoman had found the discarded Pepsi can and bag.

"It looks like he finished eating before he went into the park," Newman concluded.

There were swings and a slide just to the right of the road heading into the park, and they were crowded with small bodies, the evening air alive with the sounds of laughing children. Their parents sat on the edges of benches close by, watching carefully. Most had heard about the boy's body discovered just a few yards away from where their children were playing. They were alert for strangers, and heads turned to stare as Peter and Mark trudged past. The wading pool came next and the same scene played itself out. Children splashed in the cool shallow water, laughing in delight while their parents warily watched the two men. Neither Mark nor Peter were aware of the stares. They were engrossed in their own conversation, which was about the same tragedy that had the parents so frightened.

Peter Newman nodded toward a low building set back a few yards from the roadway. It was painted a pale mustard color with a brown cedar shake roof. The men's and women's rest rooms were separate buildings, connected by a covered walkway. Benches were built beneath the cover and there was a drinking fountain attached to an outside wall.

"There's the bathrooms," he said, pointing. "The conservatory is directly behind them."

Father Townsend was very familiar with this part of the park, he strolled through here all the time. But he studied the area as if seeing it for the first time, and he listened closely to everything Newman was telling him. They left the road and headed toward the yellow building.

There was nothing left to indicate this area had been the focus of an investigation that morning. Earlier in the day the trees and building were garlanded in yellow crime-scene tape. Police cruisers and a coroner's van crowded the drive, which was closed to public vehicles. Police roamed the park, searching in the grass, around the trees, and through the bushes for anything that might look like evidence. Garbage cans were turned upside down. The bathrooms were searched. Photos from every conceivable angle were made. Detailed sketches were drawn, mapping the location of the body in relation to everything else. Measuring tapes recorded distances. And when they were finally done, about all they had was a young boy's nearly naked body and a whole lot of questions.

The ground was too hard and dry for footprints. Dusting the public rest rooms for fingerprints was an exercise in futility. There were hundreds of smeared partials, covering almost every inch of the place. There were no witnesses that the police knew of. No murder weapon. No bits of clothing, no fibers, no hair, no particles of skin under the boy's fingernails. A rookie policewoman was assigned to gather up any of the trash she found, and about two hours into the investigation she was the one who discovered the pop can and corn-nut bag on the bench. Dutifully, she bagged them and carefully noted their location. Not until much later in the day, after Newman's and Draper's interview with Father Mark Townsend, was the connection made between the trash and the murder victim.

Mark stood next to Peter. There was nothing to see, and he was as disappointed as the countless rubberneckers who wandered past the area in hopes of seeing some telltale evidence of the violence that had occurred in the park right in their own neighborhood.

"Where was the body?" Mark asked.

Newman moved ahead, leading him past the rest rooms, down a slight slope and into a patch of ivy-covered ground. A narrow footpath threaded its way through the green growth and Peter followed it. He stopped in front of a section of exposed tree root stretching across the path. The root was still firmly embedded in the soil, although it's gnarled top was scuffed and worn from all the feet that had stumbled over it.

"We found him just on the other side of that root," he said, pointing. The path through the ivy continued on for about another nine feet before it stopped. An eight-foot cyclone fence blocked the way. "That's the cemetery on the other side. There's a bunch of these paths all along this section of fence. The maintenance crew tells us this is where people sneak into the cemetery after hours."

"What for?"

The detective shrugged his shoulders. "Who knows? Bums hide in there and sleep. It's quiet and safe. And I guess there's kids who go in to play around. Bruce Lee is buried over there, and they told us kids will go hang out by his grave at night." He pointed to an area along the fence closer to the wading pool. "If you go down there, you can see where they've dragged picnic tables next to the fence so they can climb over."

"Do you figure this kid was going into the cemetery?"

Peter shrugged again. Mark was asking the same questions the police were. "We checked for footprints, but the ground's hard as a rock. Nothing shows. And on the other side of the fence there's a cement pad, so no footprints show over there, either. But if he was going over the fence, why would he have his pants down?"

A good question. One Mark could not answer.

"We know what goes on in this park at night," Peter continued, "and our guess is that the kid was in here tricking. That would explain his being here as well as his state of undress."

Mark studied the ground in front of them. The photographs he had seen that morning came vividly to mind, and he found himself superimposing the boy's nude body on top of the earth at his feet. The scene was all too vivid for him and he closed his eyes.

"It doesn't make sense." He murmured the words so quietly that Newman could not even hear them. But he saw the priest's closed eyes and watched his lips move. Father Townsend was obviously disturbed by being here.

"We know the boy was alive and conscious for a while," he told Mark. "Originally he was about five feet back, about where that little slope is. You can see where some of the ivy leaves have been torn away. He dragged himself to this point before he died."

"So you think someone beat him up and left him?"

"Something like that. Either they figured he was dead or they just didn't care. Anyway, the kid was still alive."

"But if he was alive, he could identify whoever attacked him."

"Yeah, possibly. Although it'd be dark back here and maybe he never saw the guy's face. The nearest light is that one over by the road. It's not called anonymous sex without reason, you know.''

What Peter said made sense. But the thought of the kid being beaten and left to die alone was even more disturbing to the priest. Knowing the boy was dead was hard enough for Mark to accept. Hearing the details and envisioning the youngster crawling on his stomach over the ivy and hard-packed earth made it too brutal, too real. What kind of person would do that to a child? He searched the detective's face, as if looking for the answer.

Newman was not sure what to say to him. Bringing the priest into the park and to the crime scene was risky; something he hoped his partner and his superiors would not hear about. But there are times when instinct takes precedence over procedure, and the detective was banking that this was one of them. He knew about this Jesuit; he had watched him in action. If Father Townsend had any knowledge about this crime, Peter had to find out. And he had to find out fast. Still, it was risky.

"So, what do you think?'' he asked.

Mark blinked, still staring into Peter's face. He faltered for some way to answer.

"He . . . I can't believe someone would do something like this. Not to a child,'' Mark answered, still staring at the scene in front of him. "It doesn't make sense.''

Peter already knew that. In his two years since first meeting Father Townsend, the homicide detective had worked several cases where someone was killed during sex. They were usually prostitutes, but not always. One was a housewife and mother found next to Green Lake. And one was a plumber, married with four kids. None of them ever made sense. Peter already knew that. He also knew their cases might never be solved. He had the files to prove it.

"You've got to be pretty warped,'' Newman told the Jesuit.

They began retracing their steps back to the church.

The light was fading and soon it would be dark. The slides and swings in Volunteer Park were already being abandoned. The water in the wading pool was still, no little feet splashing through it, no shrill voices shouting in delight. In the silence, in the dark, shadows would begin emerging once again.

"Gail and I will probably be back up here tomorrow," Detective Newman advised Mark. They had reached the walk outside the priest's house. "We'll want to talk to Father Morrow, and we might have some more questions for you. Will you be around?" Mark nodded. "And I'll get someone to dust that window in the bathroom. Maybe we can find some prints."

"How long before you find out the boy's real name?"

"It shouldn't take too long," Peter said. "We've got Red Pup as his street name, now it's just a matter of finding someone who knows his real one. At least we have a nickname we can use."

"But you don't know if he's from around here?"

Peter was shaking his head. "There's no way to tell, Mark. Not until we get his real name."

"Is there anything I can do to help?"

Newman thought for a moment. "Let us know if you think of anything else. Or if you hear of anything. Maybe someone in your church saw the kid or talked to him. That'd be a big help if we could find someone who talked to him."

The priest listened carefully. Instinctively Mark recognized the risk Newman was taking by coming to him, talking about the case the way he did, visiting the church and then the park. This was not the ordinary way police did things, he was sure of that.

They wished each other good night, and Father Townsend watched the cop drive away. Father Morrow's dusty Toyota was parked in front of the house. Mark could see the light was on in the priest's second-floor bedroom. He knew he ought to fill Dan in on the murder. And he would need to know that the detectives were going to come interview him tomorrow. But he was unable to summon the energy for climbing the steps and going in to greet his fellow Jesuit. He glanced at his watch and turned back toward the church instead.

EIGHTEEN

Father Townsend had the early morning Mass. His clock radio clicked on just as Leonard V. Michael finished his sonorous introduction to Mozart's *La Clemenza di Tito* and the first few solid notes filled the bedroom. The music was full and bright and the priest's heart responded in kind. Early morning light was already flooding into his room and birds were singing. He let the music lift him up.

Not until he was standing did he remember the boy, then his energy left him suddenly. The music now sounded mocking and he slumped back onto the edge of his bed, reached over, and clicked off the radio. Roughly, he rubbed his hands across his face, wiping the remnants of sleep from his eyes. For a moment he was tempted to crawl back into bed.

His Mass that morning was more mechanical than reverent, and he went through the motions on autopilot. He saw the familiar faces in front of him, but none of them registered. The readings and prayers, the ritual gestures, even his greetings after Mass were perfunctory. He said nothing to his small congregation about the boy who had hidden in their church; and when it came time to pray aloud for personal concerns, Mark prayed in silence for the boy called Red Pup. When the liturgy was ended, instead of returning to the house, Father Townsend went to his office and closed the door. He had left a note outside of Dan's bedroom, asking to meet with him as early as possible. Father Townsend sat at his desk and waited for the knock.

Dan Morrow wandered over at 8:30. He still knew nothing and he greeted Mark cheerfully as he made himself comfortable, taking a few minutes to describe his overnight camping trip in the Cascades. If he noticed Mark's weak and unenthused responses, he did not mention them. Father Townsend waited impatiently for Dan to finish.

"Dan, the police found the kid who was hiding in the church."

"Great news," Morrow clapped his hands. "How'd they catch him?"

"That's not exactly it. They found his body in Volunteer Park."

Father Morrow grew somber as Mark began to describe what happened.

His real name was Tony Neeley and he was a fourteen-year-old runaway from Carnation, Washington. His mother reported him missing in early June, which meant Tony survived two months living on the streets.

The police found their boy's name shortly after two o'clock in the morning. Two young detectives, dressed in black jeans and sleeveless sweatshirts, began checking every place they knew they could find gutter punks. They worked their way through Pioneer Square and underneath the Alaskan Way Viaduct; they accosted kids in Waterfront Park. The two men knew several squats beneath the I-5 freeway that were used by kids and they visited those. They showed their close-ups of Red Pup's face and asked if anyone knew him. A couple of kids identified him as a grommet, a wanna-be who showed up on the scene during the summer. He did most of his panning in Pioneer Square, they said, or along the waterfront. No one knew if he turned tricks. No one really cared.

They struck pay dirt in the Steinbrueck Park next to Pike Place Market. A gang of seven gutter punks, bedecked in black, were kicking it, drinking sweet wine, and smoking dope. One of them spotted the two men resolutely walking toward them and hissed loudly, "Six up!" Roaches were hastily extinguished and bottles tucked away. None of their actions escaped the cops' notice, but they were not there to roust these kids; they wanted their cooperation instead. They studiously avoided looking at the empty wine bottles at their feet, and neither man wasted time sniffing the sweet, drug-scented air. After they described Red Pup's death in Volunteer Park, they passed around the photos. The kids grew solemn as they studied the young boy's battered face. Most of them were only three or four years older than the dead youngster, and they still wore their youth like a magic vest, somehow imagining it made them invincible. Such myths manage to survive, even on the streets, and Red Pup's death was a sobering slap in the face. The lost punks huddled closer together, staring intently at the photos, trying not to show what was registering inside. Either they had to let their myth be shredded or find some way to incorporate this sudden tear in the fabric of their own stories. Most managed to silently blame the grommet for his own death. That was the only way they could make sense out of it. That was the only way they could continue wrapping themselves in their own myths of invincibility.

One of the boys, his head shaved and covered with a tattooed spider's web, spoke for the group. "Who snuffed him?" His camouflaged army jacket was two sizes too large for him, the fabric bristling with metal studs. The coat, like his attitude, was hostile.

"We're trying to find that out," one of the cops replied. "Do you know him?"

The punk shrugged and handed the photo to a pale wraith lost in a long black dress and army boots. One side of her head was shaved and the hair on the other side was dyed scarlet. She was shaking as she passed the picture back to the policeman in the sweatshirt.

"His name's Tony," she informed him in a small, uncertain voice. A tear formed slowly in the corner of one eye and began rolling downward, streaking her thick, black mascara. "Tony Neeley."

The kid with the spider web snorted and looked disgusted.

"He's dead, for Chrissakes!" the girl shouted at him. "What difference does it make? You wanna be next?"

He kicked an empty bottle and stormed off, and the girl turned back to the cops.

"Do you know where he's from?"

She gulped and nodded, fighting to stay cool. "Carnation," she managed to say.

"Wait a minute, Mark!" Dan Morrow leaned forward in his chair, interrupting the priest's narration. "Are you saying the police think you killed this kid?"

Father Townsend tried waving off the Jesuit's question. "No, that's not it, Dan. But so far I'm the only one they've tied to the kid. You see? So far, I'm the only one with a connection."

"But what about me?" Father Morrow objected. "Hell, I'm the one who talked you into trying to catch him."

"I know. But you're not tied in the same way. The kid had my note and the twenty in his pocket."

Father Morrow slowly shook his head. "That was a dumb move, Townsend. I never give money out. Kids like that just take advantage. You should never give them money."

Mark had to struggle to remain calm. His fellow priest's self-serving advice was useless and beside the point. Father Morrow made turning down panhandlers a badge of honor; he had bragged about it for years. When Jesuits got into a round of stories of how they were taken by someone arriving at their door with a tale of woe, Dan Morrow puffed out his chest and announced he never got suckered. Father Townsend did not consider it a pastoral practice to emulate.

"The point is I did give him money, and that's what ties me to the boy."

"I wouldn't worry about it too much," Morrow said, dismissively. "Once the police look into it, they'll know you had nothing to do with his death. I'll talk to them when they come. You're not in any trouble."

Father Townsend wished he could feel reassured. His friend appeared unconcerned by any of it—the story of the boy's death, Mark's interview with the two detectives, and Peter Newman's visit. Maybe he was worrying a little too much. When the police learned more about the boy, they would certainly begin tying him to all sorts of people. The fact that Mark Townsend was the first one they came across was not going to mean they would stop looking. Once they started investigating, who knew what they would uncover? Perhaps Morrow was right.

Mark began acknowledging as much when his intercom buzzed. Helen Hart's loud voice wondered if he wanted to take a call, Penny Metcalfe was on line one. Dan was already heading out the door, mouthing a *See you later*.

"Good morning, Penny, how are you?" Mark was thankful for the distraction and his voice reflected it.

"I'm fine, Father. You sound cheerful."

"What's up?" the priest asked.

"I think I've found a lead," Penny announced. "About my parents, I mean. My birth parents."

"That's pretty quick, isn't it? I had the impression a search like that can take months."

"I guess it can," Pen Metcalfe replied, "if you don't have connections. Having a husband on the city council helps when you're trying to cut through red tape."

"So you know who they are?"

The woman laughed. "I'm not that far! Lyle would have to become governor to clear that much red tape. But no, I've got a good lead. You remember the adoption decree had me born in Shelton? Well, there's an attorney friend of Lyle's who is from there. And he's got some connections. He told me he'd look into it."

"Look into your adoption?"

"Sure!" Her voice was bright and hopeful. *La Clemenza di Tito* started up in Mark's brain.

"But I thought adoption records were sealed," Mark said. "Aren't they supposed to be locked up so people can't get access?"

"Yes," she drew the word out slowly, considering her reply, "but the doors are only locked, Mark, not nailed shut. It's like in the Bible, *Knock and it shall be opened.*"

Father Townsend was pretty sure the scriptures were not referring to legal documents sealed by a court order. Nor did he believe they became unsealed with a simple knock at the door. Unless, of course, the person was knocking with some significant political strength. He knew Pen Metcalfe was determined to mount a search for her lost birth parents, but he was surprised at the resolute way she was pursuing it. And how quickly. Mark had figured it would take her several months, which would allow time for some preparation and processing her feelings. Not only was she barging ahead, but she was moving fast.

"You're sure this is the right way to go about it?" His question sounded lame, even to himself, and he regretted asking it as soon as the words left his mouth.

"What do you mean?" Penny's voice sounded suddenly distant and suspicious.

"Forgive me, Pen. I didn't say that right. What I'm asking is if you think you're taking enough time with the process to consider the results?"

There was no response, but Mark imagined he could hear her turning his question over in her mind. He waited for her reply.

"Maybe not," she finally answered. "But what's wrong with wanting to find out who you are?" Father Townsend started to respond, but she cut him off. "How long do you think I should put this off, Mark? Until there's something medical that can't be traced biologically? Or after Lyle's dead and I'm left totally alone? Or just until it's convenient for everybody else?"

Now it was the priest's turn for silence. Father Townsend struggled to find the right words.

"Penny, I would hate to see you hurting any more than you are right now. I think if you want to search for your parents, then you have every right. But I wonder what you might discover. What if they don't want to be found? What if they reject you? Are you ready to deal with that?"

"I've thought of that. They gave me up for some reason and maybe that reason is still there. Maybe they still won't want me. But it feels like a risk I have to take?" She asked it as a question, not sure of the answer herself. "I can't explain why, it just feels like something I have to do. And putting it off is only going to make it worse."

He thought he could understand. At least he could acknowledge the doubts she was feeling.

"I'll make you a deal, Mark. If I do find them, I'll call you. I won't try contacting them without talking to you first. So we can talk this out before I move ahead. You're right, I don't need any more hurt right now. Okay?"

Townsend knew it was the best he could get, so he agreed. He wondered how Lyle Metcalfe was going to react when he learned his wife had gone ahead with her search, and with Mark's acquiescence. There was a light rap on the priest's door and Helen Hart's small head poked in from the edge of the door. Her eyes looked wide and fearful.

"Father?" She whispered, seeing he was still on the phone, "You have visitors."

Mark placed his hand over the mouthpiece and held the phone up impatiently, "I'm still on the phone, Helen. Who is it?"

She nodded nervously. "The police," she whispered. "They've come back."

NINETEEN

There were three of them this time. In addition to Draper and Newman, there was a third detective, and they introduced him to Father Townsend, explaining that he was there to gather fingerprints from inside the church. Neither Newman nor Townsend alluded to their meeting the night before. Gail Draper offered to wait with Father Townsend in the rectory while Peter took the technician over to the church to show him where to dust for prints.

Detective Draper declined Father Townsend's offer of coffee, so he led her into the visitors' parlor, away from the receptionist's desk.

"Is Father Morrow here this morning?" She sounded as if she expected Mark to make up an excuse and say no.

"He's in his office. Shall I go get him?"

"In a minute," she said, "when Detective Newman returns."

She pulled out a straight-backed desk chair to sit and Mark settled onto the low couch opposite her. He found himself sitting half a dozen inches below her eye level and self-consciously adjusted his position, sitting straighter. The detective watched his discomfort in silence.

"So, are you making any progress?" Mark asked.

Detective Draper gave him a slight nod. "A bit," she replied, her eyes locked onto his. "We're still following leads."

There was no air moving in the small room and it was uncomfortably warm. Father Townsend was wearing a black clerical shirt and could feel himself beginning to sweat. There was a faint sheen of moisture forming above the policewoman's upper lip, so he stood to open the window.

"I guess Helen forgot to open the window this morning," he apologized. Detective Draper watched him in silence. She waited until he was sitting.

"Father, one of the things we're still curious about is the skateboard. There was no board anywhere near the boy's body, and we searched the park."

Mark caught himself in time. He was about to say he already knew that, information Peter Newman had shared with him the night before.

"I never saw it," he reminded her, "but I'm sure he was riding one when he left the church. I remember hearing the wheels. And he was moving way too fast to be running. He shot down that aisle."

Gail Draper closed her eyes, as if imagining the scene. When she opened them she was looking directly into Mark's face.

"And you're convinced this is the same boy?"

Father Townsend bobbed his head. "It has to be the same one," he affirmed, "because of the note. I left it sitting in the church and you found it in his pocket. That's a direct connection."

"It connects the boy to you, Father Townsend, not necessarily to the church."

Peter Newman rapped on the parlor door and strode in as she was speaking, his eyes darting between the two of them. "Sorry for the delay."

"No problem." Detective Draper smiled up at her partner. "Father and I were just talking."

"You told him the boy's name?"

Draper shook her head.

"No, she didn't." Mark leaned forward on the couch, addressing Peter. "Who is he? Is he from here? Capital Hill, I mean?"

Detective Draper spoke crisply, cutting off her partner, who was about to speak. "We notified the parents this morning. He's from out of town."

Mark turned to Peter and waited.

"His name is Tony Neeley. His family lives in Carnation," Newman told him. He was watching his partner's face as he spoke. Draper's eyes were staring straight ahead, locked onto a photograph of the pope hanging on the wall behind the priest's head. "He was a runaway." Draper swallowed but refused to meet his eyes. "Maybe now is a good time to meet Father Morrow," her partner suggested.

Father Townsend had at least half a dozen more questions he wanted to ask about the dead boy. Now that they knew his name and where he was from, the police could piece together why the youngster was hiding in St. Joseph church. They could find out who his friends were, what his life was like. They could talk to the family. He was a runaway. Why? Mark wanted to grill the two detectives concerning what they were finding out about this Tony Neeley, but the policewoman was already standing over him, waiting. So instead of asking questions, he rose and led them down the hall to Dan Morrow's office. Introductions were made, handshakes exchanged. Until Newman said something, it did not occur to Mark that he would not be included in this interview.

"We'll see you before we go, Father," Peter said politely. "You'll still be here, won't you?"

They closed the door behind him and Mark returned to his office to wait.

Tony Neeley. The Jesuit sat at his desk and searched his memory. Neeley was not a name he knew. There

was no Neeley family that he could recall, and he had
never visited the small town of Carnation, Washington.
So there was probably no connection between himself
and the boy; not that he necessarily expected to find one.
He pushed himself away from the desk and went into
the lobby.

"Helen, does the name Neeley ring any bells for
you?"

The old woman tucked her tongue into her cheek and
thought. "No, Father, I don't recall anyone by that
name. There's a Neenan who lives over on Fourteenth,
but they don't come to church too often. You're talking
about parishioners, right?"

"Maybe someone who used to live around here."

She thought some more. Suddenly her eyes lit up.
"Was that the poor boy's name? Neeley?"

Mark admitted that it was. He wondered if the family
had lived in the parish at one time. Or if the boy knew
someone in the parish. But Helen's vast memory bank
of the parish was drawing blanks; Tony Neeley was not
a name she recognized, either. To doublecheck, she
called up the parish register on her computer. No Neeley
was registered, nor had anyone by that name been baptized, married, or buried at St. Joseph. Father Townsend
returned to his office and shut the door. Throwing himself into his chair, he started twisting furiously at the
ends of his mustache. Where was the damn connection?
There were over a dozen Catholic churches within a ten-
mile radius of downtown Seattle, and heaven only knew
how many churches, temples, and synagogues of other
religions. What would draw a street kid nicknamed Red
Pup into St. Joseph? And what possessed Tony Neeley
to choose this particular church for his hiding place?

Churches, in medieval times, were considered a safe
haven for anyone going into one. And on occasion, people fleeing from trouble actually sought sanctuary inside
them. A church provided a sort of diplomatic immunity
for anyone found inside its walls. Church sanctuary was

a place of last resort for people with nowhere left to hide. In former times no one, not even the king's own guards, would dare violate the sanctity of a church by dragging someone out against their will. Father Townsend had no way of knowing if Tony Neeley was aware of church sanctuary. He doubted it. But something drew the boy here, to this specific church. If he could find out what it was, Mark felt reasonably certain he would know at least a good portion of Red Pup's tragic story.

The two detectives interviewed Father Morrow for nearly an hour. When they were finished with him, they returned to Father Townsend's office. This time they stayed in there to talk instead of returning to the parlor. Before taking a seat, Gail Draper stood in the center of the room, examining the priest's workspace. She especially focused on a large corkboard overlaid with photographs of friends, family, and parishioners. There were photos of newlyweds, babies being baptized, and parish picnics. People sent him high school graduation photos and Mark stuck them on the board, along with the memorial cards of deceased Jesuits and the Christmas photo cards from years past. The display was a mosaic of Father Townsend's life. The detective stood in front of it, studying it as solemnly as if standing in front of a painting in a museum.

"This is quite a collection, Father," she said finally. "Are most of these parishioners?"

"Most of them, yes." He pointed to a woman with dark hair, smiling brightly in front of a For Sale sign. Then to an older couple seated at a table. "That's my sister, Pam. And those are my parents."

Gail Draper turned away and took the chair near his bookshelf. Peter Newman, already familiar with the office, had dropped into the visitor's chair nearest Mark's desk. Mark sat and waited expectantly while Detective Draper flipped through her notepad.

"Father Morrow was very helpful," she began. "He told us about the incident in the church when the two of you confronted the intruder.'' She looked up at Father Townsend. "He didn't see as much as you did, however.''

Mark met her gaze. "He was at the front of the church. I was in the middle and the kid went by me on his way out. I got a closer look.''

"He still seems unclear whether it was a boy or a girl.'' She was looking down at her notes again. "He said he could not swear either way.''

The Jesuit tried to smile. "Unless Dan has absolute certitude, he wouldn't swear to anything. And maybe even then.''

Draper eyed him, waiting.

"Mark,'' Peter spoke for the first time, "after you left the note and food for the boy, when did you first tell Father Morrow about it?''

Townsend thought a moment. "I guess it was the next morning. Dan had the early Mass and I overslept. I meant to go over with him to see if they were still where I left them.''

Draper perked up. "Why did you oversleep?''

Mark licked his lips. "Like I told you before, I was up late, and when one of us has the early Mass, the other one usually sleeps in a little longer.''

"So you got up late . . .'' Newman coached, encouraging him to continue, "then what?''

"Dan was already back from Mass and having breakfast,'' Mark remembered. "So I went over to the church and looked for the note and the stuff I'd left there. They were gone, so I knew that the kid was back.''

"You didn't think maybe Father Morrow had taken them?'' Draper again. "Or one of the other parishioners?''

"No.'' Mark reached into his desk drawer and handed her the Mercedes hood ornament, the same one he had promised to give Newman the night before. The two men exchanged looks but said nothing. "He left this sitting on the steps where I'd put the note. This is the same one we found in a pew."

The detective fingered the round silver ornament for a moment, then handed it to Peter. "Why would he leave this on the steps?"

"I think it was his way of thanking me." Both detectives looked up at him. Skepticism was written plainly on the policewoman's face, and Mark spoke directly to her. "When I left the food I tried talking to him. I didn't know for sure if he was in the building, but I talked like he was. And I offered to help him. I figured he was scared and I was trying to establish a rapport. So I left the food and the money and in return he left me this."

Newman looked satisfied but Draper was still not convinced.

"Why the need for rapport? I don't understand."

Mark extended his hands, palms up. "If a kid is hiding inside a church, then there's got to be a reason for it. I would figure he's scared, confused, and lonely. So I wanted to help. That's what priests do, Detective. I figured if I could talk to him, maybe I could help him."

Gail Draper took a deep breath, looked down at her notes but said nothing. Peter was listening intently to what Mark was saying, his lips pursed and his hands clasped under his chin. He knew Father Townsend well enough to know that was exactly what the priest would try doing for anyone in need. And he knew his partner, too. Draper would suspect ulterior motives. Why would a priest want to build up rapport with a thirteen-year-old runaway boy? Father Morrow had corroborated the story of confronting someone in the church, but he was unable to identify who that person was. Like Mark, he suspected it was the same person leaving the food wrappers in the pews. Father Morrow had also told them the person was on a skateboard; but when Draper pressed him on the point, he admitted that was only because Mark told him it was a skateboard. The associate pastor had also provided one other piece of information, and it conflicted with what Mark had just told them. According to Father Morrow, he did not find out about Mark leaving the food, note and money until he got back from his camping trip. Either one of the Jesuits was remembering wrong, or one of them was lying.

Gail Draper cleared her throat. "Father Townsend, we'd like you to come in and be fingerprinted."

"What?" The priest sat straight up. "What for?"

Her words sounded reassuring if her voice did not. "It's merely for comparison. There will be prints in the church that we will need to identify. If we know which ones are yours, that'll make things easier."

The priest was nervous abut the idea. "You want Morrow to come down, too?"

"Not at the moment," Draper replied. "We are also checking for prints on the note you wrote, as well as the Pepsi can and bag of corn nuts we found. Since you gave them to the boy, we expect to find yours on them, too."

"What about the twenty dollars?"

"No good," she replied. "Bills are made of cloth and too many people have handled them. They're so permeated with perspiration that all we'd get is a purple twenty dollar bill if we tested it."

Father Townsend looked at Newman. "Is this absolutely necessary?"

Peter shrugged. "It would help, Mark. It's a matter of trying to get a match on key pieces of evidence."

"But of course, you have the right to refuse," Detective Draper reminded him. She made it almost sound like a dare.

"No, no. That's okay," Mark assented. "I'll do it. It's just that it seems a little unnecessary."

"We appreciate your cooperation, Father." Draper gave him a smug smile. "We can give you a phone number; call today or tomorrow and tell them you need to have a set of elimination fingerprints. One of the ID techs will make an appointment for you. It's a simple procedure."

They left a few minutes later and Father Townsend saw them out the front door. He watched them drive away, then went looking for Dan Morrow. He found him in the kitchen.

"They're gone?" Dan finished rinsing his cup.

"Yeah," Mark let out a sigh of relief. "They want me to come in and be fingerprinted."

Morrow's brow wrinkled. "What the hell for?"

"They said they want to match my fingerprints to those on the stuff I left in the church."

"But they already know your prints are on there."

"I know that, Dan," Father Townsend barked in a peevish voice. Seeing the look on his friend's face, he apologized. "It feels like they're still suspecting me," he said, "and they're still asking questions about my connection with the boy."

Helen Hart started into the kitchen but came to a sudden stop when she saw the two Jesuits engrossed in conversation. "I'm sorry," she apologized, "I didn't know you were in here."

Townsend waved her on in. "It's all right, we're just talking."

"We're going to take a short walk, Helen," said Father Morrow. "We'll be back in a bit."

The men left by the side door and reached the front of the church before either one spoke.

"So what'd they ask you?" Mark wanted to know. They turned up the street, staying on the left sidewalk, out of the sun.

"They asked me a lot of questions about the night we chased the kid in the church," Dan told him. "Who thought of the idea, how we went in, how close we got to him. They wanted to know if I got a good look at his face." Mark waited. "I told them it was my idea to try and catch him. And I said I didn't know if it was a male or female. Everything happened too fast."

They reached Seventeenth and turned down a long block of fine old homes with carefully tended yards. The street was empty and they had the sidewalk to themselves.

"They wanted to know about the skateboard, too," Morrow continued. "That seems to be a major thing for them."

"I think I know why," answered Mark. "They haven't found it yet. Evidently it wasn't with the boy or anywhere in the park."

"Maybe he left it somewhere."

"He could have," Mark admitted, "or else someone took it."

"Whoever killed him?" Father Morrow gave his friend a small smile. "You're in the clear, Mark," he joked. "I'm willing to swear in court I've never seen you on a skateboard."

Father Townsend tried to force a smile, but it came off looking more like a grimace.

"Did they tell you they know who he is now?"

Morrow shook his head. "They didn't say any name to me."

"He's from Carnation," Mark continued. "His name is Tony Neeley. They told me he ran away from home at the start of the summer and was living on the streets. He got in with a crowd of kids who call themselves gutter punks."

Morrow snorted. "That sounds like the name of a band, one of those grunge groups. This Neeley kid must have been a class act. He runs away from home, joins some sort of gang, breaks into a church, and works as a prostitute in Volunteer Park." They reached the end of the block and turned left again, slowly making their way toward St. Joseph. "He probably won't be up for sainthood anytime soon."

Townsend knew he was teasing, but the priest was treating the boy's death too lightly.

"He was only fourteen, Dan. We don't know if he

was a prostitute. And he was only hiding in the church, it's not like he forced his way in.''

Father Morrow threw up his hands in mock surrender, still trying to tease. ''Okay, you win. Saint Tony it is! Virgin and martyr, patron saint of gutter punks and corn nuts.''

''Cut it out, Dan.''

The two stopped in front of St. Joe's school. The rectory was next door and neither was ready to go in quite yet.

''What about the note and the money?'' Mark said. ''Did they ask you about those?''

''And the Pepsi and corn nuts. I told them I didn't know anything about them until this morning.''

''That's not right, I told you about them before you went camping.''

''No, you didn't, Mark. You told me at the same time you said they found the boy's body in the park, remember? I told you it was stupid idea.''

He did remember. ''I've got to call Peter,'' Father Townsend said worriedly. ''When they asked me about it, I said you knew before you went camping. They're going to think I was lying.''

Dan was looking steadily at Mark. He could not remember ever seeing his fellow Jesuit so rattled. Father Morrow did not know if Townsend's lapse in memory was going to cause serious trouble with the police or not, but he could see that he was agitated.

''It'll be all right, Mark,'' he tried to sound reassuring. ''Just call and explain that you made a mistake. Peter knows you, he'll understand.''

''Yeah, I guess.''

Dan hesitated, started to speak, then stopped. Mark caught it. ''What?''

''I was just thinking,'' Morrow began again, ''after you call the detective, you might want to make another call.'' He stopped again and laid a hand on Mark's shoulder. ''I think you ought to call the provincial,

Mark, and let him know what's going on. This is the kind of stuff he'd want to know about."

The provincial superior for Jesuits working in the northwest lived in Portland, Oregon, and was responsible not only for the men in his province but their ministries as well—which meant keeping up with what was happening at two universities, four high schools, and half a dozen Jesuit parishes, in addition to the various missions, hospitals, prisons, diocesan churches, and retreat centers where his three hundred men labored. A Jesuit provincial's term only lasted six years, and if his hair was not gray when he went in, it was by the time he left. Gray, or gone. The man currently assigned to the job was formerly a university rector, well acquainted with the burdens of administrative work and negotiating with committees, boards, and commissions, as well as supervising the lives of a large number of Jesuit priests and brothers. The one thing he did not like, however, was surprises. If trouble was brewing anywhere in the province, he wanted to know about it before the pot boiled over. Hearing bad news on the television or from a reporter over the phone would mean bellows of outrage, quickly followed by threats of decapitation, plagues and pestilence, castration, and exile. Probably in that exact order.

"You're right," agreed Father Townsend, offering the priest a grim smile. "I'll call him in the morning. Right after I arrange my fingerprinting."

TWENTY

When he first considered joining the Jesuits, there were two mountainous hurdles Mark Townsend had to get over: no sex and no children. He was right out of high school when he entered the novitiate, and at the time, marriage was not that big of a draw. But sex and children were both big ticket items as he thought about his future. Over time, he found his desire for children growing less intense. That was not the case with sex. And as he grew older, he discovered that the love and companionship in marriage became more of a value for him.

But what a man values is not always what he buys. Sometimes the price is too high, and sometimes it clashes with something he already owns. Mark Townsend owned his vocation. He had invested twenty years of his life in it and considered his membership in the Jesuits as his greatest treasure. That is not to say there were no days when he was tempted to give it up. Sex continued to regularly rear its horny head. And coming home to a house of four other bachelors was not always the high point of his day. But on the whole, Father Townsend was happy and content to live his life as a Jesuit priest.

So what changed over the years was his attitude toward children. What once was clearly a paternal desire gradually developed in an avuncular pleasure. By the time he reached his mid-thirties, Mark had pretty much let go of any fantasies of rug rats clinging to his legs and calling him Daddy. There are freedoms that come with being childless; and as he aged, he grew in his appreciation of those. When he wanted to get away, there was no need to wonder who would watch the children. Parental responsibilities for clothing, housing, feeding, and educating were not part of his concerns. Nor were the finances. And as the years went by, nights of uninterrupted sleep grew more blissful and more valued. Father Townsend was happy not being a father.

What he did enjoy, and take full advantage of, was being around other people's children. He loved going into a house ringing with the shouts and laughter of younger voices. He enjoyed listening in on the mysterious language of children talking about being grossed-out and way cool. For every cornball joke they told him, he gave one back. Everything about them was fascinating to the priest. The way they flew through the house; their voracious appetites; the prepubescent patter and adolescent angst; playing with their plastic dinosaurs, video games, and squirt guns; giggling until they could no longer breathe; the clothes they wore, the music they played, and the shows they watched—Father Townsend felt like he was visiting a foreign culture. And he loved it.

He also loved being able to walk away when the cornball jokes grew tedious, toys littered the house, and the giggling turned to tears. The priest knew very well that his ability to leave when things got too loud, messy or unpleasant was a luxury. One that parents sometimes envied, sometimes resented. He caught the glint in the eyes of harried mothers and fathers trying to constrain their demon offspring while he took his leave. In some ways it was not unlike being a grandparent—enjoying your grandchildren all the more because you know you can walk away from them any time you want.

Children liked Mark and naturally gravitated to him. The priest was not like other grown ups. He was not their parent. And when he came around, the rules and restrictions were relaxed. Scoldings turned into gentle reminders when Father was in the house, and punishments were often commuted. Second helpings of dessert were encouraged with smiles, and times for bed were often extended. And the tall man with the funny mustache knew more dumb jokes than all their friends combined. He was not afraid to sit down on the floor with them, to play Nintendo or to watch "The Simpsons." The priest paid them more attention than their parents' other friends. He seemed to like them for who they were and not because they belonged to their folks.

The one thing about children that Father Townsend could never walk away from was their pain. To see a youngster hurting ripped at the Jesuit's insides. Young, lithe bodies twisted over or bent double, bleeding or burning with fever would throw him in despair. Hospital visits to sick children were especially agonizing, and the priest would often break into a cold sweat walking into their room. Seeing young bodies in the midst of disasters on the evening news made him nauseous. Try as he might, Mark had never found anything in his theology that made him feel comfortable with the suffering of children. He could never connect their pain to God's mercy; it never worked for him.

The photographs of Tony Neeley's young, bruised body continued to haunt him. The ugly details of his death were like needles jabbed into his consciousness. His unconsciousness, too. And with each passing hour the priest's discomfort grew more intense. Knowing that the boy named Red Pup had sought sanctuary at St. Joseph and that Mark had come so close to making a connection with him only made things worse. His prayers for the boy felt empty and useless. They were certainly no comfort to Mark, and he questioned whether they were of any help to Tony. If the hand of God was present in any of this, Father Townsend had a hard time seeing it. Whose ever hands were responsible had to be scarred with sin and bloody with guilt. Mark's own felt dirty by association.

He used his trip downtown as penance. The shame and embarrassment of being fingerprinted were offered up as partial reparation. That was the only way he got through the ordeal.

Mark's appointment was at ten o'clock in the Public Safety Building. Parking on the street would be impossible and the cost of a parking lot was higher than he could justify, so Father Townsend rode the bus. The Number Ten rolled right down Fifteenth, so it was an easy walk from his house to the bus stop. His hardest choice was deciding what to wear.

The standard uniform for Catholic priests is still black. Black pants, black shoes, black socks, black shirt. In addition to the religious overtones of clerical attire, there are also some practical ones. For men with little sartorial taste (and in the priesthood they are legion), there is little danger of committing sins of fashion. Unless, of course, you stray into red or blue clerical shirts with green checked pants. For single men without recourse to the help and advice of tasteful spouses, there is no need to stand in front of the closet and wonder what to wear. And laundry days are black and white. Even the most absentminded scholastic can keep that straight. Most social events are no-brainers. Weddings, clericals. Funerals, clericals. Likewise with parish meetings, formal dinners, and church on Sunday. On some occasions, wearing clericals are not necessary. Mufti is proper when playing golf, spending a day at the beach, and any time Father is at a movie with a rating below G.

But dressing that morning had Townsend stymied. There is no priest's manual of protocol that covers the proper attire for getting fingerprinted. He thought wearing his blacks would bring a certain dignity to the ordeal, but figured it might also raise a few eyebrows. Showing up in street clothes, on the other hand, could be perceived by the police as some sort of disguise, as if he had something to hide. In the end, Mark compromised, wearing black slacks and a plain white, short-sleeved shirt, without a tie. At the very least, it would do nothing to complicate his laundry day.

Getting fingerprinted is like flying. You have to pass through security first. The main entrance into Seattle's Public Safety Building is on Third, and inside the doorway the security checkpoint is just like the ones at the airport. Security gates were installed shortly after a fatal shooting in divorce court, and anyone having business with the city's legal system is now required to pass through them. Father Townsend rode the elevator to the fifth floor, wondering if sweaty hands would make the ink run. If true, his prints were going to end up looking like black rivers coursing off the page.

Peter Newman told Mark he would be at his office in the homicide division at the time of his appointment, and offered to accompany him. Before he could meet the detective, however, the priest had one more layer of security to penetrate. He lifted the phone next to the thick glass window and spoke to the receptionist behind it, asking to see Detective Newman. She barely glanced at him as she told him to wait, then walked out of sight. A few moments later, Peter opened the door.

"Come on in, Father, you're right on time."

Mark gave him a nervous smile and stepped inside. After years of watching television cop shows, he was surprised how quiet the room was. There were no loud jangling phones, police screaming to be heard over a noisy din, or shoot-outs. Seattle's Homicide Department looked like any ordinary office, and the men and women working there could have been arranging financial investments or selling real estate. Gray cloth panels formed the walls of their office cubicles, providing a modicum of privacy and muting the sounds of voices.

"Would you like some coffee?" Peter was leading Mark down a hallway with cubicles on both sides. The priest shook his head. Newman stopped walking and eyed the priest intently.

"You're nervous, aren't you? There's no need to be, you know. People do this all the time."

"Not too many priests, I'll bet."

Peter arched his eyebrows. "You'd be surprised. There's a lot of jobs today that require people to be fingerprinted. And that would include some people involved with counseling or working with children."

He appreciated Peter's efforts, but they did little to help him relax.

"Let's just get it over with," Father Townsend pleaded.

Newman led him around the corner and down a stairway to the next floor. A sign at the doorway of Room 405 read FINGERPRINTING. They veered left into a small, brightly lit lobby with several ugly vinyl chairs lining the walls. A large, heavyset man, scowling down at his hands, sat in one chair; and a young woman in tight jeans and a green silk blouse sat in another. Newman ignored them as he brushed by, stopping at the counter and waiting for Mark to catch up.

"This is Mark Townsend," he told the woman behind the counter. "He's here for case 9887-502." And he handed her a slip of paper. He had purposely left off his religious title. Mark would be forever grateful.

Father Townsend was handed a release form and asked to fill it in. The first line asked for his name. He paused at occupation, then wrote parish priest. Peter stayed with him, nodding encouragingly. When he was finished, an ID technician produced a square card and led them around the counter to a small table that stood waist-high. The top was smeared with ink. She worked quickly and proficiently. His card was attached to the left side of the table. One by one, she lifted each of the fingers of his right hand, pressing it hard against the pad of ink, then carefully but firmly rolled it gently across one of the squares on the card. Ridges and whorls stood out in black relief, and she moved to the next finger. Then the left hand, same procedure. Peter stood just behind them, watching over her shoulder, as if seeing the procedure for the first time.

When they were done with both hands, Father Townsend's fingers were coated with black printer's ink. He held them awkwardly in front of him, palms up, determined to keep them as far away from his white shirt as possible. The ID tech offered him a sympathetic smile and squirted a generous amount of liquid soap into his hands.

"It's a little hard to get off, so rub real hard," she urged him.

With a few more squirts and a lot more rubbing, Mark rid himself of all but a few faint streaks of ink, then dried his hands on the paper towels she held out to him.

"And we're done!" Peter heartily announced, slapping him on the back. There were two new customers waiting at the counter, and the tech hurried over to them as Newman led him out of the room.

"I'd take that coffee now," Mark said, "if you're still offering."

They rode the elevator down to the Fourth Avenue level and left through a doorway reserved for employees, then across a plaza to an office building that housed a Starbucks and at least two other coffee kiosks. After Peter paid for their coffee, they settled at a table looking out onto the street. He nodded to people he recognized at the next table and turned his attention to Mark.

"So how are you doing?"

"I'm okay. Better, now that that's over with." The detective sipped his coffee and waited.

Mark kept his eyes down, fixed on his cup. "I'm a little frustrated that you guys are spending so much time on me," he admitted finally. "It's an uncomfortable feeling."

Peter waited to see if there was more Mark wanted to say before he spoke.

"I don't think there should be too much more. But we have to move through this case logically, Mark, and you're the first and closest tie we have to the boy. That means you get most of our attention, at least for now."

"What happens next?"

The detective leaned back and looked out at the traffic. "We'll follow our other leads," he said. "At some point we're going to turn up something or someone who points us in the right direction."

"So you're convinced I'm not the right direction."

Newman kept his eyes turned to the outside. "I am."

Gail Draper had not come into their conversation; this was the first time either man came close to even alluding to her role in the investigation.

Mark asked, "What can I do to help?"

"Keep cooperating," Peter told him. "And if you remember anything else about the kid, be sure and let us know. Right now we're trying to track who he hung around with on the streets. But it's slow going. The gutter punks don't believe in helping cops, even when we're trying to find out who's killing them. What we know so far is that this kid, Red Pup, was friends with at least two of the other victims." He reached into the pocket of his jacket, pulling out a small notebook. "He knew that kid shot in front of the ferry terminal, and was friends with a girl we found over at Golden Gardens. There was supposed to be a group of them that hung out together, with some older guy who was sort of their leader. We haven't found any of the others yet."

"The murders could be connected . . . I mean, if they knew each other?" Mark leaned forward, waiting for Newman's reply.

"Yeah," the detective nodded, "they could be. But maybe not. I mean, yes, the kids are connected to each other, but the circumstances of their deaths seem different. We just don't know yet."

"What does that mean?"

Peter caught the note of impatience in the priest's voice and he scowled into his coffee like something was swimming around in there. He took a long swallow before replying.

"Red Pup—the Neeley kid—was what they call a grommet. That's what they call a newcomer, or a kid that's just hanging out with the real gutter punks. The other two kids were the real thing. One was from Missoula and the other from Denver. Both of them were on the streets for over two years, but Neeley only showed up in June. His mother and stepfather live outside of Carnation. It looks like a rough home life, and probably the kid wanted to get away from his family for a couple of months. There's some indication he was involved with some minor mischief around the school out there, but nothing serious. These other two are hard cases, real tough kids.

"The boy at the terminal . . . his street name was Tool . . . was gunned down at the same time as another man." Newman had to flip several pages back in his notebook. "A guy named James Robertson. He was a washed up hack who once wrote for the New York Times. He hung out around the state capital in Olympia most of the time, trying to dig up dirt on politicians. When he'd find a juicy scandal, he would sell it to whoever would offer him the best deal. Both of them were shot right in front of the terminal, within seconds of each other. There was a ton of people out there, but it happened so quick that no one can describe what really happened. We know Robertson was coming off a ferry and that there were two or maybe three guys chasing him when he was shot. The other one—Tool—might have been an innocent bystander. There were a bunch of kids in front of the terminal at the time, begging for change, and he could have been with them. They all ran when the shooting started."

"What about the girl?"

"Tracy Nelson." Newman was reading from his notes again, shaking his head as he did. "Fifteen years old. She ran away from home when she was twelve. She was the one from Denver; a nice looking kid, but into some rough stuff. Really into body piercing." Peter paused, looked up at the priest and started to turn red. "She had both her nipples pierced and another one . . . you know . . . down lower." He turned a shade redder and looked down at his notebook. "She went by the name of Slash. Real nice, huh? The postmortem showed she was pregnant, but barely. She probably didn't even know it. Before she was killed, she was beaten up, and two of her fingers were bent back until they broke."

Mark covered his eyes with his hand as he listened to the detective. The details were too graphic, more than he wanted to hear. But Newman was not done.

"Death was by strangulation. Someone choked her to death, then dumped her body in the sand, just inside the park. Then there was another kid, a boy, that we found in a Dumpster over by the Kingdome, and he was killed in the same way. He was about Red Pup's age, maybe a little older. We still don't have a name. But his right hand was smashed and he was strangled, same as the girl. And before that, there were two others. One was a girl under the freeway. We've got a thick file on her, almost all prostitution. She had her throat slit. And a boy was found floating in Elliott Bay. No name again, but we know he was a street kid. Probably about sixteen or seventeen. That one was knifed."

Finished with his litany of the dead, Detective Newman closed his notes and stuck them back in his pocket. The priest still had his eyes covered and Peter turned to stare out at the street.

"We don't know if all those cases are connected or not at this point. But because they're all street kids and they were all murdered within the last couple of weeks, Gail and I are handling them. My best guess is that at least two of the murders were done by the same person.''

Father Townsend laid his hand back on the table. "The two who were strangled.''

Newman nodded. "The others, I'm not sure about.''

"And Tony Neeley?''

"I don't know, Mark. He was obviously beaten up. Not tortured, not the way the others were, but severely beaten. And the way he was undressed and next to the men's room in the park looks like he was prostituting.''

The priest drained the last of his coffee. Newman's cup was already empty and he was glancing out the window again, looking as if he were anxious to get back out on the streets. But Father Townsend had one or two more questions he wanted to ask.

"Do you know what religion he was?''

His question caught the detective by surprise. "Neeley?'' He shook his head. "I don't know. Judging from the family, I doubt if he was much of anything. Why?''

"I've been trying to figure out why he chose St. Joe's to hide in. I thought perhaps he had some connection with the church.''

"It's close to Volunteer Park,'' Newman needlessly reminded him.

"There's two other churches just as close,'' Mark replied. "It has to be more than that. What about the skateboard? Have you found it yet?''

The policeman waved his hand impatiently, as if trying to brush away the question. "Nothing. Zilch. Nada. We turned the park upside down, it's not there. It could be that the boy's assailant took it. Or maybe he didn't have it with him.''

"Assailant. Could there have been more than one?''

"We wondered about that. The dirt is so hard around that area that we couldn't tell very much. But there was very little disturbance. The ground cover would have been torn up a lot more if there was more than one person. We think there was just one.''

*   *   *

By the time the Number Ten rolled back up Fifteenth, it was already twelve-thirty. Father Townsend's appetite was gone so he skipped lunch and walked directly from the bus stop back to the parish office. Helen Hart was away from her desk so he was able to pass through the empty lobby and make it to his office without having to explain where he had been during the morning. The receptionist had noticed his absence, though. Four pink messages were placed squarely in the middle of his desk. Mark lifted them, reading through them as he dropped into the chair.

Two caught his attention. The first was from Penny Metcalfe, who had called at 9:30. Helen had marked it Urgent and scrawled underneath: *Pls. call ASAP.* The other was from a man named Cliff Powers, who had called at ten. Mark did not recognize the name, but was seized by a sudden wave of nausea. Beneath the phone number Helen had written: *Seattle Post-Intelligencer.*

TWENTY-ONE

Jesuits have two ways they can phone their provincial superior. He has a direct line into his office and his men have access to that. Or if they choose, they can call the front desk, then ask to get rerouted through the receptionist. Rectors and those in charge of anything tend to call direct. The men less accustomed to dealing directly with their provincial prefer calling the front desk. Jesuits in trouble tend to call the front desk, too. They know they are going to end up talking to the man eventually, but being put on hold for a few moments has the feel of buying time, like sitting in the dentist's waiting room.

Mark had barely drawn a breath before his call was switched and the provincial's sonorous voice was booming through the phone. "Mark? Jack Elliott. How are you? How's St. Joe's? You guys making it through the summer okay?" The provincial liked to shotgun his men with questions at the very beginning, hoping one of them would graze the reason for the call.

"Things at the parish are fine, Jack. And the warm weather is kind of nice for a change."

After the first shotgun blast Father Elliott would narrow his sights, take aim again and fire a second round.

"What about yourself? Are you okay?" His percentage of direct hits was part of the reason he was made provincial.

"That's why I'm calling, Jack. I thought I should let you know what's going on."

And with that, Father Townsend launched into his story. He began near the end, telling his superior that the police were interviewing him about the murder of a street kid found in Volunteer Park. Then he described the circumstances of the Tony Neeley's death. He told him the boy was living inside of the church and that Mark had been trying to draw him out. He narrated the foiled attempt by Dan Morrow and himself to catch the boy. For his part, the provincial listened, salting Mark's narration with an occasional grunt, some *hmmms* and a couple of *I understand*s.

When he was finished describing how the boy escaped on his skateboard down the main aisle of the church, Mark paused. He knew he had reached the hard part of his story. But the provincial was already leading him.

"What else?"

"This morning I went down to police headquarters and let them fingerprint me. They wanted to match my prints with the ones they found on the pop can and the bag."

Father Elliott breathed a long, heavy sigh into the phone. "I don't imagine you've talked to an attorney, have you?"

His question caught Mark off guard. "No. No, I haven't. I didn't think there was any need."

"Right."

"I mean, they're not charging me with anything, but—"

Elliott cut him off. "But a kid at the church was killed near some toilets in a park late at night and now the police want to compare your fingerprints." His words peppered Mark like lead pellets, and they stung. The provincial reloaded. "What else?"

"This morning, while I was downtown, there was a

phone call . . . maybe it's not related, but—''

"Yeah, yeah," Elliott grunted. "Who's onto this?"

"I don't know for sure what it's about, but a reporter from the P-I is trying to reach me."

There was only silence. Mark held his breath and waited. This was about where he expected the cannons to explode. But Jack Elliott was not made provincial just because he could be direct. He was also deeply compassionate, especially with his own men. When he finally spoke, his voice was soft and low.

"Mark, I'm really sorry. I know this is tough on you. The main thing is to stay calm. You say you've done nothing wrong here, and I believe you. The Society is going to back you one hundred percent, no matter what happens. Now, I take it you haven't responded to the reporter yet."

"I wanted to call you first."

"Good. I'm glad you did, although a little earlier would have been nice."

Mark knew he was right. His provincial's admonition was as gentle as any Elliott could give.

"What should I do?"

There was no hesitation in the provincial's reply. "Nothing. Right now I don't want you to do anything. Except maybe pray," he added, sounding slightly gruff. "I'll do some of that myself. I'm also going to call our attorney. So you just sit tight. Pretend like you didn't get that phone call. Who all is at the house?"

Father Townsend told him most of the community was on vacation, that just he and Dan Morrow were around.

"Then you have Dan answer the phone," Elliott ordered. "The door, too. And let your secretary screen your calls, at least until we get this cleared up. Okay?"

It was more than okay. Anytime he could avoid answering a phone call was okay by Mark.

"And Mark?"

"Yes?"

"This is going to be all right." Jack Elliott's voice was now firm and calm. "Trust in God, then trust in yourself. And trust that we'll do whatever we can to help you. This is going to be okay."

Mark thanked him and they hung up. The moment he set the phone down, he plucked the reporter's pink message off his desk, crumpled it, and dropped it in the trash—and doing so brought exhilaration. Pen Metcalfe's message was directly beneath the reporter's. The priest stared at it a long moment before abruptly rising from his chair.

Helen Hart was settling back at her desk when Father Townsend startled her by striding quickly past and out the door.

"I'm out for a while, Helen," he called over his shoulder as the screen door started to close, "if anyone calls, take a message."

Penny was on her front porch when Father Townsend arrived, watering flower boxes overflowing with color. She waved when she spotted the priest, following with a wide, happy smile.

"You didn't have to come over here," she told him as he mounted the steps, "you could have called." She set down the watering can and led him into the house, "But I'm glad you did. I've got great news."

"You found your mother," Mark guessed.

The woman shot him a look of fake disappointment. "You ruined my surprise!" she complained, seating him at the kitchen table before she poured two glasses of ice tea. Excitedly, she began describing how her attorney friend had called earlier in the morning with the good news.

"Her name is Cynthia Metzler," she told Father Townsend, handing him a glass. "That sounds German, doesn't it? Ron told me there's a good chance my mother lived outside of Shelton, in a place called Wrigley, over by Hood Canal."

Penny's cheeks were flushed and her eyes were bright.

She had not stopped smiling since Mark greeted her, and despite himself, the priest found he was grinning back at her. She was bubbling like a little girl describing her new boyfriend, a favorite dress, and Christmas all at once.

"How did he find her?"

"I think it was through the county," Pen chirped. "Ron told me he worked through a judge or lawyer or somebody he knows in Shelton, and that they were able to get into the records and pull my birth certificate. Her name was written on there, and he didn't seem to have any trouble finding out where she lived."

Shelton is a small logging town of less than ten thousand, embedded at the south end of Puget Sound. Father Townsend could well imagine a homegrown attorney waltzing into the Mason County courthouse, greeting a clerk who happens to be his next door neighbor as well as his mother's best friend, then fishing through the county records until he uncovers the name of the woman who gave birth to Baby Girl Metzler in June 1958. What might take ten months in Seattle could be accomplished in ten or fifteen minutes in a small community like Shelton if you know the right people and they are your friends.

He grinned back at his smiling parishioner. "That's good news, Pen. Congratulations!"

"It is great news!" she enthused. "I can't believe it! I've been reading some of those books about adoptions and finding birth parents, and they warn that it can take months and even years to track down enough information. But this seemed so easy."

Easy if you are the wife of a powerful city councilman and able to call friends who are willing to find ways into confidential records. Rank has privileges, and as much as Father Townsend enjoyed the company of Lyle and Pen Metcalfe, he now knew that neither one was hesitant to pull rank when it was useful to them.

"So now that you have her name are you going to call her?"

"There's no listing for a Cynthia Metzler," Pen complained. "I tried Information already and they said there is no number for anyone with that last name. It was over thirty years ago, I know, but I thought maybe there might at least be a relative with the same last name."

"It sounds to me like you've hit a dead end."

Pen idly lifted a strand of long blond hair from the back of her head and began twisting the ends. She looked absorbed.

"Not entirely . . ."—her voice was tentative and Penny's eyes turned away from Mark as she continued— "I was thinking maybe of driving over there."

Father Townsend knew where this was headed. The Metcalfes only owned one car, and Mark was not even sure Pen knew how to drive. He was fumbling for a way to respond that would buy time until he could devise a way out. But the woman had had all morning to plan and was too quick for him.

"But I would need someone to go with me," she said. "Someone I could trust." Her eyes rolled back to Mark's, and she had the audacity to bat them. "Someone who already knows about this."

"Pen . . ." Mark was faltering already. She was not playing fair.

She put up a hand to stop him. "It wouldn't even take a whole day," she promised. "We could take the early ferry, look around, and come right back. You're always saying you don't get away enough. This could be like a day off or something."

One thing was clear to Mark; it would be no day off.

He was shaking his head. "I don't think this is such a—"

"Just think about it for a while," Penny pleaded. "I don't want to ask anyone else unless you really can't do it. But you've been in this with me since the beginning, and you've been so supportive. I know it's asking a lot, but I'd really like you to come.''

Father Townsend was tugging the ends of his mustache, twisting so hard it hurt. He grimaced in pain, and not just from the torture he was inflicting on his upper lip.

''Pen, I just don't think this is a good idea,'' he argued. ''You really need to think this through some more.''

''I have,'' she said decisively. ''I've done nothing else, Mark. Ever since I found those papers in mother's bedroom, I've been thinking about what to do. I wish I could make you understand, but I have spent so much time thinking about this . . . worrying about it . . . trying to figure out what to do. I didn't even know if it would be possible to track her down. But I did, and now I have a name.'' She stood up from the table and moved to the counter, looking out at her backyard. With her right hand she slowly brushed her fingertips down her left arm. ''I've even prayed about this,'' she continued in a soft voice. ''It's like God purposely allowed me to find my mother.'' She turned and looked at the priest now. ''First he took her away, and now he gives me another. That's possible, isn't it?''

He was not sure she wanted an answer, but then she asked again, ''Isn't it?''

''Anything's possible,'' he told her. ''Yes, this could be from God.''

''And if it is, then I need to pursue it, don't I?''

''If it is from God,'' Mark was speaking slowly, thoughtfully, ''then it would be right to go look for her.''

''To me, that's what it feels like.''

A little theology, as with most knowledge, can sometimes be a dangerous thing. Father Townsend often met people who knew a little bit of scripture. Without understanding its historical context and significance, they tended to interpret the words literally, and often ended up believing all sorts of funny things. The same was true with the theology of discernment. Simply equating God's will with personal feelings leads people into making all sorts of funny decisions. Sometimes with disastrous results. Father Townsend was not a good enough theologian to lead Penny Metcalfe through the theological intricacies of discernment. But he had been a Jesuit and a parish priest long enough to recognize when someone's decision had the potential of blowing up in her face. Deciding to show up at someone's door and announcing you are her long lost daughter was the atom bomb of bad discernment.

"I'll go," he said weakly.

"You'll go with me?"

Mark shook his head. "No, that's not what I mean. I'll go instead."

She was confused and made no effort to hide it.

"Here's what I'm thinking," he told her. "Let me drive to Shelton and see what I can find out. I can look around and see. If anyone knows a Cynthia Metzler, maybe I can find out where she lives. Maybe I can talk to her."

Penny Metcalfe's look of confusion shifted to one of doubt.

"I think it's a better way to go, Pen. This way it gives the woman some freedom to respond without having to face you immediately. After all, you don't know anything about her or what she might think about having her daughter show up."

She chewed at her lower lip as she mulled over what the priest was saying. Reaching into a drawer, Pen lifted out a paperback book. Mark could not read the cover, but it looked dog-eared. There were several scraps of paper sticking out from various pages. The woman opened it to a couple of different places already marked. She became so engrossed in reading that Father Townsend began to think she had forgotten he was there. When he was about to speak she looked up.

"This is one of the books on finding birth parents," she explained, "and it says here that it's better if an intermediary makes the first contact. I shouldn't presume to intrude into someone else's life without making some sort of overture first. So maybe I shouldn't go with you." She had moved from confusion to doubt, and now to disappointment. He could see it in her eyes. "You'd tell me everything that happens?"

Mark nodded.

"You'd tell her my name? And that I'm in Seattle?"

He nodded again.

"Maybe you won't even be able to find her." She laid the book back in the drawer, closing it slowly. "She might not even live there anymore. God, she could even be dead."

Mark started to speak.

"You'd tell me everything, right?"

"Pen, if I find out anything, I'll tell you. If I can locate where she lives, I'll try to see her. I'll tell her she has a daughter named Penny who lives in Seattle and who would like to come meet her."

"That would be okay."

Mark hesitated. "There is one other thing."

"Lyle."

"You're going to have to tell him," said Mark.

"I know. He comes home tomorrow night."

That would be Thursday. Closer to the weekend than he liked, but Dan Morrow was preaching, so all Mark had to do was celebrate two Masses. The timing was okay, and it might take his mind off his own troubles.

"I could go on Friday," he decided. "That gives you a little while to think about it, to decide if this is what you really want.

"It is. I know that already."

Her look had changed once more, and now it was determination.

Mark stood up. "It wouldn't hurt to pray about this," he reminded her. "Just to double-check."

She offered him a smile. "I can do that," she said, walking him to the door. "But I know it won't change anything."

Volunteer Park was nearly empty. The sun was burning bright and it was too hot for most Seattlites. The grass on both sides of the museum was turning brown. A few brave souls had thrown blankets on top of the bristling lawn, baring themselves to the sun's hot rays, but most of the park's patrons sought refuge deep in the shade under dense trees, staying as far away from the bright heat as they possibly could.

Mark tried to walk where he could remain in the shade. He was breaking a sweat nevertheless, and could feel his shirt clinging to his back. The park was too hot, but he needed time to think, and a stroll through the park provided the opportunity. Once past the museum he crossed the road, where the trees grew thicker.

Pen said that her prayers would not change anything and that bothered him. Father Townsend had grown to believe that prayer always means change. Even when your decision is already made, prayer should at least change how you look at it. When Jesuits make choices, they call them elections. When they pray about them, they look for confirmation.

He stood in front of the conservatory, facing the white opaque front, feeling the heat reflected off the panes of glass. The change comes in attitude. Before prayer, the election is only human. Afterward, it becomes part of the divine. But trying to explain that over iced tea at a kitchen table, to a woman lost in death and the grief of her own abandonment, was beyond this Jesuit's abilities. At least for today.

He turned right, past the conservatory. In front of him he could hear children shouting and laughing as they splashed through the park's wading pool. The dried grass, ivy, and dirt where Tony Neeley's nude body was discovered was to his left, and it drew him like a magnet.

The Jesuit left the road, crossing the lawn to the spot where Peter Newman told him the young boy lay. Nothing was there to mark the site. A narrow trail led through the ivy-covered ground to the chain-link fence that separated the park from the cemetery beyond it. Since the boy was from Carnation, he would more than likely be buried out there, near his family. Father Townsend had not considered the boy's family, and Peter had not told him much about them. But as he looked through the fence at the few gravestones he could see beyond, he realized the parents were faced with burying their son, probably within the next day or so. At times, life deals choices—like deciding whether or not to search for a lost mother; at other times the choices are made for us— like burying a lost son. Father Townsend believed in a divine plan, but sometimes the exact details left him feeling fuzzy. He stared hard at the ground in front of him. Maybe there was something he could do for the family.

Sounds behind him made Mark turn. An older man in plaid shorts was leaving the rest room and he gave Mark a nervous, frightened look as he hurried across the grass to rejoin his wife who was waiting beside the road. The couple crossed to the other side and walked farther into the park, looking back worriedly at the tall man standing near the bushes back by the fence. Sadly, Father Townsend watched them leave, then turned toward home.

TWENTY-TWO

The *Walla Walla* slipped away with barely the slightest tremor, so slowly that Father Townsend could hardly tell that they were moving. The deck beneath his feet vibrated and then open water appeared between the ferry's iron curves and the wooden pilings of Pier 52. Bremerton was fifty minutes away. Mark stayed at the rail and stared out as they pulled farther into Elliott Bay and the wide, grand view of downtown Seattle receded into the perspective of a panorama. The city's skyline was a mishmash of architectural styles, dominated by a handful of towering buildings near the center and flanked near each end by the city's two best-known features: the Space Needle to the north and the Kingdome to the south. The morning sun backlit the buildings, casting long shadows down into the streets. The view from the back of the *Walla Walla* was picture-postcard perfect.

There was still a morning chill coming off the water, and with a last look over his shoulder, the priest headed inside for a cup of coffee. He had risen in time to catch the 6:40 A.M. ferry to Bremerton. The car deck below was only half-filled, mostly by early commuters driving to Bremerton's shipyards and a few delivery trucks getting a jump on the morning's traffic. Most ferry traffic was coming into the city in the morning, and a lot of those were foot passengers who commuted to work from Bremerton or Bainbridge Island. The tide of traffic turned in the afternoon as the workers returned home.

The phone call had come from Lyle Metcalfe instead of Penny. She must have spoken to him shortly after he returned from his trip because the priests were just sitting down for dinner when the phone rang. Dan Morrow answered, then quickly palmed the phone over to Mark, silently mouthing the word Metcalfe.

"Hello, Penny."

"No Mark, it's Lyle."

"Welcome home." Mark scowled at Dan, who only shrugged. "How was your trip?"

"Long and hot," the man answered. "Pen's talked to me about what's gone on and I'm calling to thank you."

Mark could not tell if he was being sarcastic or not. "How so?"

"She's been busy with this adoption thing and pushed it a lot farther than I wanted her to. I knew she wasn't going to drop it like I asked, but I didn't think she'd get as far as she did. At least this soon. I'm glad you talked her out of going over to Shelton. Thanks."

Apparently no sarcasm was intended. Mark breathed a little easier. Dan Morrow was waiting patiently, and Mark signaled him to start eating as he stood up and moved away from the table.

"We talked a couple of times, but Pen pretty much had her mind made up." Mark spoke into the phone.

Metcalfe grunted. "I'm not surprised. That's my wife. Anything I tell her, she does the opposite. If I was thinking, I would have told her to hire the best detective she could and to track that woman to the end of the world. Then she probably would have dropped it completely."

"You sound like you're okay with this, Lyle. I thought you'd be upset."

Mark could hear ice clinking in Metcalfe's glass.

"Nothing I can do, is there? One thing you learn real quick in politics is when to take a stand and when to back off and regroup. Obviously she's handed me a *fait accompli*. Pardon my French."

"So you don't mind if I go over to Shelton to check things out."

"Of course' I do!" Lyle's response was loud and quick. "But what the hell good is it going to do for me to object? And it's a hell of a lot better than Pen going over herself."

"Look, Lyle, I don't want to get in the middle of something between you and Penny—"

"Nah, nah! It isn't anything like that." Mark could hear his ice rattling again." If it wasn't you, she'd hire a detective. I know she's not going to drop this. So go and find out whatever you can for her. If you find her mother, then, yeah, talk to her and see what she wants to do. The only thing I'd ask is that you not spread it around. Don't tell anyone you don't need to. And please don't mention my name to anyone. I've told Penny the same thing. Just leave me out of it."

Later that night, an apologetic Pen Metcalfe called back. She did not mean to put Mark in the middle of a disagreement with her husband. And if he wanted to forget the whole thing, she would understand.

"What would you do instead?" Mark wanted to know.

She was speaking softly. Her husband was asleep in the next room. "I'd put it off for a while. Let him get used to the idea."

"Is that what you want?"

"No. What I really want is to find this woman. But Lyle has got it in his mind that somehow this is going to make him look bad. I told him he's being irrational."

Mark could imagine how well that was received.

"He told me to go ahead and look around. Is that what you want?"

She was silent. He waited, not wanting to push.

"Yes," she said finally. "I want to know."

Two white gulls followed behind the ferry, swooping and turning, waiting to see if some choice morsel was going to appear in the ship's wake. Mark sipped his coffee slowly, enjoying the birds' antics as the ferry crossed the bay and slipped into the channel south of Bainbridge Island.

He was not clear what he was going to do when he reached Shelton. All he had was the name Cynthia Metzler and the town she was from, a place called Wrigley. Townsend had to search his map closely before he found it; the tiniest of dots on a thin black line winding out of Shelton. Even if there was no one living there by that name, in a place that small there might be someone around who still remembered her. Pen Metcalfe had given him the name of the man who had searched the Mason County records, but Lyle's admonition to avoid talking to people was not forgotten. Mark would avoid speaking to anyone unless he absolutely had to. Unless there was further information in the county records, he doubted Pen's contact could be much more help anyway.

The ferry was gliding into Bremerton's harbor and the captain's voice rang over the loudspeaker, asking drivers to return to their vehicles. Father Townsend threaded his way down the narrow stairway to the lower level, where his car was parked.

Bremerton's streets were alive with morning traffic as he followed the other cars and trucks off the boat and into downtown. He made a couple of wrong turns as he tried to find his way out of town, but eventually managed to find Highway 3, heading toward Shelton. A road sign informed him he had thirty-two miles to go. The highway narrowed to one lane running in each direction, but it remained fairly straight. Tall fir trees lined both sides of the road with the exception of plats recently logged. There, black stumps covered the landscape like beard stubble. He crossed the county line from Kitsap into Mason and the road began to curve, snaking its way into Belfair. The town seemed to have some fixation for selling cars; both sides of the road were lined with new- and used-car lots.

He followed the contours of narrow Case Inlet. Cottages lined the perimeter of the small, tidy harbor. But once past the inlet, the road cut inland again and Mark was driving through managed forests. Acres of uniform-sized trees stretched out on either side. This was timber country, where the powerful industry reigned supreme. As if to prove the point, a logging truck pulled onto the road directly in front of Father Townsend, forcing him to slam on his brakes to avoid impaling himself on a long load of Douglas fir. His small car edged up to the back of the truck's bed, loaded with logs that stretched way beyond the trailer's support, bobbling, and spilling chunks of bark onto the asphalt. There were too many curves to try to pass, so Mark slowed to a crawl, putting some distance between the huge truck and his windshield. He followed behind the behemoth for several miles before he could see clearly and far enough to gun his engine and race past. Water was off to the side again, narrow bays and inlets; the watery fringes of south Puget Sound.

A high yellow railroad bridge spanned the road as he drove into Shelton. HOMECOMING "63" was splashed in runny white paint across the cement. Below it someone had scrawled SHELTON CLASS "64". Class interest in graffiti must have run out in '65, but there were plenty of individual signatures covering the bridge. The end of Shelton's harbor was dominated by a lumber mill, and the acres around it were piled with cut lumber, stacks of plywood protectively sheathed in plastic, and mountains of sawdust. Rafts of logs floated on the water in front of the mill. At the edge of the road a large sign welcomed visitors to Shelton, CHRISTMAS TOWN U.S.A.

The town is built on two levels: the older section on

the flats close to the water, and the newer on the hilltop that towers above. Mark stopped for gas near the town's center. A kid in greasy coveralls studied him from the station's doorway, laconically eyeing Mark's black clericals as he struggled with the gas pump. He waited until Mark was finished and replacing the pump's handle before wandering over and waiting for payment with an outstretched hand.

Father Townsend counted out eight dollars into the kid's dirty hand.

"Can you tell me how to get to Wrigley?" he asked the youth.

The kid recounted the money, then carefully folded and stuffed it in his back pocket. Tilting his head to the right, he said, "Go that way."

"About how far is it?" Mark asked politely.

"About to hell and gone," the kid sneered. He locked his eyes onto Mark's white collar. "What'd ya' wanna go to Wrigley for? Ain't nothin' out there."

"I'm looking for someone."

"Lottsa luck." He turned his back on the priest and stumbled back to his same position in the doorway.

Two blocks away Mark followed a small sign pointing down Railroad Avenue and promising Information. He stopped beside an old locomotive and caboose that were parked permanently next to the street. The Visitor Information Center was inside the caboose.

A woman's tiny, white-haired head peered at him from behind a counter laden with Mason County and Shelton brochures. She offered him a welcoming smile as he entered but waited until Mark spoke first.

"Good morning. I'm trying to find my way out to Wrigley."

"Yes." She cleared her voice and her eyes blinked twice at him from behind thick lenses. "Yes," she said again. Mark could not see any part of her body behind the counter, and he had a momentary impression of talking to a disembodied head.

"There is not a lot to see in Wrigley," the woman's head told him. Her voice was high-pitched and it quavered with age. "But there is a nice lake along the way."

"I'm not a tourist," Mark explained. "I'm looking for someone."

"Yes," she said, blinking at him again.

Father Townsend looked down at a map displayed on the counter between them. "Could you give me directions?"

"Yes."

A tiny hand edged slowly over the countertop. The parchmentlike skin was nearly translucent, with thick blue veins crisscrossing over the top. Her knuckles were swollen and red and the long nails at the end of her arthritic fingers scrabbled across the map like crab legs.

"This is Wrigley." A lone finger distended from the others, but it was shaking so badly that Mark was only able to guess at the approximate vicinity. He leaned in for a closer look. A wave of lavender swept over him, and he smiled down at the old woman's sweet face. He placed one of his own fingers, twice the size of her's, on the map.

"This is the road I'd take," he guessed.

"Yes." Her own finger shifted slightly, swishing back and forth over a broken black line. "You'll find the Miriam Shining School down this road." Her eyes blinked and her smile broadened. "I used to teach at Miriam Shining."

"Did you?"

"Yes. You should visit there. The students maintain a lovely tribute to logging at the school."

"Yes," Mark replied. "You didn't happen to teach a girl named Cynthia Metzler, did you?

"Yes." The old woman blinked. "I don't recall that name. But you could ask at the office. Perhaps I did." Her smile never faded. "I taught geography, but that was so long ago."

He had to resist an overwhelming urge to reach out and gently pat the top of her tiny head. "I'll bet this train was still running back then, wasn't it?"

She smiled happily. "Yes."

He found the road leading out of Shelton and was plunged back into the forest almost immediately. Douglas fir lined both sides of the road, tall and straight and thick as weeds. He drove farther and passed hills sheared to ground level, where nothing was left standing that was any taller than the tiny woman in the caboose. A hillside to the left looked like scenery from an old war film. Tree trunks were uprooted and toppled on their sides, limbs were broken and twisted, lying scattered over a wide field. It looked like a bomb had exploded there. While on his right, dense trees formed an almost impenetrable fence, pushing to the edge of the road.

The nice lake the old woman mentioned was called Lake Wahnatsel, and its shores looked clogged with cabins. Mark pressed on, anxious to reach his destination. He was not sure what he would find at Wrigley, but after his conversations with the gas station attendant and woman in the caboose, he set his sights low. As it turned out, not low enough.

Wrigley was a four-way stop at a crossroads in a clearing surrounded by woods. On one corner sat the Wrigley General Store, a pale gray building with a decrepit ice machine at one end of the sagging porch and the huge hulk of a black mutt flopped at the other. Mark pulled to the side of the road in front of the store and turned off his engine. He stretched out his arms as he climbed out of the car, peering around at his surroundings. The mutt lifted his head, looked over at the stranger, then went back to sleep. There were no other cars anywhere in sight. It was nearly ten o'clock and the sun was high overhead. The store looked open but as he mounted the steps he could see a penciled sign stuck in the door's window: BACK IN 15 MINUTES. There was no clue how long it might have been there.

With one last look around, he got back in his car and pulled onto the road, turning left. The woman in Shelton's visitor center had told him about a school three miles farther down the road, so perhaps the center of Wrigley was closer to the school.

But if it was, it was well disguised. The Miriam Shining School was a rust-colored building with a gravel drive, surrounded by forest. There were only a couple of houses in sight and across the roadway, a fire station that looked deserted. A faded blue pickup sat parked in front of the school. That was Mark's first indication that Wrigley might still be inhabited. The front door was unlocked and he wandered in. The dark hallway was cool and smelled of floor wax and chalk. A door to the school office was open. He could hear movement inside.

A short, squat man had his back to Mark, bending over a desk and examining the contents of a cardboard box. He was dressed casually, wearing blue jeans and a faded blue work shirt. His hair was short and gray. Father Townsend cleared his throat to catch the man's attention, and he turned around. He was no man at all.

"Oh, dear!" the woman exclaimed. She was holding books in her right hand, and without taking her eyes off Mark, set them on the edge of the desk.

"I'm sorry if I frightened you," Mark apologized.

"You didn't," she replied, still staring. Her face was pleasant enough but at the moment it wore a distinct look of disappointment. "I was just sorting this shipment of books." Her eyes were fixated on Mark's white collar. "You're a minister."

"A Catholic priest, yes."

"Oh, dear!" Her disappointment increased.

"Is something the matter?"

"I didn't realize you were a priest . . ." She fumbled with how to complete her sentence, then gave up. "I just didn't know."

Mark had debated whether or not to wear his clericals. He finally decided they might provide more access to the information he was seeking. Now he was second-guessing that decision. "Is there a problem?"

She was obviously stuck for an answer. Twice she started to reply, only to fall silent, still staring at his collar. Finally she blurted out, "I'm not sure we could hire a priest to teach gym!"

His laughter echoed down the school's corridor. "I'm not looking for a job," he was finally able to say, "I stopped to ask for information."

The woman blushed a deep red, stood taller, and moved away from the desk.

"I'm so sorry," she apologized, extending her hand. "My name is Regina Bulb. I'm the principal."

Mark introduced himself. "And you thought I was here for a job?"

She blushed again and nodded. "The only reason I'm here is because a man is coming from Longview to interview for a job as our gym teacher. I thought you were him. But when I saw your clothes, I thought . . . I mean, I . . ."

Father Townsend laughed again. "That's all right, I understand.

"Thank you," she said with relief. "Would you like some coffee? I just brewed a pot."

"That'd be wonderful."

He wandered around the cluttered school office while she filled two cups. Stacks of unopened mail and shipments of books littered the countertop.

"How many students do you have?" he asked.

"Right around a hundred and twenty," she replied, "K through twelve. We're not exactly the one-room schoolhouse, but not too far from it." She pointed toward the back wall, which was lined with five rows of photographs, ten black-framed pictures in each row. They were photos of each successive year's student body, lined up on bleachers, flanked on either side by their teachers. "It allows for a pretty close community here at the school."

"I imagine," Mark said, crossing the room to stare at the photos. "How many graduates would you have in a year?"

Now that she knew he did not want to be her gym teacher, Regina Bulb was much more relaxed. She handed him his coffee and leaned against the corner of her desk. "Anywhere from seven to twelve," she told him.

Mark settled onto the edge of the desk opposite her's. "I'm trying to find someone who lived in the area almost forty years ago."

"I'm not sure I can help you, then, I've only lived here twenty." She gave him a wry smile, "I'm still a newcomer."

"The woman I'm looking for is named Cynthia Metzler."

"I may be new, but I'm not that new." The principal pointed to one of the photos on the right side of the wall. "Cindy Metzler, class of sixty-three; only she never graduated."

"You know her, then."

"I know about her," she corrected him. "She's something of a legend around these parts."

Father Townsend waited to hear more. The woman sipped her coffee, staring over the rim of her cup at the priest, sizing him up. A logging truck loudly shifted gears as it passed the school. Finally the principal spoke.

"You don't know anything about her, do you?"

"Not really." He did not want to tell her about Penny Metcalfe.

Regina Bulb took her time. Despite the students' logging exhibit, not too many visitors stopped at Miriam Shining School. No priests that she was aware of, and certainly never one who was looking for Cindy Metzler. A story this good was going to get her through the rest of the summer. But first she needed to find out everything she could.

''Why are you interested in Cindy?'' she asked inquisitively.

Father Townsend lifted himself off the desk and wandered back to the wall of photos. In every picture there was a student sitting front and center, staring into the camera and holding a small blackboard with the year etched in white chalk. He found 1963 and studied the students' faces. He could tell nothing from their looks.

''She's the one in the sweater.''

The principal was standing behind him, looking over his shoulder. There were probably a dozen girls wearing sweaters in the photograph, but Mark was able to pick out Cindy Metzler with no difficulty. She was the one in *the* sweater. Her black hair was piled high on top of her head in the style they used to call a beehive. The girl's face was plain, but heavily made up. The sweater she was wearing was tight and her breasts looked like twin Olympic ski jumps. They were the flagships of every teenaged boy's best dream. Attending the same school with such monuments would make education an honor and a privilege. In 1963, male absentees at Miriam Shining School must have been nonexistent. Mark pulled his eyes away from the photo and looked back at the principal. Her mouth was curled in an amused smile. Cindy had that same effect on most men.

''I can see what made her a legend,'' the priest said.

Regina Bulb gave a short bark of laughter. ''Right. But for an adolescent girl, they're more of a curse. And those aren't what made her the legend.''

''Then what did?''

''Ahhh,'' the principal sighed, raising her eyebrows. ''In order to tell you that, I need to hear why you want to know.''

He did not like the idea of exchanging information this way, but he could tell that Regina Bulb was not going to lay down her cards unless he gave her at least a glimpse of his.

''There is a woman in Seattle who thinks she might

be related to a Cynthia Metzler," he told her. "I'm trying to find out if this could be the woman."

The principal chewed over the nugget of information Mark fed her, trying to decide if it was enough. Still hungry, she asked, "What kind of relation?"

Mark considered before answering. There was a gleam in the woman's eye; she knew he had more.

"Maybe a daughter," he replied.

She grinned, then swallowed. "Let me tell you about Cindy."

TWENTY-THREE

The principal's tale was a sadder version of one told in just about every small town, village, and hamlet in the world. A young girl's life ruined by a series of tragic events that inevitably involves getting pregnant. The townsfolk may or may not know who the boy is, but every mother and her son knows the name of the hapless girl. The Cindy Metzlers of the world are forced to carry their shame for everyone to see. In a place the size of Wrigley, there was nowhere she could hide.

Like most other families in that part of Mason County, the Metzlers' income came from logging. Cindy's father bucked logs at the mill. Her mother was dead. Although she was not considered cute, the girl had other attributes that made her popular, at least with the boys. And by the time she was halfway through high school, she had the reputation of making easy trades for time with those attributes.

In the summer before her senior year, she was trading time with a young man who drove out from Shelton. His name was David Reid, and he was part of the family that owned most of the forests and all the mills that lay between Shelton and Wrigley. When school started in the fall, he stopped coming to Wrigley, but by then the damage was done. In late October, Cindy had to tell her father that she was pregnant.

The drive back to the Wrigley General Store took Father Townsend down a long, straight road through the managed forests that were still part of what was called the Reid Plantation. The principal had told him that David Reid now lived in San Francisco. But the mills, the trees, and the people who harvested them were still under his control.

After Cindy told her father she was pregnant, the mill-worker did not hesitate to drive into Shelton and confront David's father with his son's misconduct. Metzler's daughter was seduced and overcome by the boy, and now her life was ruined. And in addition to the ruined life, complained Mr. Metzler, there would be all those expenses.

He must have been convincing, because several large checks were cut by the Reid Corporation. Large enough to get poor Cindy through eight more months and then to pay the costs of giving birth. And large enough for her old man to quit his job and disappear, leaving eighteen-year-old Cindy with a baby and Wrigley's disapproving looks. A few days after Mr. Metzler took off, the baby was gone, too. But the disapproving looks never quite left.

Regina Bulb was not able to tell Father Townsend exactly where the Metzler house was located. Somewhere past the Wrigley General Store, she said vaguely. As far as she knew, Cindy Metzler still lived there. The post office was inside the store, and maybe they could give him directions. Mark thanked her and before he was out of the school's office, Regina Bulb was reaching for her phone.

The same tired mutt lay stretched across the end of the porch when Mark arrived back in front of Wrigley's one store. The dog had already given the man in black a good long look, so there was no need to raise his head a second time. There were still no other cars parked outside, but the sign in the window was gone.

Wrigley's post office was nothing more than a half-wall of small mail boxes and a tiny shelf built into a doorway. There was no one at that shelf, but an old man wearing a dirty apron was sitting on a high stool behind the store's counter in front. He slowly edged off the stool and stood expectantly behind his cash register when Father Townsend walked in. His white eyebrows lifted noticeably when he spotted the priest's garb. Just like at the Miriam Shining School, not many preachers visited the Wrigley General Store. Mark gave a cursory glance up and down the three aisles. The canned goods were dusty and the snack foods looked old.

"Help you?" The old man cocked his head hopefully, offering the priest a salesman's smile.

"Can you tell me how to get to Cindy Metzler's house?"

The smile turned into a leer. "Sure I can, if that's where you want to go." The old man licked his lips and eyed the priest up and down.

"It is," Mark said shortly.

The clerk's directions were not complicated, and Mark had the impression he was used to giving them. About a mile beyond the store was Wrigley's Grange Hall, a decrepit structure that leaned decisively to the south. Twenty yards beyond that, he turned left onto Beeton Loop Road, drove another quarter of a mile, crossed the railroad tracks, then took the first dirt road on his right. Billows of dust immediately rose up around him, and his car bounced and lurched from one deep rut to the next for an eighth of a mile.

The house was half hidden in a dense grove of alders. The shingle siding was old, dark, and badly stained, but the steep roof was new, made of green aluminum. A battered red pickup sat parked in front, four large barrels standing upright in the bed. The Jesuit rolled up next to the pickup and turned his motor off. He stayed inside the car, waiting for the dust to settle before opening his door. There was no porch in front of the house, just a closed wooden door centered in the middle with small dirty paned windows sitting high on both sides. A light fixture with a bare bulb hung over the door. As Father Townsend opened his car door, the house door opened, too.

Cindy Metzler had grown into a severe woman with a battered-looking face that was gaunt and pinched. She still wore too much makeup and her hair was still raven black, although it now flowed loosely over her shoulders. She was dressed in a flowered housecoat that she held closed by crossing her arms tightly in front of her chest. Her feet were bare.

"Ms. Metzler?"

She nodded. Her eyes flickered as she looked him over.

"My name is Father Mark Townsend. I'm a priest from St. Joseph Church, in Seattle."

"How'd you do," she said in a tiny girl's voice.

The sound startled the priest. He had expected her voice would be deep and husky, perhaps dark from smoke and late nights. She sounded like she belonged back in Miriam Shining's second grade. He offered her a smile.

"I was asked by one of my parishioners to come talk to you."

"What's his name?" she asked immediately.

"Her name is Penny Metcalfe," he said gently.

"I don't know any women from Seattle." But she looked at him curiously, waiting.

He had planned out what he was going to say and how he would say it, but the scene Mark had written was for a different setting, in a much different place. Before leaving Seattle he had rehearsed a conversation that took place over coffee, sitting on a chintz sofa in a small but tidy living room. He looked around at the battered truck and down the dusty drive.

"Perhaps I could come in for a while?" he suggested.

His request startled her and she took a step back into the doorway, pulling her arms even tighter against her chest, shaking her head.

"I'd rather you not," she told him in her small voice. "Things ain't too clean inside." She glanced over her shoulder at the darkness behind her, as if checking to make sure what she told the priest was true. "Who'd you say that woman's name was?"

"Penny Metcalfe," he repeated. "She lives in Seattle."

"Nope. Don't know her."

This was not the way he wanted to do this.

"Pen doesn't know you, either. But she thinks you might be related."

"My name's Metzler," she told him, "not Metcalfe. I don't know her."

Mark tried to smile again. "Metcalfe is her married name," he said. "Her maiden name was Madsen."

The woman flicked her head impatiently and her high voice sounded sharp. "Madsen, Metcalfe . . . I told you already, I'm Metzler."

There was no other way to do it.

"Penny was adopted," he told her. "She thinks you might be her mother."

Once, when he was still a little boy, Mark's father took him deer hunting in central Oregon. A large and proud buck stepped out of a stand of ponderosa pine, about seventy-five feet away. He caught their scent, but instead of bolting he stood his ground, raising his head proudly and staring straight at them. Mark's father shot him. The buck never flinched. He looked quizzically at the two humans for several seconds, then simply collapsed, his legs crumbling beneath him. Cindy Metzler stared at Father Townsend for several seconds before dropping her arms to her sides and crumpling against the door frame. He thought she was going to slide to the ground and stepped forward to catch her, but she shook her head weakly and he stepped back.

"Who are you?" She was looking at the ground, and her little girl's voice was nothing more than a gasp.

He repeated his name and where he was from. Her housecoat had fallen open when Cindy's arms dropped. She was wearing a plain white slip underneath without a bra. What had once looked so proud and brash in a high-school photograph now looked only like ponderous weights. She made no effort to cover herself.

"Why did you come here?"

"Pen . . . Penny Metcalfe asked me to. Her mother died and she found out she was adopted. She's been trying to locate you."

"No." She shook her head thickly. "I don't want nothing to do with her. I don't know who she is and I don't want her." She lifted her head and looked straight at him, "I don't got a daughter," she said. "Please go away."

"Cindy," Mark began, taking a step forward, "I know this is—"

"Get away!" she yelped. "Get away!"

Quickly he backed away from the woman.

"I don't got a daughter. No! Can't you see I don't want this!" She was pleading with him now. "Go away. You shouldn't ought to be here."

"I'm sorry. I thought it was better if I came before Penny. I was trying to help."

Cindy Metzler lifted herself away from the door frame. "Don't let her come here! I don't wanna see her. Ever! Don't tell her to come here. You understand?"

The Jesuit nodded.

"I don't have to see her and I don't want to. Just go away."

Mark was at a loss for words, but he tried again.

"You're sure this is what you want?" he asked. "You're sure you don't want to meet your daughter?"

"She ain't no daughter, I told you that." The haggard woman was nearly screeching. "All she is to me is pain. When she got borned, I hurt so bad I couldn't even stand it. My daddy left me because of her. I got nothing but hurt by her." Cindy began to cry. "She was pain when she came in my life and pain when she went out. Now I don't want no more pain. You go back and tell her I'm dead. Tell her not to ever come here. Tell her I don't need no more pain."

Tearfully she looked down at herself, grabbed the front of her housecoat, and wrapped it tightly around her body, recrossing her arms over her chest.

"Please go away," the little girl pleaded.

Four miles on the other side of Wrigley, Mark veered off the highway onto a dirt logging road. The first two hundred yards of trees were gone, and all that remained was a clutter of broken limbs and uprooted stumps. What was once tall forest was now only carnage. But farther back the firs were still standing, and Father Townsend followed the rough road back into the trees until he was entirely swallowed up by dense forest. It was dark in there and felt cooler. He stopped his car and got out. The silence felt like church.

He stepped off the road, stumbling over an exposed root but catching himself before he fell. As he wandered deeper into the woods, he heard a bird's peep and then the chatter from a chipmunk harvesting cones somewhere in the trees above him. The scent of fir was strong in the air. Mark Townsend felt numbed and very tired, and if he had not been dressed in his clerics, would have considered lying down to sleep on the ground beneath the towering trees. Instead he dropped onto a fallen log and rested his head in his hands.

There are no formulaic words that can absolve the cruelty suffered by a Cindy Metzler. Sorrow like that runs too deep, and the anguish, too long. Priests never feel more alone than when they are unable to use the skills and gifts their vocation gives them. Father Townsend felt frustrated. He was driving away from a woman he was unable to help. And carrying more pain back to another. On the log in the woods, he began to weep.

Mark stayed in the forest until hunger drove him out. In Belfair he stopped at a small diner tucked between used-car lots and ordered a large meal, too much to finish. He took his time, feeling no urge to rush back to Seattle. Once in Bellingham, he stopped again. And for over an hour he wandered the streets, letting the store windows distract him. He found a bookstore and lost himself in the aisles for half an hour. Once he boarded the ferry, he stayed in his car. The engines throbbed beneath the deck and he let their sound lull him almost to sleep. He unrolled his window and could smell the salt air.

By the time he arrived back at his house across from St. Joseph, it was nearly eight o'clock. There was still plenty of light, though, and the evening was warm. Wearily the priest climbed out of his car and started up the walk.

"Father Townsend?" A voice called out behind him.

Mark turned and spotted a man standing at the curb across the street in front of the church. The stranger looked both ways before dashing across the street.

"You're Father Townsend?"

Mark nodded.

"My name is Cliff Powers. I've been waiting to talk to you. I'm from the *Seattle Post-Intelligencer*."

TWENTY-FOUR

The newspaper's story was not as bad as Mark thought it would be. He slept in until seven, and when he finally wandered downstairs the house was empty. Dan Morrow took his early Mass but left the morning newspaper folded open and propped on the kitchen table. The story, written by Cliff Powers, was on the lower half of the front page.

INVESTIGATION CONTINUES
INTO YOUTH MURDERS

Seattle police continue to investigate the recent deaths of six homeless youths murdered during the last three weeks. According to one source, they are talking with a Roman Catholic priest they describe as "a person of interest."

Although he is not called a suspect at this time, the clergyman's relationship with 14-year-old Anthony Neeley is under investigation. The boy's body was discovered in Volunteer Park on Monday.

A source close to the investigation described the priest's connection to the boy as "a relationship we don't quite understand completely." Neeley was living inside a Catholic church on Capital Hill and was apparently being assisted by the priest.

Paula Abzug, police spokeswoman, said that Neeley was missing from his family's home in Carnation, Washington, since early June. During a part of the summer he was living in close contact with street youths in downtown Seattle. She said police are not certain when the boy moved into the Capital Hill church.

Abzug would not say if the police have tied Neeley's death to any of the other five youths murdered in recent weeks. Nor would she comment on the questioning of the clergyman connected to Neeley. "This is an ongoing investigation," Abzug said, "and I am not prepared to say anything specific about anyone we might be talking to at this time." But according to a source inside the department, the priest in question was brought to police headquarters to be fingerprinted in connection to the crime.

Seattle's Catholic Archdiocesan spokesman, Lester Kane, said he is unaware of any investigation involving a Catholic priest. "The Archdiocese has not been contacted about this matter," he said, "and I would be very surprised if the police were seriously suspecting a priest without talking to us about it."

Abzug gave no indication when an arrest might be made, but said she is confident the murders will be solved.

His name was not mentioned. Nor was the church's, although anyone with half a brain could figure it out.

The reporter promised Mark his name would not appear and said he was only seeking confirmation that he was the priest police were talking to. The trip to Wrigley had exhausted him, but Townsend still had enough sense not to say anything. He explained to the newsman that he was just returning from an all-day trip and it was not a good time to talk.

"Can I call you tomorrow?" Cliff Powers wanted to know.

"Sure," Mark replied, trying to sound nonchalant. *And if you can get past Helen Hart, I'll even talk to you.* Fortunately, the reporter was no mind reader.

The front door opened and closed and Dan Morrow appeared in the kitchen, a grim look on his face. He spotted the newspaper in front of Mark.

"You've read it."

Mark nodded

"There've already been some calls," Dan said. "I took them off the answering machine before Helen came in."

"Who's calling?" Mark was surprised how calm his own voice sounded.

"No parishioners that I know of," Dan told him. "A couple of people wanted to know if St. Joseph is the church in the newspaper. There was one sicko. And the provincial wants you to call him as soon as you can."

"He knows?" The kitchen clock had not hit eight yet and Jack Elliott had already called from Portland, Oregon. Morrow shrugged.

"Let me grab a shower and I'll come over to the office," Mark said as he got up from the table. Dan shot him a worried look.

"Why don't you stay over here for a while," he suggested.

"What for?"

Father Morrow was trying to be helpful and, at the same time, protective. "Just in case there's more reporters looking for you," he answered. "At least until Helen gets there."

"I'm not going to hide, Dan. I haven't done anything wrong."

Father Morrow was anxiously waving his hands. "No, no, I didn't mean that, Mark. I just think we ought to wait and see what happens. You can phone Elliott from over here. Talk to him and then come over to the office. It'll be all right."

Mollified, Mark agreed. He went up to his room to make the call and Dan Morrow returned to the rectory.

The provincial answered on the first ring.

"How you doing, Mark?"

"Okay," he replied. "But the paper ran an article this morning."

"Saw it," the provincial said curtly. "I've had two copies faxed already."

There are times when modern communications are faster than one might want.

"I don't think it's too bad, Jack. I didn't tell the reporter anything."

There was silence at the other end. Mark waited respectively.

"Mark, I called the rector over at Seattle U. He's got a room for you and I want you to stay over there for a few days."

"What for?" Townsend blurted out.

Seattle University was at the other end of Capital Hill. The Jesuits who worked there had a house in the center of campus, across from the library. The priests at St. Joe's occasionally went there for dinner, and once in awhile one of the university men would come to the parish to help out with Sunday Masses.

"Now that there's publicity, there'll be a lot more attention. It's going to be awkward for you and for the parish," the provincial explained. "And I don't want you getting ambushed by any more reporters. Who told them about this in the first place?"

The paper never said, but Mark had his suspicions. "I'm not sure," was all he admitted.

"Well, it doesn't help your situation, does it? I'm sure the police wouldn't want you to leave town, but they shouldn't have any problem with you moving to another house. Call and let them know where they can reach you. And call my secretary when you get settled. Let her know your phone number. Okay?"

"I don't feel very good about this," Mark told his superior. "It feels like I'm running away, and I'd rather stay here."

"If anyone asks, you can tell them you did it because I told you to. If they have any more questions, tell 'em to call me." Elliott's tone was brusque; he wanted off the phone.

"Can I go tomorrow? There's someone I need to see here today."

"The room's ready, Mark. See whomever you need to see and get over there. Today."

After the call, Father Townsend set the phone on the floor but remained on the edge of his unmade bed. Sunlight was flooding into the room and he could hear traffic through the open window. His muscles suddenly felt like mush. He fell backward, letting his body settle into the wrinkled sheets and blanket. He never wanted to move from that spot, let alone go to Seattle U. He had no energy left. Eight-thirty in the morning and all he could think about was sleep. The phone near his feet began to ring. Mark ignored it, and after the fourth ring the answering machine clicked on. He could hear Morrow's voice on the box downstairs, asking the caller to leave a message. Whomever it was hung up without responding—which was fine with Mark. He rolled his head and closed his eyes.

Penny Metcalfe would be waiting to hear from him. He had put off calling her last night, wanting to work out in his mind what he would say. And he still had not given it much thought. How do you tell someone your mother never wants to see you? With a heavy emphasis on never. Townsend rolled his head. Why would Gail Draper tell a reporter they were talking to a Catholic priest? The first time he met her she seemed angry, like he had done something wrong. He was sure Newman had talked to her, trying to reassure her that Mark was a nice guy. But for whatever reason, the detective seemed to take a personal dislike to him. How far she was willing to let that influence her investigation was not a concern for Mark, at least up until now. He wondered if there was any way to prove she was the unnamed source, and if that was enough to get her off the case.

He rolled his head again, stopping halfway, opening his eyes and staring up at the ceiling. There was something in the newspaper account that had sounded funny to him. Not wrong exactly, but not entirely accurate, either. Townsend lay there, trying to recall what it was. The phone started to ring again and Father Townsend sat up. He stepped over it on the way to the bathroom. A shower might wake him up.

He went in through the rectory's front door and Helen turned to him with a fixed smile. Her eyes betrayed her true feelings, though; they were filled with concern.

"Good morning, Father. How are you?"

"Morning, Helen." He waited. This was usually where she started waving handfuls of pink phone messages at him. This morning she just kept smiling. "Any messages?" he finally asked.

"I put two on your desk," she replied.

"Only two?"

Her face flushed. "I think it was horrid what they wrote in the newspaper," she said. "It was all rumor and innuendo, not one ounce of fact. Don't you let that story bother you, Father." She shook her finger at him, a clear indication of her disapproval.

He thanked her and headed to his office. She had

placed the two messages front and center. He wondered if Morrow was handling the rest. The top one was from the Archbishop, asking that Mark call him back. The other was from Peter Newman. No question who was first. Mark reached for the phone.

"Detective Newman speaking."

"Peter, this is Mark Townsend."

"Mark! I'm so damn sorry! How are you doing?" His voice was contrite, filled with concern.

"I'm all right, I guess. Numb more than anything. How'd this happen?"

"That's what we're trying to find out. Lieutenant Hutchings is furious."

"Was it Draper?" Mark asked.

"Probably. But she denies it—says she had nothing to do with it."

"My provincial wants me to move over to Seattle University for a while, until this dies down."

Peter's response surprised him. "Good idea. I don't blame you one bit."

There was no progress in the investigation, he informed the priest. His prints matched the ones on the pop can and cellophane bag, but that was no surprise. They were still checking the connections between Red Pup and the other victims. Newman sounded tired and after apologizing once more, he said goodbye and hung up.

The Archbishop was in a meeting and his secretary rerouted Mark's call to the chancellor, Father Ray Phillips.

"Hi, Ray, this is Mark Townsend."

"Hey, Mark, how you doing?

"I've been better."

"Yeah, I'm sorry. Look, the paper caught us by surprise, what's going on?"

"What? You don't believe everything you read?" Mark felt himself growing irritable.

"Come on, Mark. The Archbishop knows you haven't

done anything, but he wants to hear that from you. What's the story?''

''Ray, the story is that there was a kid hiding in the church. I tried to draw him out and before I could, he was killed. That's the story.''

He could hear the chancellor's voice muffled at the other end, speaking to someone.

''Ray, does the Archbishop want to talk to me?''

Father Phillips was quickly back on the line. ''No . . . okay Mark . . . sorry, someone came into my office.''

''Well, that's the story.''

''So you didn't really have any contact with the boy?'' Mark was not sure who was in the chancellor's office, whether it was just the Archbishop or whether he had diocesan attorneys in there, too. But he was speaking louder than usual, his voice clear and concise. He was being fed questions.''

''No.''

''No contact. Right.'' There was another pause. ''Then why are the police interested in you, Mark?''

Father Townsend bit his lip, trying to contain himself. ''Because I left the kid some food and money. And a note.''

More murmuring. ''So there was contact,'' said the chancellor. He made it sound sordid, like Mark was guilty of something.

''If trying to help a kid is contact, then yes. But I never met the boy or spoke to him.''

''Uh-huh. I understand. Well, that doesn't sound so bad.'' There was relief in Phillip's voice.

''Ray, I'm sorry, but I've got to go. Is there anything else?''

Father Phillips assured him of the Archbishop's support and said that they would be back in touch if there was anything more. He thanked Mark for calling back so quickly and told him again that he would call if there were more questions. Townsend slammed the phone down as soon as he was certain the chancellor had hung up his end. Damn bureaucrats!

He was on his way out to ask Helen to hold his calls when he heard her on the phone. "No, I'm sorry, I can't help you. But if you want to talk to Father Morrow, I can either put you on hold or take a message." There were a few moments as she listened. "I'm sorry," she said firmly, "but you'd have to ask Father Morrow. There's nothing I can tell you."

She was hanging up the phone and gave Mark a startled look as he rounded the corner.

"Who was that?" he wanted to know.

Helen was flustered. "Just someone asking a question," she answered.

"About the news story?"

She did not reply but looked remorsefully down at her desk.

"You're giving those calls to Dan?"

"He said he'd handle them."

Morrow was on the phone, but he waved Father Townsend into his office, pointing to a chair. Mark remained standing while the priest ended his conversation. He closed the door and waited until Dan set the phone down.

"What the hell's going on, Dan? How come you're taking all the calls?"

"I'm not," Father Morrow replied. "You just finished two, didn't you?"

"Yeah, the two you told Helen to give me."

Morrow studied Father Townsend's face. He could see the anger and hear it in Mark's voice. He could either play the marine or the teacher. He decided to be the priest.

"What's really hurting, Mark? The fact that I'm taking the calls or that people are making them? As I recalled, the provincial didn't want you answering the phone unless you needed to." He lifted a stack of phone messages off his desk. "Do you really want these? One from the other newspaper? One from a television station? One from a woman wanting to know if all priests are perverts?" He held the pages out to Mark. "You want to handle these? Really?"

Father Townsend sat in the chair, wishing it was his rumpled bed. He felt sick and had no energy for any of this. Maybe Father Elliott was right; maybe he ought to disappear.

"I'm sorry, Dan, you're right. I think I'll go back to the house, pack some gear, and head over to S.U. On the way I'll stop by Metcalfes' and talk to Pen." He looked earnestly into Morrow's face. "You're sure you're okay doing this alone? You'll call if you need help?"

His friend nodded. "I'll call you, Mark. The only thing coming up is the weekend Masses, and those aren't a problem. Maybe someone at S.U. can help out."

What Morrow was suggesting made sense. There was no way Mark could stand up in front of his parishioners and pretend to lead them in prayer. Not when the entire congregation was sitting there, wondering if he had anything to do with the dead boy in Volunteer Park. His presence in the church would be a distraction. Father Townsend realized, for the first time in his Jesuit life, that he could be an obstacle for people. He squirmed uncomfortably in the chair.

"Yeah, fine," he said, rising. "I'll call."

No one answered when Mark rang the Metcalfes' bell. He waited on the porch longer than he needed to, then fished in his pocket for paper and pen, scrawling a hasty message for Pen. *Came by to see you. Will call later. Mark.* He folded it and started to slip it through the mail slot in the door, then pulled the note back and unfolded it. Mark found himself rereading his message, making certain there was no mixed message or double entendre someone could misinterpret. At what point can paranoia push you to paralysis, he wondered, shoving the paper through the slot.

He carried a small overnight bag into the Jesuit residence on Seattle University's campus. The receptionist recognized him, smiled, and greeted Mark as he came through the door. Dora Fletcher was a younger version of St. Joe's Helen Hart. She had the key to room 305 in an envelope posted on the bulletin board with Father Townsend's name on it. If Dora knew why he was coming to bunk at the university's community house, she gave no clue. A lady with class. Mark rode the elevator up alone, getting off on the third floor. His room was directly across the hall, so with three steps he was inside, behind the closed door, safe and out of sight. The university's library loomed large outside his window, and he closed the blinds, casting the guest room into partial darkness. The room came equipped with a television, reclining lounge chair, and a bathroom, three private luxuries not commonly available in too many Jesuit houses. Maybe his time here was not going to be so bad after all. Mark tossed his bag on the bed and eased himself into the chair, tipping it back as far as it would go.

Maybe not so bad after all.

TWENTY-FIVE

By two o'clock Mark was climbing the walls. He skipped lunch, preferring not to face the Jesuit community's looks and prying questions so soon after arriving. Switching on the television, he channel surfed, working his way through all the stations three times before turning it off in disgust. Daytime TV was about as riveting as watching parked cars. He called Helen Hart, asked if there were any messages, and left his phone number for Dan Morrow. Then he found the paperback novel at the bottom of his bag and sampled a few pages, but the story did not hold him. Restlessly he tossed it aside and closed his eyes. Maybe he could nap. But as comfortable as it was, the lounger could not relax him. Mark dialed Penny Metcalfe, but there was no answer. He hung up when her answering machine kicked on.

School was not in session, so the campus was nearly deserted. Only an occasional voice rose from the walkway below his window. Feeling more and more confined, he opened the blinds and pulled them up, letting the room fill with bright sunlight. That was better. The library's facade blocked his view, but by craning his head, Mark could see up and down the esplanade that

·ran straight through the heart of the S.U. campus. Not a soul was in sight.

For a university built on the cusp of Seattle's busy downtown, someone had done a pretty good job of insulating most of the campus from the bustle and noise that scraped at the school's perimeters. A large plaza defined the heart of the university. There was a fountain in the center with a tall metal sculpture that was meant to look like flames. The water cascaded onto rocks arranged around the base. Besides looking nice, the water served a second aesthetic function by blocking some of the traffic sounds drifting in from the busy avenue a block away. There was a reflecting pool built for meditation next to the university's chapel, but Mark usually found himself drawn to this plaza instead. As he drew close, he saw a lone bicyclist slowly circling the fountain. He was about to walk on to the chapel when he took a second look. The rider kept pedaling around and around the fountain, as close as he could without getting splashed. His bicycle was faded red with fat balloon tires and on the back, training wheels to keep it upright. The rider was old Father Heschstein. The ancient Jesuit was going to be ninety-four in a couple of more months. He was a revered soul at Seattle University, and for years had worked as a fundraiser, tapping the school's alumni and benefactors for the cash to keep the place going during earlier, harder times. Eventually he shifted into the chaplain's office, offering Masses for the campus community, counseling troubled students, and marrying recent graduates. In one summer alone, Father Heschstein witnessed fifty-four marriages of S.U. alums. Only one other Jesuit, affectionately called Marrying Joe, could lay claim to more weddings than Sam Heschstein.

When age and poor eyesight finally slowed him down, Father Heschstein moved on to what one community member dubbed ''bench ministry.'' Every school morning, rain or shine, Sam would park himself on a covered bench beside the university's main thoroughfare, where he would greet the faculty and students he recognized and nod to everyone else. More often than not, someone would be sitting beside him, huddled close to Sam, unloading woes and worries onto the bent back of the pious old priest. He shouldered them all, and sent his visitors back on their way with hugs and wise words of encouragement. Few students made it through four years at S.U. without stopping at Father Heschstein's bench at least once.

Mark Townsend sat on the plaza's stone stairway and watched the old priest slowly circling the fountain. Sam was nearly bent double, shifting his weight from one side of the bike to the other. He let gravity do most of the work. He was not going to win any races, but at his age, Father Heschstein did not need to. As he looped around the third time, straining against the bike, the old priest cranked his head and stared at the man watching him. He gave a quick, unsteady wave, quickly grabbing back on to the handlebar, then steered his way over to Mark. He waited until the old man was almost directly in front of him before standing.

"You're looking good, Father Heschstein," Mark said in a loud voice.

The old priest was breathing through his mouth, peering through his thick glasses at the younger man. He took a few moments before he recognized Mark's features, then smiled happily.

"Father Townsend." His arms wobbled as he tried to dismount, and Mark moved quickly to help him. Sam grasped the younger priest's arms with a grip stronger than Mark was expecting. "What brings you to our fair neck of God's kingdom?" Together they settled back onto the steps.

"A couple of days of R and R," Mark told him. It would be too difficult trying to explain what was going on at the church.

"Yes," Father Heschstein wheezed, "even God took one day to rest." He looked over at his bicycle, as if to make certain it had not wandered off. "Of course, I don't believe God has ever showed up on the front page of the Seattle P-I."

"So you read about it."

"God blessed me with two eyes, a brain, and the ability to read; it would be a sin not to use them." He drew a long, slow breath. "Of course, not everything you read is all that efficacious," he continued, "but after sixty-seven years of reading the Divine Office, I think an old priest deserves a little titillation. Wouldn't you say?" Father Heschstein turned his head and gazed at his companion.

Mark had to smile. "Did you ever make the front page, Father?"

Heschstein slowly shook his head. "God's been very merciful."

"Maybe to you." Mark did not intend to sound bitter, but he did and the old priest caught it. His eyes narrowed as he stared at Father Townsend's face.

"I don't understand."

Mark sucked in his breath. He was not sure he wanted to get into it, not with Sam, anyway. Sometimes his old fashioned piety got to Mark. Perhaps he should have kept walking.

"I guess I feel more like Job these days, Father. You know: *'The arrows of the Almighty pierce me, and my spirit drinks in their poison; the terrors of God are arrayed against me.'*"

"Yes," said the old man, his eyes closed and his head nodding. His lips curled into the slightest smile as he offered Mark the next line: "*Does the wild ass bray when he has grass?*"

Father Townsend missed the smile, but he caught Heschstein's meaning. He should have known better than to quote scripture at the man. Sixty-seven years of reading the Bible meant that Sam could trump him chapter and verse every time. He tried another tact.

"You devote your life to try and help people," Mark

began, "but it's like that's not enough. I mean, I've got the parish to run, with all that that entails, and then there's the people who come for real help. There's a woman I'm working with now who is grieving the death of a parent and trying to come to grips with some new revelations in her own life. You give a lot of your time to people like that, but because you want to. That's our vocation. That's why I became a Jesuit. And then there's others, like that boy, who you reach out to because they need help, not necessarily because they're asking for any. I believe that's part of our vocation, too." He stopped and looked down at the priest sitting next to him. Heschstein still had his eyes closed, either listening intently or sound asleep. "What I can't figure out is why, if you're doing the work right, you end up getting crucified in the process? Instead of someone saying thanks, you get smeared in the newspaper. It doesn't seem fair."

Sam Heschstein's body slumped against Mark's, pushing him. At first Mark thought he truly was asleep; next, that the old priest was having some sort of attack. Finally he realized Heschstein was pushing against him on purpose. He shifted his own weight, allowing himself to push back, but barely.

Father Heschstein continued leaning against him as he spoke softly but clearly. There was a brittle edge to his voice and it took Mark a few seconds of listening before he realized the old priest was angry.

"I've always thought that being a Jesuit meant serving under the standard of the cross," Sam Heschstein was saying, "wherever that took us. There were lots of folks willing to stand at the gates of Jerusalem and wave palm branches. But when the good Lord got closer to the crucifixion, the crowd thinned out. I thought a Jesuit was supposed to go all the way. When everyone else drops out, we keep going, even if that means getting crucified ourselves." The old priest was pushing harder against him, and with a start Mark realized he was struggling to get to his feet. Lifting his arm was a reflex, but the old priest grabbed hold and pulled himself upright. He continued gripping Mark's arm tightly, staring down at him.

"You're not Job and this is no game, Father. If you want to be a Jesuit, then you go wherever that takes you. You're not leading the Lord, you are following." His words could puncture steel. "I suggest you go back to our Spiritual Exercises, Father, and spend a little time on the Two Standards. Perhaps you don't need R and R as much as you need a direction."

He released his grip and turned back toward his bicycle. Mark stayed where he was, shocked by the vehemence of the old man's words. He watched as Heschstein climbed back onto his bike. Sam turned back to him then, but only to deliver a final volley before pedaling off.

"One more thing, Father Townsend. If I were you, I'd advise spending less time trying to solve people's problems and more time being with them. There's a whole raft of agencies set up to help people, and they usually do a better job of it than we can. Although they're not particularly interested in being with the people they help. So there may be some who need you, Father, but not your help. If I were you, I'd spend my time worrying about them instead of what my vocation is all about. But don't expect anyone to wave palm branches at you. Not in this life, anyway."

Mark watched him circle back to the fountain, stunned. He could feel his face burning. Once he got over his immediate impulse to push the old priest off his bicycle, he stumbled to his feet, quickly turned, and hustled up the plaza steps. As he hurried away from the fountain, he drew a deep breath.

He made it back to his room without running into anyone he knew. Dropping into the chair, he leaned back and squeezed his eyes closed. Tears welled in the corners of his eyes. They burned as they slid out, but he squeezed all the harder.

TWENTY-SIX

Lyle and Pen were in the midst of dinner. Mark declined the seafood fettucini but welcomed the glass of Chardonnay Pen set in front of him. He was surprised to find them both home, pleased to see them having a quiet meal together, apparently enjoying one another's company. Maybe there were still a few things about married life he did not completely understand. For instance, how two people so divided over an issue could still feel as close as these two seemed to be. Mark flashed back to the afternoon's encounter with Heschstein. He was still feeling hurt, but now was more inclined to hug the old man than hit him.

Their dinner finished, Pen made sure all three of their wineglasses were filled before leading them into the backyard. Lawn chairs were arranged under the shade of a massive elm. Lyle quite consciously moved one of the chairs closer to his wife, reaching over and clasping her free hand in his. All three of them felt nervous. When they were settled, Pen spoke first.

"Well, Father, tell us what you found out." Her eyes were bright and searching. Mark swallowed his wine and set the glass on the ground.

"I was able to find Cynthia Metzler," he began, "and

I spoke with her.'' He saw Pen squeeze her husband's hand. ''But it didn't turn out the way you were hoping,'' he said. There was no use putting it off.

Lyle was not facing him but watching his wife's face instead. Both men could see her look of disappointment, but she gave them a brave little smile and took a sip of wine.

''What happened?'' she asked.

''Cindy doesn't seem to have a very happy life,'' Mark said. He purposely used the woman's name, trying to avoid referring to her as Pen's mother. ''She lives alone in the same house she grew up in.''

''She's not married?''

Father Townsend hesitated, then slowly shook his head. He anticipated Pen's next question before she could ask it. ''Metzler is her maiden name.''

Penny Metcalfe, like everyone else in the world, wanted to believe that her life was the direct result of two people loving each other very much. No one wants to be an accident; or worse, unwanted. She was beginning to see how it was.

''So I was born out of wedlock.''

Mark was surprised she used such an archaic expression. But at that uncomfortable moment, he was at a loss to express it any differently.

''She was only a senior in high school,'' he told her, ''and living on her own.'' He chose not to tell them that Cindy's father abandoned her when the baby was born.

Lyle continued watching his wife. He held her left hand in both of his, gently caressing it. Pen looked over at him, then back to Father Townsend.

''Who was my father?'' she asked bluntly.

''Ah, Penny, honey,'' Lyle was speaking in a low, soothing tone, ''let it go, sweetheart. It's too much, isn't it?''

But Mark had already decided how he could answer this question. He spoke before Pen could react to her husband.

"I didn't ask. I didn't think it was an appropriate question for me to ask her."

The woman in the lawn chair withdrew her hand from her husband's grasp, but she did it gently and used both hands to lift the wineglass to her lips. She took two sips before she spoke again. Although she already knew the answer, she had one more question for the priest.

"Is she willing to see me?"

For the first time since they sat down, Lyle Metcalfe turned to Father Townsend, waiting for his reply. His eyes were pleading with the priest.

"She said no, Pen." Mark leaned forward in his chair. "She is a woman who has suffered very much. The circumstances of her life—being that young, and on her own without any money—forced her to make decisions that were very painful. Just having me there disturbed her. It would hurt her a great deal if you were to try and see her."

There had not been much more to say. Pen had run out of questions, at least out of ones she was prepared to ask. And Lyle, although he said nothing, was relieved to have it over. Neither one pressed him to stay longer when Mark stood to leave. They both walked him to the house and Pen thanked him and reached up to give him a light kiss on his cheek. Then she sat back in her chair under the elm while Lyle walked Father Townsend to the front door.

"Thank you, Mark. I know that wasn't easy for you."

Father Townsend shook his head. "Will she be okay?"

"After awhile." Lyle looked toward the back of the house. "I'll talk to her."

"She needs your support, Lyle."

"I know that." There was a sharp edge to his voice and his mouth grew taut. "I didn't want her doing this, but that doesn't mean I won't support her." He stepped back and gave the priest a hard look. "Do you think I'm that self-centered?"

"No. No, Lyle."

"I don't understand how that woman could say no. Penny is her own flesh and blood, for Christ's sake." His eyes searched Mark's face. "How could she not care about her own kid?"

Mark hesitated to answer, but Lyle waited, obviously expecting a reply. "I think her own pain has forced her to shut down her other feelings," he told Lyle. "She's had so much hurt that she can't get around it."

Lyle Metcalfe took a step back, cocked his head to one side, and stared hard at the priest. A full thirty seconds passed before he spoke. "That's what happens then? You let one thing in your life get too big and everything else gets squeezed? Do our feelings have limits, Father?"

Mark did not answer him.

"Then how can you ever trust them? How do you know if what you're feeling is right or wrong? What if the voice in your head is all wrong?"

His eyes were pleading.

Father Townsend coughed and gave his friend a smile. "When it comes to your feelings, Lyle, I don't think you listen to the voice in your head. I think you listen to your heart. What is that telling you?"

Back in his car, Mark automatically headed toward the church before recalling he had a room at Seattle University. He turned back around and steered south on Fifteenth. He had tried to be truthful with Penny, to answer her questions as honestly as he could. The name of her birth father was only gossip, recounted to him by a school principal who was not even around when the event occurred. Mark had no direct knowledge of who impregnated Cindy Metzler. And after filtering out the rawness of her hurt and anger, he felt he had accurately communicated the woman's reason for not wanting to meet her daughter. "I don't want no more pain," Cindy had told him. If there was one thing Father Townsend was clear about, it was that neither woman needed any more pain at the moment. And seeing each other right then would only mean pain. Whatever might happen in the future, Mark knew, was dependent on both of them. And a healthy dose of God's grace. The same was true for Lyle Metcalfe, too. Changing your mind is one thing, but changing your heart is quite another.

He turned onto Madison and started toward the university. It was almost nine o'clock and traffic was light. But when he reached the campus, instead of turning, the Jesuit continued straight up and over the hill and into downtown Seattle. Although it was a Saturday night, traffic was light and he had no difficulty negotiating his way through the city. When he passed the bus depot Mark slowed down, leaning forward and searching for an address over the storefronts. The one he was seeking was not clearly marked, but he still had no trouble finding the Haven. A large cluster of young people were lounging in front of the building, standing on the sidewalk, leaning against the building, or sitting on the curb. Most were dressed in black. The only time Father Townsend saw that much black clothing was at the Archbishop's annual clergy dinner. The style of dress was slightly different, however.

Whoever coined the term grunge was right on. Starting at the top. Hair: long and stringy, short and bristly, or gone entirely—and in every color of the rainbow. Below the neck: T-shirts, mostly black; some plaid flannel shirts, tied around the waist and drooping nearly to the ground; a couple of the girls had on black dresses and one, a bright scarlet teddy worn over a white T-shirt two sizes too big for her. She also had on a skintight calf-length black silk skirt, slit up the side. On her feet she wore black boots that grazed the top of the skirt. Of the twenty or more kids he could see, only two were not wearing the heavy black boots called Doc Martens. One boy had on one red and one green tennis shoe and one of the girls was barefoot. Most of the boys wore black jeans, although a couple wore regular blues and one had on a pair of brown and red plaid pants that went with nothing on God's green earth.

There were enough earrings, studs, chains, bracelets, and rings to open a small store. They seemed to adorn every part of every body Mark could see. And while he refused to spend time speculating on it, he suspected there was an equal amount of hardware stuck onto body parts he could not see. Obviously none of these kids were frequent fliers; they would have triggered every airport security device they passed.

He had no trouble parking his car. This was not a part of town where the patrons of Seattle's restaurants and theaters left their Beamers. Their children might be here, but never their cars. The priest stood next to his for a few moments, feeling self-conscious and very out of place. He was wearing khaki slacks and a light green shortsleeved shirt, and stuck out like a butterfly in a box of beetles. The kids studiously ignored him, though, continuing their loud conversations over the bass thumpings coming out of a boom box in the middle of the sidewalk—until he started walking toward them. Then they stopped talking and watched in silence as he passed through their midst.

The Haven's front door was wide open. Both it and the huge window of the storefront were plastered with flyers, posters and other scraps of paper. Everything from an old Sex Pistol's poster to a leaflet offering free HIV testing. There were any number of small paper flyers labeled MISSING, usually with a picture of boy or girl printed underneath. In most of these photos, lost children gazed at the camera with bright eyes and happy smiles, in clothing very different from what was worn by those who brushed past the posters without even looking. These youngsters in the photos were missing all right, more than their families realized.

Father Townsend stood in the doorway long enough to look at each one before he tried to step inside. His way was blocked by a stubby African-American girl with extremely short, bright yellow hair, wearing baggy overalls. She had on wire-rimmed glasses, the lenses tinted pink, and she wore a diamond stud stuck through her right nostril. She stood with her legs spread apart and her arms crossed over her chest.

"Can I help you?" she asked gruffly.

"I'd like to speak to someone in charge," Mark replied.

"Clariss!" she yelled over her shoulder.

A young woman, seated at a table near the back, stood and looked toward the doorway. Her hair was blond, tied back in a ponytail. She wore blue jeans and a black T-shirt with white lettering on the front that read THE HAVEN. Spotting the stranger, she moved quickly to the door, threading her way around the couches and chairs, stepping over sleeping bodies sprawled across the floor.

"I'm Clariss Stevens," she told Mark, extending her hand, "may I help you?" The other girl melted back into the room.

"I was wondering if I could come in and talk to you for a few minutes," said Mark.

"No, I'm sorry." But she smiled as she said it. "We don't allow anyone other than our volunteers inside the Haven," she told him.

"I'm a Catholic priest," he replied, "from St. Joseph on Capital Hill."

A flicker of recognition lit her eyes. "A group from there volunteers," she said, "but I don't ever remember seeing you."

"I haven't made it yet," Mark admitted. "Jack Abel is usually the one who comes."

Hearing Abel's name apparently satisfied the woman. She gave him another smile and motioned to the street with her head. "Why don't we take a walk," she suggested. "I could use a break."

They made their way through the crowd clustered in front but not without eliciting a few catcalls and whistles. "Hey, Clariss," someone hooted behind them, "he's a little old for you, honey." They walked on, acting like neither one heard the teasing. Clariss waited until they were out of earshot from the crowd behind them.

"You'll have to excuse them," she murmured. "They take an active interest in who I meet."

"Are you the director?" Mark asked.

"Of the Haven, yes," she replied. "But we're part of a larger consortium offering services to homeless youths." It sounded like a line from a script. Mark cut in before she had a chance to deliver the rest.

"I'm trying to find out some information about someone," he told her. "I'd like to talk to some of the kids."

She was already shaking her head. "We don't do that, Father. I'm sorry." Clariss stopped walking and turned to face the priest. "Our name pretty much says it." He looked down at her T-shirt. "We try to be a safe haven for these kids. That means we provide them shelter and protect them. We don't let people in the front door, and we don't allow our clients to be interviewed." She paused, then firmly added, "By anyone."

"This situation is a little different—" Mark began.

She cut him off. "They're all a little different," she remarked, "but I can't make an exception."

Three disheveled youths were loping along the walk toward them. They slowed as they spotted Clariss Stevens talking with the stranger. She turned away from Mark and gave the kids a smile and wave, which they acknowledged as they passed on their way to the Haven. Mark waited until they were far enough past.

"I want to talk to someone who knew Tony Neeley," he told her. "He went by Red Pup."

She studied him a moment, trying to decide.

"It wouldn't work," she finally decided. "Why should they talk to you? You're an adult and they don't know you from Adam. And if you tell them you're a priest they're going to guess that you're the one the police are questioning. They'll think you're just another troll.''

"A what?''

They were walking again. "A troll. That's their word for a man who preys on boys.''

"Was Tony like that?'' Mark asked her. "Did he . . .'' Mark hesitated, searching for the words, "did he see men?''

"You mean did he do dates? Was he tricking in Volunteer Park?'' She stopped walking to turn and face him again. "That's what you want to ask these kids?'' She took a step closer to him. "Let me give you some advice, Father. Don't start nosing around unless you're ready for answers you might not want to hear. This isn't fun and games for these kids. They're fighting for their lives out here, and they do whatever it takes to survive. You can ask them if Red Pup did dates; and if they decide to answer, they might start naming names. And some of those trolls might end up being members of your own church. Heck, some might even be other priests. So don't start asking unless you really want to know.''

She turned suddenly and started taking long strides down the sidewalk, almost as if she were trying to get away. Mark had to hurry to keep up with the young woman.

"For a lot of these kids''—she continued her lecture once he caught up with her—"the smartest thing they ever did was run away. The stuff that goes on in their homes—you wouldn't believe it if I told you. I've seen kids beaten and cut and burned by their own parents. They were kept prisoners with their bedroom doors nailed shut. One girl I knew was chained to a chair in her basement for close to a year before she escaped.'' She glanced at Townsend as she hurried along the walk. "Don't talk to these kids unless you want to hear that stuff. They were right to run away. Their only mistake was running to the wrong places.

"But if you can't trust your own parents, who can you? The police? A teacher? A minister? Sorry, but a lot of them are just as bad. Or worse. You see how it is? I work with garbage, Father. Don't look so shocked; that's what they are. A lot of them got thrown out. And if you're told you're trash and you're treated like trash, you start acting like trash."

They rounded the corner and were standing beside Mark's car. Farther down the block, the youths continued milling in front of the Haven, casting furtive glances at the two of them.

"I can't let you talk to them inside," Clariss was saying. "But if you have questions you can probably get them answered on the streets. There's no law against that. Just remember who you're talking to, and what they've gone through."

"Where's the best place to meet them?" Mark wanted to know.

For the first time since they started walking, she smiled. "Well, you won't find too many of them in church, that's for sure. And probably not in Nordstrom's. Check along the waterfront and down at Pioneer Square. Some of them hang around the Westlake Center, too."

"And where do they live?"

They were approaching the crowd in front of the door, and the woman looked eager to end their conversation. "Wherever they can," she replied. "They're called squats—old buildings mostly, but under the freeway and in parks, too. Wherever they can."

Father Townsend thanked her and she ducked through the crowd and back inside the Haven. Feeling more out of place than ever, he hurried back to his car.

In a couple of minutes he was on Second Avenue, heading south. The priest drove slowly, watching the sidewalks. Street lights and brightly lit storefronts threw enough light onto the sidewalks so that he could make out people's features, and he studied the faces of the youngsters he passed. Most were banded together in groups of three or four. Not all of them looked as radical as the kids he had just left in front of the Haven; and Mark had the impression some of the ones on the street were kids coming downtown for a night's entertainment. He was having a hard time sorting them out.

Father Townsend stopped for a red light and looked over at a lone boy standing on the edge of the curb. The youngster stared straight into his car, his young face watchful. He looked like he was about sixteen. Casting a look up and down the sidewalk, he casually strolled over to the side of Mark's car. The Jesuit leaned over to roll down the passenger-side window.

"What's up, man?" the kid asked him, resting his hands on the car and peering inside.

"Nothing," Mark replied.

"So. You looking for a date or what?" The boy thrust his hips forward suggestively, then reached down and fondled himself.

Father Townsend's immediate reaction was one of cold fear. The boy's presumptions shocked him and he realized the danger he was in.

"No," he said in a loud voice. "No. Nothing. Thanks." Frantically he looked around, knowing a police car was going to appear out of the darkness, lights blinking and siren blaring. At Mark's panicked response, the kid quickly backed away from the car. The light changed and Mark sped away. He could feel sweat breaking on his forehead and his heart racing.

He never knew it was that easy. In a few more seconds, he could have had the boy in his car and taken him anywhere. And probably done anything. Mark glanced in his rearview mirror, but there was no sign of the youth in the shadows behind him. All he did was glance over at him. He had not given any signal, not even a smile or a raised eyebrow. He simply looked over and the boy was standing there, ready to climb into his car. Townsend turned a corner toward the university and wiped his sweating palms on his pant leg. Was it really that easy to find boys and girls willing to spend time with you? Were they so desperate that they would accost a stranger stopped for a light? Mark looked in the mirror again. He could see the look of fright in his own eyes, and he knew these were not the eyes of a troll. But could anyone else? That was the question that kept him awake that night.

TWENTY-SEVEN

Traffic on the floating bridge was heavy in both directions. Sunlight bounced crazily off the water of Lake Washington and the glare made driving difficult. There were plenty of distractions on both sides of the bridge, with canoes and kayaks slipping gracefully through the waves while speedboats towing skiers rushed in loops and, farther out, sailboats glided. This was Seattle at its best. If it were not for the wealth of SUVs clogging the road. The highway heading into Kirkland and Redmond was ruled by Broncos, Explorers and Scouts; and Mark's puny Civic pursued them like a beagle chasing malamutes.

He followed them all the way to the end of 520, where it empties onto Union Hill Road. By then he was running with sleek Mercedes and Jags.

Father Townsend spent a restless Sunday in the guest room at Seattle University. Long before the sun crested the Cascades and poured dawn into Seattle, the priest was up and moving about. The community chapel was on the main floor and Mark was already there when the stained-glass window started coming to life. He could not push Saturday night's incident from of his mind.

A boy not much older than Tony Neeley had propositioned him. Clariss Stevens warned him that these kids were not playing games, that they did whatever they had to just to survive. And in some abstract, antiseptic way, Mark had always known that. But none of it was real, none of it affected him. Not until Saturday.

Was the boy they called Red Pup turning tricks to pay his way on Seattle's streets? For the first time, Mark was ready to believe it possible. A runaway from a small town at the foot of the Cascades, hiding in the big city, would need money to get around, just to eat and stay alive. Underage and on his own, the kid's options were limited; selling his youth might have seemed like an easy way to go. Home would have to be pretty bad to drive a kid to that. The priest wondered just how bad it would have to be. Newman had told him very little about Neeley's family. His mother and stepfather lived outside of Carnation and life at home was rough, whatever that meant. And there was trouble at school. That hardly sounded like enough to drive a kid into the streets.

But it was more than mere curiosity that drew him to Carnation. Something Father Heschstein said continued to stick in his craw. The old priest urged him to stop worrying about helping people and to pay more attention being present to them. That felt contrary to Mark's nature, but he recognized some wisdom in Heschstein's words. He was so caught up in his own problems that he forgot there was a family mourning their son's death; a son whose last days were spent hiding inside St. Joseph Church. Curiosity about where Red Pup came from was part of Mark's motivation, but so was compassion. At least he wanted to believe it was. Father Townsend was not sure what kind of reception he might get, especially if the family read the newspaper. But he had to go there and meet them, at least to be a presence.

Signs of the big city began to diminish as country concerns took over. He passed a veterinarian's office on his left. A square sign nailed to a telephone pole in front advertised for stump grinding. Mark started up Union

Hill and both sides of the road grew dense with cedar and firs, the moss growing thick on their trunks. The roadway was narrow, steep, and windy. He had to swerve sharply to dodge two bicyclists pumping laboriously up the hill. New homes began peeking through the woods near the top. These were fenced and gated communities, with names like Hunters Wood, Hunters Glen, and Deer Meadows. Signs forbidding hunting were posted on stone walls encircling paddocks of lush green grass with fine groomed horses grazing inside. Lots of signs posted private roads on the hilltop, and Mark peered down green shaded drives meandering through thick tracts of trees. A plywood board, painted with bright colors, stood in one field: INCREDIBLE VALUES! STARTING AT ONLY $225,000!

"Incredible is right!" the Jesuit snorted.

There was a shorter route into Carnation, but Father Townsend wanted the extra time to think, and this drive was more relaxing. The freeway past Issaquah would have been faster, but the last thing he needed right now was faster. Once he was on the road, Mark began worrying about meeting Tony Neeley's family. Popping in for an unannounced visit was not unusual for a parish priest. But those were with parishioners. Showing up at the door of strangers to talk about their dead son was another matter.

He had stopped on the way to check his mail and messages at the rectory. Helen Hart looked surprised when he walked into the lobby, but she greeted him warmly and assured him everything was running smoothly. Sunday's Masses went fine. Father Morrow was visiting a shut-in, and she was not sure how many more people had called to ask about the story in the newspaper. There was nothing for him to see or do there, so Mark grabbed his mail, checked his desk, and left. In and out in under ten minutes. Not too bad at all.

The estates petered out and real working farms took over, with woodpiles, sagging barns, and dirty tractors parked next to farmhouses. Broncos turned into old pick-ups. Across a field of stubble, the priest spotted two barefoot boys with inner tubes slung over their shoulders, looking like two kids in a Rockwell painting. Farther on, he passed a middle-aged man with a ponytail hoeing around a sign promising fresh-cut flowers and organic produce. At Fall City, Mark looped across the bridge, swinging toward Carnation, Duvall, and Monroe. He saw huge sunflowers and corn stalks almost as high as an elephant's eye. Rich bottomland followed the snaking Snoqualmie River. The water looked shallow, with dry gravel bars in the river's middle, scrags of tree roots poking up.

Then he was there. CARNATION WELCOMES YOU. Just below it sat a squat pillar made of river rocks, with the word *Tolt* spelled in white gravel. Tolt Middle School was on the edge of town, HOME OF THE THUNDERBIRDS. Mark cruised slowly down the main street, passing small stores lining both sides of the road, until he came to the Carnation Grade School at the other end. A cemetery lay just beyond and Mark pull off the road, trying to spot a mound with fresh flowers. There was none. He turned around, heading back. Across from the school was the Tolt Congregational Church and beyond that the Tolt Community Club.

He was not sure where the Neeleys lived, and calling Peter Newman for directions did not seem like a very good idea. But if he was enough of a detective to find Cindy Metzler, he should have no trouble tracking down the Neeleys. Stopping at a pay phone in front of a cafe, he checked through the book's listings. There was no Neeley in Carnation. Not in Duvall or Monroe, either. No Neeley anywhere nearby. Father Townsend looked helplessly up and down the street.

The doors to the Tolt Middle School were locked. Unlike Wrigley, there was no school principal waiting to hire a new gym teacher. But there was a fire station just across the street, and Father Townsend headed toward it. He was just starting up the walk when the door opened and a bald man with slim hips and a big paunch wandered out. He leaned against the wall to light his cigarette and nodded to Mark.

"Howdy," he called out. He looked eager for company.

"Good morning," Mark replied. "Nice day."

"Too dry," the man disagreed, shaking his head. He flicked his finger against the expired match head and threw it into the grass. "Place is ripe for a fire in this kind of weather."

Mark searched the grass for a smoldering match. Seeing none, he turned back to the man.

"Have you lived here long?" he asked.

"All my life," the man answered, pulling on his cigarette.

"I was wondering about the two names, Tolt and Carnation. I take it this wasn't always called Carnation."

"You take it right, sir." The man picked at his tongue, flicking a piece of loose tobacco in the same general direction as the match. "That'd be about forty, fifty years back." He grinned broadly. "Not all of us are used to the new name quite yet. But give us time."

Father Townsend grinned back. "You sound like a supporter for the Tolt Chamber of Commerce."

"Charter member," the fireman chortled. "And pressy-dente." He snapped a salute and held out his hand. "Duane Oldham."

"Mark Townsend." The man's grip was firm. "I wonder if you might know of a family by the name of Neeley? They're supposed to live somewhere around Carnation."

"You mean Tolt, don't you?" Duane Oldham hated to see a good line end. But Mark only shrugged, so Oldham shifted his weight and gave a straight answer. "There's no Neeley family anywhere around here. Not unless they're brand-new."

"I don't think they are," Mark replied. "Their boy

attended the school over there—at least I'm pretty sure he did.''

"Ohhh, you're talking 'bout Tony Neeley. Yeah, I know all about him." He sucked a last draught from his cigarette and flicked it onto the dry lawn. Spotting Mark's look, he lifted himself off the wall of the firehouse and wandered over to plant a heavy foot on the butt, grinding it dead. "Yeah, I guess I know about Tony Neeley, all right. The family is called Scoggins, though.''

Detective Newman had told Mark the boy lived with his mother and stepfather.

"Neeley's that kid what was killed in Seattle." Oldham peered over at his visitor. "Are you a cop?''

"No. I'm just looking for the family." The Jesuit was in mufti; slacks and a sports shirt.

He leaned back against the wall and eyed Mark up and down. "Not a cop," he mused out loud. Then nodded his head wisely. "Lawyer."

Father Townsend smiled in response.

"Oh, yeah," the man said, "I can spot you guys a thousand miles. Well, you don't want Neeley, you want Scoggins. He lives up Stillwater, out the other side of town." His eyes brightened. "The other side of Tolt."

Mark gave a polite laugh. Anything that would get him the information he needed.

"The kid's the one what started that fire we had awhile back. That's why he ran away, you know."

Townsend cocked his head. "I didn't hear about a fire."

"Oh, yeah." Oldham was fishing inside his shirt pocket, which was empty. "You don't got a cigarette, by chance?" Father Townsend shook his head and the fireman dropped his hands to his sides. "Kid tried to burn down the school. Right at the end of the year." He puffed out his chest. "Lucky we caught it in time. It coulda spread and burnt the whole town, dry as it is."

"I didn't hear about that," Mark repeated.

"It was only, like, the day after classes," Oldman complained. "He came after dark and built a fire out in back, inside the Thunderbird dugout, behind first base. Hell, we got those old wood classrooms out there, and if a spark had jumped . . ." The fireman shook his head, images of the blazing inferno dancing in his brain. "No telling how bad it could have been."

"But you were able to put it out in time?"

"Oh, yeah," Oldham assured him. "We got 'er in time."

"And you're sure Tony started the fire."

The man gave him a look of surprise. "Hell, man, you're the big lawyer. You tell me. Kid comes to town, starts a fire, then runs away from home. How much proof do you want?" He shook his head in mock exasperation.

He was beginning to suspect the fireman's ladder was a couple of rungs short, but Mark continued the conversation anyway.

"Can you tell me how to get to this Stillwater?"

"Hill. Stillwater Hill," Oldham corrected. "Go right on through town and about two, three miles out the other side. There's a Lake Joy Road, turn right and, just shy of a mile, turn right again on Fay Road. You go a few hunnert feet and you'll see a mailbox with the top smashed down. That's the Scoggin's' place."

"I appreciate your help," Mark told him.

"No problemo," the man replied. "You have a nice day."

His directions were good. Father Townsend found Stillwater Hill and turned up, following directions until he found the flattened mailbox, just like the man described. A wooden hand-lettered sign was nailed to the post but hanging loose and pointing down at the ground. SCOGGINS, it read. He turned into the drive and started down the dusty road. Another sign, just before a curve, warned BEWARE OF DOG.

Around the curve, a faded pink trailer home sat in the

midst of weeds. Black stovepipes poked from one end
of the roof. The other end was covered with a tattered
blue plastic tarp. Cinder blocks, hanging down from
ropes tied to the tarp, kept it from blowing off. There
was a large satellite dish mounted to one side, aimed at
the heavens, and beneath it, the front end of an old
brown Studebaker sitting in the weeds. A dirty white
goat, tethered to the front bumper, stood on top of the
hood, eyeing Mark's Civic with what looked like envy.
A rusting horse trailer was parked nearby, but no sign
of any horses. On the other side of the trailer sat a
wooden garage, both doors sagging open on their hinges.
A gritty sign nailed on one of them announced CHAIN
SAW AND SMALL ENGINES REPAIR. Just inside the doorway was a battered wooden workbench, black with oil
and grime. Judging from the number of parts littering
the bench and ground around it, more small engines
were junked there than ever repaired.

Mr. Scoggins did not look like the type of man to
mourn their loss, either. He was tall and heavyset with
bristles of gray hair. The ones on top of his head were
only slightly longer than the ones on his pockmarked,
jowly face. He stared out from the garage at Mark's car
with rhuemy eyes and slowly licked his thick lips as if
already savoring whatever broken piece of machinery
this visitor had to offer. His arms were thick and muscular, scattered with tattoos; some from better times,
some from worse. He wiped grimy hands across grimy
coveralls and took three steps outside the garage, then
stopped. From out of the shadows behind him, a near
carbon copy followed. This one had more hair, was
about twenty years younger and twenty pounds lighter,
but Mark never doubted for a second that this was a
second Scoggins. He was as big a brute as his dad and
just as grimy.

They stood outside their garage, side by side, their
thick arms hanging at their sides, waiting. The priest
turned off his engine and climbed out.

"Good morning. Mr Scoggins?"

The older one nodded.

"I'm Father Mark Townsend, from St. Joseph parish in Seattle." He waited, but there was no response. "I'm here about your son."

At that the large man turned and gave the boy behind him a threatening look.

"Your other son, I mean. Tony."

"I ain't responsible for anything he done," the man complained in a whiny voice. "That boy ran away over two months ago, and far as I'm concerned, that was the end of it. It don't matter what he done, I ain't responsible. He's dead, besides." His speech finished, he spit a brown gob into the dust at his feet.

"I know that," Mark replied, "and I'm sorry. St. Joseph is the church where Tony was staying before he was killed. Didn't the police tell you?"

The brutish man rubbed a hand across his head, leaving a smear of grease on his forehead in the process. "They might of. To tell the truth, though, they asked more questions than they told stuff. Hell, I don't remember what they said about that. You need to ask my wife, cuz that was her boy. Neal, you remember them cops saying anything about a church?"

The younger Scoggins took a step forward and scowled at his father.

"That woman cop said St. Joseph. Yeah, I 'member that," he mumbled.

"Boy, I sure as hell don't. But if Neal says she said it, then she must of said it. He's got a good memory for stuff. Not like his old man. Hell, I'd forget my name if it wasn't sewed on my chest." He looked down at his overalls, which had no name. "Well, now, lookey there. See what I'm saying?" He gave the priest a toothy grin. "But it's Les. Les Scoggins." He stuck out his grimy hand and Mark extended his and watched it disappear inside a huge dirty paw where it was squeezed, mauled, and pumped furiously.

"What'd you say your name was?"

"Father Townsend. Mark Townsend."

"Pleased to meet you, Father. My wife's Catholic, but I ain't." He finally let go of Mark's hand. "Never really had time for it. But I gotta TV back in the shop, and I do like watching one of the preachers they got on there. He gets himself riled to hellfire sometimes, but he's all right. You watch him much?"

Mark admitted he did not.

"I guess that'd be like your competition, huh? Gotta be tough on you guys without TV. You probably need some other gimmick. Something to bring 'em in?"

Mark did not know what to say, so he said nothing. The huge man in front of him did not seem to mind, though. Apparently he enjoyed hearing himself talk, and whether or not he got a response seemed to make little difference.

"St. Joseph. That's gotta be a pretty rich church, ain't it? All we've got out here is St. Anthony, where the wife goes. It ain't all that much. Not like what you must have in the city. Now who decides what priest gets what church? Is there a ranking of some sort? It don't seem too fair if there is. I mean, we got this old priest stuck way out here and you young ones get the fancy places. But I guess there's the haves and have-nots in just about everything, huh?"

Another brown loop spattered the dust at Les Scoggins's feet. He shifted the wad in his mouth from one cheek to the other and waved a beefy hand at his son.

"Get yer butt in the house and get Janice out here. This man didn't come all the way for me to tell him how to run the churches. Did you? Go on now."

Neal Scoggins frowned and reluctantly stumbled off toward the trailer, stopping to pick up a rock and throw it at the goat.

"Go on!" his father barked. "Leave Crappy alone." He turned back to the priest. "Neal's a good boy, but thickheaded. He don't show it, but he's broke up about Tony.''

''Were they close?''

''Close?'' Scoggins thrust both arms inside the front of his coveralls and rocked back on his heels. ''Not close exactly; can't say that. But they got along all right. Neal's a tough scrapper—you can see that; and Tony ... well, Tony was pretty small and kinda sweet. Sort of a girlie boy, if you know what I mean. Neal's a lot tougher, I'd say.''

Les Scoggins had a way of stating the apparent. His own son would have towered over the younger, smaller Tony. Tougher was an understatement.

''I imagine it's been hard on the family, not knowing where Tony was or if he was safe.''

The big man spat again. ''Not for me, but for my wife, yes. She ain't been herself ever since the bugger ran away. But me? I was glad to see him go. That boy was trouble since we moved here. Picking fights and scrapping. He tried burning the school in June.'' Scoggins's eyes narrowed. ''Stole two thousand bucks from me and runned away.''

Mark heard the trailer's screen door close behind him. He had one more question and he asked it quickly.

''I take it Tony is your stepson?''

''Not even,'' Scoggins replied, looking pointedly back over the priest's shoulder. ''He belongs to her. She had him up in Alaska, before I ever met her.''

At that, Mark turned to the woman coming up behind him. She was small-boned with a dark complexion, and she moved toward them slowly, almost reluctantly. Neal dogged behind her, like a huge semi tailgating a little car. Her small face looked drawn and was pinched with a look of perpetual exhaustion. Her dark eyes were wide—from fear or worry, Mark could not tell, but his heart went out to the wasted-looking woman as she approached them. She was wearing blue cotton slacks that sagged in all the wrong places, and a blue-and-brown striped shirt that was too small for even her tiny frame. Her skinny arms poked awkwardly from the sleeves. Her black hair was pulled back loosely and tied into a ponytail. She was much too young for the strands of gray that showed in the sunlight.

"This is my wife, Janice," said Scoggins when she was· near enough. "What'd you say your name was again?"

Mark kept his eyes fixed on the woman's face. "I'm Father Mark Townsend."

He caught the flicker of recognition when she looked up at him, but then she murmured a soft hello and ducked her head back down.

"He's here about Tony. Says your boy was in his church before he was killed. This must be the one those cops were telling us about, don't ya' think? Say! That kid didn't steal anything or burn something, did he? I don't got any money to pay for nothing he did."

Father Townsend saw the hurt in Janice Scoggins's eyes.

"No, nothing like that," he replied. "I think he was staying there because he thought it was safe." He heard the Scoggins boy snicker. "Tony did nothing wrong that I'm aware of."

"He did plenty. You just don't know," Scoggins told him.

Mark ignored him and spoke to the wife. "I'm awfully sorry about your son's death. If there's anything I can do for any of you . . ."

Janice Scoggins looked up doubtfully. "Could you pray for him?" she asked in a small voice. "For my son?"

"Of course. I have been, all along."

"Our priest here at St. Anthony is praying, too."

"There's been all sorts a prayin'," Les Scoggins interrupted. "More prayin' than working ever since that boy took off. You spend half your day at that church."

She raised her chin defiantly. "It was to St. Anthony, I told you. He finds lost things."

"Your boy weren't anymore lost than he wanted to be, Janice. And that so-called saint of yours done nothing to help. That's the trouble with saints, they're all dead. Got to be if they're gonna be saints. Like your St. Anthony is dead and now so's Tony. Who knows, maybe he'll become a saint now." He sniggered at his own attempt at humor and spat a brown loop of tobacco near his wife's feet.

Mark had no idea what to say. He could see the man's words landing on his wife like blows, but he was at a loss how to stop them. The woman continued facing her husband defiantly even as her eyes filled with tears. She said nothing in response, but bit her lip as she stood listening. The younger Scoggins had sidled around until he stood between his parents, where he could see her face. He looked on impassively, one hand idly scratching his barrel chest. The priest's immediate impulse was to gather the woman into his car and drive away from the scene as quickly as possible. He made a motion to speak and Janice Scoggins turned her head.

"Would you go, please, Father?"

"I'm sorry?"

"Please go now," she pleaded. "Maybe this is not a good time to visit."

He was going to protest; he was going to insist. But the look she gave him was clear and determined, and he knew if he stayed that he would only make matters worse. Worse for her. But before he could move, Les Scoggins intervened.

"No. That wouldn't be right. You've drove out from Seattle to see us and we ain't being too friendly. I do apologize. You want to have a chat, so let's go inside and chat." He stepped to his wife's side and draped a beefy arm around his wife's shoulders. She winced but stood her ground. "We're going inside and have us a nice visit now."

TWENTY-EIGHT

The trailer was roomier than Mark imagined, with plenty of little clues about the family that inhabited it. Fortunately the senior Scoggins was occupied playing host, which gave him some time to take it all in. As soon as they were through the door, Les Scoggins directed him into a huge, sagging chair, obviously the man's own favorite and oft-used spot, located directly in front of the television. Mark protested, but the man insisted, laying a meaty hand on his shoulder and almost forcing him into the chair. Then he strode into the kitchen, intent on making coffee for their guest, but apparently without any idea where anything was. Janice hurried in after him, before her husband could tear the place apart. The younger Scoggins, Neal, slouched toward the far end of a long couch and flopped into it. With his parents banging in the kitchen beyond, he offered the priest a weird smirk but said nothing.

Janice was doing her best to turn the trailer into a home but appeared to be losing the battle. There were plenty of lace doilies and crocheted arm rests, but the majority of them were on the floor. Arrangements of plastic flowers made an attempt to brighten the place up, but they were dusty and neglected and usually pushed aside to make room for some oily machine part or a stack of magazines. The number of magazines was surprising. They were well-thumbed and seemed to be piled everywhere. Most of them were about hunting and fishing and life in the great outdoors. Several were wrestling magazines and a few dealt with various types of martial arts. Mark spotted one under the couch that seemed devoted to skateboards. A stack arrayed neatly across the coffee table were mostly religious publications with pious covers, mostly in lurid colors.

The paneled walls of the room were nearly wallpapered with posters and art work. And it was the eclectic variety that caught Father Townsend's attention and jarred his sensibilities. The competing interests of family members did battle across the four walls of the living room. Framed photographs of Les Scoggins squatting next to a dead deer hung beside a large garish poster of a blond, balding, and nearly naked wrestler in skintight briefs; above the television hung a clock made from a slice of tree trunk, with a dark picture of Jesus' head decoupaged over it. Next to the clock was a truly stunning piece of beadwork, protected behind glass. The design was Indian and was mostly small blue and yellow flowers intertwined, set against a background of red and green. The work was delicate and exact and was the one bit of true beauty in a room scarred by wrestling posters, religious kitsch, and pictures of dead animals.

While the clatter in the kitchen continued, Mark turned his attention to the hulk on the couch.

"You must be the one in the family who likes wrestling."

Neal cracked his knuckles. "Yeah, and Tae Kwon Do." He nodded to a smaller poster of a shirtless Asian in white pants and a headband lithely leaping through the air. "It's cool."

Mark had an impossible image of a Neal Scoggins dressed in white pants, flying through the air. He suppressed a shudder, imagining a 200-pound sack of cement hurled across the room.

"What about skateboarding?" Mark nodded to the magazine poking out from under the couch.

"Nah, that's Tony's," the boy answered. "He did the boarding. But he liked the kung fu stuff, too."

"Were you two close?"

Neal shook his head.

"Well, you're quite a bit older, I'd guess. What? Nineteen?"

"Twenty-two."

"Eight years." Mark tried not to sound astounded.

"He was okay for a punk kid," Neal volunteered. "We hung out some together. I mean, it ain't like there's a lot of other guys close by."

The couple in the kitchen were almost finished and Mark leaned forward in the chair.

"Why'd he run away, Neal?"

The boy cast his eyes toward the kitchen, then back to the priest.

"You know," he said, "that fire thing at the school." He glanced back at the kitchen. "An' my old man, he'd beat on 'im some. Tony couldn't take it."

There was no more time. Les led the way, followed by Janice, and they both dropped onto the couch. The three of them sat facing Father Townsend; the mother, wedged in between her husband and stepson.

"That coffee's going to be ready in a bit," Les informed him. "So we can visit till it's cooked." He pasted a phoney smile across his face.

"I was looking at your pictures. You must do a lot of hunting."

"In Alaska I did. Some down here but not as much."

"Where in Alaska? I worked up there when I was younger."

"Yeah?" Scoggins's interest seemed to go no further. "All over the state, but I lived in Galena, on the Yukon."

Mark knew vaguely where it was. The air force maintained an outpost for two F16 fighter jets in the small town, part of the country's frontline defense during the cold war.

"That's where I met Janice." Les reached over and heavily patted his wife's thigh. She tried to smile.

"So you're from around there, Janice?"

Her smile grew genuine and she nodded. "Yes. My family is from Koyuk, downriver of Galena." She paused, then added, "I'm Athabascan."

Father Townsend had never heard of Koyuk, but he knew about Athabascan Indians. Alaska was populated with more of them than Yup'ik Eskimos. Her explanation also helped clear up a question about Tony Neeley's heritage. When Detective Newman talked to Mark, he was still unclear about the boy's background.

"How long have you lived down here?" Mark asked politely.

The woman started to answer, but her husband cut her off.

"Two years," he said bluntly. "I decided it was time to get the family back to civilization. The boys were growing too wild up there."

Judging from the looks on the others' faces, Mr. Scoggins might not have been telling the whole truth.

"Were you always in machine repair?"

"I was a mechanic, and before Galena I worked on the oil pipeline. Man, that thing flowed money—which is why I went up there in the first place, to work on that thing. Then I sort a just hung around, ended up in Galena and got me a job there. I did stuff for the air base. Janice and me were both on the rebound, so we hooked up and here we are."

Another tiny piece slipped into place. "So Neeley was your first husband's name?"

"My first husband taught school in Galena," Janice told the priest in a quiet voice. "Richard got tired of the north and left me when Tony was nine. I think he went back to Chicago or somewhere, but I never heard. He, uh . . . he didn't write us. Tony missed his dad.''

Les Scoggins was frowning. ''I don't know what the hell for. The guy runs out on his family without even a 'kiss my ass' and the kid gets all weepy. His ol' man was a jerk. Same as my first wife. She took off with our dentist. Daphne and her rotten teeth. I guess she thought he'd fix 'er up, if you catch my drift.''

Father Townsend was not sure he did, but he was not about to pursue it. While Les and Janice seemed willing to give him a lot of background about their family, the only one who had provided any real clues for Tony running away was the other son. The boy had fallen silent as soon as his parents came back into the room. He slouched at the end of the couch, as far away from Janice as he possibly could and, for the most part, feigned a look of indifference. But Mark could tell from the looks that occasionally flickered across Neal's face that he was tracking every word of their conversation. Les's remarks about his mother brought out a look of bitterness, but Father Townsend could not tell which one it was directed at, Neal's absent mother or his abusive father.

''Was leaving Alaska hard, Neal?''

The boy shrugged, then shook his head no.

''The priest asked you a question!'' Les barked at his son. ''Sit up and answer 'im!''

The boy's solid body shifted a few inches. His face showed no emotion, though. ''Some,'' he mumbled. ''I had more friends up there.''

''You had shit for friends,'' his father argued. ''There weren't nothin' up there that you ain't got down here. Right?''

''I guess.''

Janice gave her husband a worried look, which he ignored, staring angrily past her at his son. ''You guess!'' he retorted.

''What about Tony?'' interrupted Mark. ''Was the move hard on him?''

"Not at all." Scoggins was speaking in a loud voice. "It didn't matter where that kid was, he was just plain unhappy from the start. Coming down here didn't make any difference."

Janice waited until she was certain her husband was finished.

"It was his first time away from the river," she pointed out, "so lots of things were new. I remember when we landed in Anchorage, at the airport he saw his first escalator. The moving stairs scared him." She smiled faintly at the memory. "He was really surprised to see those things disappearing in the floor."

"Everything scared him," her husband grumped.

"Things were so different for him." It was as close as she came to disagreeing. "Maybe Tony felt like he never fit in. He was having kind of a hard time."

"I imagine having Neal around as a big brother was a help."

At the sound of his name, the boy's head lifted and he studied the priest's face, apparently unable to decide if he was being complimented or mocked. Mark saw Janice's look of doubt.

"Neal was telling me the two of them spent time together," the priest explained to her. She still looked doubtful. Her husband saw her face, too.

"They'd lift weights together," he assured Father Townsend, "and do that judo crap sometimes. But you know, Neal's a lot older. He runs the business with me; that's his full time job." He gave the priest a broad wink. "Keeps him out of mischief."

"But from what you're telling me, Tony was having a hard time staying out of trouble."

Again Janice started to speak, only to be cut off by her husband.

"Yep! The kid was a punk. Janice may disagree"— he glanced quickly in her direction—"but that's a mama protecting her boy. But anyone lookin' at it straight can tell you he was headed wrong. I mean, that kid lied, stoled, and lit fires. And then he runs away. You tell me. If he wouldn't of died, he was headed right to the jail. Janice knows that's so.''

She sat with her hands in her lap, looking down at them, letting her husband's words rain down like lead pellets. Mark had the impression she had heard them so many times before that their sting barely registered anymore. He wished there was a way he could get her away from her husband so he could hear her own story. He had a hunch it would sound quite different.

As if on cue, Les Scoggins lifted himself off the couch. "That coffee's cooked by now." Heading for the kitchen, he called over his shoulder for his wife's help. Her eyes pleading, she turned to Neal. The boy hesitated and, with great reluctance, heaved himself up and followed his father into the kitchen.

"None of it's true!" She leaned forward, whispering. "Tony was a good boy, no matter what anyone says. No one saw him set that fire."

"Your husband said he stole two thousand dollars from him."

Janice Scoggins sat back, defeated, just as the two men barged back in, coffeepot and cups in hand.

"She tole you I was wrong, didn't she?" Scoggins said, pouring coffee, slopping it over onto the floor, "Never mind, that's what she's supposed to say. Wouldn't be a good mama if she didn't. But facts is facts, and her Tony was a half-breed juvenile delinquent. End of story."

Janice put down her coffee cup and looked like she was about to leave. Mark reacted quickly.

"Have you had the burial?" he asked her bluntly

Janice sat back as if surprised by his question.

"No. I want to take him back to the village," she told him. "I have his ashes and will bury them up there."

"She says she's gonna do the whole stick thing," Les volunteered.

Mark raised a questioning eyebrow.

"Our people have a memorial for the dead," she explained. "It's called a Stick Dance. A year or two after someone dies, you honor them at the dance. It takes about a year to prepare because you have to make lots of gifts for the people and then you do ceremonies. My auntie promised she'd show me how."

"So you'll bury Tony then?"

"No." She gave a nervous glance at her husband. "This fall I'm going up to visit and I'll do it then."

Her husband was frowning again. "I tole you, Janice, how I'm not sure we can afford for you to go. If I still had that money that Tony took . . . but now I don't know about it. You're asking for quite a chunk of change. Don't go gettin' your hopes up."

Mark listened, hesitated, then asked anyway. "One of the reasons I wanted to come out and meet you was to try and find out why your son was in our church. Can you think of any reason why Tony was hiding inside St. Joseph?"

Janice Scoggins nodded vigorously. "I told him when he was a little boy, if you're ever in trouble you can run to the church and be safe. God lives there, I told him, and He'll watch over you. That's why I think he went there. To be safe."

It was exactly what Mark did not need want to hear. Guilt ballooned inside him as he recalled chasing the frightened youngster out of his church. So much for the inviolate rule of church sanctuary.

Les was chiming in again. "Well, there you go. You can see how much good that did the boy. He sure as hell weren't too safe at your church now, was he, Padre? Goes on in there and gets himself killed like that. I guess maybe God was visiting some other church that day." He gaped over at the priest. "Maybe He was on that TV with the preacher I was tellin' about. You think?"

Father Townsend could feel the balloon of guilt deflating and a bright red one, filled with anger, inflating. The man had the sensibilities of a rock. He had baited his wife, his son, and was now turning on Mark. He was deciding how to respond when Les's son spoke from his end of the couch.

"Maybe because you weren't downtown."

All three adults turned to him.

"I'm not sure I understand," said Mark.

"Maybe that's why he went there," the young man said. "Because he didn't want to be downtown no more." He looked directly into his father's face. "And he couldn't come back here. Maybe that's why."

"There've been a number of homeless youths murdered in Seattle this summer," Mark told the family. "Perhaps Tony figured he'd be safer if he was somewhere other than right downtown. Neal could be right."

"Told you my boy's got a head on his shoulders," crowed Scoggins. "He can figure all the angles out for you."

As if embarrassed, Neal stood up. "Can I go now?" he mumbled. His father nodded and the boy clamored out the front door. He could move fast enough when he wanted to, Mark decided. The priest set down his coffee cup and looked at his watch.

"I probably need to get back," he told the couple. "I appreciate your taking the time to visit with me. I wonder, before I go, if I could look in Tony's room? Just to see where he lived?"

Les Scoggins shrugged. "Fine with me. The kid lived in a rat hole though. I made 'im keep his door closed on account of the mess." He stood, as if to lead Mark to the room, then motioned to his wife. "Why don't you let Janice show you it? I'd probably best get back out to the shop." He stuck out his hand and pumped Mark's furiously again. "It was nice of you to come out, Padre. Besides those two cops, you're the only one. 'Preciate it."

When he was gone, Janice Scoggins led Mark down the narrow hallway to the back of the trailer, apologizing for the piles of clothing on the floor and the dirt. They passed a bathroom that was desperately in need of cleaning, and the first bedroom was Neal's. The door was wide open and Mark got a good look. Gray wrinkled sheets were balled up on the bed and the floor was buried in discarded clothing. Several lurid pinups were taped on the wall next to the bed. There were magazines on the floor, a mix of mildly pornographic and martial arts. A small television balanced precariously on the edge of a dusty desk.

The next room was Tony's. The door was closed, like Les wanted. Apologizing once again for her housekeeping skills, Janice opened it. The room was like any messy teenager's—but no where near as bad as Neal's. The bed was unmade and clothes were strewn around. Dresser drawers were left open. But there were no rude pictures on the walls. There were a couple of posters of kids on skateboards—one leaping over a park bench and the other balancing dangerously across the top of a handrail. One other poster was tacked above the boy's dresser: a photograph of a wide river at sunset, the warm light reflecting off the white bark of birch trees on shore, with a handsome couple in traditional Indian garb holding hands and looking out at the scene. Scrawled across the sky was the word *Dena*. Janice saw him studying the poster and explained.

"Dena is Athabascan. It means 'The People.' "

Mark turned back to the other two posters.

"He really liked skateboards, didn't he?"

Tony's mother smiled gently. "Yes, he did. He was good on them, too; Tony would ride those things everywhere he went."

"He had one when he was at the church, Janice, but the police said they couldn't find it at the park. And we've searched the church. It's disappeared. Would you happen to remember what his looked like?"

She looked doubtful for a moment, then her eyes lit up.

"I got a picture!" she remembered. "Come with me."

She led him back to the living room and rummaged through a pile of papers and envelopes on a small table. Finding the envelope she wanted, she pulled out a photograph and presented it to Mark.

"This arrived in the mail before he died," she told him.

Tony was sitting on a park bench in front of a dense growth of shrubbery. The boy was dressed in wide baggy black jeans and a dark green sweatshirt. His black hair was parted down the middle and hung off the sides of his face, framing his big, dark eyes. Across his lap was balanced his precious skateboard. It was old and road-scarred. He had it turned upside down so that the wheels were up. Scratched into the wood and painted black was one word: *dank.*

Inquisitively Mark turned the photo over. The boy had scrawled a brief message in ballpoint ink. *I'm okay. I might come home for school, okay? Tell Crappy hi. Love, Tony*

"When did you say you got this?"

"Right before he was killed," Janice replied. "He didn't put no return on the envelope, just this one picture inside."

Mark flipped the photo over and pointed to the letters carved into the bottom of the skateboard. "Is that another Athabascan word?"

Janice looked over his shoulder at the photo. "No," she said doubtfully, "I don't think so. I don't know what that word means. Maybe it's the name of the skateboard company."

"It looks like something he put on there himself," the priest replied. He hesitated. "Janice, could I borrow this? I'll take good care of it."

"What for?" Her reluctance to let go of the picture was easy to understand.

"I want to find out what that word means, and I want

to find someone who recognizes Tony," he told her. "If this is the way he looked while he was on the streets, it might help jar someone's memory."

The mother acquiesced. "You can take it."

He put the photo in his shirt pocket and was ready to say goodbye, but Janice was not.

"You probably think I wasn't too good a mother for Tony," she said. Mark started to protest, but she rested her hand lightly on his arm, enough to stop him. "I think that myself," she admitted. "After my husband left me I was pretty bum, and I did some wrong things. I shamed my family in Koyuk with how I was. I knew Les wasn't too good when I met him, but he said he'd take care of me and my boy and I believed him. When he got fired at Galena, he told us to move down here and things would get better, and I believed him again.

"He and Tony never got along; I don't know why. They would have big arguments all the time. Les told my boy if he wasn't good that he was going to throw us both out. He said he'd kick us out without nothing, not even our own clothes. I knew he couldn't, but maybe Tony believed him that time."

She stopped talking. Her eyes were tense, and she looked as if saying so much had used all her energy. Her thin body began to tremble and Mark saw tears beginning to well. He choked back his own grief and asked if she wanted to sit. The woman shook her head no.

"You think Tony might have left so that you could stay?"

She did not reply, but her tears spilled over and began running down her cheeks.

"You can't blame yourself for what happened, Janice." Even as he said the words he knew they sounded hollow. He blinked and tried again. "I don't know what to tell you," he admitted, "but I am sorry. I will pray for you and for Tony. And if it's okay, I might try to find out more about what he was doing in Seattle."

She nodded and thanked him.

Crappy the goat was standing on top of his Studeba-ker, and from the black depths of the garage Mark could hear Les Scoggins's loud voice berating his son over something. He wasted no time saying goodbye. Father Townsend had seen enough of the Scoggins.

TWENTY-NINE

Mark took the shorter way home—out to the Interstate and past Issaquah. His thoughts were jumbled and his emotions ragged, and he was in no mood for another bucolic drive down back roads.

Mark Townsend had one sister, happily married, and two loving parents, retired and living in Arizona. The Townsend family members, when still together, lived normal lives in a quiet, normal way. While growing up, Mark had felt his family and his own life were quite boring. The Townsends had none of the excitement or drama that he heard went on in other households. A word like *dysfunctional* was not even listed in the Townsend dictionary. There were disagreements, Mark and his sister had fights like all siblings, and even his parents raised their voices on occasion. But no one was ever beaten, no one threatened. They were a family after all, and the idea of someone being exiled or held captive by intimidation was as foreign to them as the most exotic, far away place any of them could ever imagine. Not until he became a priest did Mark come to realize how blessed and fortunate his family was.

Ninety percent of everything Father Townsend heard in the confessional was family-related. Infidelities, anger, mistrust, lies, even stealing and violence—they were almost always committed against another member of the family. And most of the heartaches, the disappointments, and the brokenness Mark listened to in the parish office were traced back to family members. Families. Hard to live with them, hard to live without them.

He was racing across Mercer Island and his speedometer was at eighty. Mark veered into the far right lane and forced himself to slow down. He was driving angry, a dangerous time to be in a car. The woman at the Haven was right. Sometimes the smartest thing someone can do is run away. But as Mark Townsend and the Scoggins family now knew, where you run to can become the biggest mistake of your life.

By the time he crossed the floating bridge, Mark had calmed enough to think rationally. He was feeling better. In the hour or so that he had spent with the Scoggins, he managed to absorb inside himself the sense of hopelessness and despair that fueled the anger and undercurrent of violence emanating from those three people. With his window rolled down, the Jesuit took deep draughts of the cool moist air off Lake Washington. Out with the bad, in with the good. And it seemed to help.

He pulled out the photograph of Tony Neeley and held it at the top of the steering wheel, his eyes moving between the road and the picture. Tony's head was lifted slightly, and that gave him a somewhat confrontational attitude. The boy was staring at the camera. But his body seemed relaxed; his hands were cradling the skateboard on his knees, holding it in place. There was nothing in the picture to indicate this was a kid about to bolt. He looked in no hurry to go anywhere. There was only that word scratched in black on the underside of his board: *dank*. Mark needed to know what it meant.

Back in his room at the university, Mark threw himself across the bed. He was worn out from his encounter with the Scogginses and thought he could nap. But too many questions and too much adrenaline kept his eyes open and his body rigid—all that, and the blinking red light on the phone. He knew it meant he had messages, but he had no clue how to access them. There were no instructions written on the phone. He searched through the desk, but there was nothing there, either. Frustrated, he called the university operator and asked her to explain the procedure.

He had three messages. Peter Newman's voice sounded warm and friendly and asked Mark to call back whenever he had a chance. Dan Morrow's voice, while still friendly, sounded worried. And the provincial's was impossible to read. "Mark? This is Jack. Gimme a call." Townsend responded in reverse order.

The provincial's message was fast and hard. Jack Elliott had learned not to drag out hard news. First get it out, then deal with it.

"Thanks for calling back, Mark. I'm getting calls from some of your people at the parish. They're saying I ought to remove you. I'm not going to, not right now; but I wanted you to know it's being discussed."

Father Townsend sat against the edge of the desk, not quite believing what he was hearing.

"Could you say that again?"

"I'm sorry to dump this on you, Mark." His superior sounded genuinely contrite. "There are only two or three people in on this, but it sounds like they're trying to stir things up. I've told Dan to do whatever he can to quiet them. But the word's out that you're being tied to that boy's death, and after all the bad-priest stories, people are jumpy. A couple of them have called to ask that I transfer you out of there."

"But I haven't done anything! I haven't even been charged with anything."

Townsend could feel his face turning red. He was wide awake now.

"Calm down, Mark. These are just a couple of folks."

"But they're parishioners, Jack! They're in my parish."

"Yeah, well . . . it's their parish too, Mark. And they're concerned. I think I've got to listen to them, at least."

The provincial's approach was probably right, but Mark was having a hard time accepting it. More than anything else, he was feeling betrayed. He was not sure who was setting him up, but he wanted to point an accusing finger at someone.

"Can you tell me who they are?"

"No, Mark, I'm not going to do that. Because I know this is all going to blow over and you're still going to work there and they're still going to be parishioners. So you're going to have let go of it."

He was going to have a hard time letting go of something he was still not able to grasp. Mark had always thought of the parish members as family. The idea that some were beginning to turn against him was incomprehensible. The provincial tried to reassure him again, and after promising to stay in touch and once again urging him not to worry, he hung up. Mark sat on his desk, staring at the phone a minute or two longer. Incomprehensible.

Dan Morrow tried to sound reassuring, too. No, he did not know who the parishioners were. The provincial had called him earlier in the day and asked that he do whatever he could to reassure people in the parish. He was to explain that Father Townsend was not a suspect of any crime but only had some contact with the murdered boy and was now helping the police with their investigation. No one was to think their parish priest had done anything wrong. Dan hesitated and Mark knew there was more.

"What?"

"That reporter called again," Morrow told him.

"What'd he want?"

"He's still trying to find you. I told him you were out of the office for a few days, but he figures you're somewhere in the area because of the investigation. I told him

I couldn't help him. I'm just telling you, Mark, so you might want to keep your head down.''

First banished and now hunted. He looked around at the guest room that was suddenly feeling a lot more confining.

"Listen, Dan, keep me posted on what's going on there, will you?'' His friend assured him he would and they said goodbye.

Peter Newman was not at his desk. Mark left a quick message on his machine, letting him know he had gotten his call, asking that Peter try back later. Frustrated but no longer tired, he threw himself back onto the bed, staring at the ceiling. What a hell of a mess.

A dozen Jesuits in the university community showed up for the Mass before dinner. Mark joined them in the row of chairs surrounding the altar in the small house chapel just as the liturgy was getting underway. A couple nodded in silent greeting, then turned their attention back to the prayer. The Jesuits' Mass was relaxed and informal; religious companions coming together at the end of the day to spend time in prayer. No one had the energy or inclination for a long service or a lengthy homily, so the ceremony was short and to the point. Twenty-five minutes later they were filing out of the chapel and into the living room across the hall. The greetings were more vociferous in there, with guys welcoming him into the house, asking how he was doing. They seemed to know all about Mark's situation and recent incidents at the parish; and as they poured drinks or opened cans of pop, a few peppered him with questions.

"I heard that kid was a prostitute,'' said Father Tribble, a chemistry teacher, "Is that right?''

Mark was not sure, the police were still looking into it.

"Who the hell talked to the papers? That's what I want to know!'' Father Leotyne was a vice president and had weathered bad press of his own. "People need to keep their damn mouths shut, especially at a time like this!"

Mark smiled weakly at the grizzled veteran.

"Don't let 'em get to you, Townsend. If those sharks catch the scent of blood, they'll go off on a feeding frenzy and shred you alive."

"What's the latest on the investigation, Mark?" Phil Steigler was a classmate from novitiate days, now working in campus ministry at the university. He tipped his glass toward Mark and winked.

"I don't know where it stands right now, Phil. Last I heard, the police were still trying to track down anyone who knew Tony on the streets."

"Tony? That's the kid's name?"

"Right. Tony Neeley."

"Neeley? Neeley!" Father Leotyne cut into their conversation. "Any relation to Frank Neeley? They're big benefactors here. This Tony is no relation, is he? God! Wouldn't that be awful!"

"Not that I know of," Mark replied. "This Neeley is from Alaska, out in the bush . . ."

"Ah! No, not the same one, then. Frank Neeley lives in Bellevue. Owns computer stores. Big, big benefactor. Couldn't be the same."

Mark and Phil exchanged looks and began edging their way to another corner of the room.

"So how are you, Mark? Okay?"

"It's rough," he admitted. "The provincial called today and said some parishioners want me out of St. Joe's."

"That's nuts!" his classmate pronounced. "Elliott's not going to do it, is he?

"I don't think so. He told Morrow to deal with it."

"That's good." Steigler took another sip of his drink. "But if you're looking for other work, let me know. We can always use another priest in the campus ministry office."

"Thanks, I appreciate it, Phil."

At six o'clock the Jesuits began moving toward the dining room in groups of two or three. The two of them finished their drinks and followed the migration to the buffet.

"So what are you doing with your time?" Phil was behind him in line. "I know you're not the type to take this lying down."

"I went out and met the boy's family today," Mark told him. "I was trying to find out why he left home and what he was doing in St. Joe's."

"And?"

"And I think I can understand his running away. His mother is married to a guy who is the stepfather from hell. But why he was hiding in the church is still unclear. His mom said she told him he could always run to a church if he was in trouble."

"You sound like you don't buy that."

"No, it's not that exactly." Mark stopped in line, trying to consider how to say what he was thinking. From near the back of the line, someone loudly cleared his throat. Mark looked back in apology, then moved ahead. "That part makes some sense to me," he said, "but I can't figure out why St. Joseph? Why that church?"

"But why not?" asked Steigler.

"We're not exactly close to downtown, and there's a bunch of other places closer. Why not the cathedral?"

They were at a table and set down their plates. Both stopped talking long enough to sign themselves and silently pray grace. Then Steigler continued.

"Maybe it's like in real estate: location, location, location." He grinned at Mark and broke open his roll.

"Maybe," Mark admitted. "If he really was working in Volunteer Park, then St. Joe's would be the logical place if you wanted to hide in a church. It's close and it's safe. That'd make sense."

"What else is around there?" Steigler's question was hypothetical since he was born and raised in St. Joseph parish. "There's nothing besides the park. Unless he was really into dead people and visiting Lake View Cemetery. It seems to me the park is pretty obvious."

"Yeah," Mark did not realize how hungry he was and was giving most of his attention to the food on his plate, "I guess you're right."

He was running on fumes, so before he crested the hill he stopped for gas. When he went in to pay the cashier, Mark saw the racks of cigarettes over the attendant's back and impulsively asked for a pack.

"What kind?"

"What kind? I don't care, whatever's good. Make it four packs."

The young clerk gave the man a strange look but handed over four packs of Marlboros. Mark remembered to ask for matches.

Evening traffic downtown was still thick, and it took Father Townsend awhile to find a parking spot. He considered pulling into a lot, but their prices were exorbitant and he had no idea how long he might be. The night was still young and there was no rush, so he cruised slowly up and down the streets until he found an open space. Mark was not exactly sure how he was going to do this, but he locked his car and started off down the sidewalk. He strolled slowly, paying no attention to the store windows and their bright displays. The priest was intently looking at the people around him, studying faces, sizing up the couples and groups he passed. Finally, at Fourth and Pike, Mark found what he wanted.

The plaza in front of Westlake Center was crowded with people. Diners sat intimately around small outdoor tables in front of a couple of cafes, waiters bustling around them. Shoppers were still entering and leaving the stores. A mime was entertaining a small crowd near the main entrance to the shopping mall; and over at the other end of the plaza, two jugglers were tossing knives back and forth. Just another warm summer evening in

downtown Seattle. The monorail arrived from the Seattle
Center and unloaded another hundred or so tourists who
joined the crowded but pleasant mayhem in the plaza.
Street vendors, spotting the newcomers, began spiffing
up their wares. A fountain, arching cascades of water,
was surrounded by clusters of young people who were
letting the cool mist drift over them. Mark eyed them
carefully. A young couple got up from a stone bench
nearby and immediately he claimed it. He reached into
his jacket and pulled out one of the packs of cigarettes
and placed it on the bench next to him. Then stretching
out his long legs, he leaned back and turned his attention
to the people on the other side of the plaza. His heart
was racing and his palms itched with sweat.

A few of the kids glanced at the middle-aged man
invading their turf; but for the most part, they ignored
him once they decided he was not police. They were too
intent on their own conversations and activities to pay
him any more attention. Until one of them, a young punk
with a dagger tattooed on his cheek and chains looped
through his belt and both ears bristling with studs, noticed the old guy's cigarettes just sitting there. The kid
lifted himself up from his spot near the fountain and
sidled over to the bench.

"Can I bum a cigarette?"

Father Townsend barely glanced at him but tossed the
package to the youngster. The kid tore the cellophane
off the pack and deftly smacked the bottom, pulled one
out. Mark held a match.

"Thanks, man."

He had to wait nearly ten minutes before the next one
approached, a tiny girl in a black leather jacket studded
with silver points. Her hair was green. Again Mark
handed her the pack without a word. After that he only
had to wait five minutes for the next one. This one was
a loud and brash kid wearing a white T-shirt torn off
just above his washboard stomach and black shorts that
hung so low off his hips that Mark was not real clear

why they were not falling to his ankles. The top six
inches of silk green boxer shorts were exposed for all
the world to admire.

"Hey, dude," the kid brayed, "kick me down a
smoke!"

Mark did as he was told. The kid eyed the man as he
caught the pack with his left hand.

"I'll take the pack, man, cuz I got bros that smoke."

Townsend gave his head a short shake. "Only two,"
he said in a low voice.

The boy hesitated, then shrugged. He took three but
tossed the pack back. After that the rest of them started
wandering over every minute or so. The man, for whatever reason, was giving away his smokes. None of them
could figure out what he wanted or was doing there, but
until he started hitting on one of them, boy or girl, they
were more than happy to mooch. Mark made no effort
to do anything more than hand out cigarettes when
asked. When the first package was empty, he stood up
from the bench and stretched, wandered over to a trash
bin and tossed it in. Then he ambled back and sat down
again, reaching in his jacket for the second pack.

The guy was good for twenty more, and the kids began approaching his bench without much hesitation as
long as he was asking nothing in return. Most of them
were dressed in black or dark green clothing. Dirt was
crusted on both their clothes and their skin, and several
were in severe need of a bath and some strong deodor-
ant. They looked a lot tougher than they sounded when
they asked to borrow a smoke. None of them seemed
older than twenty. A police cruiser from a block away
was watching the activity near the fountain; but from
what the two cops could see, all the guy was doing was
giving away his cigarettes.

"Maybe he's quitting cold turkey," guessed one as
they pulled away.

By the time the third pack was open, every one of the
gutter punks who wanted to had bummed a cigarette,

and Mark's business slowed considerably. None of the kids wanted to appear too greedy, so no one had returned for a second. Until the boy in the T-shirt and half-mast shorts hopped off his spot and trotted back over. He was a little more aggressive this time.

"What the hell you doin', man? Gimme another those."

"You took three already," Mark reminded him.

"Yeah? You gave 'em to me, man."

Mark withdrew one cigarette from the package at his side and held it out. Like a wary dog, the kid eyed the outstretched hand suspiciously.

"Just hand me the pack, dude."

Mark shook his head and extended the cigarette farther. "Just one."

"Ah, man! What you messin' with me for?" He reached out suddenly, snatching it from Mark's hand. "What the hell you want?"

Father Townsend tossed him the matches. "I'm looking for someone."

"I ain't seen him, troll!" the kid retorted, turning his back.

"How do you know it's a him?" Mark asked.

"Oh, is that it?" the boy cackled. "You lookin' to score off some jailbait tonight? That what you want?"

Townsend shook his head no.

"Don't play with me, dude!"

And with that the kid hightailed it back to his crowd. Mark watched out of the corner of his eye as the kid gestured toward him, recounting his conversation with the strange man on the bench. Townsend ignored the turned heads and loud exclamations of disbelief coming from them. Calmly he reached into his pocket and set down the last pack of cigarettes.

"Can I have one?" The girl's voice was tiny and timid and came from behind him. Slowly Mark turned on the bench until he faced her.

"Sure." He offered the pack to her.

She was young, no more than fifteen, sixteen at the most. Her skin was pale, too pale, and her eyes shifted nervously. Her small hands fingered the package tentatively, as if she was not too sure what to do with it. She fumbled with the matches and her cigarette fell to the ground. She bent to pick it up, but Mark reached down before she did.

"Why don't you let me do that for you," he offered. She looked undecided, then handed the matches back to him. Her hand was shaking.

She had on a green military coat that would have been too large for a man three times her size. Her frail body looked like it could barely support the coat's weight. Underneath Mark could see blue jeans, the legs cut off at midthigh. Her small breasts were covered by a narrow halter of red elastic material. He could see her ribs beneath white, white skin. The hair on her head was clipped short and dyed bright blue, the color of a summer's sky. She had on blue lipstick, too.

"Do you want to sit down?" he asked gently.

She looked around, then turned her head from side to side.

"Can't."

"What's your name?" Mark asked, handing her the lit cigarette.

"Why do you want to know?"

"No reason. I'm Mark."

"Yeah, whatever." She took a deep pull on the cigarette pinched between two fingers. Too deep, she choked back a cough.

"I'm trying to meet someone who might have known a boy who died up at Volunteer Park a few days ago," Mark told her.

Taking a step back, she glanced over at the kids near the fountain. For an instant Mark thought she was going to run toward them. She turned back to him instead, but said nothing.

"His name was Tony. You might know his nickname, Red Pup."

She took a quick pull on her cigarette, without coughing this time.

"I'm a Catholic priest," he told the girl, "and Tony was hiding at my church. But I don't know why. I thought someone down here might be able to tell me."

She was definitely nervous.

He quickly continued, "If someone had information, I'd be willing to pay," Mark offered. "Or buy them a meal or whatever. I just want to talk."

The others were eyeing the two of them and a group of four girls extracted themselves from the crowd, coming a few feet closer.

"Hey, Skye," one of them called out, "we gotta go."

Mark looked past the nervous youngster at the four girls. Two of them were wearing high heels and all of them were in shorts and halter tops.

"Come on, girl."

She turned to leave.

"Skye," Mark called after her softly. "One question?" He waited until she looked at him. "This boy I'm talking about? He rode a skateboard and there was a word on the bottom of it. *Dank.* I don't know what that means. Do you?"

Skye flipped her cigarette away. "Means it's good," she said in a small, lost voice. "It means good stuff."

She turned and began trotting after her companions who were already shuffling away. The crowd of kids around the fountain was breaking up, dividing into smaller gangs and setting off in different directions. When no one seemed to be paying any attention, she turned suddenly and raced back to Mark's side.

"What's the name of your church?" she asked a little breathlessly.

"St. Joseph on Capital Hill."

Then she was gone. Dashing back into the crowd of youths heading toward Second Avenue, she disappeared into their midst. Townsend stood up, his calf muscles tightening in protest. He had not realized how anxious he was sitting on that bench. He felt like he had just emerged from some sort of combat in which one false move could have meant the end of everything.

Father Townsend headed back to his car, leaving the forgotten cigarettes on the bench behind him. The venture was not the success he had hoped for, but he realized he had probably set his sights too high for the first night. If he thought bribing gutter punks with cigarettes was enough to get through their defenses, he obviously had a lot to learn. Clariss Stevens called these kids survivors. They did not get that way by opening themselves up to every stranger with a cigarette. Still, he hoped the word would get out. The one with the blue hair had seemed to listen. And Mark was sure the others would ask her what he wanted. He was banking on Skye spreading the word.

THIRTY

"Where'd you hear that, Mark?" Peter Newman's laughter was coming through the phone loudly and Pen Metcalfe looked over at the priest leaning against her kitchen counter. She turned back to the loaves of bread and began unwrapping them.

"A kid downtown. I told you, Peter."

Newman was still chortling. "He called you a troll?"

Mark was tired of the joke and was growing a bit impatient.

Newman finally stopped laughing. "You're right, it's not too flattering. Why'd this kid call you that?" He shifted back into detective mode, "You weren't trying to do anything, were you?"

"I told you, Peter, I was just sitting on a bench. I was downtown and there were all sorts of people around. No, I wasn't doing anything."

"You know, Father, that's not the sort of thing you should be doing. The police are doing an investigation and you're part of that. I don't think it's a good idea for you to be trying to connect with any more kids. I've just about convinced my partner you're not involved in this, but if she hears about you approaching street kids, it's all going to start up again. Promise me you'll stay away from them."

Mark Townsend looked at the Metcalfes' kitchen counter, piled with loaves of white bread, packages of bologna, and bags of potato chips. Pen Metcalfe was laying out condiments in a sort of assembly line.

"Peter, I'm not going to do anything to get in the way of your investigation. I just wanted to see if I could find someone who knew Red Pup when he lived on the streets. So I thought I'd ask around."

"Red Pup? You're calling him Red Pup now? And kids are calling you a troll? No offense, Mark, but this is out of your league. I mean, you're dealing with some pretty hardcore characters downtown. These aren't just runaways. Those kind are outlaws. This isn't just a phase or some adolescent fad they're going through. They were misfits at home and they're misfits on the streets. And they're going to stay misfits their whole lives. You don't want to mess around with them, Mark, they're tough."

He appreciated Peter's concern, but he was talking about teenage children, not hardened criminals.

"Aren't you overstating things just a little, Peter? I mean, do you really think Tony Neeley was as bad as that? He was only fourteen."

"A grommet, Mark! He was only a grommet, a weekend wanna-be! I'm not talking about the Tony Neeleys. They're the ones who get suckered and end up becoming victims. I'm talking about your hardcore, down in the dirt gutter punks. Road warriors. You need to watch out."

The detective's cautions were worth remembering, but Mark was not going to make any promise he had no intention of keeping. He had already recruited Penny Metcalfe's help in making sandwiches, and tonight he planned on returning to the bench at Westlake Center. And the next night and the night afterward, for as long as it took. Someone down there had to have known the one they called Red Pup, and someone probably had a pretty good idea why he suddenly left the rest of the pack to hide in a church several miles away. Mark Townsend was going to find that someone and find out why. He knew his intentions were not entirely devoid of self-interest. His own reputation as a Jesuit and a priest were being called into question, and he was already being forced away from his ministry because someone suspected there might be a chance he preyed on a boy. "Troll"—it was not just the kids giving him that label.

"Peter, I appreciate your advice. I really do. Now let me ask you something. Are you guys doing anything about looking into Les Scoggins's background? He used to beat Tony, you know."

There was silence on the other end. Mark realized his mistake.

"When did you meet Les Scoggins?" Newman's voice was bristling.

"Forget I said that."

"No, Mark, I can't. Tell me how you know Mr. Scoggins."

He could see no way out of this one. "I drove out there yesterday," Mark confessed. "I wanted to meet the family and offer my condolences."

"Jeeze! I can't believe you'd do that." Peter's voice was low but the tone was one of barely contained rage. "Do you realize how totally inappropriate that was? Don't you think there's maybe something just slightly wrong about a possible suspect paying a visit to the family of a murder victim? I can't believe you went out there. Tell me you're kidding. Even if it's a lie. Just tell me."

"I drove out there yesterday morning," Mark confessed. He was not going to lie or make excuses. "I wanted to meet the family and tell them I was sorry about the death of their son. And I wanted to find out what kind of boy he was, what he was like at home."

"That's great, Mark, just terrific. So now you're

jumping in with both feet, huh? You're going to take over this investigation. Is that what you called to tell me? Is that what you want me to tell Detective Draper and my superiors? We can back off now because Father Townsend is taking over? Even though some of us might consider him the likely suspect, he's going to show us who the real bad guy is. That's just great!''

Mark waited until he was finished. He could see it from Peter's perspective and he realized the detective had a right to his opinion. But it was just as important that he at least represent his own take on the situation.

''I thought you said I wasn't a suspect, that Gail Draper was backing off me? And where is the law that says a priest can't console a family? That's what I do, Peter, and if it gets in your way then I'm sorry. But you didn't think I was in the way when you needed me in Alaska. Why is it so different down here? Because I tried to help a kid who was hiding in my own church? Because someone suspects I'm a troll? Am I supposed to stop being a priest because of what someone else thinks? I can't do that, Peter—not for you and not for anyone else.''

Pen Metcalfe was stunned by the bitterness she was hearing. She stood frozen at her kitchen counter, the knife in her hand suspended over a jar of mustard. She had never heard Father Townsend sound like this. Whenever he spoke with her, his voice was calm and soothing; she had always thought of him as a gentle man. Although he was not yelling, his voice was loud, and he was speaking to the detective in a cold voice that left no doubts that he was extremely upset with whatever the policeman had said.

They continued talking for a while longer, but nothing got resolved. Peter Newman tried to convince the Jesuit to back off and let the police do their work. And Father Townsend remained adamant that he was going to pay attention to the people who needed his help: Janice Neeley, mourning the loss of her son; and the kids living on

Seattle's streets, at least some of whom had to have known the one they called Red Pup. Neither man pushed his agenda to the point of making threats, but it was apparent to each that their conflict was straining their friendship. Both feared a rupture, so as they said goodby, each wished the other good luck and promised to let him know how things progressed.

Mark looked a little sheepish as he hung up Pen's phone. "I'm sorry you had to listen to that," he told her. "I guess the strain is getting to me."

Penny handed him a stack of bologna and pointed him toward the slices of bread already buttered. "It's okay. I probably couldn't have kept my composure as long as you did."

"I feel so helpless," he said, slapping the meat onto the bread. "No matter what I try to do, I seem to upset someone. I visit the family and Peter gets mad. I try to console the mother and the stepdad's angry." He dropped the package onto the counter and faced the woman directly. "Even when I tried to help you find your mother, Lyle got upset. Maybe those parishioners are right, I ought to go work somewhere else for a while."

"That's nonsense, Mark." Penny Metcalfe continued working, stabbing the knife into the mayonnaise jar, slapping the white stuff onto the bread. "You need to listen to your own advice. Aren't you the one always telling me I shouldn't make decisions when I'm in desolation? Isn't that one of your Jesuit rules or something? I thought you believed that stuff you tell me."

Mark grinned in spite of himself. He loved this woman for her spunk and her friendship.

"That's what I tell you, Pen. And you're right. This isn't the time for me to be making those kinds of decisions. But it's hard to shake the feeling that I've done something that's really got God mad at me."

"Like you're being punished for something you've done?"

"Yeah," Father Townsend replied, "like that."

"Well, that's easy," Pen shot back. "just ask for forgiveness. I'm sure She'll listen."

THIRTY-ONE

Three dozen bologna sandwiches, with an equal number of plastic bags of potato chips, are not particularly heavy. But by the time Mark had carried the box to his bench near the fountain in Westlake Center, his arms were sore and he dropped it with some relief. He had purposely strolled through the center of the gangs around the fountain, and they had just as purposely ignored his presence. The box looked interesting, but they would wait to see what he was going to do with it before making a move.

Mark stood beside the bench, looking around. He was hoping to spot the girl named Skye, with the blue hair and the timid voice, but she was nowhere in the area. Not that he could see. Several of the others looked familiar from the night before. Mark plucked two sandwiches from the box and laid them on the bench, out in the open. Then he waited.

They were not making any sudden rush toward him. Ten minutes and not one kid approached him. A derelict, somewhere between fifty and two hundred years old, wandered by and hit Mark up for one of his sandwiches. The priest gave him one, hoping the old man would move along and leave the area clear for the kids. Eventually the old guy gave up trying to wheedle another, and Mark swung his attention back to the kids. A few were watching him unabashedly, but no one stepped forward. Farther down the street, from their same spot as the night before, the two cops in their unmarked car studied the man at the bench. Showing up a second night, with food this time, made them pay a little more attention. He was up to something, they were sure. People seldom show up on the streets just to hand out cigarettes and sandwiches. Not unless they are bible thumpers or wanted something. This one was not carrying a Bible so that meant he was after something. Or someone.

Mark was trying to figure out what the problem was. No one was coming forward. Whenever Jack Abel and the social outreach team at St. Joseph prepared meals for the kids, they always took them directly to the Haven. As near as Mark knew, they had never attempted to hand them out on the street like this. Perhaps it was a service the kids were not used to getting. He debated whether to walk around and try distributing the sandwiches to the small knots of kids around the fountain. But the whole idea was to gain their trust, and he thought he could do that better sitting in one place. Let them come to him when they were ready.

Eventually one of the smallest of the boys broke away from his gang and headed over. Mark could not tell if he was coming on his own volition or if he was being sent, but he smiled invitingly at the kid.

"Hi. How are you doing tonight?"

The kid eyed him from several feel away. "You got any smokes?"

"Not tonight," Mark said, reaching into the box, "but how about a sandwich?"

The youngster took a step backward. "What kind?"

"Bologna. And I've got potato chips, too."

"No. Just a cigarette is all I want. Forget it." And with that he scooted back to the others.

It turned into a waiting game. Mark Townsend sat on the bench with his box of sandwiches, surrounded by small gangs of gutter punks and street kids going about their business, all the time keeping a wary eye on the guy on the bench. No one approached him. The cops stayed inside their car, waiting to see who would break first. Although obviously being rejected by the kids, the guy was making no move to leave. And they knew the kids would not break. None would go near the guy unless there was some kind of signal given that it was okay to do so. But without one, the waiting continued.

He had shown up at nine o'clock and it was now a quarter to ten. Forty-five minutes, and the only sandwich Father Townsend gave away was to the old man. Not one of the youths had asked for one. The cigarettes had worked so well the night before that Mark figured food would be an even better lure. He had felt guilty about handing out cigarettes to minors; sandwiches seemed like a better idea. But something was wrong. He would wait until ten, then give it up and go home.

There were some signs of restlessness from a larger group of punks on the other side of the plaza, closer to the shopping mall. Most of the businesses were closed by now, the lights inside their windows dimmed. These kids preferred the shadows to the light, and they tended to congregate wherever the light was low. From out of the crowd emerged half a dozen boys. They were being led by the brash boy from the night before, the kid who demanded the entire pack of cigarettes and who gave him lip. He was frowning tonight and looked mean. The ones backing him up looked none too friendly, either. For the first time since he sat down, Mark was feeling something more than nervousness. Except for the young people, the area around the Westlake Center was nearly empty. Only a few people still wandered about; and at the sight of all the kids, they tended to quicken their steps, eyes straight ahead, and hurry across the plaza. Mark started to rise.

"Sit down, man." The kid was ten feet in front of him. "What is this shit?"

Mark tipped the box so he could see inside. "I brought some sandwiches. I figured you guys might be hungry."

The punk glanced to his right and his left, checking his backup.

"You thought we'd be hungry?" His tone was cocky, mocking the man's nervousness. "How hungry did you figure we were, huh?"

Townsend did not reply. He could feel the eyes of the other youths watching them.

"What you got in those sandwiches, man?"

"They're bologna."

"Yeah, what else?"

"Nothing. Just bologna."

"Bullshit!" The word exploded across the plaza as the young man dashed forward, his leg flying up and his foot connecting with the box of food. The sandwiches and chips scattered across the bricks. The angry youth was standing over Mark, spittle flying from his mouth.

"You tryin' to kill us, man? You that man? What the hell you doin' with us?" He raised one arm and socked Mark on the side of his head. The blow was not particularly powerful, but it caught the priest by surprise and knocked him off the bench. He sprawled across the bricks and when he looked up, he saw the other boys moving forward. A couple of them released their fists and lengths of thick chain dropped down menacingly. Instinctively, Mark covered his head.

"Hold it right there!"

The voice was loud and commanding. Father Townsend heard footsteps racing, and he opened his eyes to see legs flashing as the kids scattered across the open square to the streets beyond. The plaza emptied quickly as the two cops came running.

"You all right?" one of them asked.

"Yes, I'm fine," Mark said, sitting up.

"Are you hurt? Do you need assistance?"

Mark was eager to get to his feet. "No. No, I'm fine. Really. He just got me by surprise." He felt along the side of his head. It was tender, but the skin was not broken. "I'm fine."

"What was this all about?" The two policemen were flanking him on either side.

"I was trying to give out sandwiches," Mark explained. "I guess they didn't want them. The one boy seemed to think I put something in them."

One of the cops, the shorter of the two, went behind Mark and picked up a couple of the packages. He inspected them closely, taking a cautious sniff or two. Seeing and smelling nothing suspicious, he tossed them back on the bricks. The other one continued talking to the man now resting on the bench.

"These kids are suspicious of strangers right now. There've been some unpleasant incidents in the last few weeks."

"I know that," Mark replied. "That's why I'm down here. My name is Father Townsend, I'm a priest from St. Joseph Church."

If he recognized the name or the church, the policeman did not let on. But he pulled a pad and pen from his pocket and wrote it all down. Father Townsend explained that this was his second night at Westlake Center, that he had come the night before to try meeting some of the kids. The officer did not let on that this was also the second night they had watched him. The idea of giving out sandwiches, Mark told him, was to try to find someone who knew the boy who was killed in Volunteer Park. The one who was staying in St. Joseph Church, he added.

The priest was committing no crime that they knew of, and he brushed aside their offer to file an assault charge against the young man. They helped him gather up the mess, and one of them even offered to dispose of the sandwiches. He did not bother telling Mark that they would take them to the police lab first.

Mark expressed his gratitude again. "If you hadn't yelled, I think I'd probably be needing an ambulance," he told them. "You guys came right in the nick of time."

"Yeah, well . . ." the short one replied. "We've been kind of watching things a little closer since the murders. Anytime we see a stranger hanging around the kids, we check to see what's going on. Usually if someone wants to help street kids, they do it through one of the agencies. It isn't a real good idea just to come down here and try it this way. These kids are real jumpy right now; they're scared of their own shadow. And you being a stranger and all . . ."

Father Townsend knew he was lucky. He wondered if Peter Newman and Gail Draper would hear about it. If the officers filed any kind of report about an incident involving gutter punks, chances were good that someone would flag it for the two homicide detectives. Mark did not know that much about police procedures, but he knew his friend, Newman. Anything pertaining to gutter punks would catch his attention. As would the name Mark Townsend.

The shakes did not come until he was back in his own car and heading up to Capital Hill. Then his hands started trembling on the steering wheel and he had to grip it tightly just to keep control. His body felt wired as the extra adrenaline kicked in, like he had just gulped a triple shot of straight espresso. When he reached Broadway, instead of turning right toward his room at the university, Mark signaled left and headed toward St. Joseph. He knew it would be a while before he could sleep.

The lights were still shining brightly on the front of the church when he parked his car. He saw lights on in his house across the street and debated going in to talk with Dan. But he went into the church instead, using his key to unlock the side door. The inside was dark and quiet and Mark sank gratefully into a pew near the back, resting his head in his hands, letting the silence calm him as he began his Examen.

The night was a disaster. A stupid, silly disaster. After the confrontation at Westlake Center, he was certain there was no way he would be able to approach any of the kids who heard about it. The troll with the sandwiches was up to something no good; and word would be passed along the street until every gutter punk, grommet, and street kid from Bellingham to Portland would turn tail at the first sight of him. Newman was right. He was out of his league with these kids. He had no business trying to get involved where he was not wanted.

The Jesuit was disgusted with himself. Once again he had disregarded the good advice of those who knew the situation much better than he, presuming good intentions and God's grace would get him over the humps. At the Haven, Clariss Stevens warned against trying to connect with the kids on the street. He ignored her. Peter Newman told him it was dangerous. Mark ignored him, too. Even Sam Heschstein had tried to reason with him. *This is no game, Father.* Mark had never felt he was particularly susceptible to the sin of pride, but tonight, alone in the silent church, he was beginning to have his doubts. Were pride and stubbornness his principle motivations? Did the fact that some members of the parish want him out have anything to do with chasing after kids with sandwiches? Was he so protective of his good name, his reputation, that he ignored common sense? St. Ignatius thought humility was a grace, and he described three levels. The best, naturally, was to prefer poverty to riches, dishonor to honor. Good Ignatius was probably not too pleased with this particular son of his. Not tonight, anyway.

There was a loud creak and for a moment Mark ignored it, imagining it was one of the overhead beams settling as the temperature inside the church began to drop. But it was followed by another, softer this time, and coming from somewhere closer than the ceiling. The priest froze in the pew, his ears straining to listen. He remained absolutely still, scarcely breathing, waiting. There it was again, a softer sound, like one foot carefully being placed in front of another. Townsend held his breath, trying to pinpoint what direction the sound was coming from.

The silence seemed interminable, but then it came again; a soft footstep. This one was followed by a bump. Mark's heart, not entirely slowed from the night's earlier excitement, was racing again. He was having a hard time hearing anything over the blood pounding in his ears, and he could feel the hair on his arms beginning to stand. Was it possible? Could the person hiding in St. Joseph be someone other than Tony Neeley? Townsend had been so sure. But there was definitely someone else inside the dark church now. Someone creeping slowly, cautiously, obviously aware that he was no longer alone.

Father Townsend sensed him more than heard him. He was overhead, in the choir loft. Now that he knew where, Mark tried focusing his attention in that direction. Slowly he moved his head until his right ear was straining up and toward the back. There was a door on either side of the loft, and whoever was up there had to be moving toward one of them. Stairwells ran down both sides of the loft all the way into the church basement, where doors opened to the outside. The night Morrow and Townsend chased the kid on the skateboard, the youth had escaped down the stairs on the north side. If he had run up instead of down, he would have gone directly into the loft. The priests never bothered locking the door on that side. The music director's office was on the south side, in a small room just outside the choir loft, so that was the side they kept locked.

The loft was a perfect hiding place. People seldom went up there during the week, and there was room to move around. By standing back in the shadows, you could see over the railing and get a clear view of the rest of the church. The only area you could not see was directly below you. But if you heard footsteps, or someone treading on corn nuts, you would know someone was entering the church. Mark never thought to look up there. Other than the huge pipe organ and some chairs on raised platforms, there was nothing to see. Except tonight. Mark heard two more distinct footsteps, close to the far side, near the door to the north. He was going to try to make his escape down the same stairwell as the time before.

Cautiously the Jesuit stood and slowly began edging his way out of the pew. He made sure the kneeler was up; he was not going to trip over it a second time. Father Townsend made it into the aisle without bumping anything. The side door to his left, connecting to the stairwell, was about fifty feet away from where he stood. He would need to skirt around the back end of the pews to reach it. He assumed it was still unlocked, and he was guessing that the door in the basement was propped open, giving whoever was upstairs an easy escape to the outside. Would Mark be smarter to sneak out the back and around the side, to catch the person when he left the building? Or better to race over to the door now, hoping to confront the individual when he made his dash down the stairwell?

His decision was made for him in the next instance. Mark heard a loud groan as the loft's door was yanked open, followed immediately by the sound of distant footsteps flying down the stairwell. The priest bolted for the north door, managing to dodge the pews without banging his hip. The footsteps down the concrete steps were louder now, and Mark dashed for the door. He grabbed the handle and threw it open just in time to see a dark figure hurdle past, dodging around the corner of the stairwell, continuing down to the next level. He followed, taking two steps at a time, trying to close the space between them. Whoever was in front of him was scrambling fast, though; and without lights, the stairwell was almost in complete darkness. There were only a few small and narrow windows of stained glass that allowed pale light from the outside to seep through. Mark's foot slipped, but he caught the rail and kept going. They were both nearing the bottom and Mark could hear their footsteps echoing crazily back up the shaft.

By the time he reached the bottom, the small dark figure was only a few feet away. But he hit the outside door hard, without slowing, and was free of the church. The kid had no skateboard this time, so it was a foot race. And Mark's legs were longer. The door was still wide open when Father Townsend sailed through. The cool night air hit him full force and he dodged to the right, instinctively knowing the kid would head downhill instead of up. He saw the dark shadow tearing across the lawn and Mark leapt after it. He was gaining, and he could hear the kid's hard and frightened breathing. They were a few feet away from the sidewalk. Mark decided it was now or never. He had not played football since high-school days, but the old moves came back. Mark crunched down and pushed off with his right foot, stretching out his long body and extending both arms straight in front of him, flying almost parallel to the ground. His fingers slipped past hips. He willed himself to keep flying until his left shoulder connected with the small of the kid's back, then he wrapped his arms tightly around the kid's waist, locking on and letting his own weight freefall, dragging them both to the ground. They hit the grass hard. Mark's right shoulder bore the brunt of his weight, but he held on tight. The fall knocked the wind out of the youngster and out of Mark, too. And they both lay on the lawn, gasping for breath, too exhausted to struggle against each other. The priest did shift his weight a little, getting on top of the kid so he could not escape. Then he lay there, trying to catch his breath, until the kid started squirming beneath him.

Father Townsend eased himself up, still straddling the body below him, his legs clamped securely on either side. The kid was dressed in dark clothes with a stocking cap pulled down low over his face. There was next to no light, and Mark could make out none of his features. Reaching down, he grabbed the cap and yanked it off, tossing it aside.

Blue hair. Even in the darkness, Mark could make out that familiar soft shade of blue that reminded him of summer days.

"Skye!"

The body beneath him struggled all the more. Father Townsend continued pinning the side of her body with his knees, but he lifted himself up, easing his weight off her small frame.

"Calm down," he urged the girl, "I'm not going to hurt you."

He realized then that she was crying.

"Did I hurt you? Are you okay?"

Grabbing hold of one arm, he rolled off the girl. She was plainly sobbing, but Mark could not tell if it was from pain or fright. In either case, her fight was gone as she lay in the grass, no longer struggling against him. He let go of her arm and it dropped onto her chest.

"I'm sorry, I didn't know who you were." Mark got to his knees. "Are you hurt?" he asked again.

She shook her head, still crying. "No," she sobbed.

"Can you move?"

Slowly the girl raised herself until she was sitting. Nothing seemed to be broken. And although her breathing was still ragged, she seemed to be calming some. Mark knelt next to her. His eyes were adjusting to the dark and he could see tears glistening on her dirt-streaked face.

"I didn't know it was you. I could hear you running and I had to stop you. But I'm sorry if I hurt you."

"I'm not . . ." Skye choked back her tears and took a deep breath, "I'm not hurt. You scared me."

"You scared me, too," Mark admitted. He was suddenly aware that his right shoulder was beginning to throb and he shifted it uncomfortably. Nothing seemed to be broken, but there was definitely pain. First his head and now his shoulder; kids were becoming hazardous to his health. "Do you want to try to stand up?"

Leaning on each other, both managed to get to their feet. Skye's left forearm was scraped, but otherwise she was okay. Mark's legs were a bit wobbly in addition to his shoulder, but the two of them hobbled back up the hill, across the street and into Mark's house.

Dan Morrow was sprawled in front of the television in his bathrobe, his pale bare legs stretched out on top of the coffee table. The lights were off; the room lit with the glow of the television. He greeted Mark without noticing the girl at his side. It was only when Mark turned a bit that Dan realized someone else was in the room. He sat up, took his feet off the table, and drew the robe a little tighter around him.

"Father Morrow, this is Skye."

Morrow was staring at her hair. The girl was still sniffling, more frightened than hurt.

"I found her up in our choir loft," Mark told his fellow Jesuit, "and ended up chasing her outside."

Father Morrow was still fixated on the hair. "She was the one hiding over there?"

"Yes," Mark said.

Skye answered at the same time. "No."

Father Townsend looked down at the girl. "But I caught you in there, Skye. Tell him the truth."

The girl's tears started anew. "I was in there tonight, but never before."

The two Jesuits exchanged looks over the top of her head. Crying girls with blue hair were out of their league.

"What were you doing in there?" Father Morrow demanded.

Skye looked down, refusing to answer.

"I asked you a question, young lady." Father Morrow the principal was speaking.

Mark jumped in before the Marine landed. "Dan . . ." he cautioned.

"We're going to have to call the police, Mark." Morrow was playing it to the hilt. Skye's head snapped up, fear in her eyes. "Unless, of course, you're willing to tell us why you were hiding in our church."

"I wasn't hiding!"

"Then what you were doing in there?"

Her head dropped again. Silence.

"Well . . ." Morrow's bluff was called and he was stymied. He looked across at Mark.

"Skye, why don't you sit down here with Father Morrow for a minute. I want to make a phone call." She looked at him, panic in her eyes. "Not the police," he assured her.

Lyle Metcalfe answered the phone on the first ring. Mark hesitated, then asked to speak to Penny. Lyle hesitated, too, then asked the priest to wait. Mark heard him set the phone down, his receeding footsteps. A few moments later, Penny was one the line.

"Pen, I hope I didn't wake you."

"You didn't, Father. I was lying here reading. What's up?"

She let Mark talk without interrupting. He knew he was presuming on their friendship. When he was finished, her reply was exactly what he expected from a friend.

"Of course!"

THIRTY-TWO

They did not want to turn Skye over to the police, nor did they want to turn her loose. Asking the Metcalfes to house her for the night seemed like the best solution. There was no way the two priests were going to let a young homeless girl sleep in the rectory overnight. To everyone's surprise, the young girl made no protest, but rather, seemed almost eager to accept Lyle and Pen's hospitality. By the time Mark lead her up the front steps, she had stopped crying and turned quiet and shy.

Lyle and Pen met them at the door. Penny, spotting the bloody scrape on the child's arm, immediately took charge, leading her back to the bathroom, where the wound was washed and properly treated. While the two men waited in the living room, Mark apologized for the intrusion, then offered a quick recounting of what had just occurred at the church.

"So she was the one hiding in there? Not the boy?" Lyle was listening intently.

"She says not," Mark answered. "According to her, tonight was her first time inside the church."

"Do you believe her?"

"Not really," Father Townsend admitted. "She's given me no reason for being in there tonight."

"You're going to call the police, aren't you, Mark? I mean, it seems to me this changes everything. If it was the girl hiding in there and not the boy, then that means you're exonerated."

Mark doubted it was that simple. Tony Neeley had both the note and the money Mark had left. There was still that direct connection from the priest to the dead youth.

"I wonder if both of them were hiding in there," Father Townsend mused.

"What do you want us to do?"

"If you can just let her stay here tonight," suggested the Jesuit, "I'll try and sort things out in the morning." He touched the side of his head. "Right now I'm not thinking too clearly."

Penny led the girl into the room. She had taken a washcloth not only to Skye's arm but to her face, too. Skye was much calmer now, almost demure under the scrutiny of the three adults.

"I'm going to show Skye to her room," Penny informed the two of them, "and then I'm going to bed myself." She wrapped an arm around the girl's shoulder and looked pointedly at the men. Mark got the hint and rose to his feet.

"You'll be all right here, won't you?" he asked the girl.

Eyes fixed on the floor, she nodded.

"I'll come by in the morning," Father Townsend told the Metcalfes. "Thanks. . . . If you need me, I'll be at the house tonight."

One night away from Seattle University would make no difference. Besides, it was late, nearly one o'clock, and Townsend was exhausted. He drove the few short blocks back to St. Joseph and fell eagerly into his own bed in his own room. As comfortable as things were in the university's Jesuit community, it was not home. St. Ignatius supposedly once said that a Jesuit's home was on the road. In at least that one regard, Father Townsend felt more like a Benedictine than a Jesuit. But the Society would never agree to a vow of stability. He shifted and rolled in his own familiar, comfortable bed. He could always dream.

And dream he did. But they were bothersome ones, not the comforts of a settled, peaceful life. Small, dark phantoms darted through his dreams, first hiding their faces, then peering out with wide, frightened eyes. There was sudden violence too, flash floods of dark red liquid. He heard the sounds of skateboards and then silence and then laughter—hollow, taunting laughter. His head and his shoulder hurt. His mother came in to sooth the pain, to make it go away. She lay her cool, healing hands on him, gently rubbing his aching muscles, crooning to him in a soft low voice, promising him things would get better. Her hands rubbed over him and felt so good, helping him relax—until they moved to his neck and their grip tightened, and he found himself choking. He struggled against her and, freeing one arm, began to thrash at her, only to have her features turn from those of his mother into someone else. Someone he could not see clearly. Someone he knew he desperately needed to see.

Father Townsend awoke with a start. He was bathed in sweat and the bedding was kicked aside, half onto the floor. He drew two deep breaths and sat up. He was okay, in his own room, but it was only two-thirty in the morning. Mark lay back down, his eyes wide open, staring up at the ceiling. He could not help wondering if everyone was asleep at the Metcalfes.

The girl with blue hair offered no resistance when he told her he was taking her to another house for the night. She had actually looked relieved and seemed quite willing to do as she was told. There was nothing about her that seemed dangerous or threatening, otherwise Mark would not have asked his friends to watch her. For a kid used to living on the streets, she appeared quite docile.

But he wondered if she would still be there in the morning. He knew Pen would keep an eye on her, and Lyle would sleep lightly, one ear tuned for any sound of movement in his house. He was sure Skye would be safe there; he hoped she would cause no trouble for her hosts.

Mark was having a hard time fitting her into the sequence of events that had occurred in the last week or so. There was obviously some connection, though. Both Skye and Red Pup were homeless kids, hanging out in Seattle. He could tie both of them to St. Joseph. The boy had the note and money Mark had left. And he had caught the girl hiding in the choir loft—even if she denied she was hiding.

There was another connection, though; but for the life of him, Mark could not find it. He was wide awake now, his mind sorting aimlessly back and forth over stray pieces of information, chunks of images, and impressions. He felt like a rock hound turning over stones, looking for that one gem that lay buried in gravel.

Both kids were afraid—they had that in common. As were the ones at Westlake Center, too. When Mark showed up with cigarettes, they were all over him. But they treated the sandwiches like poison. If someone was trying to kill them, homemade sandwiches would probably be an effective way to do it. They were right to be suspicious; none of them knew Mark or anything about him. Until the police caught whoever was killing kids, they were smarter not to trust anyone—which led him right back to Skye. Why was she so ready to go into a strange house and stay with people she knew nothing about? What made her decide she was safe with them? And to trust Mark enough to accompany him there in the first place? His mind was racing and his head hurt. Sleep was impossible. Father Townsend kicked off the remaining covers.

The neighborhood was quiet, the streets deserted. Mark strolled up to Fifteenth and turned north toward the park, lost in his thoughts. A car slowed as it cruised past, a man's white face peering out from his side window. The priest glanced up but kept walking. The street lights dotted Fifteenth with bright circles of light, and he could see clearly along both sides of the road. Not a soul was in sight. A dog barked somewhere in the distance, but that was the only other indication of life. As he approached the entrance to Volunteer Park, Mark was about to cross the street and go in. But he remembered that the park was closed at this time of night. He searched for the sign confirming what he already knew. There it was. But there was no way to prevent anyone from entering, no fences or locked gates. And people went in all the time, Mark knew that. He continued along Fifteenth, staying on the opposite side of the road from the park. Tony Neeley went into the park after it closed and was clubbed and beaten to death, his nearly nude body left in the weeds between the cemetery fence and the men's restroom. There had to have been others in the park that same night. Mark wondered if the two detectives assigned to the case had made any effort to locate someone who might have heard or seen something.

For a brief moment the priest considered entering the park and doing his own search. Maybe he could find someone who knew something. But it was a bad idea. The way his luck was running that night, he would end up getting mugged. Then how would he explain what he was doing in there after hours? Definitely a bad idea. He continued past the park until he was opposite Lake View Cemetery. That was closed, too. But with a high fence and locked iron gate, getting inside there at night was a lot harder than getting into Volunteer Park. A lot harder, but not impossible. Mark knew that kids climbed over from the park after hours. They pulled picnic tables next to the fence and then scrambled across. Something about sneaking into a cemetery was thrilling; and the idea of wandering among the dead at night had excited generations of youngsters. Many classic ghost stories took place in cemeteries after dark. Washington Irving,

Mary Shelley, and Stephen King built their reputations with such tales.

Father Townsend smiled to himself. Lake View would be a good setting for a cemetery thriller. The lawns were dotted with the markers of Seattle's early pioneers, not to mention the famed Bruce Lee and his son, Brandon. Mark had spent enough of his own time ambling over the grounds to know where most of the well-known markers were set. He could probably write the story himself, but Jesuits had better things to do than write fiction. The priest yawned and turned back toward home. Maybe he could sleep now.

Father Townsend made it as far as the roadway that turned into the park, at the point where the cemetery fence ended and the park began. There he stopped and stood looking into the park, his eyes following the line of chain-link fence that separated the two pieces of property. There was enough light coming from nearby streetlamps that he could see a little way into the park, as far as the small outbuilding and the bench where police found the can and wrapper Tony Neeley left there. Where they imagined he was waiting to meet someone. Whether that someone was an anonymous troll willing to pay for sexual favors, or somebody bent on murdering homeless youths, or someone else entirely, no one knew yet. Townsend crossed the street, hesitated long enough to look up and down Fifteenth, then entered the park.

He stayed back off the roadway, moving through the trees in case a patrol car came cruising through the park. Cautiously watching for other movement around him, he made his way past the children's swings and wading pool. The restrooms were in front of him now, and Mark dodged farther to his right, closer to the park's perimeter. Just in front was the cemetery fence, and he slowed even more as he approached it. The priest continued walking, but kept his eyes fixed along the top of the fence. Three strands of barbed wire were stretched along the top, put there to discourage people from climbing over. But there were several places where the rusted strands were bent, pushed down by the weight of bodies. At one spot, a strip of old carpeting was tossed over, rendering the barbs useless.

He stopped when he reached the place where Tony's body was found. There was barely any light by the fence and Mark was having a hard time seeing. He let his hands run along the cyclone fence, feeling the wires with his fingers. They touched solid metal, an upright pipe. His hands felt lower along the pipe and found the gate's latch. But there was a rusty padlock, too. At one time this was another entrance into Lake View, but now it was closed, locked tight, and apparently forgotten. He stepped back and strained to see the top against the night sky. The wires on top of the gate were mashed down by countless crossings. Father Townsend studied them, pulling at the ends of his mustache. Why bother locking the gate when you could so easily climb over the top?

THIRTY-THREE

To say he was impatient would be an understatement. First he tried calling Peter Newman at the police department. All he got was his voice recording. Then he tried Gail Draper and got the same thing. Although it was only seven-thirty, Mark had thought at least one of them would be in the office by that time. The idea of homicide detectives working regular hours never even occurred to him.

Penny and Lyle were up. The husband answered Mark's call, but his greeting sounded tired and less than enthused. Neither he nor his wife had slept that well, both imagining every small sound to be from the girl trying to sneak away. Mark confessed that his own night was shortened considerably by his predawn prowling. The only one who seemed to have gotten a full night's rest was Skye. Pen, who had gotten out of bed half a dozen times during the night to look in on their guest, reported the girl was still sleeping soundly.

"The poor child's exhausted," she told Mark when Lyle handed her the phone. "Didn't you see those dark circles under her eyes? I don't think she's slept in days."

Mark remembered blue hair but no dark circles.

"She was starving, too," Pen continued. "I offered

her a sandwich before bed, and she ate two. Then a huge
slice of cake. The poor thing!''

''Did you find out where she's from?''

''No. We didn't talk about anything personal.''

''She didn't say anything about Carnation? Or knowing Tony Neeley?''

''No,'' Pen repeated. ''She hardly talked at all, she
just ate. And I didn't want to ask too many questions, I
could see she was tired.''

Penny would have a sensitivity about such things. Father Townsend would have bowled the poor girl over
with questions, which was what he wanted to do now.
But Pen told him to wait. Skye was still in bed and she
wanted her to sleep as long as she could without inter-
ruption. The Jesuit thought his friend was sounding a
little protective of the child, but he let it pass. He told
her he would come by later on.

The Lake View Cemetery gates were open when an
agitated Mark Townsend arrived. Anyone used to watching the tall man amble about would have been surprised
to see him today. There was nothing indecisive about
him. He turned to the left once through the gates, following the drive that led him toward the back end of
Volunteer Park. The roadway took a turn to the right
and Father Townsend followed, but with his eyes fixed
on the cyclone fence beyond the last row of graves. He
was looking for the gate he had found in the dark the
night before, and when Mark spotted the milky white
glass of the park's conservatory on the other side of the
fence, he left the road and started across the lawn. He
knew he was close. On the park's side, the restrooms
would be just to the side of the conservatory. Mark spotted the locked gate behind a stand of trees, the mangled
wires on top easy to see in the morning light. There was
a cement pad on this side of the fence, as opposed to
the hard packed dirt on the park's side. But on either
side, footprints were impossible. Whoever used this area
as a crossing point between the park and cemetery

grounds would leave no clear signs of where he or she jumped down from the fence. Father Townsend turned his back, looking out over the grounds. Lake View was not a huge cemetery, but big enough, and with enough small hills for joggers to get some decent exercise. Which areas might be frequented after hours was hard to say, although Mark had a pretty good idea of one site that would draw the attention of young people.

Bruce Lee's grave was almost in a straight line from the locked gate. Townsend had only to follow the road a short way and then cross a narrow patch of lawn before he was standing in front of the two chest-high obelisks that marked the graves of Bruce Lee and his son. There was a small stone bench placed at the foot of the graves; the father's marker on the left, his son's on the right. Both stones were tall pieces of polished granite. Bruce Lee's had a picture of the man set above his name. And on the base below, a sculpture of an open book. The base of his son's stone was inscribed with a long tribute to the young man buried underneath. The graves were separated only by a few inches, and both were covered with flowers left by admirers. A candle in a jar was set between the two of them and coins were scattered about. A playing card—the ace of spades—was left lying on the sculpted book as well as several scraps of paper with handwritten messages. There were also two photographs of Asian women lying on Brandon's grave, anchored with small stones. So many were intent on leaving some small part of themselves there. It was obvious to Father Townsend that the site remained popular with the fans of both Lee men.

But if Tony Neeley ever visited this spot, there was nothing here now to indicate it. Before he left, Mark offered a quick prayer for Bruce and Brandon Lee. His own concepts of God were probably far different from the men he prayed for, but he was fairly certain that the same highest power that watched over the dead as well as the living was the one listening, no matter by what name.

As he started back toward the entrance, the cemetery's stillness was disrupted by the loud rumble of a power mower. A groundskeeper, on a tractor mower, rose over a low hill, carefully guiding his machine between the stones. The man was wearing headphones to cut down the noise, so it was not until Mark stood almost directly in front of him that he rolled to a stop. Mark was trying to talk over the roar, so he turned the engine off and removed his headphones.

"Thank you," said Father Townsend. "I'm sorry to bother you, but I had a question."

"That's okay. No problem." He was a young man, lean, muscular, and tanned. Working among the dead looked like it could have its rewards. "What can I do for you?"

"I was wondering about all those things on Bruce Lee's grave. I walk through here quite often, and I'm surprised at the amount of stuff that people leave. Are there really that many people who visit?

"Yeah, it's a lot, isn't it?" The young man straddled his machine and idly scratched his chest through his T-shirt. "I could probably sit in the airport all day and never see half the foreigners that come through here. Sometimes they come by the busloads. Hell, I'd guess after Jesus and Elvis, Bruce Lee is probably the most famous man in the world."

Mark raised a skeptical eyebrow but kept his opinion to himself. Instead he asked, "What happens to all the stuff that people leave?"

"Well, the flowers we toss. When they get wilted, of course. And most of the rest we throw into a box back at the equipment shed." He pointed vaguely over his shoulder. "Except for the money. That goes into a coffee can, and when we get enough saved up, the crew gets to order pizza for lunch." He gave Mark a broad smile filled with dazzling white teeth.

"Is there any way I could get a look at those boxes?" Father Townsend asked. "I'm looking for something that might have been left there."

The young man shrugged. "Shouldn't be a problem," he replied. "Go over behind that row of trees and you'll see the equipment shed. I think Ray's still in there. He'll show you what's around."

Townsend thanked him and headed to the shed, the sound of the mower starting up behind him. The equipment shed was actually quite a large building that served not only for storing mowers and other maintenance equipment but also as the general office for the grounds-keeping crew. There were a couple of pickups parked in front, as well as a battered Volkswagen van. Mark stopped at the wide entrance to the building and called in. A voice answered from the dark recesses, and eventually a man with a gray ponytail wandered into the light.

"Are you Ray?"

"Depends who wants him," the man replied, wiping his hands on his blue jeans. But he was smiling as he said it.

"I'm Father Townsend from St. Joseph. The man mowing the lawn told me you have a box back here with stuff from Bruce Lee's grave."

"A box? Heck, we've got five boxes! I don't know why they want us to keep all that junk, but they do. Then about every couple of years someone comes in and tells us to throw it all away." He shook his head, unable to understand the intricate minds of upper management. "All except the dough, of course."

"Yes, he was telling me about the pizza fund."

"The Bruce Lee Pizza Fund."

"Would you mind if I took a look at those boxes?"

"Look all you like," invited Ray. "If you see anything you want, help yourself. It's all going to end up in the trash eventually."

He led the priest to a wooden workbench near the

back of one wall. Piled underneath were five cardboard boxes, which Ray pulled out and stacked on top of the bench.

"Most of it is just notes and pictures and stuff. This box here is mostly stuffed animals." He lifted out a small panda bear. "If you got any kids, they might like some of these." Blushing, he dropped the animal back in the box. "But I guess you probably don't. Sorry, I forgot you were a priest."

Two of the bigger boxes were nearly full with paper—letters, cards, drawings, and photographs. Another one had candles and other small tokens left by Lee admirers. But the one thing that was not in any of the boxes was a skateboard. It had been a long shot anyway.

"See anything you want?" the man asked Mark.

"No. But thanks for letting me look."

"Anytime, Father."

Mark was nearing the cemetery entrance when the young man on the mower rode up beside him.

"Did you find Ray?" he yelled over the engine's loud noise.

Mark nodded.

"Did you find what you wanted?"

He shook his head no, and the mower scooted on ahead of him. If there had been a skateboard in one of the boxes, one with *dank* scratched underneath, it would have put Tony Neeley inside the cemetery. Not that any questions could necessarily be answered, but it would be one more piece of information, one more piece of the puzzle that Mark did not have now. He thought it was worth a try, even though it did not pan out. The mower had stopped about fifty feet in front of Mark. As Father Townsend walked by, the young groundskeeper was pouring gas into the tank from a five gallon drum left at the edge of the road.

"Thanks again for the help," Mark told him as he passed.

"Sure," the boy said, concentrating on his pouring,

trying to avoid spilling gas. "What were you looking for anyway?"

"I was hoping there was a skateboard, but there wasn't."

The young man stopped what he was doing. "You mean left at Bruce Lee's grave?"

The priest stopped walking and nodded.

"There was one about a week ago, but that's not where I found it. It was about twenty-five, thirty feet away from there, closer to Doc Maynard's grave. That's why I didn't put it in the box."

Townsend could not believe his luck. But there was still no guarantee it was the same board.

"Can you describe it?" he asked.

"It's just a skateboard. Kind of beat up. There's something scratched on the bottom . . . some kind of word."

"Dank?"

"Yeah, I think that's it."

"Where is it now?"

The young man looked embarrassed. "I took it home," he said. "It was just lying on the grass and there was no way of knowing who owned it. I didn't put it in the box because it wasn't on the Lee's grave. And I kind of wanted to use it. I didn't know whose it was."

"That's okay," Father Townsend assured him. "It's not mine either. But it might have belonged to a boy who died; the one they found over in the park."

"Yeah, I know about that kid. The police looked around over here, but no one said anything about a skateboard, though. I never thought it might be that kid's." His embarrassment was turning to nervousness. "I'm not going to get in any trouble, am I?"

"No, of course not," Mark assured him, "you didn't know whose it was. But you do need to get it to the police. How far away do you live?"

"I'm over in the U district. I could get it at lunch and bring it back here."

They agreed to meet in the afternoon, after the young man had time to go home and get the board. Mark was banking on it being Tony's. He hurried back to the equipment shed.

"I need to look at those boxes again," he told Ray.

He was not quite as genial this time. Ray was busy replacing a broken wheel on a small tractor and told the priest he would have to get the boxes out himself.

"Don't make a mess back there," he grumbled as Mark headed for the workbench.

Father Townsend only lifted up the two filled with paper. If Tony Neeley left a plush animal or a candle or some other trinket, there would be no way of identifying it as his. But if there was something else, a note or a photograph . . . There was no need to dig to the bottom, because both Ray and the boy said that the crew just tossed stuff into the boxes. Anything collected over the past two weeks would have to be near the top. The Jesuit plunged his hands about three inches into the boxes, lifting out the contents and dumping them onto the workbench. There was still a good-sized mound of material in front of him and Mark set to work. He started by sorting the photographs into one pile and the notes and letters into another. He did not take time to examine them but simply separated them into two piles. Everything else, greeting cards, playing cards (what was with the ace of spades?) and printed tributes, he threw back into the boxes at his feet. Only when everything was separated did he start reading. The Jesuit was surprised how many languages were represented, but it made his work even easier. Most were unsigned, and those he quickly disposed of, too. He was looking for Tony or Red Pup, but after ten minutes he reached the bottom of the pile. If Tony Neeley had left a note, he had not signed it. Next Mark turned to the photos. The process was even easier this time. A quick glance at the picture and it was back into the box. Mark searched for five minutes before he suddenly stopped. There was a girl with blue hair. He looked closer and, yes, it was Skye. Her head was tucked down as she looked back up at the camera with wide eyes and a shy smile; it was a young girl's demure look. She was sitting on a park bench and behind her were bushes. There was no one else in the picture. Mark studied it a few moments longer, then set it aside and started looking again. Two minutes later he found Red Pup. The photograph looked almost identical to the one Tony's mother had given Mark. And it was the same setting as Skye's picture. The young boy was leaning back on the park bench, the legs of his baggy black jeans spread apart, the skateboard resting in his lap. His head was raised and there was a wide grin pasted on his face. If Skye's look was demure, Tony's was cocky.

Mark quickly tucked both pictures into his pocket and scooped the rest back into the box. He thanked Ray on his way out, informing him he had found two photographs he wanted. The old man was still hunched over the broken wheel and only grunted.

THIRTY-FOUR

Penny Metcalfe was in her kitchen, sipping coffee and reading the newspaper when Father Townsend rang the bell. His breathing was labored and there was a fine sheen of perspiration covering his face. As hard as it was to believe, it looked like the priest had been running. She led him back to the kitchen, informing him Skye was still not awake. Mark turned down her offer of coffee and asked for a glass of ice water instead. When Penny brought it, he had the two photographs propped side by side on her table.

"Where did you get those?" she asked, bending closer to examine the two pictures.

"At Lake View cemetery. They were left at Bruce Lee's grave."

"Is that the boy?"

Mark realized she had never seen him.

"That's Tony Neeley. And this proves that they knew each other."

"Of course it does," Pen murmured.

"And it also means they were in the cemetery."

She looked at Father Townsend skeptically. If that was significant, Pen failed to understand why. He spotted her questioning look.

"It means that Tony wasn't spending all his time in the park," Mark explained. "Because his body was found on the other side of the fence, the police presumed he was in the park. But what if he was actually in the cemetery and was caught when he was climbing over the fence?"

"By whom?"

Father Townsend shook his head. "I'm not sure," he admitted, picking up the boy's picture.

"You don't think the girl had anything to do with this, do you?"

That thought had already occurred to him. "I don't think she killed him, if that's what you mean. She isn't that strong. But if she was there, she could have been involved. I think that's a possibility."

Penny reached across him and plucked the girl's picture from the table, staring hard at it. The girl's look was not that of a killer.

"I think she was his girlfriend." Pen was guessing. "Look at the way she's looking straight ahead. Tony was the one taking her picture, right?"

The priest held his photograph up next to her's; the park bench and the shrubs were identical. They both agreed that Skye photographed Red Pup and that Red Pup photographed Skye.

"I think you should wake her up," Mark said. Penny looked doubtful. "We need to get to the bottom of this, Pen, and we need to do it quick. When the police find out about her, they're going to want to take her in."

Penny stepped back from the table with a look of consternation. "You didn't tell them about her, did you?"

"No, not yet. I haven't had a chance."

"Well you can't, Mark. She's just a tired, frightened little girl. You can't let the police take her. Think of what that would do to her."

When Father Townsend had asked Penny to put the girl up for the night, he was banking on his friend's generous nature. He knew she was still reeling from the experiences of her own mother's death and learning about her adoption. And Cindy Metzler's rejection was cruel. Asking Penny to care for the girl had the added benefit of getting her to focus on something else besides herself. But Father Townsend had not anticipated she would establish such a close bond in so short of a short time. Penny was acting as protective as a mother, and Mark was beginning to see that there could be trouble ahead.

"The police are going to have to be told about her, Pen. I mean, she was with the boy and obviously knew him. That's important information."

"That doesn't mean she knows anything about his murder," the woman argued. "Maybe she was just a friend."

"Penny . . ." Mark warned, looking past her. A very sleepy-looking, tousled girl with blue hair was standing behind her. She was wearing one of Lyle's old white shirts, and it hung down to her knees. The sleeves draped off her arms and completely covered her hands.

"Good morning, Skye," Penny Metcalfe said airily. "Come on in."

The girl took a couple of steps into the sunlit kitchen and then stopped.

"You guys are talking about Red Pup." She spotted the photographs and stared at them for several seconds but said nothing.

"Come here and sit down," Mark said firmly, "we need to talk."

She hesitated, looking from one adult to the other. For a moment Skye acted like she might turn and run from the room; but after glancing down at the long shirt she was wearing, she shrugged and moved slowly to the table. Mark waited until she was sitting.

"I found these at the cemetery this morning. You and Tony put them on Bruce Lee's grave, didn't you?"

The girl shook her head.

"Skye?"

"He did, not me. I wasn't there."

"When were these taken?" Pen was hovering over the girl's shoulder.

"Can I have some of that coffee?" Skye turned to the woman. "Please?"

Penny was about to protest, thought better of it, then poured the girl a cup.

"Any milk?" While Penny was at the refrigerator, the girl took a sip from her coffee, then began dumping in sugar, spoonful after spoonful. When Pen returned with the carton, Skye filled her cup with milk until the coffee was a pale brown and threatening to overflow the brim. Cautiously she leaned forward and slurped noisily.

"Tell us when you and Tony took these pictures."

She leaned back in her chair. "I don't know, it was before he got killed. Maybe four days or something. We were hanging at the park."

"But you didn't go into the cemetery?"

"Yeah, but not when the Pup put the pictures there. I guess that was after. I went with him that day we were at the park to look at the graves. He wanted to show me the kung fu one."

"Bruce Lee's?"

"Yeah, he said the guy's movies were dank."

Penny's brow wrinkled. "What does that mean? 'Dank?' "

The youngster turned in her seat until she could see Penny's face. "You know, dank . . . like in dakine . . . good."

The woman did not know but smiled back doubtfully.

"Okay, now," Mark began, "we know you and Red Pup were friends and that you were hanging out together at the park. Now tell us why you were hiding in the church."

"He was hiding there. Not me." The girl's voice was emphatic.

"What were you doing in there if you weren't hiding?" Father Townsend asked.

She shrugged again. "Just looking around. I wanted to see his squat."

"His what?" Pen's voice sounded alarmed.

"Where he stayed." Mark answered. "Right?"

Skye nodded.

Mark thought for a moment. When he first discovered the girl in the church, she was still up in the choir loft. He knew it was possible that Tony hid up there during the day. In fact, it made a lot of sense. People who wandered in to visit the church during regular weekdays would never go up there. The space was secluded and safe for anyone not wanting to be found.

"So why was Tony hiding in the choir loft?" He was watching for the girl's reaction when he mentioned the choir loft. She never even blinked.

"He was scared," Skye told the priest. "He thought someone was after him. Some of his gang got popped, and Pup was afraid he was next."

Penny could no longer contain herself. "I don't understand any of this," she protested. "You're just kids! What were you doing that you've got to hide in churches and live the way you do? Can't you see how dangerous that is? Where is your family?"

As Penny continued, Mark watched the young girl shutting down. Skye was withdrawing into some quiet place where Pen's histrionics could not touch her. He saw her eyes go flat and her face blank. The girl knew more than she was telling them, he was sure of it. She seemed willing to answer their questions, but so far had volunteered nothing on her own. He was not surprised. The priest did not know a lot about teenagers but he knew enough to recognize that they were not inclined toward long, informative conversations with adults. Townsend began tugging at the ends of his mustache. Jesuit high-school teachers were always complaining how hard it was to get their students to open up. He ought to sic Dan Morrow on the girl—that would be a picture.

Mark caught himself. Pen was still carrying on and the girl was staring down into her coffee.

"Pen! Stop it!" he ordered. His friend abruptly quit, and Skye looked up in surprise. At least he had her attention. "Who took the pictures of you two when you were in the park?" Mark asked the girl.

Her eyes narrowed and one hand began fidgeting with the coffee mug. "We did," she answered.

"You and Pup?"

"Yeah."

"And with whose camera?" Mark asked.

"His. He had one."

Do runaways usually pack their cameras? Somehow, Mark had his doubts.

"You're sure it was his, Skye?"

She was nodding her head, but Father Townsend was watching her eyes.

"Then where is it now?"

Her eyes shifted, but they never blinked. "I don't know for sure."

The tall priest leaned back in his chair, studying the girl. He was twisting hard at the end of his mustache, weighing her answers and trying to decide how hard to push.

Finally he spoke. "If I guess it right, will you tell me?"

With something that looked a lot like relief, the girl nodded.

"Tony was hiding in the choir loft, and you think that's where he hid the camera. And that's why you were up there." Mark was still guessing, but so far the girl was with him. "Skye, that's where it is. You think it's still in the choir loft, don't you?"

THIRTY-FIVE

When St. Ignatius was a much younger man, he wanted to be a courtier. He had all the fantasies of a young boy growing up in the days of castles and kings and pretty, young damsels. His dream was to move out of the family home and into a nobleman's castle, where he would drink fine wine, eat great food, and chase the girls. And when his lordship needed help defending his kingdom, the dashing young Ignatius would be right there at his side with sword in hand, loyal to the end.

They were fine dreams, and the young man from Loyola did his best to act on them. He attached himself to a nobleman and he did live in court. He chased the girls and had his share of fine wine and good food. And he went to battle. Then a cannonball shattered his leg—and with it, all his dreams. Afterward, back in his family's house, alone and crippled, a young and sobered Ignatius had to find new dreams.

Growing up has never been easy. Not in any age. A rare few are actually able to bring their dreams to life and live them to the end, but a lot more have to grow up with their dreams abandoned. Adulthood, for many of us, becomes nothing more than letting go of dreams. The very lucky in this world get to build new dreams.

The unlucky die trying. Youth is a cruel sanctuary.

Father Townsend did not have all the answers, and he doubted that he ever would. But he was pretty sure he knew who killed Tony Neeley, the boy whose dreams never even got off the ground.

He had three phone calls to make. The first one was to his provincial in Portland, asking permission to move back to his own room at St. Joseph. He explained to Father Elliott that the crisis was coming to an end and assured him that there would be no parishioners left wondering if their priest was suitable for ministry at their church. The Jesuit told his superior that he would need to stay there if he was going to effect the healing that needed to take place; and Father Elliott, after listening, agreed.

Next, he called Peter Newman. That conversation was a lot harder. The detective was not too happy to hear that Father Townsend was continuing, in his words, "to poke his nose where it wasn't wanted." But although irritated, he listened to what the priest had to say. Mark told him plenty. He thought he had the evidence Newman would need to find out who was behind the murders of Seattle's street kids. He now knew how Tony Neeley was involved, and he was reasonably sure he could explain why the young people were killed. The Jesuit said he also knew who killed Tony. But he had one more phone call to make first, and he wanted Peter Newman and Gail Draper to help. Only with great reluctance, and more than a little perturbation, did the detective agree.

The hardest of all was the third call. Mark dialed the number and listened as the phone at the other end began to ring. He was dreading this. There was no answer after the fourth ring, but Father Townsend did not hang up. After the eighth ring, he heard the receiver being lifted.

"'lo?"

The voice was low and husky. Mark could hear canned laughter from the television. This was not the one he had expected would answer.

"Hello, is this Neal?"

"Uhh." More of a grunt than an assent.

A wave of doubt swept over Mark. He had not prepared himself for talking to the boy. He imagined either Les or Janice Scoggins would answer the phone. Quickly he began revising what he wanted to say, trying to make it suitable for Neal.

"I was hoping to talk to your dad," Father Townsend began, "is he there?"

"Nope."

"What about your mother, Neal. Is she home?"

"No," the young man replied.

Mark was thinking fast. "It's important that I talk to one of them," he said, "as soon as I can. I have some information about Tony. Is there some place I can reach them."

"She's down at church, praying." Neal had moved off one-word replies, his interest obviously piqued. "My dad's in Monroe, getting parts." There was a pause. "You want me to give 'em a message?"

"Yes," Mark decided, "I guess you better. This is a message for your dad, Neal, so please make sure he gets it. Tell him that I called to say I found some of his missing money inside the church. Okay? It's not the whole two thousand, but a lot of it. Tony had it hidden up in the choir loft along with a camera and some pictures. Do you understand?"

He could hear the boy's quickened breath on the other end. "Yeah, I do." His voice sounded unsure, though.

"Neal, tell your father that since this money is his, I'm not going to give it to the police. Not unless that's what he wants me to do. But if he prefers, he can come here to St. Joseph and pick it up."

"Yeah, okay. I can tell him. What time you want him to come?"

"It's three o'clock now, what time do you think he'll be home?"

"Maybe in an hour, or maybe at five. I don't know exactly. He didn't say."

"What about this evening? Would that be better?"

"I think so," Neal told him. "Maybe later on is better."

"Well, if that's what he wants to do. Or else I can hand it over to the police, whatever Les decides. Why don't you tell him I'll be inside the church at eight o'clock. If he wants, he can meet me in there. But if he doesn't come then, I'll go ahead and call the police. Does that sound all right? You can give him that message?"

"That's good," the boy said. There was a long pause, as if he was writing it down. "Eight o'clock, right?"

"Yes."

"Okay, I'll tell 'im. Thanks."

"Thank you, Neal. You take it easy."

Mark's hands were sweaty when he hung up the phone. When he had imagined making the call, he envisioned Janice Scoggins inside the trailer and the two Scoggins men outside in their shop. He had thought she would be the one to answer and had prepared what to say to her. On the off chance that Les Scoggins answered, Mark was also ready to speak to him. Having to give the message to the boy was hard, and Father Townsend was not sure he did it right. Tonight would tell.

THIRTY-SIX

Prayer ordinarily came easy to Mark inside St. Joseph Church. Especially in the quiet of the evening, after a hard day. There was a sense of peace, of comfort, sitting in a pew, gathering up the day's details and offering them to God. *Off my plate and onto yours.* He never actually said those words aloud, but they were often part of his night prayer. And sometimes, on the hardest of days when he was the most tired, they were all he could manage.

Tonight he was too tense to pray. And although he tried relaxing, there was no position Mark found that gave any comfort at all. The pew was hard and unforgiving, and the priest's tense body fought against it. He would be glad when this was over.

The spirits loose inside St. Joseph tonight were not comfortable, either. Their empty, hallowed space was being violated, and they protested as loudly as they could. There were creaks and loud pops in the church rafters, and the wooden pews groaned. Traffic noises from outside sounded like they were coming right down the main aisle. The flames in the vigil lamps tugged at their waxy wicks as if in a desperate struggle to escape. In every way it could, the church registered its complaints. Sanctuary was being violated and no one, no thing was too happy about it. Mark included.

His plan might not be the way to go about it. Earlier, the church context seemed right. But tonight, sitting in the unyielding pew and waiting, it felt all wrong. But it was way too late to change anything now.

He sensed the footsteps before he heard them. Perhaps there was a slight sigh as an outside door eased shut. Perhaps the candle flames jumped a little quicker when an inside door opened. But someone new was in the church and Mark's heart began to race. Now he could hear footsteps. Coming closer, along the side aisle; heavy ones, with no effort to disguise or soften the sound. Father Townsend raised his eyes to the red sanctuary lamp: *Off my plate and onto yours.* Then he turned in his pew.

Neal Scoggins was five pews behind him and continuing forward. Mark stood and faced the boy.

"Dad couldn't come," he told the priest, still walking forward, "so he sent me instead."

Mark motioned to the pew directly behind his own and said gently, "Sit down, Neal."

The boy remained standing. "I kinda got to go," he answered. "If you can just give me the money—"

"You can sit for a minute," Mark told him. As if by example, he sat back down. Neal hesitated, then did likewise, taking the pew behind his as Mark had directed.

"You didn't have any trouble finding the church, did you?" Father Townsend was speaking calmly and quietly. He leaned his arm over the wooden back, turning so he could face Neal fully.

"No, I found it okay."

"Is this your first time here?" the priest asked.

Neal licked his lips and nodded, looking nervously around at the darkened church.

"Really?" Mark leaned closer. "I thought maybe you might have come here to meet Tony."

The young man's eyes grew wide. "I've never been in here."

Father Townsend forced himself to relax. "Okay. I just thought maybe this was where you met."

"Why are you saying that?"

"Because I know you saw him, Neal. And I know Tony didn't steal two thousand dollars."

He tried to shrug. "Pop said he took two thousand," he mumbled.

"I think that's how much your father lost," Mark agreed, "but Tony didn't take it." He pointed over Neal's shoulder. "Look back up there. That's the choir loft where Tony was hiding. You see those big organ pipes sticking out? There's a little door that opens into a crawl space behind them. That's where your brother was sleeping. It's pretty tight back there." Neal turned back to face the priest. "Why would your brother hide in a tiny, dirty place like that if he had two thousand dollars to spend?"

"Maybe he was saving it," Neal suggested.

"Why? So he could run away from home? He'd already done that."

"I don't know. Maybe he wanted to buy something."

"Like what, Neal?"

"I don't know!" His voice rose, loud and angry.

Mark tried not to flinch. He waited for the boy to calm down; and when he spoke, he kept his words soft and low, the same tone of voice he used in the confessional.

"If a guy had two thousand dollars, he could really run away. He could sure get a lot farther from Carnation than downtown Seattle. And if he had that kind of money, he wouldn't have to be begging on the street for spare change. You see, Neal? That's why I don't think Tony took the money. I suspect when he left home, all he took was his skateboard and the clothes he was wearing."

"You said there was a camera. Tony must of spent some for that camera. That's what happened."

"What would he buy a camera for?" Mark was keeping his voice low, trying to avoid sounding argumentative. "No. This is one he found. The police know it belonged to a man who was shot at the ferry terminal. Tony somehow ended up with it. The problem was that the film inside was of some people who didn't want to be photographed. That's probably why they killed the man at the ferry terminal, and that's probably why they were looking for your brother. And while they were looking for Tony, they killed some of the kids who knew him. I think that's when Tony started hiding in here. Because he was really afraid. And because his mother told him he should run to a church if he was ever in trouble."

"You said there's more money," Neal protested, "that there's a bunch of it."

"I know. But that was to get you to come."

Neal Scoggins stood up suddenly. He was looming over Mark, who sat rooted in his pew, surprised and unable to move. "You lied to me," he hissed. Townsend swallowed hard, trying not to show his fear. "You said there was money for my dad!"

Mark was afraid to look up. "Tony didn't have any money. I only found the camera and some pictures. I'm sorry, Neal." He waited, expecting the boy to either take a swing or start running out of the church. Instead Neal did neither, falling heavily back into the pew.

"You lied."

"Yes." Mark was still unable to look at him.

"Priests aren't supposed to lie."

"No, they're not. And brothers aren't supposed to kill brothers."

The young man looked into the priest's face and blinked, swallowed hard. "It was an accident."

"You didn't mean to kill him?"

"No. He hit his head. We were fighting and I did a kick to his chest; and when he fell, his head hit on a grave."

"So you were in the cemetery."

The young man nodded. He was blinking steadily now, trying his best to hold back tears.

"After—after he fell, he didn't move. But he was still breathing, you know? And I thought he was just knocked out."

"Why didn't you go get help?" Mark asked.

Neal shook his head helplessly. "I—I couldn't. By then my old man knew the money was gone and he was blaming the kid. He would of found out it was me."

"So what did you do?"

"I picked him up and carried him back over to the fence." Tears were coursing down Neal's face. "I thought someone would find him if I threw him in the park. They'd figure the fags got him. My dad said he was a sissy anyway."

"That's why you pulled his pants down?"

The boy nodded.

"So you knew Tony was up here, hiding out in the church. Then you met and went to the cemetery, where you fought."

"No. See, Tony called me and said he had to get away. He said he had a place to hide but that he couldn't stay there too long. He was afraid he was getting caught. You guys chased him or something. He told me to come help him and to meet at Bruce Lee's grave."

Mark interrupted. "And you knew where that was? . . ."

"Cuz we used to do kung fu stuff," Neal said, finishing Mark's sentence. "I taught him some Tae Kwon Do, and we used to practice. Yeah, him and me used to come see the grave sometimes."

Mark tried to steer him back on course. "So that's where you agreed to meet?"

"Yeah. He was waiting in the park for me. We climbed over the fence when I got there, then we went to the grave. He said he knew I was thinking about leaving home and wanted to go with me." Neal hesitated, then continued. "When I told him no, he started hitting at me. Then I hit back and he started kicking and trying to punch me out. Next thing, I kicked him and he fell."

"Neal, when you threw him back over the fence, was he still alive?"

"I think so," the young man admitted. "Yeah, I think he was."

Both of them fell silent then, leaning back in their pews, watching each other in the nearly darkened church. Confession may be good for the soul, but it is exhausting. Each in his own way felt the heaviness of what was said and of what had happened, and neither could do anything. Finally, though, Mark spoke.

"What do you think you should do?"

"Do?" The young man sounded confused. "I was going to get the money you promised and then head out. I got my car packed already." He motioned with his head toward the back of the church. "I've got to get away."

"Do you think that's a good idea, Neal?"

"What? You think I oughta stick around? Tony's dead, there ain't nothing that's going to change that. And I can't stay at my dad's no more. If he finds out about this . . ." He looked squarely at the priest. "Are you going to tell him?"

Mark had already lied once and that was enough for one day. "Yes, probably I am," he replied.

The boy chewed on his lower lip as if deciding what to do. "Will you wait until tomorrow?" he asked. "So I can put on some miles?"

Mark slowly shook his head. "I can't do that, Neal. I'm sorry."

"How much time will you give me?"

Neal Scoggins was already out of time. The two detectives, Peter Newman and Gail Draper, stepped out of the shadows and took control. There was no sense waiting any longer. The young man made no effort to resist.

But until they led him from the church, Neal Scoggins's eyes never left Mark Townsend's face. He wore a look of complete betrayal, and he stared hard at the priest, as if trying to memorize everything about him. Father Townsend, aware of what the boy was doing, tried to keep his attention focused on Newman and Draper. Once or twice his eyes met Neal's, but it was nothing he could sustain for very long.

Two other officers arrived, and when they came inside, Father Dan Morrow slipped in with them. He stayed at the back of the church, however, watching from a distance. Neal Scoggins was handcuffed and led away, and only then did Morrow come forward to stand beside Mark Townsend.

Most of the questions around Tony Neeley's death were already answered, although Mark's statement would need to be taken in some detail. And whatever charges were going to be made against Neal Scoggins would be determined by someone else. The surprising thing about homicide is how cut and dried the process becomes once it is solved. Legal procedures are so intricate and departmentalized that it becomes quite easy for those involved to step back, to remain detached and unemotional. That is the only way the business of homicide can get done. It works much the same way for police, attorneys, and judges. It does not work for surviving relatives and friends of the victims. For them, the nightmares never go away.

For Father Mark Townsend, the bad dreams went away after the third night. But a week later, he was still unable to sleep through an entire night; and he spent long hours lying in the dark, both praying and pondering.

The day after Neal Scoggins's arrest, Janice left her husband and flew back to her family in Koyuk, Alaska. There was nothing left for her in Carnation. Les Scoggins closed his shop and withdrew into his faded pink trailer, seldom venturing out unless he needed food or liquor. The girl with blue hair, whose true name was Rachel McKenzie, went home to her family in Mountain Home, Idaho. For a fifteen-year-old, she had seen enough of life, and she wanted to go home. Her mother and father welcomed her back with open arms. Skye's blue hair was changed back to her natural blond. And the rest of Seattle's several hundred street kids—gutter punks and grommets included—continued spaynging, turning tricks, and trying to survive. Mark prayed for them all, over and over, until he could sleep some more.

THIRTY-SEVEN

Lyle and Penny Metcalfe were not great pizza lovers, but they knew Father Townsend's proclivity for the Olympic's pizzas, especially the number twenty-five with extra pepperoni, so that was where they met him. It was a week later and at the end of August. Seattle's weather was beginning to turn, and while there was still no rain, the evenings were cooler and the morning clouds hung around longer. Seattle's news media were crowing over the juicy details of a prominent state senator arrested for racketeering and conspiracy to commit murder. Two organized-crime figures were also arrested, and a third had fled the country. Both of Seattle's newspapers splashed large color photos across their front pages, showing the senator huddled in an intense conversation with the mobsters on board a luxury yacht docked indiscreetly in Winslow's harbor on Bainbridge Island. Such photos are the stuff of indictments, and a middle-aged photojournalist and several young people were killed because of them. Twenty of Washington state's Indian tribes had opened gambling casinos, and the distinguished senator was willing to help his undistinguished friends find their way into the action. But for a price, of course. The news was a hot topic for everyone's dinner conversation, but it was not what the Metcalfes wanted to talk about with Mark. Not at first, anyway.

When the Jesuit arrived, he saw the couple already sitting at an umbrella-covered table on the sidewalk in front. Rich tomato and garlicky aromas wafted out from the pizza oven inside. Lyle and Pen were seated beside each other, holding hands, an open bottle of wine between them. For a brief moment, their friend was tempted to turn back and let them enjoy the evening by themselves. But Pen spotted the priest and gave an eager wave. Her husband smiled broadly.

Mark ducked his head under the umbrella as Penny Metcalfe pulled him down and planted a wet kiss on his cheek.

"What took you?" she scolded. "I'm famished!"

"Sorry," Mark apologized, "but the Pope called and I couldn't get off the phone. You know how that man loves to talk."

Pen laughed and Lyle grinned. "What's he got, a big case in Rome that needs solving?" Lyle poured the priest a glass of Chianti then lifted his own in salute. The three of them tipped their glasses together.

"Actually I was on the phone with Detective Draper," Mark said truthfully. "She said that the prosecutors have decided to charge Neal Scoggins with second-degree murder." He was shaking his head. "It seems excessive to me."

"That seems stiff to me, too," Lyle agreed. "I thought they'd go for voluntary manslaughter."

"Well, Detective Draper said that throwing Tony's body into the park and leaving him to die was what tipped it. But I don't know . . . I feel for the kid."

"How is he doing?" Penny asked.

"Not all that well. His dad still hasn't seen him. The poor guy's locked in there by himself. I tried to visit, but he wouldn't see me. I feel sorry for him."

"I feel sorrier for his brother," Pen responded, "and

for the rest of those children. What a terrible tragedy.''

Their waiter arrived and was quickly dispatched. A large number twenty-five, extra pepperoni, and another bottle of Chianti. Mark smiled happily.

"You two are grinning like Cheshire cats. What's up?"

The couple exchanged glances, then Lyle took the lead.

"Pen and I have made a couple of decisions," he announced. "The first is that I've decided not to run for mayor."

The look of surprise on Mark's face was genuine. He had expected to hear the opposite.

"I don't know what to say," he admitted. "That's . . . that's quite a decision. How did you come to it?"

Penny Metcalfe intertwined her arm around her husband's, locking his hand in her's. She smiled contentedly as Lyle's cheek grazed her own.

"I didn't think I should take on two new positions at once," Lyle said. "The other seemed more important, so I'll put off running for mayor. At least for now."

"What other position are you taking, Lyle?"

"I've decided to run for father," his friend replied with a huge grin. "Pen and I have decided to have a baby."

"My gosh, that's great news," Mark enthused. "When did this happen?"

"Well, we don't think it's happened yet," Lyle quipped, "but we're working at it as hard as we can."

"Lyle!" Pen was blushing furiously, but there was a smile on her lips and a glow in her eyes. "I don't think that's quite what Mark was asking." She turned her attention to the Jesuit. "I think having Skye in the house is what did it. Both of us felt so sorry for her, especially after she told us what a hard time she had with her own parents. But living on the streets wasn't the answer, and she knew it. If she had stayed down there, she would have gotten in a lot more trouble. I think that's why she was so cooperative. And why she agreed to let you bring her to our house. She was tired and looking for a way off the streets.

"Then, after she left, Lyle and I talked about it. We decided we certainly couldn't be any worse parents than Skye's, and probably even better."

"I was always afraid of it," Lyle confessed. "I didn't think I could be both a politician and a good father." He gave Father Townsend a knowing smile. "I think maybe it was a case of letting one thing in my life get too big and squeezing out some other things." The councilman tipped his head to the priest. "I decided you were right. I was listening a little too much with my head. So now I guess we'll see. I'll stay on the city council and see how things work out; and if it seems right, then maybe I'll run for something else later on. But neither of us are getting younger—and if we're going to be parents, now's the time." He smiled at his wife. "Anyway, that's what my heart is saying."

Father Townsend raised his glass. "To the Metcalfes," he said, "and to your future."

He had seen it work before, when couples floundered in their marriage and finally managed to navigate their way over the shoals and past the jagged rocks. Deciding to have a baby to save a marriage never seemed to work. But having one did often seem to strengthen them. Mark hoped it would work for these two. They were good people and they deserved to be happy.

"Lyle told me I can't ask you any questions about the kids," Penny said. She pulled her mouth down in a fake pout. "So I won't. I'm not going to ask how you figured out it was the brother. I won't do it."

Mark laughed. "Fine. Then I won't have to tell you it was the skateboard that gave it away."

"What skateboard?" Lyle asked, forgetting his own edict.

Penny arched her eyebrows and glared at her husband. "Omigod!" he cried, covering his face with his hands,

"That look! I give up, I surrender! Ask anything you want."

Mark was smiling. "I knew the boy had a skateboard," he told the couple, "and it was bothering me that the police hadn't found it. When his mother showed me a picture he sent her from Seattle, he was cradling the thing on his lap like it was his prize possession. And as a matter of fact, it probably was. So why wasn't it with him when they found the body? It meant either someone stole it or he left it somewhere. I couldn't imagine anyone beating up a kid for a skateboard, so I figured it had to be somewhere else. And wherever that was, I figured it was going to tell me something about Tony that we didn't know."

"So he left it in the cemetery?" Penny was trying to follow the priest's reasoning.

"Not exactly," Mark replied. "Tony had it on the night he met his brother. But after they fought and Neal knocked him down, he decided to move the body away from Bruce Lee's grave. Leaving Tony there was too obvious.

"But instead of getting rid of the skateboard, all Neal did was pick up the board and hurl it away from where he was standing. The groundskeeper told me he found it about thirty feet away from Bruce Lee's grave. Then Neal picked up Tony's body and carried it back to the fence. After he pulled down his pants, he lifted Tony and threw him over. The police never found any footprints by the fence because there's cement there. All they found was a boy badly beaten who looked like he'd been hit with something on the back of his head."

"But why did knowing Tony was in the cemetery point to his brother?" asked Lyle.

"I knew they both liked martial arts. And after I found the photos of Tony and Skye left at the grave, I knew that was one of the places Tony went to visit. I could think of only two people who would have gone into the cemetery with Tony. Skye was one and his brother was the other.

When I heard the skateboard was found near Bruce Lee's grave, I figured whatever happened to Tony was done there and not over in the park. His death had nothing to do with Tony picking up men. Leaving him half-naked in the park was meant to confuse things, to make it look like the boy was attacked in the park."

"Well, it worked," Penny proclaimed. "Everyone presumed that's what happened."

Mark continued. "I didn't think Skye did it because she was too small. She could never have lifted Tony and thrown him over the fence. Only someone the size of Neal could do that. So as much as I hated to, I had to consider him."

Lyle leaned forward, intent on Mark's explanation. "And not the dad?"

"I don't think he could have climbed over the fence," Mark said bluntly. "Besides, he had written the kid off. I think he was glad when Tony ran away."

"Even though he thought Tony stole his money?"

Mark nodded to Penny. He knew what she was asking. "That part made no sense. If a fourteen-year-old boy has two thousand dollars, he won't be hitting up strangers for quarters. I never believed Tony had the money. If you want to know the truth, when Les Scoggins told me he was missing two thousand dollars, I suspected his wife had it. At least I hoped she did. She deserved a lot more than that, believe me."

"So the old man had no motive," Lyle reasoned.

Mark replied with a curt nod. "No motive. And Skye was too small. And the mother . . . never. That only left Neal." The priest offered his friends a tight smile and a small shrug. "The process of elimination," he said.

"Tell us about the pictures," Penny asked, "then we'll leave you alone. Why didn't Tony take them to the police?"

"I can answer that one," her husband said. "Because he was fourteen and a runaway."

Mark agreed. "And there was nothing in the pictures

that looked that dangerous. They were just photos of a bunch of men sitting on a boat. A couple of them looked like whoever was taking the pictures was being chased. When Tony found the camera, the roll of film wasn't even full yet, so he finished shooting the roll himself. The last pictures were the ones of Skye and him sitting on a park bench. He kept those, but left the camera and the pictures he didn't want stuck in back of the pipe organ. That's what Skye was looking for when I caught her inside St. Joe's. She knew Tony was hiding in a church on Capital Hill. But it wasn't until I bumped into her downtown that she found out which church.''

''Skye told me that if she found the pictures, she was going to mail them to the police,'' Pen contributed. ''She figured out that they had to have something to do with the kids getting murdered.'' Pen raised her glass to her lips. ''She said she knew some of them.''

''That would make sense,'' replied Mark. ''From what I gathered, the kids do try to watch out for each other. They're so vulnerable down there on the streets.''

''What about those others who were murdered?'' Lyle asked. ''Did Detective Draper tell you anything about those investigations?''

''They've tied three of them to those same thugs involved with the gambling scandal. The men who shot the photographer and the boy in front of the ferry terminal killed two others. They were trying to find Tony Neeley, but none of the kids knew where he was hiding.''

''And the others?''

Father Townsend looked down at the table, then shook his head. ''The police don't know,'' he said finally. ''Someone picked them up off the street, used them, and for whatever reason, killed them.''

Pen shivered. ''I can't imagine what that must be like for them. I look at a little girl like Skye . . . it's hard to think of someone that young being brutalized.''

Her husband grabbed her hand and held it tightly.

"She was smart enough to know when it was time to get out," he observed. "Despite her problems, she was a very smart girl."

Father Townsend leaned back in his chair. A slight breeze fluttered the awning above them. The evening was warm and he was with friends. He lifted his wineglass, not to taste but simply to enjoy the aroma. For the first time in several days, he was relaxed.

"Those kids are not dumb," he agreed. "They're hurt and confused, and they've lost their way. But they're not dumb."

"I'd hate to be a kid today," Lyle said pensively, looking down at his glass.

"Me too. I think the pressure on some of these kids is unbearable." Father Townsend looked fondly at the Metcalfes. "Given what Tony Neeley was facing, I might have done the same thing. If you were that young and you didn't feel safe in your own home . . . I don't know . . ." He shook his head. "What would you do?"

Their pizza arrived. Fortunately neither the Metcalfes nor Father Townsend had to answer that question. Not right then, anyway.

BRAD REYNOLDS, S.J., lives in Portland, Oregon, where he presently serves as the formation director for the Jesuits in the Pacific Northwest. As a Jesuit priest, he has also worked as a writer and photographer, publishing over 300 articles and 500 photographs in magazines and newspapers throughout the U.S. His work in Alaska for *National Geographic* helped form the basis for the first Father Mark Townsend mystery, *The Story Knife*.